A Land Fit for Heroes

Book 1

ESCAPE TO THE WILD WOOD

A Land Fit for Heroes

Book I

ESCAPE TO THE WILD WOOD

PHILLIP MANN

VICTOR GOLLANCZ

LONDON

First published in Great Britain 1993
by Victor Gollancz
A Cassell imprint
Villiers House, 41/47 Strand, London WC2N 5JE

A catalogue record for this book is
available from the British Library

ISBN 0 575 05515 4

Photoset in Great Britain by
Rowland Phototypesetting Ltd, Bury St Edmunds, Suffolk
and printed in Great Britain by
St Edmundsbury Press Ltd, Bury St Edmunds, Suffolk

For Dick Rothrock, friend and teacher,
now sadly missed.
And for Janice Rothrock, whose courage
shines like a beacon.
Also for Tom and Megan, currently
making things happen in LA.

1 *Twelve Seconds Distant*

Welcome to the Earth.

But it is not quite the Earth which you and I know, though viewed from the moon you could not tell the difference. This world belongs in one of those parallel universes which exist, infinite in quantity, yet each in its own discrete time-shell, just slightly out of temporal phase with our own world and with each other.

This world, which we are now approaching, is displaced from our own by a mere twelve seconds. But that short time is sufficient to make this world wholly different from our own while yet remaining, in some ways, quite familiar. For instance, the hills and rivers and plains are largely the same, but the men and women who inhabit them are different. Their history and customs too are different, but in subtle and strange ways.

In this world the Roman legions never quit Britannia. Far from it. The Roman legions marched on and, after stamping their mark on Britannia, conquered the rest of the world. Wherever they trod they established their social systems, their laws and their military organization.

Though for a while Roma tottered before the northern tribes, it nevertheless survived to become the capital city of a vast eclectic civilization. Roma became renowned as a great seat of learning; as a cultural melting-pot and place in the sun for all races; as a home of good food, rare spices and fine red wine; as the place for hot gossip, love, philosophy and lust; as the centre of fabulous, profligate wealth and awesome world-rattling power.

Which is all well and good, but this book is not much concerned with Roma, or with the rest of the world come to that, but with just one small corner in the distant north-east of the moist and wooded province of Britannia.

When military resistance in Britannia ended with the defeat of the Celtic tribes, the province prospered. The Romans built their roads throughout the length and breadth of the country and ruled in the neat cities, small towns and military camps. Gradually they created an organized society based on urban living.

In the early days after the conquest, the political leader of this society, the Praefectus Comitum as he was called, was appointed from Roma. But soon this position was filled by members of the great aristocratic, military families that settled in Britannia and began to call that province home. These families controlled vast estates and enjoyed almost unlimited power. Their privilege was supported by two classes in the population: the Citizens and the Soldiers. These two classes were mainly drawn from native families who, in the early days, forsook the tribal life and accepted the *pax Romana* with relish. They became 'civilized'. As the decades stretched into centuries and the centuries ticked past, Roman rule began to seem like a law of nature. Given material comforts, security and a guaranteed place in society, the Citizens were hardly aware of the strict rules and regulations and limits under which they lived. Thus the clerks and sewermen, the cooks, cleaners, nurses, gardeners and candlestick-makers who made civilized life possible for the Roman military aristocracy hardly ever questioned their condition. As for the Soldiers, they were not encouraged to think about anything other than a pride in service and a delight in efficiency. They controlled the roads and the city gates.

But where the city walls ended, the wild wood began. Still, in the forests and moors and swamps which surrounded the Roman towns, life continued pretty much as it had for centuries: as it had since before the coming of the Celts and the earlier generations of men who built Stonehenge, yea back even unto the time of giants. In the different regions of what the Romans called Britannia, the old, green and ever youthful spirits of tree, glade and river maintained their dignity and held sway among the people who lived close to the soil. To those who lived in the vast forests, their ancestors, almost as old as the hills, could be heard whispering in the trees and among the bubbling streams.

At nightfall they murmured together in the shadows of the long barrows. Even so, golden lads and lasses made love in the meadows and on the hilltops and in the quiet places behind the barrows, and never thought about grave-dust.

To the ancient Roman families and the Citizens and Soldiers who served them, these woodlanders were primitive savages who could be tolerated because they posed no threat.

Christianity sprang up in some quarters but nowhere did it become as great a political force as it achieved in our world. Indeed, where it did survive, Christianity took its place as one sect among many, each of which celebrated in its own special way the sacrifice of a man or woman who chose death in order that humankind might be saved. These various creeds rubbed shoulders with older religions of earth and sky and of the Great Mother.

And all races and creeds walked the Roman roads.

We come to the present.

Throughout the world, Roman rationalism and Roman law are reaching their limits. They have become a kind of prison of the spirit, and that spirit, in some quarters at least, is now rattling its chains and shaking its bars. At the same time, ecstatic forces are bubbling up, lava-like and threatening to destroy the Roman order as surely as Vesuvius destroyed Pompeii.

Of course, on a day-to-day level, nothing seems very different. The sun rises and sets as it always has. The moon waxes and wanes and heaves the seas round the world. Spring follows winter and is itself followed by summer and autumn until winter comes again. But deep change is inevitable and remorseless. It is a law of Nature, there as here.

Shortly we will join this world . . .

2 *Above the Wild Wood*

. . . but for the moment we are drifting slowly above the vast wild woods of the north of Britannia. We are a few miles east and a bit north of the great city of Eburacum which in this world is the capital city of Britannia. In our world this area is known as the Vale of Pickering in the county of Yorkshire and the great city is called York. The time is mid-afternoon and the season springtime. After a bright warm day, the sun's rays fall slanting into the forest, lighting up the tumbling dust and pollen and the dancing insects in a golden haze.

The forest is an overwhelming presence. It stretches as far as the eye can see, sometimes bright with the pale green of new leaves, sometimes sombre. Holly and hazel trees are much in evidence, their fruits praised by man and bird. Yew trees, ancient by any human standard, brood in the shadows of the taller trees. Willows with their steep branches mark the courses of streams and reach across to join with the common alder, while stands of beech and oak provide a contrast of shape and colour and presence. The forest is rich and mysterious. When the winds blow the canopy stirs and the branches flex and groan and scrape – the forest is a single creature then, a mighty green organism, which measures its time by season and century.

From time to time we drift over stout hedges of clipped haw-thorn and hazel and sometimes holly trees. These trees are a barrier. They hold back the mighty forest and protect small villages. Each village is roughly circular and the houses are packed tightly together but with sufficient room for small gardens and fruit trees. Many of the tall trees close to the village have had their branches chopped back to allow the daylight in. But not so the favoured oak trees. They loom high beyond the hedge and cast their shadows into the enclosures. In autumn the roofs of the houses patter with falling acorns which block the gutters.

The houses are made of wood and brick and lath. The roofs are tiled. Many of the houses are built to a circular pattern and rise above the ground on stilts. Beneath them is room for animals. The houses have small windows and high chimneys from which blue wood-smoke rises. Outside the front doors are clumps of rosemary, thyme, lemon balm and mint. Fences define small allotments where turnips grow beside winter sprouts and where the picked-out stumps of autumn crops lie mouldering.

Spring ploughing is well under way and in some places early rye and barley, planted in the autumn, are already pushing their bright green spears up through the dark soil. Piles of damp vegetation, rotting marigold leaves, soiled pea-straw and the sodden tangle from ditch bottoms are heaped up at the sides of the fields ready for the compost bins.

The village is crowded with people, for the day's work is ended and it is a time for talking and drinking in the village square. The air is filled with the smell of cooking. Chickens squawk, pecking beneath tables which have been set up in the sunshine. Children sing and cry. Somewhere there is hammering and an argument breaks out. Elsewhere there is laughter. These are the 'savages', as the Romans call them, the woodlanders whose fires burn at Beltane. These men and women are descended from the Celts who invaded Britannia centuries before the Romans, as well as from Vikings and escaped slaves from Africa and the Orient. In their veins flows blood from the earliest inhabitants of the land, the men and women who built the stone circles and forts in the hills. These woodlanders continue a culture already ancient when the Romans came a-calling and which can trace its ancestry, some say, even back to old Atlantis. Nor are they the only inhabitants of the forest.

In the village, spring flowers are sweetening the air as are the pigs which grunt and nuzzle among the oak trees. Cows lumber in the water-meadows outside the village wall. Sheep bleat within fences made of osiers. Bearded goats strain against their leashes, hungry for whatever is beyond their reach. A dog runs from the back of a house and hunkers down in the grass when a voice calls.

Narrow lanes which join the isolated cottages into a network meander from beneath the trees of the forest. The paths are all well trodden and each is just wide enough to allow two pack-horses to scrape by one another. Entry to the village is by means of a gate and this is closed every evening when the sun goes down. The gate is topped with spikes and is sufficiently tall and stoutly built to stop a rutting stag in its tracks or a pack of howling wolves. Beyond the villages the lanes meander away and are lost under the trees, only to re-emerge at the next village.

To the north the vast dappled forest merges with the misty grey and purple of the Moors: the trees give way to bracken and heather. To the east the forest presses right to the edge of the cliffs which border the grey North Sea. There the trees are stunted and wind-burnt, carved into fantastic shapes by the salt breeze. To the south and west the forest laps round the lower slopes of the Wolds and skirts the salt-marshes where the River Ouse becomes tidal. Then it presses south enclosing hill and river beneath its branches. It is said that if you step out under the greenwood just beyond the walls of Eburacum, you need never leave the cover of the forest until you come to the edge of the far southern sea.

This vast tangle of trees and undergrowth is the way the land recovered after the last ice age. The forest is home to wildcats, giant wolves and bears. Even a tiger with long shaggy dappled coat and curving teeth has been seen loping under the fir trees near Kirkdale. There are other creatures too, creatures which are rarely seen unless they want to be seen and which move silently.

But, though the forest teems with life, as we drift above the trees we see only the flutter of birds and the occasional sparkle of sun on water. In the distance we might see the stain of smoke rising above the canopy of leaves, for today is the first day of May and the fires celebrating Beltane are burning.

Abruptly we come to a place where several acres of forest have been cleared. Within this area there is a sharply defined rectangle. Being fanciful, we might imagine that one of the old gods, a Jupiter or a Vulcan say, has used a giant cutter to remove a precise area of forest. The perimeter is defined by high walls of stone and soldiers patrol behind the battlements. There are watch-towers at the corners. Within this cleared area are square fields, long rows of glasshouses, oval ponds where fish are growing, irrigation ditches, graduated water-races and windmills. At the centre of the enclosure are several prefabricated cottages which gather round a central area of green grass which is a playing-field. This small community looks like a village but it is actually a single farm, one of many scattered throughout the province, whose sole purpose is to produce the food demanded by the State. It provides the highest-quality fresh meat and vegetables for consumption in Eburacum and the nearby military camp. Each state farm has a name and a number. Apart from competing in agriculture, the state farms compete in sport and hence the importance given to the central playing-field. Here wrestling contests take place, and races. Two team sports, akin to rugby and cricket, are particularly popular. Just now the rugby posts have been lowered and gardeners are inspecting the damage done over the winter to the central cricket square.

Much of all this might be recognizable to us. Unfamiliar would be the tall pylons which surround the entire farm enclosure and which carry on their tops the black plates of solar-energy cells. Solar energy is widespread and advanced in this world and provides the power for most of the farm.

Roads join up the various state farms into larger units. These cut, straight as ruled lines, through the rough dappled forest. As we move from the wild heart of the forest towards Eburacum and its neighbouring towns, order, planning and a care for economy are becoming more evident. The roads are an assertion: reason over wild Nature; and this is a comforting thought to those who hold that wild Nature ought to be tamed. To the careful observer, however, it is apparent that the vegetation is at its most impenetrable where the forest meets the clipped edge of the roads. It is as though the wild wood is insulating the green glades within from the noisy, peopled roads.

The farm roads join larger highways which cover the entire province, and these in turn link up with the major expressways which lead ultimately to the great cities of the Empire: glittering

Byzantium, vast Roma, marbled Athenae and distant fragrant Xi An, to name but a few.

We drift over one such expressway and notice that it is crowded with vehicles, and all are travelling in the same direction which is away from the city of Eburacum and towards Derventio, the town which we know as Malton. Crowded the road may be, but there is no panic. All the vehicles move down the road at a constant speed, like beads on a string, each vehicle separated from the one in front and the one behind by the same distance.

In appearance the vehicles look like motorized chariots such as we might see at a fairground. But we notice that the wheels on the sides are merely painted disks and that they do not actually touch the ground. The vehicles slide silently, each on its own cushion of air and each held firmly in the magnetic grip of an expressway monitor. Balloons and streamers, thrusting out from the windows, bounce and strain in the breeze. We can hear singing too and laughing and the occasional pop of a champagne cork.

Rising from the median strip in the centre of the road are tall pylons, similar to those found in the state farms except that these are much taller and are capped with twin domes of black and silver. They look like spindly mushrooms and reach well above the highest oak trees in the forest canopy. They are spaced regularly some 200 yards apart. In the breeze they flex and sway as though they are animate and are tasting and filtering the air.

These pylons serve many functions. They receive daylight and convert the sun's energy into power which is used to manage all the different mechanisms of the road including the highway monitor. The Romans have made transport technology into a high art. Accidents are rare on their roads since speed and proximity are both controlled. When a driver has logged his destination into his vehicle's controls, he can lie back on the soft fur-covered couches and drink champagne, leaving the tedious business of actually controlling the vehicle to the road monitor. The pylons also radiate energy on a specific wavelength thereby providing a 'road in the sky', as it is called, along which special air-vehicles glide at astonishing speeds. The sky-road is narrow, extending little more than twenty feet to either side of the pylons. It does not reach out into the wild wood nor does it need to, for there are land roads a-plenty in Britannia and, as the cliché has it, the shortest distance between two points is the Roman road. In any case, the Romans who rule and the Citizens who serve their needs find little of interest in the wild tribes that blow their horns and beat their drums and light their fires beyond the city walls. Finally, the thin pylons support bright lights which blaze down on the road when dusk falls. All the major roads in Britannia are illuminated in this way, which means that at night-time the whole of the province is covered with a spangled web of bright white lights.

Where are all the vehicles going? Obviously there is something exciting at their destination. The road describes a gentle curve east by north and encounters a major junction. Here traffic streaming up from the south joins with the vehicles arriving from Eburacum. The junction takes the form of a vast round-about. The majority of vehicles which enter the roundabout select an exit called Battle Street. Those few which do not, continue north. Soon small roads will branch off the expressway. One of these will head east towards Derventio and the coastal fishing towns. Another will drive directly up on to the Moors where snow still lingers in hollows. Its destination is the famous Caligula Detention and Punishment Camp located near the ancient tumuli above the town which we call Rosedale Abbey. The main expressway continues north via Cataractonium to the towns of Caledonia.

However, we follow the vehicles which have turned off down Battle Street. This road becomes smaller and uncharacteristically picturesque weaving back and forth round pretty lakes and manicured lawns and stands of yew and elm. The traffic moves more slowly now. It is reaching its destination: the Battle Dome.

The Battle Dome is a vast hemisphere. It covers many acres and its sides rise sheer and smooth from the tightly packed trees of the wild forest. There are many tall oak and beech trees in the forest, but they cannot match the dome for height. It rises, unblemished and sterile, white and alien, high above the trees and then curves majestically inwards to its apex.

In the summer there is rain which drums and froths and sluices down the sides. In the winter there is snow which pelts and freezes and caps the surface of the dome with ice causing a shallow depression. At such times the dome's lights are switched on providing warmth. The frozen mass melts and comes slithering down the sides in crumpled sheets of snow and slush to land with a thump round the dome's base. After a few moments the roof of the dome reasserts its true shape with a muffled snap.

For tonight, a clear starbright sky is forecast with perhaps a few degrees of frost to make patterns on the windows. There are no clouds and there is no wind. The trees stand stiff and still while a crescent moon rises to the south above the distant Wolds.

The day is waning and the sun is almost gone. In the light which people call Blind Man's Holiday, the dome glows a milky blue while part of its surface is stained pink by the last rays of the setting sun.

3 The Battle Dome

For the young officers and cadets studying at the Marcus Aurelius Military Academy at Eburacum, tonight was the most important night of the year, for this was the night when the graduation combat took place – a combat for which they had trained all year. The celebration, always held at the end of April or in early May, marked their coming of age as members of the administrative Roman élite, and was one of the main activities associated with that ancient fertility festival, the Reformed Lupercalia. It was *reformed* only in the sense that the date had been changed. The Lupercalia of old Italia had been held in February: but that date was too cold in the more northern Britannia. Hence the change.

Wherever you looked there were people hurrying about. Fairy lights twinkled and bobbed in the trees while projectors played coloured images over the curved surface of the dome.

The land-vehicles, arriving in their hundreds, glided to a halt under the trees and sank on to their false wheels. They disgorged their passengers before lifting again and moving to a ramp which led down to the vast underground chariot-park.

Flyers from Eburacum and the distant cities of Londinium, Viroconium, Aquae Sulis and Deva swooped in along the charged sky-road and settled in a clearing close to the dome. Men and women emerged wearing fine bright clothes. Many were carrying lanterns while others unfurled multicoloured banners on which were emblazoned insignia. These identified which of the major families the revellers supported. There was the red-on-black banner of the Caesar clan and the white-on-black banner of the Manavia. The Gallica banner was much in evidence in black on gold, as was the Agricola in red on white. Ulysses, green on black, vied with the Severus banner of red on green. And there were many, many more. Everywhere there was colour and pageantry and the buzz of excited voices. Almost everyone attending had at one time been a student at the Eburacum Military Academy and had fought in the Battle Dome. They all carried the swords awarded to them at their graduation and the swords were keenly sharp, for they were not toys and would see action this night.

Attendants wearing the smart maroon uniforms of the Battle Dome staff greeted each of the flyers and took charge of it and guided it down to its parking-place where its battery could be recharged.

A squadron of black beetle-like flyers dipped down to the surface of the dome and passed through a special portal which opened like a small mouth on the dome's surface. These vehicles, jet-black save for the silver axe device on their under-surfaces, ferried those students from the Military Academy who would fight this evening. Once the black vehicles were inside the dome, the aperture closed.

Shouting taunts and insults, singing battle-hymns and carrying glasses and bottles in their hands, the revellers stepped out on to a moving transit path and were carried towards the dome. The transit path resembled a ruby-red carpet and was called the Blood Path of Honour. It twisted round the boles of the trees and carried the revellers through a low arch and into the Battle Dome proper. Once inside, they stepped off the transit path at a tiled piazza where were tables laden with pig-meat and bull-meat, tripes, wholemeal bread, creamy butter, fruits from Arabia and the South Seas, cakes from Parma shaped like butterflies, steamed mussels with pepper and garlic sauce, braised pheasant, jugged hare, Scotch eggs and a delicacy from Cathay called spiced pangolin. There was a special dark fruit-cake in which gold coins were hidden. Bottles of chilled white wine from Germania, upon which condensation had formed, stood in gleaming ice-water beside bowls of rich red wine from Gallia and Hispania. They were available for the thirsty, as was beer. Following ancient custom, a special brew had been put down for this occasion. Wooden barrels decorated to resemble the bellies of bulls were set up on chocks and the first was broached as the first revellers arrived. Pints were drawn, the froth blown off, and the flavour debated. It was a dark beer, suitable for spring, suitable for the Reformed Lupercalia, and it received its proper accolade: empty pint glasses proffered for more.

Overseeing the food and drink was a master chef dressed in a white jacket, blue checked pants and sporting the traditional chef's hat. He beamed like a host, his hands on his ample waist, and nothing was too much trouble for him. He was flattered to be called by name, Walter, by the old and young of the Roman military class. At his disposal were carvers and doughmen, brewers and porters. At his nod, waiters hurried between tables to deliver special delicacies or replace dropped forks. Other chefs, his equal in skill but lacking his rank, stood ready to tenderize or crispen or satisfy a sudden whim for an omelette or a crêpe. Though the excited Romans might vomit his sauces through over-indulgence, Walter's eyes only became chill if he saw any of his staff failing in their duty. His dream, like the dream of his father before him, was that the cuisine at the Eburacum Battle Dome be regarded as the best in the world, service befitting the capital city of Britannia.

Beyond the piazza where the food was served were tiers of seats. They reached high up the wall of the dome and appeared to be firmly set on the side of a grassy hill. But the hill was false. It could be trundled on rails round the perimeter of the dome to any location and thus the battlescape could be changed each year. At the very top of the hill was a chalet with high sloping roofs and a wooden balcony which jutted out over the seats below. This building was reserved for the most distinguished guests from other parts of the Empire and for those champions who survived the evening battles.

Some of the revellers, balancing plates and glasses as well as their banners, climbed up to their seats and sat studying the arena. Facing them was a fantastic landscape which had been carefully scaled to the human and compressed into false perspective. It was a landscape which had all the immediacy of a Chinese willow-pattern plate or a medieval morality painting where dark valleys meet aspiring mountains and where caves and rivers and strange rocks offer adventures unimaginable. Each year the battlescape was different, its possibilities limited only by the imagination of the architect and the technical competence of the engineers. For this year, the main design intention was to recreate an Alpine valley.

To the left there was a mountain. Its shoulder joined the side of the dome and its crest, soaring up towards the high curving roof, owed something to the Matterhorn. Its peak appeared snowbound and fleecy clouds drifted round it. Lower down, diminutive pine trees grew round the mountain's steep slopes and merged with half-sized oak, ash and elm trees at the foothills. The black pine trees were new for this year as also were a ring of monoliths which stood on the grassy meadow at the foot of the mountain. They looked like a newly built Stonehenge and would provide an interesting hazard in the coming battles and contests.

Two rivers tumbled from the mountain's heights in impressive waterfalls. They meandered when they reached the plain, passing behind the circle of standing stones, and finally fed into a lake which lay half hidden in the distance behind gracious weeping willows.

Beyond the lake were more tree-covered hills. And beyond the hills there was a mistiness in which one could just detect the gaunt shapes of cliffs and romantic canyons . . . but these disappeared as soon as perceived, hidden behind veils of artificial mist. Here the dome's architects were working, inventing the battlescape for a year hence.

The artificial grass was bright green round the foothills and on the plain. It had been rolled to a perfect flatness and pulled and teased so that there were no wrinkles which showed where it had been sewn together. Some of the guests wandered out on to the plain and tested the springy turf by stamping and felt its texture between finger and thumb.

The overall visual effect facing the onlookers was of wildness contained. It might have been a dramatic golf course or a museum diorama with heroic implications. It was a toy landscape, a place of derring-do, a land fit for heroes.

Outside the dome the day was giving way to evening and the daylight gradually faded from the sky. The food on the tables was consumed and newcomers dwindled to a few stragglers. While dessert was being taken, musicians assembled at a pavilion near the barbecue pits and set out their instruments. They were all members of a brass band from the walled city of Deva. They struck up some cheerful military airs while the waiters and attendants scurried among the banks of seats collecting plates and glasses. This music was the cue for everyone to finish their eating and take their places. There was much jostling and shouting and climbing over seats and, while the last clashing cymbal notes of the Imperial March faded, the lights in the dome gradually dimmed until only an orange 'pre-show special' remained, lighting up the bottom of the mountain at a place where there were many tumbled rocks.

Suddenly this light intensified to a searing whiteness. A large boulder twitched and then moved, rolling to one side with a mighty rumbling to reveal a cave. Inside the cave was tethered a white bull. A single high note on a trumpet sounded and on this cue a second searchlight blinked on and picked out a man dressed in silver who came gliding down from the apex of the dome astride a milk-white horse with widespread wings. The horse flapped its wings lazily and flew high over the spectators and round the walls and then dropped down lower to land finally near the cave. The horse dropped to its knees and the man stepped from the saddle and on to the ground. This was Mithras, the god of the legions. Rays of light shone from his hair. He carried a bright sword.

The god stepped away from the horse and advanced to the cave. Aware of him, and perhaps with some premonition of its fate, the bull stamped and blew and lowered its head. Its breath was grey about its face. Mithras released the bull, slicing through the leather thongs which held it, and slapped its buttocks with the flat of his sword. It ran and he ran beside it and then with one bound he leaped up on to its back and before the surprised bull could so much as roar and arch its back, the god reached down and round, and slit the bull's throat with one movement of his bright sword. The bull stood stock still for a moment. It seemed to cough and then it buckled while the blood poured from the wound and steam rose from the ground where the blood ran. The bull sank on to its knees, its silly head twisted without control, and the man rode it down to the ground. Finally it toppled over and lay dead with one rear leg quivering.

There came a great breathing-out from the assembled spectators. The simple rite was ended and the sacrifice made. Blood was spilt and the god intact. Mithras stood in the blood and with his sword cut open the body of the bull and revealed the heart which still beat convulsively. With the tip of his sword he excavated the heart and lifted it above his head. Blood dripped on to his tunic. Then, still carrying the heart, he mounted the winged horse which beat its wings. Support cables tightened and the horse and rider rose slowly and began to fly in a widening spiral.

Again the god flew over the spectators. With a heave he threw the heart wide and away from him to fall down into the crowd. There spectators clamoured for it for it was a great prize worth much gold at game's end and assuring fertility and fortune for the year ahead.

The rider and the white horse faded into the gloom in the roof of the dome. On the ground, the light slowly faded on the tragic, ecstatic scene of the slaughtered bull. And only when the light was finally extinguished did cheering and stamping begin. The carcass of the bull would remain on the field during the entire evening's festivities.

Now the spectators were primed and looking for action. Rockets soared into the sky from behind the mountain and exploded into a burst of coloured stars. A trumpet played a savage fanfare like the screaming of a horse and the festivities began. From darkness the lights blazed to full, revealing every detail of the plain and mountain and lake. The spectators settled back in their comfortable seats.

First on the bill was an equestrian show presented by the first-year cadets of the Military Academy. They galloped their horses round the lake through the circle of monoliths and on to the plain. Then they slowed to a trot and finally drew into a line before the spectators. The horses bowed to the terraces, lowering their heads to the ground, and the cadets raised their sabres. Many spectators responded with the same gesture, waving their swords above their heads and shouting 'Prima. Prima.'

The cadets came to attention and began to walk their mounts slowly following strict patterns on the plain in front of the terraces. They held their sabres advanced and began weaving in and out of one another. It was a dangerous movement. Then they moved from a walk to a trot and from a trot to a canter and finally to a full gallop. Only once did a cadet have to rein in to protect a colleague's steed. They ended the manoeuvre with all the horses wheeling into a full battle-charge straight at the onlookers. The cadets screamed and waved their sabres and pulled up their steeds just feet from the first row of seats. The manoeuvre was received with applause. It was a traditional ending but one which never failed to bring a rouse. The spectators hurled flowers and bouquets down on to the horses which again bowed prettily before turning and rearing and then galloping away past the lake.

Trumpets blared. Drums beat a galloping rhythm. And before the dust could settle after the cadets' departure, there came another drumming of hooves and a cracking of whips and chariots burst into the arena and began a circuit of the plain.

At the same time, men and women wearing the green uniform which signified that they were gardeners hurried out from a hidden location in the mountainside and placed markers round the standing stones. These stones became the inner perimeter for a chariot run which extended round the entire plain.

This entertainment, a chariot contest, was presented by the junior officers of the second year. Each chariot had a driver who was an instructor at the Academy. The vehicles had short knives at the wheels and were open at the back. The style had hardly changed in two thousand years except that the chariots now had hydraulic brakes and the wheels had pneumatic tyres. The harness too was improved and gave the charioteer greater control over the powerful horses.

The chariots drew up in a line at right angles to the rows of seats and the drivers nimbly jumped from their vehicles and held the horses by the bridle for they were excited and fired up and pawed the ground and shook their heads, whinnying.

The second-year officers now entered at a run. They were

stripped for fighting, wearing only the traditional leather tunics and greaves, and with dampened leather thongs bound round their knuckles. They lined up in front of the terraces and then knelt down on the grass with their arms spread wide. The drumming reached a climax and stopped leaving an awful silence. In that silence the horses became still.

A voice rang out, echoing round the dome. 'We the officers of the second year . . .'

The kneeling officers repeated the words. 'We the officers . . .'

'Swear by the blood of the bull of Mithras . . .'

'Swear by the . . .'

'That we will fight to the death if needs be . . .'

'That we will fight . . .'

'For the honour of the victor's crown . . .'

'For the honour . . .'

'And the glory of the Senate and the People of Roma.'

'And the glory of the Senate and the People of Roma.'

The oath ended. A fight marshal ran forwards and waved a red flag. The drum beat once and on this cue the charioteers sprang into their chariots, holding their horses firmly by the bit.

The marshal signalled a second time and the officers of the second year stood up and braced themselves in running position. He signalled a third time and the game was on. The charioteers cracked their whips and the chariots began to move, milling about. The first objective for the officers was to run and leap aboard a chariot. However, there were fewer chariots than Officers and this meant that fighting took place as two contestants sought to occupy the same chariot. Inevitably some officers missed out in this very first round and this was their disgrace and frequently the end of their participation. Those who did succeed each jumped into his chariot and there selected a pennant which he stuffed into a small leather bag at his waist. Each chariot had its own named pennants and the winner at the end of the contest was the officer who had the largest number of different pennants. Cheating, such as throwing pennants away so that others could not get them, led to immediate dismissal from the Academy.

Once a chariot had an officer on board, the driver whipped

the horses up and they began to charge round the circuit. Now the officers began the difficult and dangerous task of leaping and scrambling from chariot to chariot. Some climbed out along the shafts and leaped on to the horses of a neighbouring chariot and thence began to fight their way back to the chariot proper. Others vaulted directly from vehicle to vehicle. When two young officers met in a chariot they wrestled until one was ousted from the back of the vehicle and sent sprawling on to the ground. If a chariot became empty either because it was abandoned or because both its occupants had fallen out, it withdrew. Thus, as with our musical chairs, there were always more fighters than chariots. The game could last for twenty circuits, but so great was the depletion rate that the game rarely went the full number before there was a clear victor.

The chariot contest was a gambling event and many of the spectators backed a young warrior with the name Victor Ulysses. Almost as many backed a tall golden-haired youth called Alexander Diotimus.

The young Ulysses was a stocky, dark-haired, handsome youth. He swung from chariot to chariot with the agility and strength of a monkey. He wrestled well, too, having a naturally low centre of gravity. When he defeated Alexander after a long and brutally fought contest in the back of a pitching chariot, a great cry went up from the audience. Victor Ulysses was obviously hurt, but adrenalin and the blood-lust were keeping him going. Those who fancied him were rewarded for he managed to retain the last chariot. He up-ended his opponent, Diana by name, and then kicked her in the stomach when she rose so that she fell backwards out of the chariot and rolled on the ground. Even so his victory was narrow and depended on the decision of the judges. Both he and Diana received a standing ovation for both had shown outstanding stamina and courage.

Victor Ulysses moves with an easy confidence as he takes Diana by the hand and they salute the audience. He knows he is good and only requires opportunities to show how good. Casually he brushes back the dark curls from his brow revealing a profile that would have delighted Praxiteles as he planned his statue of Hermes. But as with many conventionally handsome men, there is a hint of weakness too, a latent decadence, perhaps suggesting that the real flesh-and-blood man cannot live up, either morally or physically, to the expectations inspired by his mien. This young man is sole male heir to the Ulysses family, one of the wealthiest families in all Britannia. We have called him Victor Ulysses but among his family he is called simply Viti.

When the chariots had departed there remained only the mercy vehicles with their bright blue and white flags. The injured were patched up. They limped or were carried to a high chalet where they could watch the rest of the entertainment. Two contestants had died, kicked or trampled when they fell from the back of a chariot, and their parents, present among the spectators, stood up and left the dome sad-faced but dry-eyed. One of the young dead was the much-favoured athlete called Alexander, of whom more later.

As the ambulances departed, the brass band struck up with a fanfare announcing the opportunity for final refreshments before the next entertainment of the evening. Winnings were claimed, wine and beer were drunk and the relative skills of the young officers were debated. Then a fanfare blared again played by many bugles. It began like the Last Post and changed to a voluntary before returning to final, lingering, plangent notes. The spectators hurried to their places. A series of individual contests was about to begin. These were contests assigned by the Praefectus Comitum himself and were fought between adult members of the Roman families. The battles could be the result of grudges or insults. Alternatively they could take place simply to display the latest technology, for all the battles involved machinery of one sort or another. Always they involved spectacular shows of skill. During most of the year, the Battle Dome was host to such contests on a monthly basis, but on this, the night of the graduation, such battles were by way of a side entertainment and the contestants were drawn from former champions of the Academy. In the popular tongue these contests were called the Battle of the Beasts.

As the sound of bugles faded, the thousands of spectators quietened and their attention again became focused on the battlescape which was again brilliantly illuminated. All that could be seen of the spectators on the chalet high above was a row of binoculars resting on the balcony rail. No one knew how the contest would begin. Surprise was one of the main ingredients.

It was the massed crowds on the terraces who first saw movement among the dark pine trees high on the mountain. Trees shook where there was no breeze. Artificial snow, dislodged, fell in a cascade. Something was moving: some giant beast. It was working its way down the mountainside using the pine trees for cover. It moved stealthily despite its bulk and only occasionally was a tree seen to jerk and then fall.

Binoculars searched the depth of the battlescape looking for the opponent. But nothing moved.

The creature in the pine trees reached the foothills where the pine woods ended and a squat triangular lizard's head poked out briefly from the undergrowth. On its horned crown it bore the device of the Ulysses family and this was greeted with a cheer from that family's many supporters. The creature sniffed the air and then the entire beast advanced.

A monster, fancifully modelled on prehistoric forms, emerged dragging its long tail which flexed back and forth, scything down small trees and bushes. The beast looked like a dragon and if plumes of smoke had belched from its nostrils then this would have seemed quite appropriate. Indeed, one of the horns on its head was equipped to shoot flame but this was strictly prohibited in the Battle Dome. The creature had six legs which worked in pairs, and each leg had black talons of carbon steel which left imprints in the turf as it moved. The rear legs were mighty haunches. They were jointed and could move independently or together and could hurl the creature forwards at tremendous speed, at a leap if needs be. They could also crush an opponent, for individually they could be raised high like a hammer to come smashing down. The middle pair of legs was mainly for support. They had spiked wheels between the talons and could be raised telescopically, giving the creature a humped appearance. The spiked wheels were chain-driven and provided the dragon with a steady sustained speed. Slung between the middle legs was a retractable wheel-and-track mechanism. This was particularly useful if the creature had to climb up a hill or needed to anchor itself in the ground to withstand a charge. The half-track also allowed the beast to inch forward, a movement far too subtle for the mighty drive-haunches or requiring too much traction for the middle legs. The front pair of legs was simply for support and guidance. They too were telescopic and could lift the creature some thirty feet off the ground. When both the front and the middle legs were extended the dragon appeared to be begging. High on its front the creature carried a pair of claws. These were simply for fighting. The claws closed like knives folding together and the entire joint could swivel and extend from the body of the beast.

In its appearance the dragon was quite beautiful and it was painted afresh after every fight. Scales of different sizes covered its entire body. The colours of these ranged from aquamarine round the belly to burnished red at the spine. On the head and neck the scales were golden. Rising above the spine were pentagonal plates which looked like defensive armour but whose primary function was to serve as heat-exchange units. When the creature was at rest these units also served as steps. In movement the creature gave an awesome impression of fluid grace and great power while yet being somewhat comic.

Free from the restrictions of the wood the dragon trundled into open space and looked about. Then it raised its massive head and opened its jaws, displaying interlocking teeth, and roared. The meaning of the roar was unmistakable. It was a challenge. It said, 'Come out and fight, whoever you are.' Silence greeted this challenge.

This was not normal. Usually by now the shape of a battle was forming and a challenge was answered with a challenge. A hum of conversation broke out as people began to wonder if something had gone wrong. Then again, others reasoned, this was a grudge match to settle a long-standing argument between the Ulysses family and the Caesars, and in such cases there was considerable latitude in interpreting the rules. The result was that the contestants more or less played as they saw fit, grabbing advantage when it presented itself, and to hell with the code of conduct. While most battles ended with an act of surrender, more than once in recent history a battle had resulted in the death of the loser and the total dismemberment of his vehicle. One never knew, battle-fever being unpredictable. It was widely speculated in the crowd (though only in whispers) that this contest would end in a death, for the Ulysses and the Caesars were old rivals and had many reasons to hate.

So people muttered and waited and then the more observant began pointing towards the lake. A ripple line had appeared, forming a V on the lake's surface. Whatever was below the surface was unmistakably driving for the lake's edge where the trees hung out over the water and provided cover.

The monster saw nothing of this. It stamped on the plain near the standing stones and again bellowed its challenge with back arched and mouth open wide. It smashed its front claws together and the air shimmered above its spines as it shed energy. For a few moments it paused with one rear leg raised, immobile as a statue, and the onlookers guessed that the Ulysses who was driving the beast was checking with battle headquarters to make sure that there had not been some foul-up in the organization and that a battle was really on.

That pause was all the creature in the lake needed. It launched itself from the water using the dappled shade from the trees as camouflage and the standing stones for cover. It was low like a crab but ran like a spider. It had a horned head with a frill of bone to protect its spine. Tusks stood out from its lower jaw and with these it could lever and pitch. On giant arms in front it sported a pair of claws which were spiked and razor-sharp.

It came like a shadow over the grass and the Dragon with the burnished scales found itself attacked before it could move. The Crab sank its tusks near the place where the monster's tail joined its body and it attempted to rip part of the scales free. But the Dragon read the plan and planted one of its giant hind feet squarely on one of the Crab's pincers and crushed it with its weight. Sparks flew and the claw became detached. At this a murmur rose from the spectators.

The giant Crab pulled back leaving its claw behind and sat back on its rear legs with its spiny head advanced. It looked for advantage and what damage it might have caused.

The Dragon was wounded, that was clear. It rounded to face the Crab but it dragged one of its rear legs slightly. A hole had been opened up in the dragon's plating and several red scales now lay scattered and bent on the grass. Those spectators with binoculars could see one of the high-pressure air-pistons which powered the leg flailing about inside the dragon. Its couplings were broken but power was still being fed to it. The terrible clattering of the loose piston-arm could be heard by everyone.

The Dragon roared and lowered its head. The tractor mechanism under its belly whirred into life and began to churn the earth, dragging the beast round. There came a wrenching of gears and the Dragon began to advance with jaws open. To the experts on the terraces this seemed like a stupid manoeuvre. The Dragon seemed to be making itself vulnerable. It seemed to be inviting attack. The giant Crab skittered round, suspicious, trying to approach the monster on its damaged flank, but the Dragon kept it at bay.

Then with a suddenness which caught the onlookers by surprise, the Dragon heaved forwards using its rear legs in a single leap. It took the spines of the Crab's head in its mouth and with its front claws tried to shake it. For its part the Crab did not retreat but leaped forwards and its tusks opened a wound low on the monster's throat. Black oil spurted. Pressing its advantage, the giant Crab caught the Dragon round the throat and shoulders with its remaining claw and began to twist its neck. Methodically the Crab heaved part of its bulk up on to the Dragon's back, locking its legs in the heat-exchange units and bending the plates back. It was seeking unbreakable leverage. And then, just when it looked as though the Dragon would be torn open in the throat, the Dragon heaved and rolled. This was a move rarely seen, a dangerous move, for the torque of neck and tail had left many such creatures with compound dislocations. Easy prey; easy meat. Defeated. Sometimes, too, the gimbals which held the giant flywheel that gave the Dragon its power fractured, sending the wheel bounding free to destroy everything within the body of the beast.

But this roll was carefully executed. Every part of the beast joined in the convulsion so that a mighty peristalsis took place, and the Dragon rolled over the Crab and squashed it. The cracking of the carapace could be heard by everyone. The legs on one side crumpled and hydraulic pistons broke through the skin and began pouring oil. The remaining claw opened and closed jerkily. To add final insult to injury, the Dragon shook itself free and then turned its back on the Crab, raised its tail and brought it smashing down like the blunt back of an axe on an enamel garden bucket. The Crab ruptured in every seam. The Dragon limped away. The battle was over. It had lasted just seven minutes.

The crowds on the terraces came to their feet. Those who supported the Ulysses family cheered and applauded and shouted their appreciation. Others were more thoughtful, especially those of the Caesar clan. They recognized the skill and daring of the last manoeuvre. But they also realized that a senior member of the family had just been killed. None could foresee the consequences of this. Would a blood feud now erupt to go clattering down the centuries until both families were tired, depleted and ruined? It had happened before, to others.

Any such speculation was certainly not in the mind of the man who controlled the Dragon. The Dragon bayed. It was hurt but it could still manage a loping run. The half-track withdrew into its belly and it lumbered in a circle round the broken body of the Crab and tore the grass with its claws. Its tail snaked back and forth, bruising the grass, and knocking over two of the monoliths like skittles. In mid-flight it suddenly halted. One by one its claws closed and dug into the earth, anchoring it. The half-track emerged from the belly and sank to the earth. Finally, the fierce head lowered and came to rest on the ground. The eyes closed with a snap.

A few moments later a hatch in the high part of the back flipped open and a white-garbed arm emerged and waved. The arm was followed by a head wearing a crash-helmet. Finally a portly figure in white overalls clambered through and climbed painfully to its feet. The figure stood with legs spread on the sleeping Dragon and waved to the crowds in the terraces.

On this cue, a hinged section of the foothills beneath the mountain cranked open on hydraulic arms. Low-slung vehicles with large wheels came rolling out. The vehicles were accompanied by teams of workers in blue overalls who either rode on the sides or trotted beside the vehicles. One vehicle came up to the Dragon and a nurse, who had ridden aboard it, stepped across and climbed up the back of the Dragon. She checked the portly driver quickly and then helped him climb down the steps set in the neck of the beast and thence to a small flyer which had landed nearby. Immediately they were safely inside, the small craft lifted and carried them both up to the chalet.

A tall, strongly built young man with red hair, the same man who had driven the safety vehicle, now climbed up the Dragon's back and lowered himself into the cockpit. Moments later the creature raised its head, though the eyes remained shut. Then it began to pace, somewhat unevenly and noisily, towards the open hillside. Behind it, it left a trail of black oil. Finally, with a last proud swish of its tail, it vanished down the ramp and into the hillside workshops.

The young man driving the monster is named Angus and he is an apprentice mechanic at the Battle Dome. He has celebrated his eighteenth birthday just a few weeks earlier. He is well over six feet tall and has a raw strength in his muscles and a quick temper which of necessity he keeps well in check. Beneath his shock of red hair his eyes are wide-spread and green and his jaw is firm, suggesting stubbornness.

The Crab was greatly damaged. Vehicles clustered about it like ants round a piece of meat. The carapace could not be hinged open in the normal manner and so large-bladed cutting-machines were used to force entry. They cut through its skin sending up plumes of orange sparks, and fork-jawed lifters prised the sections apart. The driver of the machine was located just below the spined head. His lower body was crushed as though a vice had closed on it. The purple face retained some hint of anger and surprise, but that was all. The death had been swift and merciful. The warrior was fortunate. His name was Gaius Julius Caesar XIX, which meant that he was the nineteenth by descent to hold that name.

Ambulance workers took charge of his remains and the body was soon removed. Blue-garbed workers swarmed all over the Crab, checking its suspension and hydraulic systems. Its central structure was distorted and there was no way it could be made to move on its own. After a brief discussion among the mechanics, sections of the Crab were jacked up and large-wheeled bogies were edged underneath. These took its weight. When the creature was completely supported, the leader of the mechanics, a man with a slight limp from an accident many years earlier, blew on his whistle and waved his arms like the conductor of an orchestra. The ungainly Crab began to move slowly, rocking slightly on the soft suspension of the support vehicles. It made a slow and painful exit into the giant hangar in the hillside. It was clear that the vehicle was a complete write-off.

As soon as the convoy of large-wheeled machines departed, other smaller vehicles moved on to the plain and began to scurry about. These came from behind the mountain where the gardeners had their hydroponics tanks and seed-beds. They set about mending the turf: cutting out damaged patches and stitching in new sections of synthetic grass. They smoothed the scars where the Dragon's claws had gouged. They reset and replaced the damaged monoliths. The ground now crawled with green-garbed workers. No amphitheatre in ancient Roma ever presented a more busy scene. And as soon as their work was completed, the teams of workers departed, clinging to the backs and sides of their vehicles. Last to leave, standing in his green and orange command vehicle, was the master gardener.

Satisfied that all was in order, he departed and a rocket roared and sputtered from the middle of the standing stones. The rocket exploded into a cascade of stars high in the roof of the dome. This was the signal that the arena was ready for the next contest. Only half an hour had elapsed since the breaking of the Crab and the death of Gaius Julius Caesar XIX.

Again there was silence as eyes devoured the landscape for movement.

33

At the margin of the forest, earth was thrown back and a creature like a centipede drilled its way from the ground. As it emerged, spines rose from its back, each one moving independently of its neighbour. The spines were projectiles which could be fired. It ran for a hundred yards or so until it was close to the standing stones and then it dipped its head and burrowed into the earth. Within seconds it was gone, leaving a tell-tale mound of freshly turned earth and a slight whiff of burnt oil.

No sooner had it vanished than a bat-winged creature with claws and saw-toothed bill flapped lazily into view from behind the mountain. Its head cast about from side to side as its heat sensors studied the ground.

The next battle between Spurius Romulus Glabrio and Calpurnia Gallica was on.

And after this battle, three more took place between different creatures, each with its particular strength and character. The last of these was a comedy duel between a pair of creatures which resembled porcupines and which ended with them trying to copulate strenuously while they fired their quills all over the plain and hillside.

After this the field was again cleared and made ready for the climax of the evening's entertainment, the tactical gladiatorial battles of the graduating class.

These latter were strict contests in which detachments of forty fully armed soldiers were matched against one another. Each graduating student had trained his or her soldiers for months. The battles were to the death: not for the commanders, but for the soldiers, and hence it was in the soldiers' own interests to fight as ferociously as possible. The blood-lust of the spectators grew as they watched and gambled and drank, and they were not disappointed. The green plain where chariots had run and a fairy-tale dragon had trampled became a churned and blood-red killing-field. After each battle, the green-overalled gardeners mended the turf and hosed down the grass but the stain and smell of blood was everywhere and could not be removed.

In this graduating class only sixteen students had survived to the final year. Of these only one could win the coveted wreath of

Victor Ludorum. Sixteen armies became eight. Eight became four. Four became two and finally, like a repeat of the battle between the Horatii and the Curiatii, a single unscarred commander whose troops were all dead was matched against three wounded opponents. Having a knowledge of history, the sole commander separated his enemies by running before them and goading them with insults. Then he turned and cut them down one by one by one.

This last bloody contest ended at about four o'clock in the morning.

It was followed by the last rite.

While the Romans ate and drank for the last time and vomited and argued about the last contest, prisoners condemned to death during the year were marched across the bloody field and penned behind iron grilles within the standing stones. These were men and women who had violated state laws by stealing weapons or who had opposed the Romans in some way or who had struck out at one of them. Many were young people brought that day from the nearby Caligula Detention and Punishment Camp up on the Moors.

A final trumpet sounded. Hearing this the Roman warriors turned from their food and drink and licked their lips. A terrible silence descended on the Battle Dome. One by one the Romans drew their graduation swords and stepped away from the tables or climbed down from the terraces. Some stripped off to reveal beneath their party clothes the tunics and insignia of their student legions. Others donned white plastic overalls which they had brought with them in small pocket-bags. They advanced, bright-eyed with fatigue and lust, until they stood round the standing stones. Then in one movement the iron grilles clattered down and they charged forwards and killed in their favourite fashion. Some struck once, aiming for jugular vein or heart. Others hacked. There were some who drank the warm blood. There were women daubed in red who used nail and tooth. Some men had erections. Some men shouted the names of their gods as they lunged and cut. Some taunted their victims: some victims, with hands chained, tried to bite and kick. Others knelt and bowed their head.

At the end there were no prisoners left standing, or kneeling. Their bodies lay tangled, open-eyed and bloody. The Romans sat panting and satiated, each alone as he or she slowly returned to reality. In their own time they wiped their blades and returned to their places and got changed and joined their friends.

The games were over for a year.

In small groups the revellers slowly made their way out of the dome and were conducted to their personal flyers and chariots. A few tried to continue the party, calling for food and drink and music to dance to. But they were out of luck. The chefs had all gone home and only the undertakers remained. They began to sort the bodies for cremation. The festivity was at an end, for this year.

In the middle of the field the lone carcass of the sacrificial bull had its rear legs tied together and then it was dragged away behind a tractor to a door behind the hillside. Its steaks and tripes were a traditional perk for the gardeners.

As the revellers sauntered into the chill morning air outside the dome, they encountered some of the woodlanders who had gathered at the entrance to watch the activities within. The tired members of the military caste paid them scant attention as they stepped on to the red carpet which now carried them away from the dome and towards their vehicles. For their part the woodlanders watched the Romans and their faces held no expression. They were neither envious nor afraid. Had the latter-day Romans chosen to look closely they would have noticed that the men were generally tall and broad of shoulder with fine features. The women were full-bodied and bold-faced. There was no hint of malnutrition or premature ageing through hardship. And bright-eyed children peeped from the folds of their garments.

One of the forest people is standing apart from the rest. He is a stranger among the strange. His only garment is the skin of an Arctic deer which is laced at the neck and lashed to his wrists. Where the head of the deer has been removed, a hood of white fur has been stitched into place. This hood can be removed and the antlered head replaced if ceremony requires. The skin trails on the ground behind him. This is a garment for the deep forest. When travelling, the man can wrap himself up in the skin for the night and sleep dry and warm at the foot of a tree though the wind howls in the branches and the rain falls in torrents. He stands with his hands on his hips revealing that his own skin, on his chest and legs, is covered with a pale down like a baby goat. The legs do not end in cloven hoofs, however, but in normal feet which are encased in loose sandals. He wears shorts of stitched hide which cover his midriff to his knees. He shows firm, hard muscles in his legs as though he is used to running.

This night his hood is thrown back revealing a brown face with thoughtful grey eyes. His hair is fair and straight and he wears it parted at the sides and plaited on top. At his side is a woven bag and across his back he carries a set of bagpipes made from the hide of a wild pig. Though he carries no weapons, he yet gives the impression that he is fully armed or that he does not need arms should he need to defend himself at a moment's notice. In age he might be thirty-five, or fifty or older. It is impossible to tell. This is Lyf, a witch-man of the green-woods. The other people of the forest pay him no attention. It is as though they cannot see him.

Lyf watched the last of the revellers depart and then, as the sleepy gate-wardens moved to close the dome gate, he stepped to the opening and peered through. He could see up the terraces to the chalet where lights were still blazing. A party was in full swing and would continue until the last guest had been carried away.

'Come on, old man. Shift yourself,' called one of the gate-wardens as he swung the gate into place. Lyf touched his fingers to his tongue and then snapped his fingers together. He bowed and moved away and glided into the dark shadows. The last thing he wanted was to attract undue attention to himself.

High in the chalet the party was in its boisterous phase. A well-known dance-band was playing popular classics from an earlier age and the dance-floor was packed.

Almost unrecognizable were the warriors and students who had fought that night. Gone were the utilitarian battle-costumes and in their place were the plumes of military showmanship. Both men and women wore the long purple or grey or green cloaks of their year. These were a link back to their Roman ancestors. Beneath their cloaks the men wore tight-fitting doublet and hose of black velvet. Their honour medals were in silver. The women wore full skirts of the same black velvet but with sashes of scarlet or yellow silk. Everyone except the older men was dancing.

The older warriors, those who had been settling grudges or were fighting just for the hell of it, were gathered round the bar, reliving the contests.

Prominent among this group was a large man, now somewhat run to fat though still muscular, but with a face and profile that might have been cast from bronze. He was pulling on a large cigar and puffing the blue smoke above the heads of his colleagues. Between puffs he drank wine copiously. This was Marcus Augustus Ulysses, the head of the Ulysses family. Talking to him was a gracious, aquiline-featured woman with tumbling grey hair and a suggestively deep voice. Both had fought that day and both had been victors. Marcus Augustus Ulysses had commanded the Dragon and Calpurnia Gallica had flown the Pterodactyl in the second contest. They were old enemies and lovers.

'I thought we had lost you today, Marcus,' said Calpurnia, with a twinkle in her eye. 'I thought that Dragon roll was a young man's stunt.'

'It is,' he replied smoothly, 'and is still in my repertoire.'

'Bah. You were desperate and lucky. Gaius had you, didn't he? Go on, admit it. You gambled everything on that . . .'

'And won,' said Marcus Ulysses with finality. 'That is all that matters.' He drank quickly. There was silence between them. Finally he said, 'Are you very sorry I killed Julius? He *knew* you, I take it.'

'Are you asking me whether I'm glad you survived, for I suppose you agreed the fight was to the death?'

'We did.'

'Well, I don't know. You have more mana than he. But he was more fun as a man than you will ever be. I hope that hurts you a bit. But yes, I'm glad you came through.' She reached up and kissed him suddenly on the lips. 'We're all getting a bit old for the arena. I've decided that today was my last time. From today I'm going to devote myself to the arts. *Ars longa, vita brevis*, as they say. Well, I reckon I've got about fifteen more years of *vita* before my *brevis* is up. I want to be ready for the pyre without too many regrets. I want to write my memoirs and compose a book of recipes, one for each day of the year, and travel. I'm going to take the South Seas cruise next year and visit some of the Palm Tree Islands and the Great Southern Ice Continent and the Land of the Long White Cloud. My daughters can manage affairs here and they'll be glad to see the back of me for a while, I shouldn't wonder. What about you?'

Marcus Ulysses considered and puffed smoke. He signalled for an attendant to bring an ashtray. 'No,' he said finally. 'I don't want a decline. I still like the feel of the harness. I like the power. I like the killing if that's not too crass a thing to say. If there is one thing I regret it's that we don't have any decent wars going.'

'I think you are incurably romantic,' said Calpurnia. 'If you are not careful I shall write an elegy for you and publish it the day after you are killed in your dragon, crushed like poor Julius. Then everyone will remember my words and forget that you were once flesh and blood, skin and bone. You will only live because a woman took care of your name.'

'Perhaps,' said Ulysses and laughed. 'You talk too much. You always have. You are a strange woman.'

'And a thirsty one,' said Calpurnia holding up her glass.

Ulysses signalled for more drinks and a waiter was instantly beside them. 'There is another thing that keeps me going,' he said. 'I want to keep an eye on my son. He's the last. I have great hopes for him.'

Calpurnia nodded. 'He is a fine-looking young man,' she said, sipping her drink. 'He reminds me of you. A bit shorter perhaps, but a bit brighter too I think. He already seems more adult. Tell

39

me, Marcus: were we more naïve at their age? Did we know as much? Was the world brighter and more innocent when we were young?'

'You are getting drunk.'

'That is my business and it is your business, as a gentleman, not to behave like my conscience or a block of smoking concrete. Relax man: I'm not going to eat you. I want you to answer me.'

Any answer which Marcus Ulysses might have offered was pre-empted by a loud drum solo. This marked the end of the first band's gig. The drummer beat the skins weaving rhythms within rhythms while the sweat stood out on his black forehead and dripped from his nose. The solo ended with cacophony: the trumpet and sax leaping in and tearing at one another melodically while the double bass pulled the tempo down to the earth. Wonderful music, and the audience of bandaged and cut warriors stood round the bandstand and clapped as well as they could.

Ulysses and Calpurnia clapped, both remembering the time of their own graduation from the Military Academy. They had both been champions and very much in love. But because they were so competitive in their natures, that love had had no chance to prosper. In their later lives they enjoyed brief, private, passionate meetings which suited them both in one way but yet left a hunger. Such meetings merely revealed more clearly their deep and unrequited need for companionship. Calpurnia thought of this and felt sadness in her stomach. How many nights had she lain alone in bed or beside a man whom she did not love? Too many. What was wrong with her? What was wrong with all of them? She looked round the assorted men and women, all now deep in their cups, and she felt a feeling akin to vertigo. She was aware of waste. She was aware also that she was letting her awareness show. *Ars longa, vita brevis*, she thought for the second time that night. Well to hell with the art, it's the short life that worries me. Aloud she said, 'Your son still has a year to go?'

Ulysses nodded.

'And you hope he will carry off the Victor Ludorum like you did?'

'Naturally.'

'I would like to meet him again. It must be seven years since the last time. He was all knees and elbows and catapults then.'

Ulysses snapped his fingers and immediately a young woman was at his side. She was one of the general attendants responsible for bringing fresh drinks or cigars or a snack from the buffet. She had dark curly hair and a clear brow. When she was serious she looked sad, but when she smiled her whole face lit up, making her look roguish. She had a loud laugh which often embarrassed her. Her name was Miranda.

'Ask my son to come over here please and bring his partner,' said Ulysses.

Miranda curtsied prettily and nodded in a way which in anyone else might have been too familiar and hence rude but which in her case was simple enthusiasm. Miranda was having the time of her life. At seventeen she was the youngest attendant present and the only one from her year. She would have such a lot to tell her mum and dad and Angus and the other girls at the Eburacum Polytech where she was studying domestic science and catering. It is also fair to say that Miranda had no real understanding of how attractive she was to the bullish males who were present. It was in part her innocent good humour that turned heads but mainly it was an impression that she gave of a sensuality awaiting.

Miranda spoke to the young Ulysses, touching him to gain attention. He was standing with his arm round a beautiful slim blonde woman called Diana. They were near the small stage where the band were busy packing up their instruments. Viti looked surprised and glanced across to his father. Usually a parental summons meant a rebuke, and he could think of nothing that he had done wrong today of all days. Surely today he would receive a word of warmth from his father.

The young Ulysses saw that his father was smiling as he helped himself to another cigar and that he was deep in conversation with the eccentric old woman called Calpurnia who dressed too young for her age but who had flown the Pterodactyl with great skill today. He remembered meeting her once before when he was a boy.

'The pater wants to see me. And you,' he explained to Diana. 'Come on. He's an old rogue. He probably just wants to get an eyeful of you. Don't be offended if he slobbers.'

'He's quite attractive in a ruthless, brutal sort of way,' said Diana being deliberately provocative. Then she held back. 'Did he mean to kill Julius XIX, today? Caesar was my uncle, you know. A kind man. I'll miss him. I always thought the oldies played for honour only.'

'They do. But there was a grudge in that match. Something to do with land. Come on. Pater gets mad if he's kept waiting.' He began to push through the crowd, holding her by the hand, pulling her behind him. She broke his grip by pressing up against the thumb and fingers. That stopped him and he turned back to her.

'You haven't answered my question,' she said. 'Did he mean to kill?'

'Pater rarely kills unintentionally. Yes. He meant to kill. And there is nothing can be done about it. Your uncle knew the odds as well as anyone, and he would have killed the pater given the chance. I'm sure they'd agreed the fight was to the death. The battle marshal would have said something by now if it wasn't. So . . .' He shrugged. 'Come on. Let's get it over with.' Diana looked at him for a moment and then nodded. Hand in hand they approached the two senior Romans.

'I haven't had a chance to compliment you,' rumbled Marcus Ulysses directing his attention to Diana. 'A well-fought contest in the chariots. You almost made my son look a monkey. He was lucky you slipped.'

'I didn't slip,' said Diana, looking at his granite and unyielding but compellingly handsome face. 'I wish I had. He might have missed me with his kick and then I would have been able to catch him in a leg-lock and pitch him out. But he was too quick for me.' She said this brightly and Calpurnia smiled, recognizing the young woman's courtesy. It was an opening for the father to praise the son. But Ulysses senior looked at the ground, unable to smile and unable to congratulate. Finally he cleared his throat and said, 'Would anyone like a cigar?'

Diana accepted. Young Ulysses refused. He was, but for quite different reasons, as embarrassed as his father. He wanted to escape.

'Well I *at least* will congratulate you,' said Calpurnia, speaking directly to the young man and with clear emphasis. 'I know you think I'm a silly old woman in my flying-machine.' Viti began to protest but she waved him down. 'But I can recognize talent when I see it, and you have the potential to be better than your father. *N'est-ce pas?*' She nudged the elder Ulysses in the midriff, demanding his grudging acquiescence, but that man was into conversation with Diana.

'Sorry I killed your uncle,' he said. 'But we had agreed, you know.' He coughed on his cigar. 'He was once my friend. We adventured together in Africa.' He paused. Drink was having its effect. He was on the edge of being maudlin . . . either that or he was preparing to launch into one of his Africa stories in the hope of impressing Diana.

Calpurnia stopped him in his tracks. 'Forget Africa,' she said. 'It was a long time ago and you've told all the stories already, and besides, tonight belongs to these young ones.' She turned away and said with finality, 'It was nice to meet you both. I wish you happiness and hope we will meet next year when, who knows, one of you two might be Victor Ludorum. Now go and enjoy yourselves. Dance till you drop. There is a new band over from the West Coast I'm told, the Beaters or some such. I'm told they're good. Very original. I'll probably come and dance myself before long. Now bye-bye.'

The two made their farewells. Old Ulysses was staring into his glass and grunted. He was somewhat at a loss for words, not being used to having the initiative taken from him by a strong woman and having drunk too much too quickly for any but a muttered riposte. There was also guilt seeping into him like black oil travelling up a wick.

Calpurnia sized him up. 'Do you want to sit down or do you want to dance?' she asked.

'Neither. I want to talk.'

'Then you must talk to yourself, my dear, because I want to dance. Just remember to tell me if you decide to leave.' Calpurnia wandered away, threading her way through the crowd who were already beginning to shout and clap as the drummer checked the tension on his drums and rapped out a snappy break.

Left alone old Ulysses looked round. Everyone seemed to be enjoying themselves and that made him feel even more morose. As life grows short, what does a hero have except the memories of deeds long ago? How empty is memory! A verse from an ancient sad epic drifted into his mind.

> *Happy the hero,*
> *Dead in his prime,*
> *Who need never whisper,*
> *'There once was a time . . .'*

The words fitted his mood perfectly. Marcus Ulysses felt a slight panic.

He looked round and caught the eye of Miranda. He beckoned and she hurried to him though her eyes lingered briefly and longingly on the stage where two of the lead musicians were clowning.

'What is your name?' asked Marcus Ulysses.

'Miranda, sir.'

'Good. Now get me another drink and come back here. I want to tell you all about Africa . . .'

4 Three Tales

The tale of Angus, the apprentice engineer

His full name was Angus Macnamara and he was born at Portus Lemanis which was close to the town which we call Dymchurch beside the Romney Marsh. Both his mother and father were devout members of the Citizen class and deeply loyal to the Roman institutions in which they served. Their family origins were lost after being traced back a few generations. Even so, there were stories which had been handed down over the generations from mouth to mouth.

According to an oft-repeated account, Connie Macnamara was descended from a Celtic tribe called the Demetae though where they had lived she had no idea. When pressed she waved her hand airily and said, 'Over there. To the west. Beyond the magic hills.' Connie Macnamara was a small woman with crinkly dark hair and sharp features and a wide pale forehead. Once when Angus was little, Connie had taught him some dance-steps and sang a few lines from a song in a language that he had never heard. She confessed she did not know the meaning of the words but said, 'Those were the words of my people. Once.' Angus's mother worked as a senior nurse in the casualty wing of the Citizens' Hospital.

Angus's father's origins were both more precise and more mysterious. Five generations earlier his great-great-great-grandfather along with his three brothers had been drafted down to Portus Lemanis from the far northern town of Trimontium. The Macnamara brothers were engineers by training, hardened by winters in the Highlands, and their main occupation in Portus Lemanis was the building of stone dykes. The family history they left behind them in Trimontium was never known and since Citizens rarely travelled beyond the confines of their own town, any contact was lost. Two of the brothers died in an accident shortly after their arrival at Portus Lemanis. The remaining two married, but their accents were so thick as to be almost opaque to their southern wives and neighbours, and story-telling to the children was almost non-existent. Neither lived to an old age.

Engineering ran in the family. Angus's father worked as an engineer on the Great Channel Bridge which, having been thrust out into the channel just north of Dubris, was now curving across to the coast of Gallia.

During all his formative years, Angus was aware of the slow advance of the Channel Bridge. Indeed, the bridge was like a fourth and bossy member of the family. It dominated conversation at mealtime. It provided material for jokes and songs, and gave Angus his first experience of tragedy, for the death-rate among the bridge workers was extremely high and his only uncle was lost when a coal-barge collided with the section on which he was working and he was flung down into the rough sea.

The bridge emerges from the land like a giant blood-vessel. The platform where vehicles move is completely enclosed within a canopy made from the same tough laminate as the Battle Dome. Sturdy legs jab down giving the entire structure an organic appearance as though it had grown roots like a banyan tree. The bridge reaches out over the sea, never rising more than 150 feet above the waves. It does not look like any of the bridges we know and that is because some aspects of the technology of this world are different from ours. The bridge is a tube which has been slightly flattened so that in section it is oval. Within this tube are roads and railways and pipelines. Each of the legs which support it is bedded deep in the silt of the Channel. Where the legs join the tube there is engineering brilliance: it is a combination of the organic and the inorganic, quite unlike anything we know. The legs of the bridge are of thick, pre-stressed ferroconcrete: growing up them are carefully cultivated arms of kelp. At the place where the kelp meets the under-structure of the bridge, the plant has been cut open and oils rubbed into the wound to stimulate the production of a healing gum. This gum flows and is piped into channels and sumps in the base of the bridge. There it hardens. It becomes dense and fibrous like the tough foot of a kelp and joins the two parts of the bridge.

Anchored again to its satisfaction and its wound healed, the kelp grows on and wraps round the entire upper tube of the bridge, lashing it to the legs. The joints thus made are strong and flexible. They can absorb complex patterns of torque and stress. The bridge can flex and move in storms and spring-tides. This bridge, which has already been two generations in the building, will replace the old bridge which was destroyed in a terrible storm during the last century.

However . . .

It was from his father that Angus gained his love of machines, and that love showed itself early. His mother used to tell the story of how, when he was very little, he ran away from home one time and hid aboard one of the giant foundation-barges just before it put to sea. He was not found for a day, and when found sat quietly watching with fascination the noisy pumps with their clattering whirling wheels, each pump lifting 600 gallons of sea-water in thirty seconds. The water helped to cool the power-driver which excavated the sea-bed.

His favourite toys were pieces of machinery which his father brought home from work. He would take them to bits and then slowly reassemble them with seemingly infinite patience.

He also made models of the flyers used by the senior Roman military leaders which he observed taking off from the Cantiacorum Turnabout and thence flying north-west towards the complex Londinium Changeover. The flyers were sleek creatures which rode on an electromagnetic cushion. They could not fly freely but depended on the power lines which ran along the old roads. As a boy of seven Angus had an exact and practical knowledge of magnetism.

Also at the age of seven he sat the PEE exam which is the Primary Evaluation Examination. Not surprisingly he scored highly in the practical areas. Using special materials not unlike Meccano and Lego, he built a mobile crane and a river lock. He was good at sums, too, with a quick understanding of the decimal point. In botany and biology he was average. In the linguistic areas he scored almost zero. His essay on 'The Coastline near Portus Lemanis' consisted of a few uninspired words. This failure at writing was not because he was a dullard by nature but because he had never had the opportunity to develop linguistic skills. Quite simply, the Roman military aristocracy saw no advantage in training abstract thinkers. Indeed, those who were in charge of education rather feared words, for words are the vehicles for ideas. Ideas lead to questions and questions can end up anywhere. They can even be dangerous ... very dangerous. Freedom of expression and individuality were not seen as virtues in this world. The good Citizen was the one who knew his duty, was skilled in his craft and took pride in offering good service. Plumbers and chefs and butchers and engineers were what the State needed, as well as nurses and gardeners and farmers and midwives. In this world, children learned to sing songs, but not how to write music. They learned how to calculate distances but not how to generate equations. They could write reports but not short stories and only in painting did originality show, for the human drive to self-expression is finally unstoppable.

The exams revealed Angus's remarkable aptitude for engineering and this had disastrous consequences for his family. Some two months after his PEE exam, officials from the State Education Authority came knocking at his door and the boy was taken from his parents and sent to the Engineering Academy at Crookesmoor, close to the city which we would know as Sheffield. There he joined with other seven-year-olds of a similar aptitude and ended up living in a large draughty dormitory. He was to remain at the Crookesmoor Academy until the age of eighteen.

The regimen at the Academy was strict. 6.30 A clanging dormitory bell wakes everyone up. 7.00 Breakfast. 8.00–12.00 Classes. One hour for lunch. 1.00–3.00 Classes. 3.30–4.45 Sports (weather and season permitting). 5.30 Evening meal. 7.00 Preparation for the next day. 8.00 Bed. 8.30 Lights out and woe betide any little boy caught talking. However, boys being boys and these being especially bright little boys, they managed to circumvent this rule. One of them built a series of low-power radio transceivers and they conversed from their beds in giggles.

The strict Academy regimen worked. What it lacked in love

was slightly compensated for by the sense of security which prevailed. The youngsters knew where they were and what was expected of them. The rules were strict and punishment was swift for transgressors. But the system was not vindictive. The careful and conscientious boy who kept his nose clean (so to speak) could avoid trouble.

The parents got to see their children twice a year and these were deliberately made into awkward occasions by the officials who managed the Crookesmoor Academy. Their ideal was to wean the children from their mothers and fathers within two years. To the boys, the sad and nervous parents who came to see them were as visitors from some distant land. No intimacy or bonding could occur within the forbidding scoured refectory where the air smelled of boiled turnips and every sound had an echo. The boys sat on polished benches on one side of long tables while their parents sat opposite. The boys twisted their feet and hands and looked anywhere rather than at the strangers who had come to see them and who themselves sat tongue-tied and ill at ease. For most of the parents, the visits ceased after the boys were eleven. Any boys who by that age had not adjusted to the ways of the Academy failed their tests and were discreetly removed. They moved to lower-grade training. Eventually they found their niche in one of the trades. Those at the bottom, the dreamy ones with no real aptitude for anything which the State might consider useful, ended up cleaning the public urinals and pulling up weeds in the state farms. They rarely lived long as the work was hard and the rewards were nil.

The real malcontents in the Academy, those in whom a primeval fire of rebellion burned, were quickly dispatched to camps in Hibernia and Caledonia and to the famous Caligula Detention Centre on the Moors not far from Eburacum. There they joined others expelled from the different training institutes scattered throughout civilized Britannia. And of them more later. But be it noted that few of these survived beyond thirty. Fewer still managed to transmit their genes. Thus it had been for centuries.

By and large a passive society of contented and mild-mannered citizens had been engendered. The price paid for this security was creativity, for there is a close link between the creative act and rebellion since both require a new vision of what might be. But still there were throw-backs. Truly is it said that it is not poverty that leads to rebellion but awareness of poverty. There were still men and women born with independent minds who asked very basic questions such as 'Do not all children come into this world equal?' and 'Is not death the only certainty faced by all?' Such thinkers began to question the very basis of Roman rule. 'Why,' they asked, 'do we not have a society that seeks the good of all, rather than the good of a few?' 'What should justify the worth of a man? His heredity or his ability?' 'How may those who have no power redress their wrongs except with gunfire?' And of course these questioners paid a high price for their ideas. One such was a quietly spoken and unworldly schoolmaster called Thomas. This man, alive some two hundred years before Angus, taught languages during the day and at night worked on in the school, using the printing-press to turn out short revolutionary works which he distributed under the name 'The Citizen's Friend'. One night, the school-master was caught by a detachment of the Civilian Militia as he was loading some of his works on to a market dray which was ready to carry goods to the nearby seaport. He was taken in chains to Eburacum and there he was placed within the belly of a brass bull and slowly roasted. This was to celebrate his capture. A feast was held in the city square while the fire under the bull heated. To the very end he denied the Romans their pleasure, for not a sound was heard from the belly of the bull.

Despite tortures such as this, every generation threw up its quota of original thinkers who were dispatched to the punish-ment centres and thence each year to the Battle Domes – for while the Battle Dome at Eburacum was the grandest, it was only one of many scattered throughout Britannia and indeed the entire civilized world.

But assuming a young person accepted the status quo without question (as most did), what could that person expect of his or her life? The answer can be given in one word: security. If the promise of youth were borne out, he or she might become a teacher and researcher at any one of the Institutes of Higher Learning. However, this research was not a disinterested quest for knowledge. It was directed to very immediate and very practical goals. Though there were machines which used solar power and magnetic force fields, though technology and gardening had achieved a limited fusion, though medicine had made great strides in conquering the common cold through a combination of garlic and hot vapour, there was no real theoretical base for these activities. Quarks were a thing unknown, as were viruses.

How can you have science without theory? Well you can't, and the people of this world did not have what we would understand by science. By and large they did not think about underlying causes, but if they did, their logic led them to mysticism. If something worked, that was good enough for them. Research was a matter of applying logic to what was known. Thus the wheel implied the road. The pulley implied architecture. And so on ... This world had one lucky break, however, a unique convergence of thinking. On the one side, old Dunstan's steam-engine led to the electric generator which in turn led to the application of magnetism which led to the transit system we have already seen. On the other, the study of agriculture led to sophisticated wind-machines and (most important of all) the solar cell. It was found that certain flowers of the lily family, now alas extinct on our world, could convert sunlight into an electric charge. Nodules on the roots acted like capacitors. The rest was simply a matter of application. Had these developments not taken place then the entire globe might have been stripped of its tree cover to feed the furnaces and this world would have choked on its own smoke. But it did not and the great forests remained, pre-eminently in Britannia, let it be said, but also in those parts of Europe which had not been exclusively dedicated to sheep and cattle.

So, the men and women of this world accepted the phenomena of Nature in the same way that they accepted themselves. On the rare occasions when they worried about a deeper cause, it could always be found in the will of the gods who dwelt above the sky and below the earth. An unforeseen event was the act of a god and that was the end of it. Of course the great danger in this thinking is that it creates a mentality of conservatism and acquiescence. If you believe that things are ordained by Fate then you do nothing to change them . . . and what an infinite world of discovery is then denied.

In the society in which young Angus was maturing, there were no real material wants. For centuries, equal work had meant equal pay, though payment was less important than in our world. There were some very fixed ideas about what was man's work and what was woman's work. Thus, for example, men became engineers and women became nurses. Men went to sea to fish and women made clothes. No one seriously questioned such things and, to be fair, there was some mobility and easing of categories though the fundamental reality of this society, the division into three classes, the Romans who ruled and the Citizens and Soldiers who served, remained unyielding and impervious to time.

Below the level of the military aristocrats there was relative equality of opportunity. Food was almost free and when there was a lack of (say) fresh meat, everyone experienced it. Education (such as it was) was free. Health care was free. Holidays were free in a variety of leisure and sports camps. Travel between the different parts of Britannia was almost non-existent except for the Romans, and any journeys undertaken by the Citizens had to be carefully planned and applied for many months in advance. Where one worked was where one lived and jobs were rarely changed. As a consequence, knowledge of the geography and topography of Britannia was limited. Caledonia was 'up there'. The Pennine Chain was a reality only to those who lived close to it. And the Moors and the Mendips were names of mystery.

By rough census, the total population of the civilized world of Britannia was little over seven million, and that meant there was a lot of wild land. No one knew the population of the Woodlanders. And no one really cared. The Woodlanders did not cause trouble and were rarely seen except on market days. Occasionally there were patterns of their fires on the hilltops in spring and autumn and occasionally singing and drumming could be heard. As far as the Citizens were concerned, the Wood-landers belonged to an inferior race.

To return to Angus . . .

The boy did well at the Crookesmoor Academy, steadily accumulating merit points for careful work, being punctual and showing a thorough grasp of mechanics and electrical engineering. He was also a fine sportsman representing his academy in games akin to rugby and cricket. In both these sports he displayed a controlled aggression and this was observed by his tutors with pleasure. Not one of them could have foreseen how far his *un*controlled aggression would one day carry this red-haired and raw-boned young man.

He graduated magna cum laude when still seventeen and was apprenticed to the Battle Dome at Eburacum under the particular guardianship of Wallace who was third chief mechanic. Wallace was the man with the limp we saw at the Battle Dome. Wallace was a good master and teacher. He had a cheerful sense of humour and was much given to whistling tunelessly when confronting a mechanical problem which required ingenuity. He worked hard himself and expected the same dedication from others. His philosophy was that the good mechanic was he whose feet you saw sticking out from under a machine and who needed ten minutes to clean the oil and grease from his hands at the end of the day.

Angus could not believe his good fortune. He threw himself into his new work, studying the circuitry and mechanical layout of the 327 mechanical creatures that were stabled at the Battle Dome. He spent his first days climbing into and out of the machines, studying every part of their structure. He polished the bright steel ball-joints until they shone like crystal. He cleaned the oil-ducts and filters and found and repaired a malfunction in an oil-pump. Wallace took a shine to young Angus who was obviously as keen on the work at the Battle Dome as he was.

For his part, young Angus took a shine to Wallace's daughter named Miranda. As an apprentice, Angus lived in an annexe to the semi-detached house occupied by Wallace and his wife Eve and daughter Miranda. It was a convenient arrangement, for it was understood that by being appointed to be Wallace's apprentice Angus might one day take over the position of third mechanic. It meant, however, that at the evening meal and on weekends Angus found himself sitting by and chatting to the lively Miranda. Angus's knowledge of girls, let alone sex, was non-existent if you set to one side the enormous misinformation of the boy's academy and his vague memories of his mother. He had only a dim understanding of the explosive changes his manhood was making in him. By day he worked. In the evening he studied. At night he heaved in bed thinking of the lovely Miranda with the dazzling smile and he ached to touch her and feel the warmth of her hands and her smile. His special fantasy was that one night she would creep into his bed asking for his caress.

Miranda was not unaware of Angus's feelings, nor was her mother who looked on thoughtfully. But love for a man or need of one was not part of Miranda's world at this time and she found it easy to keep the brakes on. She was flattered by his moony attention. She was worldly enough to know that he was good-looking in a rough sort of way. More deeply, she was also aware of his sexual energy. It almost mesmerized her at times, especially when Angus was preoccupied and thoughtful as when mending an electric plug or replacing a pane of glass in her father's greenhouse. She would study him, drinking in his casual elegance and youthful grace and half wishing she was the plug or the pane of glass. And she would blush to herself . . . But she kept her appreciation well hidden: Angus never suspected.

So you can understand how complex were Angus's feelings on that particular evening when the fighting took place in the Battle Dome. This was the first real test of his skill and status. Colleagues from his academy, those who had been appointed to lower positions at the Battle Dome, were watching him enviously, some no doubt hoping he would make a mess of things. Older mechanics were watching to see whether the young apprentice was as tough and competent as he looked. Wallace was watching to see whether he had given the young man too much responsibility too soon. And of course, Miranda was watching from the high chalet.

The call to action came as the Dragon smashed its tail down on the Crab. The mechanics in the workshop inside the hill had been observing the action through the lens of a large periscope. This was disguised within an artificial fir tree on the hillside above and allowed the mechanics to view most of the action in the Battle Dome. They sat relaxed on the various big-wheeled retrieval machines but they shouted when they saw the Crab's back break for all of them had worked on that machine in some capacity or other and they knew how strong it was. The end was obviously near and the drivers powered up their vehicles.

Then an alarm sounded and a red light began to flash, warning them that the battle was over and only a brief victory ceremony remained. They watched the Dragon charge in a circle and then stop. They saw the head lower and a hatch in the high back open and the portly man in white overalls climb stiffly out and stand and wave to the crowds. At that moment the red light changed to green and an entire section of the wall began to lift on hydraulic pistons. The mechanics engaged the gears of their machines and stared up the ramp into the Battle Dome which seemed vast and misty and chill after the brilliant arc-lights and muggy warmth and solid walls of the workshop.

When the door in the hillside was high enough, they drove out. In his excitement Angus jumped the clutch on his vehicle and it lurched but did not stall. Wallace, riding beside him, turned and winked and gave him the thumbs-up and then signalled for him to calm down. Angus got the vehicle rolling. The moment of nerves was over. The vehicle rode softly on its suspension over the ruts and gullies where the creatures had torn the earth in their fight.

Beside Angus in the vehicle was an older woman wearing the white and blue insignia of the nursing staff. She was there to give immediate medical attention to any cuts and bruises the driver of the dragon had sustained. 'Your first time?' she asked.

Angus nodded, his attention solely on the terrain in front,

making sure he didn't jar his companions, especially Wallace, too much.

'We'll pull round to the right of the creature. That's where the best landing is.' Then she pointed up into the darkness of the dome where twin green lights were descending. 'See,' she said. 'There's one of the Ulysses' flyers coming down to land.'

Angus glanced to Wallace who nodded and Angus did as he was bid. The vehicle turned sharply round the prone head of the Dragon and slowed by its side. It was dwarfed by the giant hams of the beast and the steep scaly sides. 'Now wait until I've got Ulysses off,' said the nurse. 'Don't rush. It's all part of the scene. Everyone up there,' she gestured towards the terraces and chalet, 'wants to see how badly hurt he is. They want to see if he can walk. The Crab nearly mauled him. They don't want to be distracted by you. Savvy?'

Angus nodded.

'When I've got him safe in the flyer you can take over.' She smiled, aware of Angus's nervousness, and the vehicle stopped. Angus was vaguely reminded of his own mother who had talked in the same kind and precise way many years earlier.

The nurse stepped directly from the tray of the transport vehicle up on to the back of the Dragon and climbed to where the white-garbed Ulysses was standing. He was holding a guide-rail for support and was swaying slightly. Angus could see his face was ashen and that he had been sick down the front of his uniform. The nurse checked him quickly, studying information concerning pulse, temperature, blood-pressure and bodily secretions provided by a small electrical medipack strapped to Ulysses' side. A few light touches established that no bones were broken. She was satisfied that he could move and helped him down the shallow steps and across to the flyer. As Ulysses climbed into the vehicle the nurse gave Angus a nod and a wink and it was his turn.

Wallace and the other mechanics who had travelled on the transport vehicle were already down on the ground checking the oil-leaks and studying the mechanical status panel which was located under one of the dark scales close to the base of the tail. The main pressure systems were OK. There was considerable structural damage and the electrical systems which controlled the movements of the Dragon's eyes and the front claws were completely blown. Many scales had been lost and some of the internal pistons which fed power to the rear legs were shattered. But the Dragon could still move under its own power and could leave the field triumphant. That was the main thing.

'Take her away, son,' said Wallace as he limped back to the transport vehicle and swung up into it. 'Go very easy. The controls may be a bit jumpy so use the tractor. She'll rattle and bang like a can of loose nuts, but she'll make it all right. Park her in the back bay. We'll be taking the whole tail off tomorrow and stripping her right down to the flywheel.' He engaged the gears of the transporter and prepared to move away to inspect the Crab. Angus stood nodding. 'Well don't stand there looking gormless, lad, get to it. We've got work to do tonight. And whatever you do, don't crash her.' Then Wallace winked.

Angus came to himself. He'd almost been overawed by the situation. 'Right,' he said, and then added as an afterthought, 'Do you want me to come back after I've parked it?'

'No,' said Wallace. 'I reckon we can cope. Good luck.'

Angus stepped over the narrow gap between the vehicles and Wallace accelerated away. Angus stood on the Dragon. He felt very much on his own as he climbed up the shallow steps which led to the entrance hatch. He noted the scratches and the bent scales. 'Plenty of panel-beating tomorrow, too,' he thought. Then he was high on the creature, standing on the small platform and with the scaled sides sloping steeply away from him. He felt very exposed and the focus of all eyes. Every other time he had been aboard the Dragon, it had been within the comfortable confines of the machine-shop or doing practice runs with only mechanics for company. Here he could smell the torn grass and the spilled hot oil and hear the band playing and the murmur of a vast crowd talking excitedly. The atmosphere thrilled him.

Angus did not linger though his movements seemed to take a long time. He climbed down into the cockpit and felt the pneumatic seat shape itself about him and lock to his shape. He saw where Marcus Ulysses had vomited over the controls and his nose told him that the Ulysses had also shat himself in his fear. He used a wad of mechanic's shoddy to clean the controls. There was nothing he could do about the smell.

No matter. To his left, inset into the control deck, was a carved wooden box similar in shape to a cigar-box but deeper. The lid was open and revealed inside was a black object which Angus knew was the dried phallus of a sacrificed bull. This was the old Ulysses' *fascinum*, a charm used to ward off the evil eye and turn back on ill-wishers their own malediction. Just as the Roman generals had carried such charms under their chariots, so Ulysses senior carried this one in his Dragon. The man was nothing if not superstitious, and the fact that the box was open meant that he had been praying to whatever gods would listen and had been so shaken at the end of the contest that he had forgotten to protect this, his most powerful talisman. It was the first time that Angus had seen it for normally the box containing the sacred object was kept locked and only old Ulysses had the key. Wallace, explaining the Dragon to Angus, had warned him not to tamper. Carefully Angus closed the box and turned the key and heard the magnetic bolts slam home. He put the key in his pocket. He would give it to Wallace when he returned to the workshop.

Angus checked the controls, noting that the flywheel had only lost 11 per cent of its energy. He could hear its hum and feel the harmonics of its vibration. Though he had driven the Dragon many times before for test runs and had helped Wallace and the other mechanics check the trim of the flywheel, he still felt a massive thrill at being so close to such raw power, to so much mechanical energy in so small a place. The fighting-machines at battle readiness gave him a joy like no other.

Those parts of the Dragon's drive system that had been damaged in the combat were now isolated from the main hydraulics. The servo-control mechanism was intact. Angus touched the prime switch and heard the electric generators which controlled the hydraulics engage with the flywheel. There was a brief shudder. With a sudden rush all the systems came alive. The air tingled and the dials in front of him danced, monitoring revs and pressure. The various cathode-ray screens round him blinked and settled providing direct visual and infra-red scanning of the entire area round the beast. The cameras were located in a steel girdle just below where he sat.

Angus lowered the direction harness over his head. It rested lightly on his shoulders and a soft cap gripped his upper skull. Sensors with limpet heads attached themselves lightly to his temples and to the nape of his neck. He tightened the safety-belt across his waist and felt braced. This was exactly the feeling a Roman warrior experienced when he tightened the straps of his breastplate until his muscles bulged. Finally Angus slipped his hands into the control gloves. These were unpleasantly damp as they tightened round his wrist. Beneath the tips of his fingers and thumbs he could feel the tingle of the charged steel drive-studs. Soft pressure-pads of cork pressed against the base of his thumbs. Beneath his feet were pedals.

This was it. THIS WAS IT. He closed his thumbs and at the same time drew his hands towards him. He felt the lurching movement as the Dragon's front legs straightened and the neck and head rose. He released and the movement stopped. Angus thanked Vulcan and whatever other gods there were that looked after young mechanics. If he had continued that movement any further the creature could have overreached and become unstable. It could even have toppled and that would have been a terrible disgrace.

His view had changed. He was now seeing the dome from some twenty feet above the field. He could see the terraces and the high chalet. He hoped, oh how he hoped that Miranda was looking at him. He could feel the beast hum and quiver round him. He could feel his own heart hammer too.

With pressure on all fingers and inclining his hands forwards and pressing his toes down on the pedals, he made the Dragon lift its rear legs which locked into a neutral travel position. Then he fed power to the tractor. He heard the clatter of relay switches as valves were opened and closed and pistons activated. He relaxed his left hand slightly and after a brief delay the Dragon turned slightly to the right. He gripped again and, again after a delay, it straightened. The delay was the mechanical time. The Dragon's movements responded to the slightest changes in any of his control movements.

In the vision-plate Angus could see the entrance to the repair hangar directly in front of him. He pressed with his feet and the tempo of the movements increased slightly. He listened to the clatter of the machine and corrected a tendency for the creature to slew round to the left.

Suddenly the hangar was before him and he slowed and lowered the Dragon's head, withdrawing it back as far as possible. The creature came to the ramp and tipped downwards, its treads suddenly noisy on the ribbed steel gangway. It was sheer bravado born of relief, or perhaps that controlled aggression mentioned earlier, which made Angus crook his little fingers and cause the Dragon to flourish its tail like a whip as it disappeared within the workshop.

The tale of Viti Ulysses, the Student Warrior

Viti was the third son, and the only surviving son of the Ulysses family.

His eldest brother, Quintus, died in a flying accident close to a loch in Caledonia. According to rumour he was drunk at the controls and attempted to land among fir trees. The flyer tore to bits in the trees and fell into the loch and the body was never recovered. Quintus was as handsome as his father and brilliant in many ways, but he had an erratic, angry streak to his personality. He had prophesied that he would not live long and made sure his prophecy was fulfilled.

Viti's second brother, Felix, was assassinated by a terrorist group shortly after being appointed governor of one of the distant regions of the New West Empire. Felix was a brilliant linguist and diplomat. His competence with the short sword left something to be desired but when he spoke, even the greybeards listened. One irony in his death was that the group that claimed responsibility was the very same group whose right to free expression he had vigorously defended. While it would be wrong to think of him as a liberal in the way we might understand that word, he was nevertheless concerned with questions of justice for all Citizens.

Felix could sing and play the cello and piano. He was a composer and a playwright. His death was regarded as a great loss to the Empire and three legions were sent to exact reprisal. It is said that the vultures had food enough for the year when the legions departed. A second irony in his death is that Felix would not have approved of the forces of reprisal which were unleashed.

Viti's eldest sister, Florea, had married an African king and now lived in a magnificent palace south of Tunis on the beautiful Gulf of Hammamet. On the eve of each Reformed Lupercalia she sent home sugared sweetmeats and ornaments carved from black ivory. These were entrusted to the care of biancanegro servants who transported them by ship and who themselves remained as curios to serve the family on one or other of their estates.

Viti's youngest sister, Thalia, was only six at the time the events in this story took place and spent most of her time on her pet pony at the family estate west of Aquae Sulis.

Each of the children had a different mother, for Marcus Augustus Ulysses, who fathered them, had never discovered domestic happiness: a fault which must be laid at his own private door. Unfaithful as he was in his own relations, he yet doted on his offspring though he lacked the means to express his love. Viti was the last of the male line, which explains why old Marcus sought out young women when he could and fornicated whenever he was able, but finally had to acknowledge his impotence.

Why was the boy called Viti? In a family such as the Ulysses even trivial events can take on mythic proportions. According to one story, the name dates from when the young Victor Ulysses was four and the family was enjoying the Reformed Lupercalia on their estate at Farland Head in Caledonia. Among his presents, the young Victor had been given a cloak and breastplate and a sword, each item being a miniature replica of those worn by the great Julius Caesar who pacified Britannia.

The little boy ran down the halls and through the rooms shouting 'Veni, viti, vici', and no amount of persuading could make him say 'vidi'. So Viti he became. The family liked the name because it had implications of strength. However, according to another story, the name Viti is simply a childish simplification of Victor: but that is far less romantic as a story.

Victor Ulysses is heir to one of the richest and hence most powerful families in Britannia. From a boy he has learned little except hunting, fishing, some literature and fighting. When his father dies he will take possession of some twenty-one different estates, the smallest of which is seven acres while the largest occupies many thousands of acres.

Viti can trace his line by direct descent back to Julius Caesar's invasion of Britannia on 26 August in 55 BC, when the centurion Junius Parventius, who was commonly known as Ulysses, served as one of Caesar's most trusted soldiers. Thus the name Ulysses was originally a nickname. During the crossing, Junius Parventius's ship became separated from the rest of Caesar's fleet and was blown far north. It endured many strange adventures, including the first recorded complete circumnavigation of the Britannic Isles. These adventures are all recorded in the volumes of the family's history and the original manuscripts are kept in the family museum. When Junius Parventius and his soldiers rejoined the main army during 54 BC, they were just in time for the decisive battles. This warrior was a great breaker of heads and a crusher of bones. He was a cunning gambler, for which he gained the appellation 'the Fox'. Hence for diverse reasons the name Ulysses.

In whatever campaign he was engaged, he maintained a harem of twenty captured native women whom he slaughtered to the god of war before each major battle. After the battle he replenished his resources. It was said that he ate the flesh of his victims when he had a mind to. Even the great Caesar, who was not renowned for delicacy in his habits, held him in a certain awe. The barbarians recognized him as one of their own. When Caesar needed a victory he sent in 'Ulysses' Parventius to soften up the opposition.

Strange is the blood that flows in young Viti's veins and daunting the accomplishments to which he must aspire if he is to be worthy of the name Ulysses.

Viti's father, Marcus Augustus Ulysses, is generally regarded as a throw-back to an earlier age. His blood-lust can be tolerated because he is popular and powerful. The son is different, and the father knows it. Viti is not a killer by nature though he has killed. If we could strip away tradition and all the expectations that tradition builds into a man, we would see that Viti has the caring mind of a scholar, the grace of a dancer and the spirit of a singer. But these attributes are buried deep and Viti strives to ignore them. Viti has a warrior's muscles and the face of a champion, but he does not have a warrior's will. Everything he does is to please his father and satisfy tradition, but he is not aware of this. He does his best to deny his true creative nature and to emulate the tiger.

Viti's early schooling was with tutors. He learned enough of the classical language to satisfy the official requirements of his position. He showed an aptitude for mathematics and astronomy. He enjoyed an easy, untroubled boyhood spent mainly on the family estate at Farland Head in Caledonia but with occasional long holidays on some of the other estates. The most traumatic event was when he was five and was caught by his father dressing up in some of his elder sister's clothes. His father shouted and servants were whipped. Viti did not know what he had done wrong but he knew he had displeased his father. He feared the withdrawal of love and thereafter tried to win his father's affection with feats of strength.

At seven he was sent to a military prep. school at Camboritum, in the eastern wetlands once controlled by the powerful Iceni. There he was schooled in history and horsemanship and the arts of being a member of the warrior class. He learned languages and swordsmanship and anatomy. He was also initiated into some of the mysteries of Mithras and was taught how to read the auguries.

At fourteen he set out on a tour of the old world with his father and several cousins. He visited Roma, Athenae, Masada and Alexandria. He sailed a short distance up the Nile and stared at the pyramids with wonder. At Aphroditopolis he joined the great Via Africana, the trans-Africa highway which ran beside the river for a while before cutting away to the south-west. With many twists and turns and exotic resting places, the road traversed the entire African continent and finally emerged at the safe harbour called Portus Tutus close to the town which we know as Abidjan. There, a boat was waiting and he finally returned to Britannia by sea. The entire journey had taken two years. When he set out he was pale and slightly effete. When he returned he was bronzed and hardened. He could swear and arm-wrestle, but under the worldly swagger he was still just a boy. He was yet unknown to woman having been zealously chaperoned every sleeping and waking moment by two giant Nubians. The only morality in this was the morality of survival, for venereal disease was rife throughout the whole of the Old World and struck down the rich and poor without care or favour. Old Marcus Ulysses did not want to see his youngest (and last) son sweating his life away on a stretcher while blow-flies buzzed. Despite the rich evidence of carnal joy which surrounded him, Viti displayed no great interest in girls or things sexual. 'But that will change,' thought father Ulysses, supping wine with his favourite houris, remembering his own explosive adolescence.

Viti returned to cool, damp, green Britannia as summer was settling into autumn, just in time to enter the Military Academy at Eburacum. He spent the last week of his vacation on the estate in Caledonia and there he was robbed of his virginity by three of his father's women. 'Take him in hand,' said Marcus Ulysses with a wink and that they did and more. What Viti thought of this is not recorded. Equally, he was never heard to complain and all the evidence would suggest that he was a willing student. In this alone did Viti show he was a true son of his father.

And so at the age of sixteen Viti found himself staring down at the outskirts of Eburacum from the vantage-point of the control deck of his father's flagship, the *Ithaca*. This craft dominated the sky-road coming in from the north, forcing other craft to give way. Gradually it slowed and the navigator selected the correct sky-road for the Eburacum Military Academy.

The city, destined for greatness, began its existence in the early days of the Empire as a fifty-acre legionary fortress. Established by Petillius Cerialis, it might have remained a damp and draughty military camp had not Fate taken a hand. Shortly after the occupation of Britannia and Hibernia had been completed, several towns in Britannia were contending for the title of capital. In the south-west there was Aquae Sulis with its warm baths and gentle climate. To the south was Londinium, already making a name as a centre for trade. To the east was Lindum which was a great centre of learning.

Now it so happened that one night the Emperor Lucius Septimus Severus, who was using Eburacum as his military base, dreamed that he was visited by the great Gaius Julius Caesar in person. Caesar came to him wearing a toga of cloth of gold and with a silver helmet, shield and sword. Caesar held out his silver sword before the startled eyes of Severus, and it flashed and shimmered. Julius Caesar said, 'Where next you see this flashing sword, there establish your greatest city. Call it Eburacum in honour of the yew trees. It will rival Roma and be the home of great leaders.' Then he vanished.

Some three weeks later it so happened that Severus was leading a punitive expedition against some Parisi woodlanders who had set up as pirates in the estuary near Petuaria. It was a cloudy day with scudding rain blowing in from the north. Severus came to the bridge near where the River Foss joins the River Ouse, and there, just as he was about to urge his horse on to the bridge, the sun suddenly broke through the clouds and the river lit up with a brilliant silver light. Reflected in the water was the unmistakable shape of a sword.

Severus reined in. He climbed from the saddle. He summoned his aides and pointed, declaring that here he would build a great city.

And so it happened. The military camp became a capital city. From the beginning Eburacum prospered. The rivers were given stone banks and the marshes were drained. City walls were built and then torn down and expanded as the city became a bustling market-place. Severus began the building of a palace and this was continued by his successors. Little by little the administration of the province became settled there. New roads spread out from Eburacum, linking that city to the southern cities and to the northern islands. One road became a vast bridge which joined the north-west of Britannia to the island of Manavia and thence to the mainland of Hibernia.

People came to visit this beautiful new city, some from distant parts of the Empire, and stayed to settle, for the climate was gentle, the soil was good, slave labour was plentiful and the amenities the best that could be provided. Stately Roman villas sprang up beside the Ouse and the Foss and in the carefully landscaped parks and gardens. Easy access to the sea and to the expressways which cut through the dense forests meant a regular supply of fresh fish, wine, meat and luxury goods from the continental mainland. The people lacked for nothing. Eburacum became a peaceful, gracious city which retained something of its rural origins. The streets had the smell of the country. You could as easily meet a horse-drawn cart piled with apples as one of the flashy chariots which rode the energy lanes. And in the evenings, when the mist came up the river, fishermen, retired Roman commanders, gathered in the numerous restaurants and inns which lined the Foss and retold their day's fortunes.

Beyond the Roman villas and clustering round the city walls were the houses of the Citizens. These were small dwellings, each with its own plot of land, or else several houses clustered round private courtyards. There was no heavy industry in the city and so most of the Citizens who lived here were employed in the service industries: manning the rail- and river-transport system, giving secretarial and administrative assistance in the State offices, providing an army of cleaners, gardeners, chefs and housemaids to the large villas. Then of course there was the staff that maintained the Battle Dome and who looked after the animals and playing-fields at the Military Academy.

As Viti looked out of his window, he saw the shadow of the *Ithaca* elongated into an egg shape, cast by the last rays of the autumn sun. It passed over the straight neat streets of the Citizens' houses and the ancient, biscuit-coloured stone walls of the city. These walls and the gates which pierced them were now protected as part of the city's ancient heritage. It glided over the site of the first Roman camp and on over parks and lakes.

Finally, the *Ithaca* passed over a high brick wall topped with guard-posts and barbed wire. Within the walls were neat lawns and playing-fields and deciduous trees now shedding their leaves. The *Ithaca* manoeuvred round to land in the courtyard of an ancient building with solid stone walls and tiled roofs. This was the famous Military Academy and it was here that Viti would spend the next three years of his life, learning to be a warrior, learning to be a champion, learning to take his place as a leading member of one of the greatest families of Britannia.

The Academy occupied an expansive flat area on the eastern side of the River Ouse just to the south of the old city. In its regimen, the school was a strange mixture of the austere and the opulent. The boys and girls who attended were drilled and pampered by turns for these boys and girls were the élite of their generation and a fine balance needed to be struck between suppression and tolerance.

The first year taught traditional skills and Viti excelled in wrestling, boxing, fighting with the net and trident, ballistics, map-reading, orienteering and horsemanship. He gained a reputation as a ruthless fighter and a heartless and profligate lover. He was treated as a natural leader by his peers and discovered that what he regarded as pig-headed and wilful stubbornness in himself could be admired as strength and determination by other people. He discovered that he felt contempt for people that he could manipulate and that manipulation was easy if you set your mind to it.

In the second year he reached his tallest growth and worked to improve his acrobatic skills. He began to study strategy and military history. He learned to fly the battle-tanks which could lay a magnetic track in front of them and hence advance over open country. He learned first aid, mathematics, selected languages and how to debate. He also learned etiquette and drinking and how to judge a good wine and a good beer. But the boy remained fundamentally a loner, as his skills testified. He was an awkward speaker and his attempts at wit were often misplaced. He made no close friends and kept his distance from his tutors who observed his isolation with some concern. The boy was a contradiction. He should have been popular and happy with all the advantages of wealth, good looks and natural talent to support him. But he seemed morose and introspective and achievement brought him no apparent joy. Briefly he experimented with homosexuality, yielding to the seductive heroworship of one of the cadets. Then he fell in love for the first time, with the wife of one of his tutors, and when he finally seduced her, discovered that he had fallen out of love and wanted to run away from her. His emotions were stormy and unpredictable. He began to distrust his own feelings. Perhaps worse, he began to believe he had no natural feelings. Was temporary gratification all he could feel? He could see beauty and grace in women, but he could not feel them as a vital part of his sensual life. He wanted to love, but couldn't. Sometimes he lay in his bed at night longing to be taken and hurt and torn apart by a demanding woman. But despite his numerous adventures, dawn invariably found him dry-eyed and unsatisfied. Viti came to prefer his own company and when he exercised, it was always against an abstract foe whom, for convenience, we might call Perfection.

So we come to the night at the Battle Dome.

Viti had trained like no other. To win was everything. Even so, there was no guarantee that he would win. A young man called Alexander was as good as he.

In the changing-rooms under the Battle Dome Viti talked instructions to himself as he oiled his body and donned the simple acrobatic singlet. Alexander came to see him and slid his arm round Viti's shoulders. 'Remember not to kill,' he murmured. 'Kick, but don't kick through. Hold the neck but don't twist. Punch, but hold something in reserve. That way we all win. Remember. I'll do the same for you. I want to link little fingers with you after this is all over, no matter which of us wins the prize. OK? Oh, and watch out for Diana. She's been praying to the moon at night, I hear, and dancing on the backs of bulls by day. She wants to lead the women's legion and nothing will play better into her hand than to beat one of us. Remember that.' Alexander winked and touched his lips and walked away, binding leather thongs round his knuckles.

Viti did not reply to his speech. But when Alexander had gone Viti smiled to himself. The enemy had revealed himself and he knew whom to beware of and whom to go hunting.

Viti built his adrenalin by punching and head-butting a bag filled with damp horsehair. His tutor spent a few minutes kicking at him while he parried and slammed into him. Then the warning call came. This told that the cadets were performing their final charge and all second-year students should take their places immediately. Viti hurried and found his place. The leather was tight round his wrists. Woven thongs bit into his biceps. The belt tightened his stomach to a ball. He breathed through his teeth. Battle-lust was almost on him. He was ready.

Come the signal, Viti bounded up the ramp and into the Battle Dome. He heard the roaring of the crowd and it could have been the passing of a river over his head. He knelt and took the oath. He saw the chariots line up and the chariot-masters take their whips in hand and then, on cue, leap to their positions and crack their whips behind the horses' ears.

Viti let the first and the second chariots pass for they were jerking, uncertain between canter and gallop. The third was driven by the tutor called Harpalus who was no friend of his and who might swerve when he saw who was trying to scramble aboard. No chance there. Already his companions were jumping for the bridles or the running-boards of the passing chariots as they gathered speed. The fourth chariot was already occupied but it was driven by his favourite tutor, Servius by name, and Viti decided to strike. He matched pace with the horse and threw himself against the embossed side of the chariot avoiding the wheels. One kick and he was over the rail and landing inside. The other boy who had scrambled aboard had scraped his right side against the chariot wheel and had opened deep cuts on his thigh and forearm. Viti did not pause. A fist drove for the nose. A knee drove for the genitals. A chop to the back of the head sent the convulsed boy on his way to the dark, churned turf.

Viti held on tight with his left hand and selected a pennant which he stuffed into the pouch at his waist. Time to move.

His tutor edged the chariot out into the middle of the circuit and ran parallel with two others. Viti made his choice and jumped, touching ground briefly to give him extra spring. As luck would have it, the moment he gained the chariot its former occupant departed, grabbing for the traces of a neighbouring steed. Viti thanked Juno and Mars and Mithras, to whom he had prayed the previous evening, for his good fortune. He selected a pennant at leisure and looked about. There were fewer chariots.

One came close, throwing up dirt from its wheels. Two men were fighting in the back. Viti urged his driver to pull in front and then he leaped from the back, bounded once and threw himself up on to the horses. He scrambled back and was able to take the two fighting men by surprise and push them both out. Again he chose a pennant. He was doing well. He was unwounded. His courage was high.

He heard the charioteer who was driving give a shout. The man was pointing to a chariot that was bearing down on them. Its rider was obviously preparing to jump for Viti's chariot. Viti ducked down behind the side. He heard the chariots lock together, and when the opposing warrior came leaping aboard he head-butted him neatly and the man lost his grip and fell backwards. Viti now swung across to the empty chariot and took a pennant. It was time to take stock and look about. He had no idea how many laps had been completed. Now that there were fewer chariots the driving was more tactical, with drivers making sudden rushes and slamming the chariots together.

Viti was looking ahead when suddenly he felt a jarring barge as a chariot from behind collided with his and sent his vehicle skittering sideways, skidding on its spinning wheels. Viti was thrown down to his knees and banged his head on the side-rail. Groggily he was aware of danger. A tall golden figure stepped almost casually into his chariot and selected a pennant. It was Alexander.

Then Viti felt hands about his head, and fingers feeling for the soft membrane inside his ears. He twisted by instinct and reached up, groping for eyes or nose or anything soft he could tear or jab. 'Remember our agreement,' murmured Alexander, and he changed grip and held Viti's head to his chest and began to twist.

Viti, who was still crouched, kicked with his legs and sent the pair of them crashing back against the side of the chariot. The movement winded Alexander who released his grip momentarily. That was enough for Viti. He scrambled free and turned. He slammed a quick blow to Alexander's face and followed this with a jab to his heart.

But Alexander had an advantage in reach. He used that advantage to hold on, smothering any blows that Viti might throw while he recovered. And then he began to pepper Viti with quick hard blows to the head, tempting Viti to duck into what would be a stunning, crippling right-handed smash.

Viti was aware. He covered up and sensed the moment when the chariot, charging round the monoliths, gave him maximum advantage. The centrifugal force threw Alexander back and at the same moment Viti plunged under Alexander's defence and then, instead of slugging for the solar plexus, he drove up with his head forcing Alexander back. Then, twisting to the side, he punched as hard as he could for the throat.

Perhaps the lurching of the chariot helped him, but the blow sank home, crushing Alexander's Adam's apple back into his throat and making him gag.

Alexander could not breathe. His eyes took on a frightened unbelieving stare as his muscles pumped and laboured but no air passed down his throat. Viti hit him again in the face and felt the nose collapse. Then it was a round-armed back-hander which clubbed Alexander to his knees and finally a push with the foot which sent the labouring body out of the back of the chariot.

Vaguely Viti was aware of the shouting of the crowd. The race was reaching its climax. There was now only one other chariot left in the contest.

Viti was in no shape to fight. His vision was blurred and he seemed to see two chariots converging on him. He gripped the safety-rail and blinked his eyes, trying to clear his head. He saw a figure leap through the dust and grip the guard-rail of his chariot and swing aboard. It was Diana, of course, and she picked up the last pennant.

She took her time deciding how to attack. She saw that Viti's eyes were almost closed from the punches inflicted by Alexander and so she attacked the head. That was her mistake, for Viti butted and struck blindly, with all the despairing passion of an *andabata*. One blow struck home, sending Diana to her knees, and as she rose he kicked. It was not the calculated kick of a fighter who knows just what he is attacking but more the kick of a rugby-player punting a ball. Still, the blow was effective, catching Diana in her naked midriff and sending her head over heels backwards.

Viti became aware that he had won. His chariot did a lap of honour during which he came to his senses. He saw Diana stand up, and was glad. He saw the hunched mound that was Alexander and that did not move. He was indifferent.

Then there was the cheering and the rich heady smell of horses and blood and he felt strong and fierce again.

His chariot came to a halt beside Diana and she reached up to him. In her hand she held five pennants. Viti felt his heart sink for he could only produce four. Nevertheless, the games marshal, after consulting the panel of judges, declared that Viti was the victor since his was the last chariot and he had defeated all comers. The result was broadcast through the dome. Hearing it, Viti took Diana's outstretched hand and stepped down from his chariot with all the arrogance of Agamemnon of old.

They acknowledged the crowd and then ran to a place close to the ring of monoliths where ramps led down to the baths and the saunas and the expert attention of masseurs.

'See you up top in the chalet later,' said Viti.

'Have me a drink waiting,' said Diana. 'Something long and strong and bitter and with lots of ice.'

'Will do,' said Viti, and vanished down the men's ramp.

Some time later, when Viti was washed and steamed and lying on the masseur's slab, the adrenalin finally started to drain out of him and he began to shake uncontrollably. His masseur, one of the Nubians who had looked after him in Africa, sized him up with an expert's eye. He knew that he could fix up the young man's body but he could not touch the deep seat of his trouble. That was within. Viti would have to do that for himself, some time.

The Nubian worked methodically, releasing the knotted tense muscles, and as he did so he talked. 'Cry, if you've a mind to,' he said. 'That helps. The times I've cried. Howled the house down. Crying's natural. Not crying's not normal. Think on that.' But Viti lay mute.

The masseur repaired the damaged skin with soothing oint-ments and balms. Finally he wiped his hands and took a deep breath. Suddenly he gripped Viti by the ankles and wrists and stretched him backwards like a bow, lifting him bodily off the bench. He squeezed. 'Fight me and cry,' ordered the slave.

Viti struggled, trying to turn, shocked and powerless. And then suddenly sobs racked him, uncontrollable hacking tears. The giant masseur held him firm and unyielding while he gulped and coughed. And after some minutes Viti felt better and the masseur released him. He flopped on the bench and sat up and was embarrassed to discover that his cock had become stiff and erect for no reason that he could think of. His Nubian servant observed this development with mock, wide-eyed horror. 'My my,' he observed to no one in particular, 'that one-eyed snake's got a mind of its own. Now you go, and make some girl happy this night. OK? Hey, and make yourself happy too. That's what the Buddha says and don't you forget it.'

Viti grinned. It had taken the shock of being for a few moments powerless and naked to break and wake him. 'I won't,' he said.

Wrapped in a vast white towel, like some ancient senator in his toga, he left to get changed.

But Viti did not find it easy to relax. He had killed Alexander and the knowledge that Alexander would have killed him, given the chance, made no difference at all. There was still a hole made.

He was quite a hero and many people wanted him to retell the fight against Alexander. They were disappointed when he said, 'It's all a blur. I don't really remember anything.'

When he had the chance, Viti slipped away and found a private corner of the chalet where he could look down on to the battleground. He watched his father's contest with mixed feelings. Guiltily he found himself half hoping that his father would be killed. But that did not happen. 'Like father, like son,' thought Viti as the Dragon smashed the Crab with its tail.

He saw Angus climb into the Dragon and the beast rear up. 'Next year,' he thought. 'Next year I'll get to drive that creature. I'll make it dance.'

Someone slipped an arm through his and led him away from the balcony. 'Come on. Don't think too deeply,' said a soft voice. It was Diana. The change in her was extraordinary. Gone was the tight-muscled warrior and in her place was a woman as supple as a serpent and who smelled of Egypt. Viti marvelled and was glad. He was especially glad to be rescued from himself. 'You're going to dance with me,' she said, 'and I won't accept any excuses like slipped discs and pulled muscles. So tough! You've a lot of work in front of you this night, my lad.'

Viti hoped that meant what he thought it meant.

Later that night, long after the meeting with his father in the chalet and the celebratory meal, Viti found himself finally alone with Diana. They were outside the Battle Dome making haphazard progress to where a taxi flyer, summoned from Eburacum, was patiently waiting. Dawn was pink above the trees and the branches stood out like black fretwork. The woman was tired and tousled and amorous. She had broken her shoes dancing and now carried them in one hand. At the present moment her other hand was up behind Viti's neck and she was kissing him full on the lips as though drinking. She had no regrets about the evening in the Battle Dome. She felt no guilt and lived and devoured each moment of her life with little thought for cause or consequence. Now she was preparing to end the evening with one last blaze of passion. She was prepared to stoke the man's fires, if that were necessary. She ached for his hands to be on her. She ached to feel his driving weight.

Viti envied Diana her directness and tried to cast aside the melancholy which gripped him. In truth, Viti was appalled at himself. Here he was, alone at last with a woman he'd lusted after all year and who was ready, willing and wanting . . . her body as available as his own, and what was he doing? He was musing. He was letting thoughts get in the way. Perhaps he'd drunk too much . . . He remembered the words of his masseur. That released something in him, or perhaps it was Diana's hands working, or whatever . . . something was released and his juices finally began to flow. He forgot his father. He forgot the pretence of being a hero of the old school. He forgot the Academy. He forgot himself . . .

'Carry me,' whispered Diana, and he scooped her up and ran. He ran into the lightening wood and there he tripped on the root of an old yew tree. They tumbled laughing on the ground. They could not be hurt. The trunk of the yew tree was split open and the ground within was soft and sweet-scented. She was tiger and horse: he was lion and stag. Within moments they were locked in the old fierce embrace of opposites, shouting and thrusting and wanting to bite. Tomorrow they could count the new bruises with pleasure.

Sitting some hundred yards away from them on the fallen trunk of an oak tree was the white-coated figure of Lyf. He was looking at them, and his look was neither envious nor prurient: it was appreciative. He was observing patterns of energy, as old as time, curling like incense-smoke in the clear dawn air. And as the energy built to its climax he pulled the hood of his cloak down over his eyes and gave them privacy.

The tale of Miranda, trainee housekeeper at the Eburacum Women's Polytechnic

Miranda is the only child of Wallace and Eve Duff.

It was a difficult birth and one consequence was that Eve, a most gentle and natural of mothers, could have no more children. For both the parents that was a great disappointment for they had set their hearts on three children, but they had, at least,

Miranda. They lived in one of the small houses on the outskirts of the Severus district of Eburacum.

Miranda grew up protected from the world. She was the centre of her parents' love. From an early age she showed two particular qualities. She had an instinctive sensitivity for the feelings of others. She was the first to stop the tears when a neighbouring child broke a toy or scrubbed its knees. Her sensitivity made her something of a healer, able to charm headaches and lift depression. She was bright and cheerful and occasionally fell into a brown study in which she sat smiling as though listening to music that only she could hear. The second quality is allied to this, and it is innocence. Now in a way all children are innocent but there are two types of innocence. There is the innocence which comes from ignorance and which is gradually worn away, like gilt from a statue, as time and experience work on us. Thus the ignorant child may become the cunning adult. There is, however, another type of innocence which comes from not accepting the world on its own terms, of permanently looking beyond, or respecting a deeper reality than appearance. To this kind of innocence the world is a source of infinite surprise and the fall of a sparrow is deemed at least as important as the death of politicians or princes. Such was Miranda's innocence.

Do not think of her as a slightly fey do-gooder with milky blood and aspirations to sanctity. Her blood was red. Her tears were wet. Her laughter was loud. Her periods hurt and she dreamed of horses. Her heart was in the here and now, and for those who could see, her passions were palpable. Miranda was very much down to earth, but she was not *of* the earth. She was a woman of air and fire.

Miranda followed her mother in showing a great liking for the domestic crafts. She enjoyed sewing and cooking. She joined her mother in managing the small garden at the back of the house where there were flowers and vegetables and a much-prized grape-vine which produced sweet black grapes.

Eve had trained as a sempstress, making clothes in one of the factories on the outskirts of Eburacum, to be sent to the frontiers of the Empire. She had retired from this, however, when arthritis made the working of the machines too painful. She stayed home and was happy bringing up Miranda during the daytime. This was as well, for at about the time Eve had to relinquish her work, Wallace was appointed third mechanic at the Battle Dome and life in the Duff household became more complicated. For one thing, more people began to visit the small house and her father ended up spending more time away.

Miranda grew up with an awareness of greasy overalls which needed washing every night to prevent the stains setting. She knew the laughter of men relaxing over a beer after work and retelling the day's adventures. She saw the briskness of her mother who managed the household with flair and humour. She took charge of a small area, the preparation of her father's lunch. She learned to brew beer and she learned the songs and chants that accompanied the brief services to various gods in the evening and morning.

For entertainment her father would often take her to the Battle Dome to watch the monsters clash. Occasionally, perhaps once a year, they went to the State Theatre when there was a play staged especially for children. Beyond that, like most children born into the Citizen class, Miranda grew up in a quiet world where she was expected to make her own entertainment and gradually, little by little, define her individuality within the traditional constraints of home and work. There was no television or radio in the home. A form of these existed but was for the exclusive use of the Roman military aristocracy or for work. That was the way things were and few thought to question it. A newspaper was published in the evening but this gave local news only. Almost everything in her life focused on the present and the immediate.

If Miranda got sick, she went to the doctor and the doctor treated her: and she either got well or she didn't, for medicine, beyond the setting of bones at which the doctors were expert, was a complex mixture of alchemy, astrology, herbalism and luck. There was no question of payment. Doctors were provided by the State as were the undertakers. Death had no surprises for Miranda either. She saw death at the Battle Dome and it was commonplace among the Citizen class either from accidents at work or in the home. When this happened, again the State took over. The bodies were taken to the civic crematorium where, after a few words to various gods and goddesses, they were burned. The ashes were taken to one of the large State farms to be dug in and the saddened family saw the name of their loved one inscribed in a civic roll. Life went on.

When she was five, Miranda watched her auntie die of a brain tumour and felt that it was her fault. When she was seven, two of her playmates were killed. One was drowned in the Foss and the other, having wandered outside her small community, was crushed by a military vehicle. No one thought to put fences up.

The various comings and goings of the Romans meant nothing to Miranda. They were elsewhere. They obeyed their own laws. They did not come between her and the sun. They were part of what was. She admired them in a vague way, and on the one occasion when two junior Romans who were involved in the administration of the Battle Dome visited her house, she and her mother spent the entire day cleaning and getting the house ready and then Miranda hid in the cupboard under the stairs too shy to meet the visitors.

She knew the Romans mainly through the opinions of her father and that man divided the world into those who were careful with machines and those who were insensitive to machines.

At the age of fourteen Miranda chose to enter the Eburacum Poly and study to become a housekeeper. It was a five-year course followed by a three year apprenticeship which could be in any part of Britannia. Housekeepers were always in demand in the houses of the Roman aristocrats.

The Polytech was situated outside the old city walls just beyond the place which we know as Walmgate Bar. Miranda was a day student and each morning she travelled by underground train from her home north of the city in the district called Severus to the stop at Foss Island.

By her third year of study she was already noted as a most promising student and it was in recognition of her talents that she was given the signal honour of being allowed to serve at the

Battle Dome on the night of the graduation battles. Her mother and father were delighted, as too was Angus who had joined the Duff household some seven months earlier.

Miranda was giddy with delight on the day of the battles. She was up before dawn and spent hours pressing her Polytech uniform and making herself look her best. She wanted to be attractive for a variety of reasons. She placed the carefully ironed uniform in a suitcase and then added some ear-rings, a cameo brooch that her grandmother had given her, a modest necklace and, wrapped in paper, a pair of not-so-sensible shoes just in case the serving-maids were invited to dance with the general staff when their duties were over, as sometimes happened.

The entire family, plus Angus, travelled to the Battle Dome together that day. The station was at the limit of the underground system. Beyond Battle Dome the high-speed trains emerged above ground and darted to the market town of Derventio which was the end of the line. If you wanted to travel on to the fishing towns on the east coast you went by road.

The two men followed an underground passage which ran directly from the underground station to the main machine-shops. They arrived just as the night-time security staff were signing off. Some of the day security men were already on their rounds. Others were checking the water-level in the tea-urn and the supply of sugar.

'All quiet?' asked Wallace as he identified himself and entered the machine-shop where the fighting-creatures were stored and maintained.

'Not a mouse stirring,' said the security guard and both men laughed. Angus looked questioning, and as he and Wallace entered the main workshop Wallace explained.

'I suppose you are wondering why I keep mousetraps all over the place. Well there is a reason and I'll tell you. There was once a battle here – long before my time . . . mid last century – and one of the creatures being driven was a big brass bull. I've seen pictures of it. It were a grand piece of work. They'd given it six legs for stability and the horns could rotate. Anyway, a mouse got into the drive controls the night before the battle and chavelled up some of the wiring. Well, come the battle, out trots the Bull, steam coming from its ears and bum and the driver – one of the Valentinian line I think – he revs it up to full speed and away it goes, straight across the Battle Dome, gathering speed and straight through the bloody wall. Left a great big hole you could drive a train through. Aye, and it didn't stop there either. It went across the clearing where the new parking-lot now is and through the hazel copse and down into that muddy little mere. They say you could hear the splash from way down here. Aye, and they reckon that the way it were going, it wouldn't have stopped till it hit the walls of Eburacum. Anyway, minutes later, the driver comes staggering in through the hole in the wall, water dripping off him and spitting out weed and swearing that he'd been sabotaged. Then there came this big bang as the Bull blew its engine. They say one leg landed in Deva and another in Derventio. The tail went half-way to Londinium and the head came down right here through the roof. The driver never lived the humiliation down ... beaten by a mouse, eh ...'

'You're having me on,' said Angus as he brought the work-shop lights to full and switched on the air-conditioning. 'That's never a true story.'

The vastness of the hangar was revealed. Suspended, each in its separate bay, were all the creatures that would fight that evening. All had been thoroughly checked a week earlier and all were oiled and with their batteries charged and ready to go.

Wallace looked about. 'True as I'm standing here,' he said. 'Anyway, that's why we have all the rat-poison and traps, and that's why we close all the machines before we leave at night. To keep the mice out.'

Angus was not impressed. 'Pull the other one. I reckon that if a mouse wants to get into one of these smelly brutes and chew the wiring she must be pretty desperate. And a desperate mouse will find a way, no matter what.'

Wallace sighed. 'Aye Angus. That's what I'm saying. That's why I keep the traps all over the place. And that's why we lock the creatures up.'

'But I've never seen a mouse in any of the traps, let alone any of the droppings—'

'That's because we're careful.'

'No, the point I'm trying to make is . . .'

There we must leave them, arguing in a friendly, roundabout way. Other mechanics were arriving and clocking on. The building was coming alive with a friendly hum of voices. The reason everyone was happy was because there would be little work to do beyond running test programmes and perhaps a bit more polishing. Bonuses of wine and poultry were paid after each battle night.

Wallace runs a tight shop. This is the way he likes things: as little as possible left to chance. The mousetraps that he keeps about the workshop are in some ways rather like touching wood after tempting providence or tossing salt over one's left shoulder after a spill to blind the devil: namely a precaution.

If the men could have an easy day, there was plenty of work for the women. Eve Duff had been taken on for the morning to help with the cleaning. She and Miranda and the rest of the serving-staff spent the morning up in the chalet counting out cutlery, folding napkins, polishing silver, buffing glasses and making sure that privately owned tankards were in the correct place.

Most of the women who were serving had attended at a battle banquet before but to Miranda it was all new. She spent a long time just getting to know the passages and walkways which lay beyond the dark green swing-doors at the back of the chalet. Miranda poked her head into any room that took her fancy and if it was occupied said, 'Ooops, sorry, wrong room.' And then retired after a good long look. Here were kitchens and cool-stores, pantries and wineries. There was a small but well-equipped medical suite for any of the Romans who became sick through overeating or who started bleeding while dancing when their stitches came out.

There were also sundry sumptuous bedrooms which could be booked by the hour.

At the very back of the chalet, escalators toiled down to the ground and back again. Miranda did not need to use these as her work was entirely in the dining-room and ballroom. Only porters used the escalators.

At 2 p.m. a siren sounded through the entire Battle Dome. It signified the start of the rest period. Those whose jobs were completed were now free for a few hours. Those whose jobs were not complete worked on. Everything that Miranda and Eve had to do was well finished and Eve took her leave of her daughter. She became fussy, obviously concerned, as this was the first time her daughter had worked away from home. Eve was under no illusions. She knew that the battle banquets usually became licentious and that a seventeen-year-old virgin on her own and a bit giddy could be meat for predators. 'Now you'll be sure to look out for your father and Angus?'

'Yes, Mum.' This for what seemed to be the hundredth time.

'And if anyone starts er . . . talking to you, you know, "talking". Well, you make sure they know you're a student from the Polytech and that your father is third mechanic down below and that he's picking you up.'

'Yes, Mum.'

'And be careful if anyone asks you to drink.'

'Yes, Mum.'

'And don't . . .'

'I won't.'

'Anyway. I've had a word with Sandy Parkin in catering. We were at school together. She'll keep an eye on you.'

'Mum!'

'All right. I'm going. I'll see you when you get home. Have a good rest and have a good time.'

'Yes, Mum.'

Eve departed and Miranda was left alone for the first time in the small closet that had been assigned to her for the rest period. She opened the suitcase and removed and hung up her uniform.

She was too excited to rest and so went for a walk through the chalet. She wandered through the dining-room with its soft carpet and crisp white table-linen and then into the long bar where she encountered an apprentice wine waiter, young as herself, who was desperately studying and trying to memorize the vintage list. He was speaking the names and dates of the wines in a loud whisper. He looked up in embarrassment when he realized that Miranda was near and had heard him but she smiled and gave him the thumbs-up and sauntered on.

The dance-floor had been polished once by machine and it gleamed, but granules of polish had been scattered for later sweeping and these crunched under her feet. Miranda danced a few steps from a dance she had learned at school, dipping low and with arms outstretched as though with a partner. These steps and a final turn carried her across the floor and to the sliding doors which gave access to the veranda. She wandered outside.

Resting her elbows on the railing which surrounded the platform, Miranda looked out and down into the vast amphitheatre. The sounds which reached her ears were softened as though heard through fog: men calling, the crackle of radio transmissions, the boom of speakers being tuned and somewhere a lone trumpeter practising a glissando in preparation for the lively martial music of the evening. In the technical control booth set high in the wall of the dome, one of the technicians was running a lighting check, flashing up each of the lanterns in the roof in turn to make sure that the bulbs had not blown and the circuits were intact. The patterns seemed random and, as each of the lanterns flashed on, so parts of the arena came alive as though lit from within. To Miranda the effect was magical. Down on the field a design assistant was texturing one of the monoliths, his pots of paint on the ground by his feet. Gardeners were at work on the mountainside anchoring bushes. Others were down on the plain teasing out a ruckle that had appeared in the smooth green surface. Excited voices, thin and distant, sounded from the tiled area near the entrance to the Battle Dome where the bull-bellied barrels of beer had arrived from Calcaria. These were being unloaded from a truck and set up on their trestles.

Everything was purposeful and businesslike. It gave Miranda a great sense of security. She yawned and realized that despite her excitement she was tired. So she made her way back to her small closet and lay down on the trestle bed.

She awoke to a siren. For a moment she didn't know where she was and then she remembered, and with a rush realized that if she didn't get a move on she would be late. As she hurried into her neatly pressed uniform she was angry with herself. She had promised herself plenty of time to get ready, carefully and without fuss, and now here she was scrambling. She smoothed her uniform straight against her sides and legs and looked in the mirror. She pulled pins from her hair and shook her head, freeing her dark curls. She had plans for her hair for tonight.

There was talk of Roman blood in her veins from her mother's side and this made her brush her hair up and pin it back to reveal her profile. The effect was immediate and remarkable. Had she been wearing a Roman robe instead of the pink and green uniform of the Polytech she could have taken her place at any of the ancient Imperial feasts so coldly depicted in marble throughout the city.

She donned the ear-rings and the cameo brooch from her grandmother and after debating with herself decided to leave the necklace off. She pressed her feet into her sensible shoes knowing there would be a lot of running about, especially after the first exhibit ended and the cadets arrived. Then, with a last glance at herself and a final touch to her hair, she stepped outside and hurried down to the bar.

There was no one there, of course, except the apprentice waiter who had just run in and whose hair was slicked back with water. He smiled a bit sheepishly and Miranda grinned too, glad she was not alone.

But things were happening. Down below at the Battle Dome entrance rowdy Romans were arriving and the beer was starting to flow.

A flyer settled at the landing-platform of the chalet and the Vice-Chancellor of the Academy and the entire Board of Studies climbed out. These were seven old men and two old women. Most needed sticks to help them and some had crutches. They were all eager and all demanded a quick stiff drink. Miranda found herself busy.

A second and very official-looking flyer arrived. First out was a young black servant who unrolled a length of red carpet fringed with gold tassels. He was followed by men and women wearing traditional togas and long gowns. They formed a guard of honour and waited. Finally a very fat man in a white toga and with a plaited crown of golden leaves round his forehead climbed out. He was helped by two young boys. This was the Praefectus Urbi, the chairman of the senate of the city of Eburacum.

Guests began to arrive in quick order. Between fetching drinks and snacks Miranda was just able to catch the opening movements and the final charge of the cadets. Then more flyers arrived at the chalet carrying senior Romans who had been attending a banquet in Eburacum and she had to run, bringing drinks and cigars and emptying ashtrays and once helping one of the older women to the ladies' room.

No one drank during the chariot contest and Miranda was able to watch it from the end of the balcony. She did not enjoy the fighting but she thought Viti was the most handsome man she had ever seen. Later she brought him a snack of olives and tomatoes and peppers when he sat alone on the balcony. She saw how bruised was his face and was surprised that his hand trembled when he lifted his glass. For his part, Viti was ignorant of her existence as a being, as something more than a waitress.

Miranda also saw the end of the contest between the Dragon and the Crab and watched Angus mount and climb into the Dragon. She knew how nervous he was and sent a kind thought to him. Thereafter she had no chance to watch what was going on in the Battle Dome.

Miranda had no real problems. She dropped a glass once. And once when she was reaching over a table to collect a used plate she felt a hand slide between her legs and stroke the inside of her knee. She was so surprised she cried out and there were smirks and angry glances at the table.

Later a younger dance-band arrived. Miranda would have liked to curl up in a chair close to the front and just watch, but the large sad man, the Ulysses father, commanded her attention. He talked about Africa, telling her things she could not understand but which seemed important to him. She could feel his deep sadness and his aching need to talk and so she listened as well as she could and nodded, and with just a small part of her attention followed the music.

Marcus Ulysses insisted that she have a drink with him and Miranda contrived to have fruit juice rather than the stiff gin he proffered. Old Ulysses talked and gradually became maudlin as he got drunk. He began fishing for compliments and his hand rested briefly on her shoulder and his fingers touched her lips. 'You remind me,' he said, 'of a woman I once knew in Tashkent.'

'Do I?' said Miranda with surprise, having no idea where Tashkent was.

It was only the arrival of Calpurnia Gallica that released her. That experienced lady sized up the situation and insisted that the old Ulysses should dance and got him to his feet. He was like a groggy bear, just out of hibernation in springtime.

'I'll be back,' he said thickly to Miranda. 'Don't go away.'

'She can do what she likes,' said Calpurnia firmly and nodded to Miranda, dismissing her. Speaking solely to the old Ulysses and quietly she said, 'Can't you see she's just a child from the Polytech. Retain some dignity at least. It's probably time she was leaving anyway – way past her bedtime.' They moved off.

Miranda stood up. Since she had been monopolized by the old Ulysses no one had asked her to fetch or bring. Nor did they now. She was in a sense marked, though she did not know it.

The quality of the party was changing. The professional waitresses, who had families waiting for them, were being replaced by the night-time women who were fresh and perfumed and ready for any kind of action. But had Miranda chosen to stay, there were none among the Romans who would have objected. It was accepted that an attractive woman could use her good looks to make her way. Calpurnia Gallica was more thoughtful in her morality than most of her colleagues. She had recognized innocence in Miranda and did not want to see innocence wantonly ruined by a drunken old man who would, in any case, perform badly. If it had been young Viti dazzling Miranda then Calpurnia would probably have held her peace.

One of Miranda's older colleagues, Sandy Parkin, the buxom blond-headed woman that her mother had mentioned, came over to her and told her that the shift was over and that her father and Angus had been waiting in the back rooms for over half an hour. Sandy made it clear that it was time to go. Miranda hurried out. She had not realized it was so late. She still had a lot of energy in her.

Her father was enjoying a beer and Angus was tucking into a pie. They were both relaxed and full of good humour, their work being done.

'Are you ready to leave?' asked Wallace.

'Is it after one already?' asked Miranda. 'I'm contracted to stay till one.'

'It's a quarter to two,' said Angus.

'I think there might be a bit of a dance for us,' said Miranda boldly. 'I'd like to stay for a few more minutes. And I don't have to be up early tomorrow. None of us do.'

And that rather clinched the matter. They stayed another half-hour.

While an orgy got under way in the front part of the chalet, the maids and general workers had a party at the back. There was no lack of food or drink or good music. Angus danced with Miranda and Wallace enjoyed a couple more beers and did a few turns round the room with Sandy.

Something was released in Miranda that night, some warm spring of her womanhood. The scent of potent males on the prowl, the music and the season of the year all played their part, without doubt, as well as her own sensual disposition. She danced like a hungry woman, which in a way she was.

Angus sensed it without having a name for it and when his strong mechanic's arm half lifted her to him, she flowed along. They didn't quite kiss since it is hard to kiss when you are dancing, and besides, there were too many people in the room. But had they been alone they would have kissed, and now all they needed was an opportunity.

Wallace looked at his pocket-watch. He yawned. It was time

to go and they all knew it. They called goodbye to colleagues and then made their way to the lift which would carry them down to the ground and to the Battle Dome underground station. Sandy accompanied them as she lived quite close to the Duffs and didn't like travelling alone on the underground late at night. While Wallace and Sandy walked in front, talking about the night's battles, Angus and Miranda held back. As they walked their arms bumped and finally it was Miranda who took the initiative and eased the situation by linking her arm with Angus. Angus, to show that he was grateful for her boldness, squeezed her arm and pressed her hand. They talked about the music.

On the underground train they sat together and Miranda's head rested lightly on his shoulder. Angus could feel her breath on his cheek. Wallace, thinking that Miranda was falling asleep, winked and nodded to his apprentice as though commiserating. Women, ha! He gave a big artificial snore and pretended to nuzzle his head into the shoulder of Sandy Parkin. That lady cuffed him off with a laugh. 'Ah get enough of that at 'ome without thee startin',' she said.

A few hundred yards from the station they bade good-night to Sandy and heard her front door bang. A light was still on at her house so obviously her husband had stayed up for her.

At the Duffs' house Eve was glad to see them. She opened the door and stood in her slippers and pinnie when she heard them approaching. 'Have you had a good night?' she asked.

They all nodded. Within minutes of being home, the Duffs made their way to bed. Angus made pretence of looking for a magazine in the sitting-room while Miranda got herself a drink of water. They met briefly at the kitchen door. Miranda was holding a glass.

Angus acted without thinking. He put his arms round her. He kissed her neck. He pulled her in to him until he could feel her breasts against him. Miranda responded with her arms and the result was that she tipped part of the contents of the glass down the neck of his shirt. This was funny to both of them and they laughed trying not to make a sound. And then, before the laughter died, Miranda lifted her lips and kissed Angus fairly and squarely. He responded and for a few moments they were quiet before they parted to draw breath. For both of them this was an important moment. It was the first time they had kissed and felt the wind of abandonment fan them.

Then Miranda parted from him. She refilled her glass with water, and with a smile and a blown kiss ran upstairs. She was asleep within five minutes.

Not so Angus. He spent a restless but happy night alone with his imagination.

5   Biography of a Year

Spring advanced into summer, in this world just as in ours, but with this difference: the presence of the forest meant that wildlife was more plentiful than we have ever known. Deer could be seen in the evening from the walls of Eburacum as they made their way down to the river to drink. Red squirrels occupied the trees in their thousands, bobbing about in the branches and diving into the hollows left by fallen branches. Foxes came and went by day as well as night, silent as shadows, and the bird life was such that the dawn chorus vied with the morning bells of the city for supremacy.

The sound of the forest changed with the seasons. In winter there was the rattle and creak of branches while the wind howled and moaned through the stands of bare-branched trees and drove the snow like wraiths from the high moors. Then in spring there came softer sounds with the growth of the new leaves. The wind changed its pitch, baffled by the forest. The patter of rain on leaves was a gentle susurration. In the summer the trees rustled and sighed together and crackled in the heat from the sun. Then in autumn there was the rattle of dying leaves stripped from the trees and pelted through the woodlands, and the pop of seed-pods and the plop of ripe nuts and fruit as they fell to earth. The sounds of the forest were like the sounds of the sea, always there, always different and always changing; accepted as such a normal part of the everyday world that life could not be imagined without them.

So . . .

One Sunday morning early in June, Angus took Miranda for a sail up the Ouse. Apart from the oars, the boat that they hired had a single central sail which Angus could control from the tiller seat in the rear. A south-east wind sent the small boat shooting up against the current. They soon passed the last of the magnificent Roman villas on the left bank and found themselves entering a shady area where the willow trees hung low over the water and trailed in the river. They had entered the place where the river flowed through a neck of the wild wood.

Even though it was Sunday, the river was busy. Small steamers chugged with the stream carrying early apricots, beech-oil, leatherware and dried eels from the small towns down for the Monday markets at Eburacum.

Among the willows there were many private places, places where the river turned back on itself and swirled lazily under the weeping willows creating a haven away from the main stream.

Angus beached the boat at one such secret place and tied it to a young alder tree. He and Miranda climbed the bank carrying the picnic basket between them. They came to a glade above the water where the grass smelled warm and where the black-thorn and elder bushes blocked the breeze. Insects darted in the still air while birds argued in song, declaring their territory.

In the short time since the graduation night at the Battle Dome, Angus and Miranda had become lovers in everything except the deed. Pleasing to both of them was the fact that Miranda's parents seemed happy to see them spending time together. Angus had shown himself to be a fine and imaginative mechanic. Miranda had decided to specialize in cooking. Both were doing well in their different vocations and both seemed to be growing into maturity without too much fuss and bother. However, Wallace and Eve did not enquire too deeply, trusting to their daughter's good sense and remembering their own passionate and furtive courting.

In the evenings Angus and Miranda went for walks. They spent hours longing and yet holding back, touching and sighing and trying to understand what was happening to them. They kissed and joked. They danced together. They shared intimacies, but they did not make love.

Given the opportunity, Angus would have barged into love-making with all the finesse of a hippopotamus plunging into a river. It was Miranda that was shy and her shyness was the result of her deep passion. Miranda was frightened of the forces she felt stirring inside herself. Once she almost fainted when Angus's hand slipped down her body and between her legs. Her open-mouthed cry frightened Angus for he thought he had hurt her in some way that he could not understand. In a hundred ways Miranda explored and considered her passion. She thought about babies and she thought about what it would feel like if Angus were to reject her afterwards. She wondered if love would besot her and feared that it might. As for Angus, he could not control his thoughts or his erections. They came unbidden and embarrassing, sometimes at work, sometimes at mealtime. Only at night could he let his imagination flow and his deep sensuality have an airing.

But there came the day when such speculation became intolerable. Life was immediate. It did not lend itself to planning. Dreams were insubstantial in the light of day. Frustration grew and came to seem like a contempt for life. These two people, green with love, aching for one another, needed only a place where they could be close and alone.

This fine day in early summer just happened to be the day and the place was a grassy bank close by a clump of nettles under a towering elm tree. It could have been a lot worse.

They set the hamper down on the ground. Miranda spread the blanket. Angus smoothed it, kneeling on the ground. Miranda put her arms round him. He kissed her and suddenly a painful urgency possessed both of them.

Some minutes later when they lay tangled together and panting, the thought struck Angus that he wished they were in a comfortable bed and with the entire night before them. Somehow he had contrived to brush the stinging nettles with his arm. He lay on his back, indecent as a dog, and Miranda lay beside him, like water lapping round him, holding him tenderly. That first love-making was artless and clumsy and more than a bit painful for both of them. 'If this is all there is to it,' they both thought, 'then why all the fuss?' But they didn't say that, of course. No, they told one another how terrific it was.

After sandwiches, and much kissing, they were freer and less artless while trusting their passion more. Soon they were noisy enough to startle the birds in the elm tree.

Later in the drowsy warm afternoon they dozed and when they woke up they were both stiff of muscle. Miranda lay for a long time in Angus's arms without speaking. Angus did not know what was going through her mind, but she seemed contented with his arms about her and with holding him, and for the time being that was sufficient. But then, reluctantly, Angus found his attention drifting to the coming evening and the journey home and the need to get the boat back. Finally he kissed her and eased her arms from round him and was truly astonished to find that she had been crying.

'Why are you crying? Are you sorry we . . . ?' His voice trailed away, begging the question.

'I'm crying because, because I'm happy. And no, I'm not sorry, I'm glad. It was wonderful. You are so beautiful.'

These words quite astounded Angus and he could think of nothing to say. But he felt like a young god. For her part, Miranda felt like a lake.

They dressed quickly, pausing only to kiss, while a sudden breeze from the north told of a change in the weather. The evening came quickly and the first stars were out as they pushed the boat out from under the willows.

Angus took to the oars and soon the small boat was speeding down the river. Even so, the journey took longer than they had expected. Finally, they passed under a bridge which supported one of the main east–west highways and the lights from the road shone down on the river and the small jetty where the boats were moored. In starlight the boat bumped the bank and a dark figure emerged from the boat-shed, grabbed the painter and pulled the boat roughly to its mooring. Miranda, in the act of standing, sat down with a bump.

'You should've been back before sundown,' growled the grumpy attendant. 'I'm charging you extra for this.'

Angus didn't know whether he should push the man into the river for his churlishness or offer him a handsome tip. In the event his good humour won out and he paid the man and thanked him and handed Miranda from the boat with fond and elaborate courtesy.

They arrived home just in time for a supper of ham and lettuce and the first of the year's tomatoes. 'Have you had a good day?' asked Eve. 'I was just beginning to wonder.'

'Terrific,' said Angus. 'Great,' said Miranda. Both over-lapping.

'Well that's all right then,' said Eve, thoughtfully.

Wallace raised his eyes from the evening paper. 'See there's been some trouble last night,' he said. 'That young Ulysses boy who won the chariot event has been in a fight. The city guards are holding him. There's a couple of youngsters dead apparently. It doesn't say who.'

Angus, tucking in to ham, stopped eating. 'I know him,' he said. 'I was teaching him just yesterday evening. He often comes down to the dome to practise on his dad's machine. I took him out for a training run. He's pretty clumsy. I think he fancies himself a bit, though.'

Wallace, who hardly ever attended training sessions, screwed his face up as though trying to call his face to mind. 'You remember him,' said Angus. 'He's a shortish fellow with cropped hair. Big chest. Thick arms. Looks a bit like an otter. His mates called him Viti. He damaged the Dragon a week last Wednesday and we had to get a special part over from Danum.'

Light dawned for Wallace. 'Oh *him*,' he said. 'Strained the spinal torque-shaft last time he had the Dragon out.'

'That's the one. Tried to make it turn while it was doing a high-knee canter.'

Both men laughed. 'I remember,' said Wallace. 'Well, he's been arrested. Sounds serious.'

And indeed it was.

The trouble had begun in mid-April, shortly after the commencement of the spring term. Viti Ulysses was now a third-year student which meant that he had private quarters of his own. Like all the other third-years, he also had two servants from the first-year students. As chance would have it, one of these two was a relative of Julius Caesar XIX who had been killed by Viti's father. This young man, ironically called Brutus, was looking out for any opportunity to humiliate Viti and he found it on the occasion of the first full-dress parade which occurred in May. He fed Viti's horse on fennel and half-cooked beans just before the parade so that the poor animal farted loudly during the entire ceremony and Viti could do nothing except sit aboard his charger in acute embarrassment while it voided its guts noisily and spattered the parade-ground.

This could have been forgiven. Practical jokes were not uncommon and the unwritten code of honour which went with them meant that Viti would have accepted any punishment meted out to him without revealing the true culprit even if he had known who it was. Equally legitimate in the unwritten code was that Viti could now come hunting and deal tit-for-tat if he discovered the identity of his tormentor.

Let it be said that the young Brutus was neither intelligent nor imaginative. In his next tricks he revealed a fascination for excrement which most humans grow out of by late adolescence.

He put dog-turds in Viti's armoured riding-boots and in his leather and steel-banded jousting-gloves. He contrived to do this during the opening ceremony just before a contest against the Military Academy at Camboritum. Being heavy equipment the boots and gloves were not normally donned until the very last moment.

The trumpets were calling for the first tourney when Viti strapped on his boots, uncertain what felt wrong. He was atop his charger and heading out to the lists when he plunged his hands into his gloves and the smell hit him. There was no time to change. As it was a non-stop tourney, Viti had to ride continuously until defeated. This occurred half-way through the morning when he was up-ended by a second-year student from Camboritum who rode away from him fanning his nose. Later this same student made it known that Viti had shat himself. Viti's fury made him white of face. He stormed away from the contest and some of the warrior lads from Camboritum jeered at him for being a bad loser. That made him angrier still and later, in the hot steaming shower, he vowed to kill whoever was tormenting him.

Viti was not a fool. Aware that he had an enemy, he narrowed down the suspects and set a trap. To be fair, he was suspicious of young Brutus, if only because that boy offered sycophantic phrases but in a sexless, cold and humourless way. In contrast, his other servant, a sloppy but handsome Greek youth called Aristogeiton, made it clear that he venerated the very ground that Viti walked on and was ready for any debauchery. Viti, however, was not.

So Viti announced one day that he was going to entertain at home and was inviting some of the senior third-year students including the magnificent Diana. On the night of the feast he hid in a broom-cupboard inside his dining-room and watched as his servants set the table. He saw nothing wrong and Viti was just about to give up when Brutus entered the room quickly and closed the door. Then he removed a bottle of fine Caledonian whisky from Viti's cabinet and replaced it with a bottle that he had brought in hidden under a cloth on his trolly. He wiped the bottle and set it in place. Then he went about his work again.

When the room was empty Viti stepped out of hiding. He checked the bottle and his worst fears were confirmed. He let half an hour pass and then called his two servants to join him.

'Tonight being a special celebration,' he said, 'in which I intend to rid myself of certain encumbrances, I propose we have a small drink together to celebrate the future. Now you, Aristogeiton, I know you like the vintages of the Po valley so you may open any bottle you like. You, Brutus, like many of us pure-bred Romans, enjoy the tart whisky of the North. This is the bottle for you.' Viti selected, after some careful delay and pondering, the bottle which the hapless Brutus had installed.

'I think, sir, today I would prefer a white wine. My head is jaded,' said Brutus.

'Not at all,' said Viti, screwing open the top. 'No better cure for a jaded head than aged Caledonian whisky. Never let it be said that a Roman turned his back on the hard stuff when offered.'

'Then will you join me, sir?' asked Brutus.

'No. I will just take mineral water. I want a clear head for tonight.'

So, while Aristogeiton drank his fill of old Roman wine, Brutus manfully swallowed his first glass of urine. Viti refilled his glass immediately. 'Drink,' he ordered.

Only then did Brutus finally realize that Viti had somehow discovered the substitution. He backed away but Viti was faster. He caught the young man by the front of his shirt and then locked his head. 'You will drink now the entire bottle,' said Viti. 'Or die in the attempt. No man turns down my hospitality.' He tipped back Brutus's head and forced the bottle-neck into his mouth. Aristogeiton looked on in surprise. The bottle gurgled and Brutus gulped and gagged and the contents flooded down his face and into his clothes. Viti squeezed harder until Brutus's face was flushed. 'What are you drinking?' he asked.

'Horse-piss.'

Viti struck him across the face with the back of his hand. A ring on his index-finger opened a wound on Brutus's cheek. 'And what else?'

'That's all.'

'Why?'

'I hate you.'

'Why?'

Brutus spat up into Viti's face. 'That's why,' he said.

The ensuing fight was short-lived. Viti, who, if he had lived in our world, could have excelled as a street-fighter in New York, belted the young Brutus three or four times round the face, making him bleed from nose and mouth and ear. Then he emptied the last of the bottle over the prone body and walked out. It was left to the incredulous Aristogeiton to clean up the mess.

The young Brutus was later accepted into the Academy hospital where his stomach was pumped and his wounds dressed.

That evening, at his dinner-party, when Viti was asked where his other servant was he told the full story, never thinking that there could be some connection between Brutus and the dead Julius. But Diana made the connection immediately. When she heard that young Brutus was wounded and had been taken to hospital with fractured jaw and broken nose she set down her napkin and left the meal. 'You should have thought twice,' she said angrily, 'before you decided to attack another member of my family. And to boast of it too ... Did you have to injure the boy for a schoolboy's prank? Well, your family will pay this time.' With that she left. With her went three of the remaining guests. They were members of families closely allied to the Caesar family.

This division escalated within the Military Academy, especially among the third-year students. Contests began to diverge along family lines, those who favoured the Caesars against those who favoured the Ulysses. This was no longer a childish matter of dog-turds. The fighting was in earnest whether with sword or leather-wrapped knuckles.

Viti did his best to hold matters in check. But he was powerless to stop the skirmishing. Nor did the Ulysses family lack friends who wanted a chance to have a go at the Caesar clan. The instructors at the Academy tried to quieten things down but they were curiously impotent. The antagonism was fuelled from without the Academy, and in a way the Academy was merely a pawn in a deep and ongoing feud.

One night, quite late, Viti was walking home through the streets of Eburacum when he was set upon by three assailants. He had been training that evening at the Battle Dome, with Angus as it happened, and after returning to the city he had spent an hour (as well as a considerable sum of money) at one of the waterfront brothels. Whistling and invigorated by the night air, he was strolling back to the Academy when the assailants pounced. They were not trying to kill him but to kidnap him.

A net was thrown over his shoulders and his feet were kicked away from him. Viti shouted with all his might. When he fell he rolled and managed to free his knife from his wrist-sheath. He cut the twine sufficiently to free one arm and when one of the assailants came at him, hefting a short springy cosh, Viti stabbed.

The attacker fell with a gurgle. A second moved in and Viti was able to entangle him in the net and then silence him with a hip throw and a kick. The third began to run and Viti, now free of the net, gave chase. They ran through the narrow streets cluttered with shop-stalls and pails of garbage set out for the night collectors. There were few people about and the sound of their running steps and panting was loud in the night. There were other shouts too, the shouts of city guards, and somewhere a siren started.

Viti caught his attacker just inside the gate through the old city walls at the place which we call Bootham Bar. They fought hard and without quarter. But Viti was the stronger. He inflicted most damage. Then, as he moved in for the kill, a searchlight blazed down from above. It did not stop him. The knife flashed and was buried to the hilt between the ribs of his enemy. It cut the heart and lungs and the man died quickly, slipping off the blade as he slumped. Then there were city guards dropping about them. The flyer landed with a whine of its siren and the noise of its engine was like thunder rolling between the houses. Lights flashed on in bedroom windows, for this was a part of town where many of the Citizens lived, and windows slammed open.

Street vehicles arrived from different parts of town, and an ambulance with a flashing green light. Viti was taken in charge, but when it was realized who he was there was no one dared lay a finger on him. He was, however, advised that it was in his own interests to go quietly. He was to some extent protected by a long-standing agreement between the Academy and the city that the Academy would discipline its own students if the city authorities would hand them over. This arrangement was complicated only by the fact that the two young men that Viti had stabbed were both sons of city prefects, and their fathers were supporters of the Caesar clan and would undoubtedly demand the most extreme penalty. Young Viti could not have committed a worse deed had he tried.

That Viti was the last son of the ageing Ulysses made him a prime target for those who wanted to damage and destroy the Ulysses family. The stakes were high in anyone's game and lesser players kept well clear.

All this occurred on a Saturday in June, the very day before Angus and Miranda went for their sail up the River Ouse.

Viti was held for two weeks confined to his rooms at the Academy while the pros and cons of his case were argued. The death penalty could be invoked since Roman law involved elements of the 'eye for an eye and tooth for a tooth' philosophy. Old Ulysses made it known that if such a verdict were passed he would raise legions in the North and would destroy the armies and cities of Britannia and personally kill anyone who opposed him. His enemies said they would raise armies in Gallia and do the same if the extreme penalty were not passed.

Stalemate. And then old Marcus Ulysses took the initiative and solved the problem with a stroke of genius of the kind which could only work with the Romans.

One night, secretly, he had a solid gold statue erected to the memory of Julius Caesar XIX whom he had killed. It was a statue of Caesar in a chariot drawn by bulls. This monument was placed on a small hill just outside the city of Eburacum on the road to Calcaria. The nearby trees were cut down so the statue glinted in the morning sun. A simple plaque announced, *'Marcus Augustus Ulysses salutes his comrade of the African campaign, Gaius Julius Caesar XIX. May the all-wise gods smile on frail and mortal man.'* As word of the statue spread through the city, people poured through the gates to look at it. The city fathers arrived and their faces were beaming for they saw the solution to their dilemma. This magnanimous gesture was an act of truce. No one could expect old Ulysses to apologize (he had never been known to apologize in his life), but this was the next best thing. This was an honouring of a noble kinsman and no one could say he had stinted the cost. There were several tons of gold in the statue. It was, of course, an ancient statue and those who had studied such things recognized the statue of Marcus Aurelius. The head of the emperor had been removed and a new likeness of the contemporary Caesar had been set in its place. This was a common practice among the Romans where political fortunes could change faster than sculptors could sculpt. Most statues had detachable heads and no one thought it amiss.

That same day Viti was freed from solitary confinement, and while there was still tension when he encountered members of the Caesar clan, there was also a recognition that anyone who started hostilities could expect no sympathy from either party. Young Brutus had prudently withdrawn from the Academy for this year and would pick up his studies again next year when Viti had left.

That evening Viti dined in the city at a restaurant on the river, sitting outside in the warm summer air. Conspicuously, Diana joined him later for the long dessert. Afterwards they went out to see the statue, which was floodlit, and photographs of them looking up at it were taken by the city archivist for distribution to the daily papers. All seemed to be well . . .

. . . but it was not. This whole series of events affected Viti badly. He became colder and more calculating. He adopted a cynical shell to protect the gentler being within. But it wasn't just a shell: he was genuinely harder too, less forgiving.

He stepped up his training programme. He made himself competent at driving his father's Dragon machine. He practised unarmed combat with a zeal that astonished his tutors and made him feared. Anger and resentment burned in him like fire and he could not forgive and forget and recover his tough innocence. But his anger had no focus and hence no release. Indeed, what was he angry about? Insults to his name? Being imprisoned? Being frightened of execution? Upset that his father never visited him? Upset that those who he thought were friends proved to be fickle? Upset that there was no friendship anyway, only politics? All this and more. Much more. He was angry with himself. He was angry with the imperfect world. In short, he was angry with everything.

When, in the autumn, his forty infantry soldiers were assigned to him in preparation for the final graduating battle in the Battle Dome, Viti began a thorough programme of training. He had studied previous battles and devised a new stratagem based on fighting in threes. His aim was to create a flexible fighting force which, if it once gained the upper hand, would be unbeatable. He also, secretly, introduced a new weapon, the shuriken. This was a device much favoured on islands in one of the distant Eastern provinces. It was a star of metal with razor-sharp sides and needle points. Thrown from close quarters it could damage a leg or lodge in the vulnerable space between helmet and shoulder-guard. It could be fatal to a fleeing opponent with an exposed back. Viti intended to win the title of Victor Ludorum and his dedication to this end showed the dimension of his anger.

Of course, all preparations were conducted in secret at

scheduled times in the Battle Dome and the Academy's rules were very strict on this. Any student caught spying or attempting bribery of Battle Dome staff could be expelled from the Academy on the spot and have his rights severely restricted. Few cheated, therefore. In any case, it was usually the soldiers who died, hacking one another to pieces. They were selected from the prisons of north Britannia and no one counted their deaths a great loss. The Roman officers were judged on their generalship.

The year worked slowly through. The days of autumn shortened and a chill came into the air. Viti trained. Angus completed his first year as an apprentice and was promoted. Miranda studied the fine arts of cooking and remembered the summer.

Winter arrived with snow in Caledonia and north-east gales belting the coast of northern Britannia. The seas were mountains of grey and white and the clouds low-bellied and dark. The smell of snow was in the air. One night the rain which had spattered during the day changed to snow and in the morning the world was white-over. It was only mid-December.

When Wallace and Angus arrived at the dome, their breath formed white clouds in the morning air. There was shouting in the dome. Viti and his team of warriors were already at work, practising moves aimed at dividing an enemy before the *coup de grâce*. Angus watched for a while. None of it made much sense to him. It looked as though the infantrymen were dancing.

This was a day for maintenance in the machine-shop. Angus's job was to start up each creature and check its different systems. Some, those that had undergone recent repair, he would take for a test run. All the machines were suspended in their maintenance cradles and the vast hangar looked like the morgue for a zoo. From each creature there rose a thick black tube which was connected with high-pressure clips to a central tube which ran along the middle of the ceiling for the entire length of the hangar. This central tube guided the compressed air that was used to get the flywheels of the different fighting-machines turning. The compressed air came from an artificial waterfall in the nearby hills. The system was very simple and had originally been developed in the Pennines during the eleventh century to assist the blast furnaces of Danum. A column of water fell on to a piston, thereby compressing the air on the piston's interior side up to several atmospheres. Once a working pressure had been achieved in the system, the compressed air was fed to any one of several outlets. In the Battle Dome it was used to lift water for decorative waterfalls and to provide a high-velocity jet to start the flywheels of the fighting-beasts. However, for routine maintenance such as Angus was engaged on, the flywheels were not started. Every fighting-machine had internal batteries which could provide power to the mechanical systems.

Standing on the workshop floor, Angus powered up the first creature by remote control and studied it critically as its legs scampered in the air. This beast was a new version, only recently delivered, of the same Crab in which Julius Caesar XIX had died. Angus put it through its paces, making the legs move for advance and retreat and turn. The creature had an uncanny life, especially when he made the head bob and the hornèd jaws advance and retract.

Angus was particularly vigilant, for the repair workshop had had a lot of trouble with this machine since its first commissioning. There was some problem in the relay system which controlled the complex leg movements. For 99 per cent of the time the machine worked perfectly. At maximum acceleration on flat ground, the Crab could attain a speed of fifty-five miles an hour. This was fifteen miles an hour faster than the beast in which Julius had died. But there was that 1 per cent error which meant that sometimes two of the legs seized up and ruptured, or worse, they performed out of sync so that the Crab ran with a humpy movement which led inevitably to its flipping on to its back. The mechanics in the workshop had replaced the entire relay control unit but still the error persisted, which meant that it was in one of the thousands of small switches which fed back to the main control centre the information it needed to keep everything running smoothly.

Just now, with the Crab idling, everything was fine but as soon as Angus applied acceleration two of the legs locked out of phase for half a second and then with a grinding of gears jumped back into sync. Angus eyed the giant Crab and his eyes gleamed. He would solve the problem with its leg movements one day even if he had to dismantle the creature's entire electric circuitry by hand.

Before switching the Crab off and moving on, he noted that the relay-battery terminals were again showing corrosion and that there was some oil leaking from the rear 'sting' mechanism. This surprised him as he had overhauled the lubrication system only a week earlier and replaced several of the rubber seals.

This 'sting' was a nice development dreamed up in one of the design labs. The 'sting' was really nothing more than a large electrode which could be advanced on a telescopic arm. It was powered by the centrifugal dynamo located low down in the Crab's carapace. When the Crab made contact with another creature it could release the sting which, if it touched the opposing animal's body, discharged violently. The hope was that some of the opponent's electrical systems would be knocked out by the sudden surge of current. Had old Gaius Julius Caesar's Crab been equipped with a 'sting' then he probably could have neutralized the Ulysses' Dragon just long enough to snip its head off.

Angus found the cause of the oil-leak. It was not serious: just excess lubricant easing out under the rubber sleeves which protected the telescopic mechanism. He wiped it away with a rag. Angus eyed the blunt, black sting and wondered. 'If the dynamo sometimes draws current erratically causing a surge . . . mmm . . . or if there's a capacitor failure and it discharges internally . . .' Angus became excited as he followed his line of thought. 'It would be . . . as if the creature had stung itself. That could throw two of the legs out of sync. Hell's bells. Worth a check. Hell yes, worth a check.' For several minutes Angus laboured to write his ideas in the report book and finally drew a small, neat picture. It was enough to remind him. He would follow his ideas up the next time he came to work on the Crab. Then he switched the creature to idle and finally turned it off and watched the legs work through slow motion to stillness.

Some machines did not need testing for they were already damaged and in need of major overhaul. One such was an ancient machine built to resemble a hydra and which seventy years earlier had been given the name Jesse.

In its day Jesse had been a pinnacle of engineering skill. The creature consisted of a central mobile cabin which was heavily armoured and travelled on caterpillar tracks. Reaching out from the roof of the cabin were six long flexible arms, four of which were telescopic and two of which operated on the principle of a pantograph. All of the arms were equipped with electromagnetic hooks, each of which was linked to a steel cable, and the cables were stored in drums under the main body. When Jesse was in a fight, it would send its arms round its enemy and some of the hooks would detach and anchor. The cables would uncoil and enmesh the opponent. Finally the opponent would be unable to move and Jesse would then reveal an oxy-acetylene cutter. Crude but effective. If the opponent did not give in then Jesse simply chewed its way into the creature until vital systems were severed. Such was the theory, and Jesse had an impressive list of victories to show how well theory and practice could go hand in hand.

Wallace was working on Jesse. He had all the arms detached and extended and was sitting in a cradle in the middle of them welding some eye-brackets into place to strengthen the steel hawser connections. Another mechanic was underneath replacing brake-shoes on the interlocking pressure plates which controlled the speed at which cable was paid out after a hook had been taken. Yet a third mechanic, his face black with oil and rivered with sweat, was repairing the servo mechanism which drove the tracks. Jesse had to be ready for an exhibition tourney in two days' time and so the work, while it was not hurried, did not slow down. Angus merely waved and enquired how the repairs were going before moving on.

By lunch-time Angus was half-way through his checking and was perched high in a machine called the Porcupine eating his sandwiches. He heard his name called and thrust his head through the open porthole of the cockpit and looked down. It was Miranda looking smart and cool in her neat Polytech uniform. Her arrival at the Battle Dome during work hours was a departure from normal affairs and he wondered what the occasion was. She was smiling, so the visit did not signify a problem.

Since they now made love regularly and whenever they could and never took precautions, it was, in Angus's mind, only a matter of time before nature went clickety-click and he found himself a father-to-be. He assumed, correctly, that Miranda had made the same evaluation of their situation. In an uncomplicated way he looked forward to the event which would push his life in a new direction.

Angus waved and beckoned. 'Climb up,' he shouted. 'Use the ladder. It's bolted tight.' He pointed to a narrow ladder which reached from the ground to a hatch in the stomach between the creature's six legs. Miranda climbed but it was obvious from her movements and from the way she gripped the sides of the ladder that she did not have a good head for heights or trust the flimsy-looking rungs. Once through the hatch she scrambled along a narrow walkway past the large pneumatic pistons which drove the armour-piercing quills. At the end she came to a second ladder. This was made of flexible steel links and was awkward to climb. It led up to the control cabin where Angus was sitting. The young man reached down and she took his arm and he guided her up the swaying ladder. She joined him in the narrow cabin and sat on a webbing seat with her legs dangling.

'What's up?' he asked, offering her a sandwich. 'I thought you'd be at the Poly all day. Is it still snowing?'

She accepted the sandwich and wrinkled her nose. 'What's that smell?' she asked.

Angus sniffed. And then began clowning, sniffing his own armpits, sniffing the walls, sniffing like a dog sniffing another dog. Clearly he could smell nothing out of the ordinary. She pushed him off. 'Seriously.'

'Probably hydraulic fluid. There's always leaks. Or it could be some of the compressed air. That always smells bad. I was bleeding the main compressor cylinders earlier. Nothing to worry about. Anyway, what brings you here?'

'They've given me the half-day off.'

'How come? Talk about lucky.' He bit into one of his sandwiches. 'I'd like a half-day off. We could go out in the snow.'

Miranda pulled a face at this. 'Snow's nearly all gone, anyway,' she said.

'Well come on, tell us.'

'I've got all the assignments in and this afternoon's for staff—student conferences and my conference was this morning. So . . . here I am.'

'And?' This while chewing.

'And what?

'How was it? Your conference.'

'Well, they're not expelling me.' She paused and he waited. 'I've come top in my division.'

'They must have made a mistake,' said he.

'What . . . ?' Miranda pretended to punch him and he reached over quickly and gave her a crumbed kiss. She disentangled herself.

'And what else?' he asked.

'They want me to do the Battle Dome duty again . . .'

Angus's face lit up at this. 'Hey, perhaps we can stay longer this time and really have a good dance . . .'

'That was what I thought. And, I'm going out on section next term. To the Academy. I'll be assistant to the main banquet cook. She's the top in all Britannia. So that should be good.' Miranda was obviously pleased and beamed at him.

Angus beamed back, though to be honest he did not know what to make of this last piece of information. He thought the Academy sounded boring, but then he was not interested in domestic management. He accepted his ignorance. He made no pretences to false interest. As far as he was concerned, if Miranda was happy that was good enough for him. He shared, as well as he could, her delight. He wanted to give her a treat.

'Come on,' he said. 'I'll take you for a celebration run. I'll make this thing scamper. You can hold on to your sandwich.'

Angus put the remains of his lunch away in a locker and sealed it. Then he helped Miranda into a helmet and adjusted webbing straps across her shoulders and lap and between her legs.

'What are you doing?' she asked, her voice mildly mischievous.

'Strapping you in. I don't want you distracting me. You'll see why. This creature can do cartwheels.' When he was certain that she was secure he climbed down to the lower compartment and attached the high-pressure air line to the protected chamber which housed the flywheel and all its local generators. Angus used the emergency batteries to start the wheel turning for he was in a hurry and then, when the flywheel was close to 100 r.p.m., he fed a high-speed stream of air into the wheel chamber. All the flywheels which powered the fighting-beasts had a system of vanes which trapped the air when the wheel was starting but which dropped flat when it was up to speed. The wheel gradually increased its spin until it achieved its optimum working speed of 600 r.p.m. At this speed Angus disconnected the air hose and thrust it outside. Tension-support cables lifted the air pipe in festoons well clear of the creature. Angus closed the lower access door and spun the wheel which locked it. Then he climbed back up to the cabin, gave Miranda a quick kiss and strapped himself into the control seat. He checked that all systems were operating smoothly, cocked a trained ear to hear and feel the vibrations of the spinning wheel, and then lowered the communications helmet over his head and inserted his hands into the guidance gloves.

Gently Angus fed energy from the flywheel generators to the legs. Slowly, like a creature waking from sleep, the Porcupine stood up. In front of Angus all the dials flickered except the one which registered oil pressure in the main quill-cylinders. Angus tapped the dial with his knuckle and it sprang into life. 'Never fails,' he said to Miranda. 'Magic knuckles. You ask your dad.'

Two junior mechanics who were doing some welding under one of the neighbouring creatures pulled their gear out of the way and waved. Like Angus, they were thrilled by the power of the machines, and looked forward to the day when they could take the creatures for a 'spin'.

Angus was in radio contact with the security officer who managed the gates which connected the workshops below with the battlefields above. He asked her for gate three to be opened and moments later a section of the wall to their right slid up.

All systems within the Porcupine were now warm and had

reached operational pressure, including the pneumatic cylinders which fired the quills like bolts from a crossbow. Thoughtfully, Angus deactivated that system. He did not want an accident. Quills from the Porcupine could tear holes in the dome wall. The Porcupine was one of the most dangerous and feared beasts in the entire fighting-zoo and was only matched against creatures reinforced with special armour-plating. Angus nudged the controls and the the creature began to walk. It required six legs to give it a smooth and balanced movement. Basically the creature had three patterns of leg movement and each pattern had its own range of speeds. It was one of the delights of the Battle Dome to see the Porcupine (or indeed any of the six-legged creatures) move from a fast walk to a canter to a gallop, for then the leg patterns went through a phased shift. The sound changed, the rhythm changed, the speed changed and the creature's entire profile underwent a shift as it altered its centre of gravity.

The controls facing Angus had television screens at about eye-level and these gave him a 360-degree view. Below these, the controls resembled the keys and manuals and pedals of a wind-organ, from which indeed the idea had been filched. Each key and pedal controlled a different quill. Pressure on a key sent the matching quill darting out to its maximum length with armour-piercing power. Sustained pressure on the key locked the quill extended and it remained out until the key was pressed again. A quick dab meant that the quill would extend at full speed but then draw back slowly while its pressure cylinder recharged. Some quills, those controlled by the foot-pedals, could actually be fired and it was this system that Angus had stood down. The Porcupine had a hard, pointed nose with which it could ram an opponent. And it could, as Angus had explained to Miranda, roll completely over and come up running.

The creature walked slowly and steadily out of the workshop and up the ramp and into the wide field of the Battle Dome.

Part of the space inside the dome had been marked off with white flags as a training area for the third-year students at the Eburacum Academy. Viti was still there, drilling his troops. For the rest, the dome was in the process of transformation. It resembled a gigantic building-site. Scaffolding-pipes rose round the walls and on to these would be mounted the new hills for next year's battles. Some parts of the fighting-field had been completely lifted and the synthetic turf rolled back so that hydraulic technicians could install special high-pressure pipes. These would allow geysers to jet high into the air in the middle of the dome.

Angus walked the Porcupine between the white pennants and out into clear territory. Then, when it was a safe distance away from the building-gangs, he nudged the controls and the creature went through its first pattern-shift and began to canter. Gradually he increased its speed until there came a second brief shudder as it moved to a gallop and altered its centre of gravity. 'Hold on,' he shouted. 'I'll make it perform.'

The ground was a blur under the machine as it ran. Angus suddenly advanced all the quills on one side while throwing the machine into a sharp turn. The quills acted like an outrigger. It turned so sharply that Miranda lost the sandwich she had been eating. Then he made it wheel the other way, digging its extended quills into the soil and pivoting on them. At the same time its six legs kicked. 'Now watch this,' he shouted as he gathered speed. Again he swung the machine into a tight bend and used the quills so that he changed the Porcupine's centre of gravity. It rolled. The noise as the quills slammed home inside the beast during the roll deafened Miranda and she screamed. The Porcupine came out of the roll running and turned again and again, rolled and this time twisted in the roll so that when it came to its six legs again with a crushing jar, it was facing the opposite direction. '*Fire*,' shouted Angus and he pretended to hit the foot-pedals.

'That sends these front quills out at about half the speed of sound,' he said, his voice lively with battle-envy. 'If there'd been a creature in front I'd have gutted it. It makes for a quick kill. But you've got to be careful. One of the quills could blow a hole in the dome or hit the dining area if you ballsed it up. It's all in the timing. And the surprise. Terrific, isn't it?'

Miranda didn't reply. He glanced at her while he automatically brought the Porcupine down to a slow canter. 'Hey, what's up, love?'

'I feel sick,' she said in a small voice. 'Can we go back?' She looked green. Angus quickly brought the machine to a halt. 'I think it's the smell and all that . . .' she waved her hands. 'I don't know how you can drive these things.'

'Sit tight and get your bearings,' said Angus. 'Here.' He reached forward and touched one of the control buttons. Immediately a compartment opened in front of her. Inside were grease-paper bags, paper tissues, a sealed container of fresh iced water and a small phial containing white pills. 'Take one of these,' he said, handing her one of the pills and the water. 'They're very quick-acting. The drivers often get sick.'

She gulped the pill down and wiped her lips. She sat still with her eyes closed and breathed deeply. Angus looked on anxiously, not knowing what to do next.

Within minutes Miranda was feeling better. When she opened her eyes she was more herself. 'Danger past,' she said, 'and I won't need the bag. But no more high jinks on the way back. OK? I'm not saying I can't get used to it in time. But that's enough for one day. I'll come out with you again another day.' She looked at Angus and Angus was crestfallen.

'Sorry,' he said. 'I should have thought. Silly of me to show off like that on your first time out. It's not bad when you're driving . . . but I suppose when you're just sitting there it's . . .' Angus's voice trailed away.

Miranda leaned across and kissed him. Her good spirits were obviously returning. 'I think you are a very good driver,' she said. 'I felt very safe with you. You're almost as good at driving this thing as you are at making love.' Angus was not expecting to hear this and he blushed with sudden happiness. 'But enough for one day. OK?'

He walked the machine slowly back to the workshop hangar, not wanting the journey to end or indeed to make a single bump. On the way he showed her how to control the pneumatic quills. She touched some of the control keys and heard the hiss and ram as the quills extended and locked and then drew back with a sound like waves on shingle.

*

When they arrived back at the dome workshop they found Viti Ulysses waiting for them. He was wearing battle-overalls and was obviously none too pleased to have been kept waiting. Having finished his manoeuvres for the day and still having some energy to burn up, Viti wanted to know if his father's Dragon was in a fit state to drive. The junior mechanics had explained to him that Angus was out testing the Porcupine and would be back before long. Being tactful, and because they liked Angus, they did not contact Wallace, for obvious reasons.

Angus saw Viti waiting and guessed his purpose but he did not let that hurry him. He walked the Porcupine to its place in the workshop and anchored it in its support harness. He closed the machine down methodically and let the flywheel idle, using the stored energy to charge the beast's own batteries and those of the entire Battle Dome.

'Right. We'd better get down there and see what his nibs wants,' he said with a wink. Then he began helping Miranda divest herself of the protective harness.

'He's one of the best of the fighters, isn't he?' she said. 'I remember him last year, in that chariot game. He looked so big and strong. But then when I saw him afterwards next to his father, he was like a boy. He's only the same age as us, isn't he?'

Angus grunted and released the last of the webbing straps. 'Yes, well, I think there's something wrong with him now,' he said. 'If he isn't fighting or preparing for a fight, he doesn't know what to do with himself. He's angry all the time. He takes it out on his squad and he takes it out on the Dragon. I've already had to warn him once that he's pushing the tolerances too far. I think that business with the Caesars really made him bitter.'

'Bah! Silliness,' said Miranda. 'They take their squabbles too seriously.' She gave Angus a quick kiss and then began to climb down. 'He can't make trouble for you, can he?' she asked.

'Over what?'

'You not being here when he wanted you and me being with you.'

Angus laughed. 'I'd like to see him try. He's too sensible for that. He knows how much he depends on my savvy. No, he won't cause trouble. He'll just be a bit snotty, and that we can cope with. Right, you go down first and I'll follow. There's a couple of security relays to close.'

Miranda, completely recovered, made her way past the banks of pneumatic cylinders which drove the quills and then turned round to climb down the exit ladder from the Porcupine.

It was thus that Viti's first real sight of Miranda was of her legs as she cautiously descended. The Polytech uniform had not been designed to give modest concealment to a woman climbing down a ladder. Viti could not drag his eyes away. The sexual charge he felt as he looked at her was as overpowering as it was unexpected. He stared until, seeing Miranda's flushed and startled face looking at him, he blushed and looked at the ground. She too blushed. She finished climbing down the ladder and moved away. Neither spoke.

Miranda was annoyed and she was saddened, too: annoyed because of the embarrassment, saddened because a young man whom she had admired had lowered himself in her estimation to little better than a peeping Tom. But she knew she would say nothing to Angus.

Angus swung down the ladder easily and jumped to the floor. He made a formal bow to Viti, a salute which Viti acknowledged.

'I trust you have had a pleasant ride,' said Viti smoothly.

'Yes thank you, sir. I am pleased to report that the Porcupine is in fine running order. One of the best in the shop.'

'Good. I was hoping to have a run on my father's Dragon if it, too, is in fine running order.'

'It was looked at a week ago. There were some minor repairs needed in the cooling-system. I did them myself. It should be ready to go.'

'Can we check?'

'By all means.' Angus glanced across at Miranda who stood to one side looking at neither of them. 'I'll be about ten minutes,' he said and winked conspicuously. Miranda nodded.

The two men set off through the workshop and Miranda followed them with her gaze. Angus, tall, lean, ginger-haired and confident, striding through the world of the workshop in which he felt at home. Beside him dark-haired and olive-skinned Viti, shorter than Angus but equally broad of shoulder and with a springy swaying gait which told of his strength and yet which remained earthbound. She felt her anger evaporate. She found herself looking at the slim buttocks of the two men and smiled to herself, despite herself.

Winter gave way to spring and the date for the annual graduating battle night drew near. Preparations at the Battle Dome went into high gear. Practice sessions and private battles between individual warriors came to an end. The gardeners and architectural engineers took over the dome and their teams of assistants worked round the clock.

During the winter the banked seating area and the chalet had been moved some ninety degrees to their new position. They were now looking down into what seemed to be a lightly wooded valley between high peaks. At the far end of the valley, at the limit of their view, a waterfall cascaded down from a rocky cwm into a wide pool. Above the cwm was a rim of stone peaks. A special effect had been introduced for this year. It was a region of bubbling hot pools which occupied part of the lower valley wall and vented steam in loud spurts. The steam then drifted down into the valley providing camouflage for a stealthy attack. Occasionally a geyser exploded with a roar from the hot pools and sent a plume of water jetting straight up into the air.

Battle night began as tradition demanded with the god Mithras flying round the dome and the sacrifice of a bull. That accomplished, the evening's festivities got under way.

Observers in the terraces noted that there was an air of restraint about this year's proceedings. No one expected the battles to be as anguished as the previous year.

In the opening contests between the mechanical creatures, no one was killed though the fighting had spirit. The Porcupine could have achieved a devastating kill against a giant hornèd beetle by almost replicating Angus's manoeuvres. But it held back. In a later battle old Jesse flailed with its hooks but was no match for a creature called the Golden Scorpion which clipped Jesse's cables and then ceremoniously symbolized the kill by a light tapping on Jesse's cabin with its barbed sting.

Nor was there so much colour among the guests. Old Marcus Ulysses was ill with gout and arrived late. Accompanying him was a tall Negress with tribal scars on her face. She seemed to be his nurse. He called her Julia. Also in attendance were two stone-faced bodyguards who made no effort to disguise the weapons they were carrying. Old Marcus was insufferable. Having been ordered by his doctor not to drink, he spent the entire evening moving from group to group trying to get someone to say that the odd nip would do him good. No one obliged.

The new Praefectus Comitum, Tripontifex Britannicus by name, also arrived late. He scrambled from his flyer smiling in apology. Surrounding him were his sycophants and official bodyguard. Tripontifex was a grey bureaucrat: a compromise candidate elected to keep the peace between the Caesars and the Ulysses. Everyone but he seemed to know that he would be turfed from office by the powerful families as soon as more settled times arrived.

Missing from the assembly was the grand Calpurnia Gallica. She was away exploring with one of her daughters down the Amazon basin.

One man whose presence did cause comment was Marmellius Caesar. He had recently returned from an administrative post in the Western Empire and was now, since the death of Julius XIX, the head of the Caesar clan.

All the guests remembered the clash that had occurred between Viti and the younger members of the Caesar family in mid-year. Everyone was careful to be polite. The truce was still delicate.

While the earlier contests occasioned some gambling, most interest centred on the battles between the rival troops of the third-year cadets. This year there were once again sixteen teams and their battle-order had been decided so that the most favoured contenders could not meet until the final battle. Rumours were rife. Word in the streets was that Diana had trained a team of Amazons and it was whispered that the young Viti Ulysses had some tricks up his sleeve.

As indeed he had. When he first appeared at the march-past before the fighting started, there was an audible drawing-in of breath. Viti appeared wearing armour of an antique kind. His helmet had plumes in the family colours of green and black. His breastplate and greaves were golden. Defying tradition and the gods he wore a purple cloak attached to his shoulders. His sword-blade glinted blue and silver and the edge sparkled. In deliberately dressing this way, Viti was making a statement. First he was making himself more vulnerable than necessary and that alone was an open challenge to all the other commanders. But more importantly, by choosing antique armour, reminiscent of the early centurions and of the great Marcus Antonius himself, Viti was identifying himself with ancient virtues. He was saying, 'I believe I am the equal of our great heroes. If I am defeated tonight I will die in the fighting or on my own sword.' He looked, let it be said, magnificent. The armour had been made for him by one of the old craftsmen armourers in the southern part of Eburacum and the muscular structure revealed in the breastplate and greaves matched his own body perfectly.

Just occasionally the Romans did such things as this. They chose a moment which was to define them, creating either their living fame or their epitaph. They had a high sense of drama.

Diana too was flamboyant in her battle apparel. She was iridescent as a snake. Apart from a crested helmet, she wore a light uniform made from crimson and blue laminated carbon-fibre disks. These could not be penetrated by point or blade and were so designed that they spread the impact of a blow. She also carried a light shield which was as tall as she was and which bore the emblem of the Caesars in commemoration of the dead Julius. She did not carry a sword but held a baton which was connected to a power pack and which could deliver a charge able to stun the nervous system of an opponent.

The first two detachments lined up and a trumpet-call sent them clashing together. It was a suitably bloody sight. When a winner was declared the next two teams joined battle and so on until the sixteen teams had been reduced to eight and the pitch was churning to dark red mud.

During this first round of fighting it became obvious that Diana's and Viti's troops were far and away the best-trained. They inflicted severe punishment on their opponents without revealing any special trickery, and were themselves relatively unscathed.

In the second and third rounds they cut and sundered their opponents like a band-saw chewing through timber and inevitably, in the fourth round, it was their detachments which met. Viti and Diana may have shared intimacy in private, but on the battlefield it was war with no quarter asked or given. Still, neither of the teams had revealed any special skills or surprises. They won simply because they were the best-prepared and the best-led.

This final battle would decide the Victor Ludorum for the year and it was prepared for with great solemnity. Wounds were dressed while martial music played and blue incense-smoke rose from golden dishes. Already a blood-lust was possessing the spectators. Knives were out and eyes were bright. The night was moving to climax. After this battle would come the communal slaying of the convicts.

Finally the two small detachments were called to order. They lined up, facing one another across the centre of the valley. Though some of the combatants on both sides were bloodied and injured, the detachments were complete. A brief prayer was sung and then, on the signal of a trumpet-call, Viti and Diana shouted orders and their troops began to advance.

Well trained though they were, fatigue was setting in. Some of the soldiers were so doped with their own adrenalin that they were almost suicidal in their battle-rage. The key question for the onlookers was whether the warriors would engage in battle directly or skirmish and run, trying to gain the high ground.

Viti sent his troops forward at a gentle trot, swords out. Diana split her Amazons into two detachments, left and right, and retreated. The right wing began to retreat to higher ground where the steam roared from the hot pools. Seeing her forces divided, Viti pounced, sending three-quarters of his detachment against Diana's right wing. He could not believe his good fortune. He looked to gain from the first skirmish the small numerical advantage which would allow his three-on-one strategy to work. A quarter of his troops were held back in reserve. To the crowd on the terraces it seemed that Diana had made an uncharacteristic error and those who had gambled on her side let out a howl of rage. To make matters worse, the retreating right wing seemed to stagger and get bogged down as the Amazons backed up the hill towards the hot pools. Viti was suspicious. He tried to see things through Diana's eyes. Why had she split her forces? Perhaps she had hoped to catch him in a pincer movement. Perhaps she had gambled that he would split his forces fifty-fifty, like her. Well the gamble had not paid off. He was on the attack. He had thirty warriors attacking her twenty. Perhaps the speed of his troops had caught Diana's Amazons napping. No matter how you weighed it, Viti knew he had the advantage.

Viti smelt victory. With a clear command he sent his troops running for the kill screaming, and at that same moment there came a clear high whistle from Diana. Immediately her left wing, the Amazons that had remained on the plain, sheathed their batons and slung their shields across their backs. With their arms free they produced from their belts lanyards of white rope with round weights at the ends. These they began to twirl, one in each hand, flexing the wrists, until each of them seemed to be surrounded by a pair of propellers. On a whistle-call they all let go. Released, the white lanyards spun above the ground, seeming almost to glide, and when they encountered the running legs of Viti's soldiers they wrapped and bound. The weights caught at ankles and wrists and tangled over the edges of shields.

The ploy was seen for what it was. Diana's right wing stopped their staggering retreat and suddenly began to advance at a run down the hill. They screamed as they ran and when they came to where Viti's soldiers where enmeshed in cords they jabbed down with their charged batons leaving men slumped and paralysed.

Viti issued two orders. He called for a retreat along the hill for those of his soldiers who had managed to survive the sweeping attack. At the same time, he ordered the small detachment he had held in reserve to use their shurikens against the Amazons who had thrown the bolas. Those Amazons had made the fatal mistake of pausing to watch the effect of their handiwork. They had not immediately covered up with their shields. Viti's small troupe hurled the small spinning blades which flashed through the air like a shoal of bright silver fish. The effect was devastating. Where the metal touched flesh it cut and gouged. The shurikens cut power-pack cables and lodged in armour. And there was not just one wave of attack. Each of Viti's warriors carried twenty shurikens. The second flight, thrown more carefully at exposed targets, began to kill and incapacitate.

The watchers on the terraces did not know what to make of this since they were too far away to see what was being thrown, but when they saw the Amazons begin to fall, the screaming and shouting was deafening.

Meanwhile, the right wing of Diana's forces arrived at the foot of the slope and Viti was forced to retreat in a crescent-shaped manoeuvre. This meant that he was able to join up the remnants of his split forces. All that was in his favour was that he now held the high ground and he led his soldiers at a loping run up to the very crest of the hill where the hot pools chuckled. Of his original forty soldiers he now had only fifteen in a fit state to fight. Looking down he was able to count Diana's forces. She had twenty-seven Amazons. There was no way that Viti could gain the numerical superiority he had hoped for. The fighting would now be direct, hand to hand. He might gain some slight advantage from close-quarters use of the shurikens, but the Amazons would be ready. He wondered if Diana had any more tricks with which to dazzle him and hoped not. He hoped that from now on she would trust to good generalship and the traditional virtues of courage and expert swordsmanship.

Viti spoke to his men. 'We will hold the hill and force them to attack us. Each one of you, if you see an opening for a shuriken, don't wait for an order, throw. Remember your training. Fight for yourself and fight for the comrade on your left. I will be in the middle. Fight for me. Remember your training. If we pull this one off then they'll rewrite the songbook. To your positions. They're coming.'

This little speech brought some optimism to his men and they crouched behind their shields with their swords drawn and ready.

Diana's forces split into four detachments. Two of these advanced slowly up the hill, their shields touching and forming a solid wall. The other two moved right and left with the obvious intention of outflanking Viti's troops.

Those advancing up the centre, among whose number was Diana, began to beat on the inside of their shields with their batons. It was a monotonous, numbing rhythm with something implacable and irresistible about it. When they were only four metres from Viti's line of defence they stopped but the drumming continued. Those on the flanks began to run and as they ran they unfurled the crimson lanyards of new bolas and began to whirl them. The air was suddenly filled with a whistling shriek and a roaring from the spinning cords and weights. Then the bolas were thrown high into the air. For a few moments Viti and his troops' attention was caught by the movement and the noise. And that was all the time needed for the front troops suddenly to advance like a wall and bang down on Viti's soldiers.

The fighting began. Hand to hand Viti's troops were more than a match for Diana's Amazons. But the Amazons had the slight edge of surprise. Their batons darted in and out. Men who had been stunned could fight no more but lolled open-eyed and semi-conscious. Wounded Amazons on the other hand could for the most part parry and stab even while they bled.

Inexorably numbers told. Viti saw the end coming even as he cut down one of the Amazons. He backed away from the fighting and into the misty area where the pools bubbled hotly and steam rose. He felt a mixture of sorrow and anger as he loosed his breastplate and prepared to take his own life. He had hoped for so much and now his hopes were ashes.

He thought in these last few moments that he was hallucinating for he seemed to see living shapes in the wraiths of steam. He heard voices in the bubbling water. Ancestors? Were these the ancestors he had sought to emulate and who were now gathering to mock him in his moment of abasement? Viti growled to himself, and it was the sound of an animal and the sound of the earth as it heaves. He tore open the last of the catches and flung the golden breastplate aside.

'Viti.'

It *was* a voice and the call was unmistakable. And there was a dancing shape in the steam. As Viti placed the point of his sword in the place below his heart and prepared to fall, he saw before him the dusty, bleeding and angry figure of Diana. As a simple extension of her movement of arrival she reached down with her stun-baton and touched his arm. Viti's vision darkened to night. Even as he tried to fall, his muscles turned to water. The cry died on his lips. He collapsed and the unheld sword fell flat beneath him.

Diana heaved a sigh of relief. Her face showed the strain as she crouched down and checked his pulse. She smiled a weary smile and pulled out a small whistle from her tunic and blew on it. Her Amazons, who were still fighting the remnants of Viti's forces, heard the call and suddenly pulled back, jumping several paces down the hill. They held their weapons on guard.

Viti's warriors understood. They crouched down on the grass. Some cried in sheer exhaustion and began to shake. Others plunged their swords in the soil and stripped open their throats hoping for a mercifully quick dispatch. One stabbed himself in the throat and died with an ugly retching sound.

Diana appeared through the steam. She was carrying Viti. She set him down gently.

When the distant crowd on the terraces saw this there was a stunned and incredulous silence. Then bedlam as every man warned his neighbour of civil war. Then silence again as a groggy Viti shook his head and struggled to his knees and looked about like a bleary-eyed drunk who is wondering where the party has gone.

And then there was cheering.

Later there was partying, and a complex, emotional party it was too.

Diana was declared Victrix Ludorum. She was only the

seventh woman in the one-thousand-year-old history of the Military Academy to achieve this honour. Viti, who had sprained his arm when he fell stunned, led the applause by beating on the table with his good hand. For this generous attitude he received much honour. Even so, he found it impossible to smile and a high colour never left his cheek.

Diana was gracious in victory. She thanked her patron goddess and she thanked her Amazons, honouring by name each of those who had died. Lastly she acknowledged the quality of those she had fought against.

Old Marcus Ulysses sat stoical, sober and alone for most of the evening. He watched the festivities with unresponsive attention. No one knew what he was thinking and no one approached him except Viti who stood before him but the father would not speak. Before he left he was seen to cry a few tears and he danced a round with Diana and he drank some wine too, saying, 'I'll pay in the night.' And then he departed with his bodyguards and nurse.

Even Viti's enemies might have felt compassion for the teenager. Viti kept up a show of bravado when his father left but he was white-faced and brittle of temper. Miranda saw him and something in her melted before his suffering. She took the opportunity to serve him and whispered, 'Nothing is ever as good or as bad as you expect.' Viti was startled by this; not by the words which he didn't understand but by being spoken to in such a direct way and by a serving-girl. Such had not happened before. He nodded rudely and turned away though he remembered Miranda well enough.

Diana observed. She was getting drunk and salacious. Someone months earlier had dared her to dance naked on a table if she won the supreme prize. She had accepted the dare then and was now working up to it. She came up to Viti and breathed on him. 'So a kitchen-maid's got the hots for you too, eh? Good job I didn't sting you on the cock.'

'You should have let me die,' growled Viti.

'Tell me that in the morning,' said Diana with a wink and she wandered away, casually undoing a brooch at her shoulder.

*

For those who served the Romans, relations were not so complex.

Many of the young men who worked at the Battle Dome had brought their girl-friends. They sat about in the servants' hall drinking beer from bottles and pecking at the remains of the buffet meal that had been served to the young élite. Some hung round the doors listening to the band inside and practising dance-steps. Later they would push the tables back and have their own dance.

When Miranda came off duty, Angus was waiting for her. While she changed out of her Polytech uniform she told him about Diana's dance of the seven veils and how Diana had insisted that the rest of the students from the Military Academy take off their clothes as she did. She told him how like his father Viti was as he sat alone and apart, his arm in a sling and his head bowed. 'He tried to kill himself today,' she concluded.

Angus shrugged. To him a Roman more or less was neither here nor there. His job was with machines.

'Well, you might say something,' said Miranda.

'Well, if he had topped himself,' said Angus slowly, 'then he wouldn't be coming around in a few days' time to bugger up his dad's machine.' He cracked the top from a fresh bottle of beer. 'How's that for sympathy them?'

Miranda threw her bundled-up uniform at him.

Later they danced and sang and drank in the servants' quarters until late in the night. Then word came that the people from the forest were having a party out near the train station and that it was a sight worth seeing. This was one of their Beltane celebrations.

The forest people had a bonfire blazing and there were men playing bagpipes while couples danced in the flickering firelight. Occasionally a shout went up and then everything became silent and the couples stopped dancing while a man, naked save for a loincloth and with his body daubed with white streaks, ran at the fire and dived over it turning a somersault. While Angus and Miranda watched, a young man failed in his take-off and crashed into the blazing wood and rolled out of the ashes. He was immediately doused with water from buckets held by other contestants. Overseeing everything was the enigmatic figure of Lyf who stood by the woodpile and fed the flames.

'Why do they do it?' asked Miranda.

'A test of manhood, I guess,' replied Angus. 'They have a lot of primitive ceremonies.'

Another man prepared to run. He held his hands and arms open to the sky and shouted words in a language that neither Angus or Miranda could understand before settling down and sprinting. The prayer, if it was a prayer that he uttered, was effective for he hit the springboard at full run and dived upwards, gripping his knees to his chest so that he turned 360 degrees through the smoke and landed safe and running on the ciders. A cheer went up and the dancing recommenced.

'That was fantastic,' said Angus and there was excitement in his voice.

'Don't even think it,' said Miranda as she snuggled in to him. 'I like you done but not burnt.'

Other workers from the Battle Dome arrived and some of the men were very drunk and started shouting. The shouting became derisory when one of the jumpers after a good somersault failed to land properly on his feet and toppled backwards and landed on his bottom in the embers. He scrambled from the fire to catcalls.

Some of the forest people shouted back while others doused their burnt comrade, and although the exact meaning of their words was not clear the intention was obvious enough. Then one of the men from the Battle Dome was seen to urinate on the perimeter of the dance area and suddenly the entire situation turned ugly. Suddenly there were many more of the woodlanders, men and women, some with staves, some with crossbows, some holding burning brands, gathered round the small group from the Battle Dome. A fight was imminent and Angus released Miranda.

Then the one called Lyf intervened. He was laughing. He stood between the two groups with his staff upraised. 'There'll be no fighting this night,' he said in a thick accent which suddenly struck Angus as comic. Others who also spoke the accented Britannic Latin found it comic also and laughed. Then Lyf repeated his words in the language of his people and accompanied the words with a dance which consisted of hops and jumps and punches thrown in the air. This also brought merriment and the tension drained away. The groups drifted apart.

With arms round one another, Angus and Miranda made their sleepy and amorous way down into the train station and home. Behind them they left a blazing fire and dancing men and the strange sad and thrilling noise of the bagpipes.

So ended the year, Spring matching spring.

6 At Viti's Banquet

While the games in the Battle Dome marked the climax of the training at the Military Academy, they were not the final event in a student's life. The last four weeks were given over to formal events.

First there were the long sessions at which each student had to stand before senior tutors and receive their evaluations face to face. These sessions could be difficult as they involved not only assessments of skill but evaluations of character also. The main qualities that the Military Academy sought to develop were leadership, will-power and fortitude, and any students who were found wanting were told so in no uncertain terms. Viti was praised, both for his courage and his dedication, but one old tutor wagged a finger at him. 'You have a romantic softness that worries me,' he said. 'Consider your attempted suicide. You have too much imagination for your own good. But don't expect that there will always be a woman to rescue you from your folly. One day you will have to stand alone.'

Viti shrugged upon hearing this. 'I've been alone all my life,' he muttered.

Following the days of assessment there came the ceremonial handing-back of equipment. Items such as saddles and battle-shields which belonged to the Marcus Aurelius Academy and had been loaned to a student on entering the Academy were first taken to an engraver in the city. There the student's name was carefully inscribed on all their equipment. Then the pieces were returned to the armourer who signed a receipt which included the pedigree of each piece of equipment. The armourer then made whatever repairs were necessary and got the pieces ready for the next year's intake of students. Tradition was most important. Equipment worn by Viti's father was at present being used by one of the first-year cadets. Some items such as the practice helmets were centuries old.

A memorial service for those class-mates who had died during the three years at the Academy took place in a grove close to the playing-fields at the Academy. It was a long service and those who had been responsible for the death of a fellow student had to speak about their victims. Thus Viti found himself talking about Alexander whom he had killed in his second year during the chariot contest. He extolled Alexander's courage and skill and generosity. Inwardly Viti cringed at his own hypocrisy. But what could he do? The Academy followed old Solon's law, *'De mortuis, nil nisi bonum'* – 'Concerning the dead, nothing unless good'. And so Viti lied.

Every evening there were opportunities to carouse with the living and bury old enmities. It was another law of the Academy that only those who had buried their enmity could graduate.

The last formal ceremony was the Presentation of the Sword. Each graduand received his own individually crafted sword which was the equivalent of a diploma. At the same time he or she swore an oath to uphold the laws of the Empire and the honour of the Emperor. These swords were not ornamental but were practical fighting weapons. Receipt of the sword marked the end of the student's life at the Academy.

During these last four weeks, Viti came in for special attention. While he had lost the final battle to the boisterous Diana (and nothing could change that), attempts were made to ensure that he did not feel disgraced. He had fought well as had his troops. There were those who thought that Diana's display was too theatrical and who questioned the use of stun-batons for final contests. His three-on-one plan, which he explained at a post-battle seminar, was regarded as exemplary of its kind and completely in accord with the traditions of the games. Had Viti been up against anyone but Diana and her Amazons with their silver and crimson bolas, he would have won, no question. Moreover, Viti's attempted suicide was respected.

Viti remained the most powerful and skilful fighter among the male graduates of his year. So why was he not more happy? Everyone wondered. A special banquet was held in his honour. It was not a big affair but was very select. Only the graduating males and some of the tutors were invited. The wine was the best available and the meal was served from golden plates.

It so happened that this banquet coincided with Miranda's beginning her time of service at the Academy and this was her first major function. It was her responsibility to plan the menu and the wine list. She also arranged the entertainers who would perform during the long meal.

The evening was a great success.

So much so that after the dessert, which was a white swan made of frosted sugar and which contained lemon ice-cream and whipped chocolate as well as sugar balls containing the finest liqueurs, Miranda was called into the banqueting-room to receive the thanks of the assembly.

Such was not unknown and Miranda was warned well in advance that she would be called. She wore her demure Polytech dress uniform, well pressed but slightly shortened, and took trouble to make sure that her hair and make-up would not let her down. The effect was stunning: for Miranda, without really trying, possessed that strange quality understood in all times and cultures and languages as 'sex appeal'. The applause from the cigar-puffing and drunken graduates which greeted her entry could be heard beyond the Academy walls.

Miranda received their thanks. She sat briefly beside Viti at the top table. She accepted and sipped a glass of the raisin-scented red wine of southern Italy. And at that moment the band struck up some dance music and before she could protest she found herself in the middle of the dance-floor and dancing with one of the handsome sons of the Paganini family. The boy had the face of Pan and wore flowers in his hair. He did not so much dance with her as use her for the dance, and something in Miranda responded. The formal part of the evening was over and the male graduates slipped out of their dress togas and danced in simple short tunics which revealed their muscles and allowed them great freedom of movement.

Partners changed. There was wine and laughter and toasts and cheers. Other girls began to arrive too, girls from the city, and Miranda, while she knew she was probably going beyond the limits of what the Polytech authorities would consider acceptable, felt safe and decided to enjoy herself. This was, after all, a special night for her. She half wished that Angus could be present. At the same time, she realized that if he were there she would not feel quite so free. 'Angus tomorrow,' she thought. 'Me for tonight and where's the harm?'

The music was brilliant. The beat was like a drug and the musicians played until the sweat was pouring off them. The dancers and the musicians joined in a shout at the end of one of the numbers.

Miranda knew it was time for her to think about leaving. As the number finished with a clash of cymbals, she thanked her partner and clapped the band and then turned away. She found herself suddenly facing dark Viti. He was only inches taller than her, and his arm slipped round her waist and she could feel the contained strength in his muscles. He had been strange to her during the entire evening: friendly one minute and distant the next. He had made a point of asking, within Miranda's earshot, other women to dance and had then danced close to her so that she would be aware of him. Probably no one but Miranda would have noticed this, but she did, and that is all that matters. She was not feeling particularly well disposed to Viti Ulysses no matter how handsome and powerful he might be.

She wanted to leave and told him so. But he asked her to stay for one last dance and she finally agreed. As luck would have it the next dance was slow, and Viti and Miranda floated round the dance-floor, brushing against one another and holding the beat inside them like a pulse, like a flickering flame, so that when the next number started, a sexy blues about 'a woman who loved a man like the sea loved the shore', they were both primed and ready to go. Viti did not have to ask her to stay for 'just one more'.

Miranda danced. She let her spirit flow and she was oblivious of the knowing looks and gestures from the men who clustered round the perimeter of the dance-floor. Viti was a fine and virile dancer and matched her exuberance.

At the end of the dance Viti lifted her off her feet and turned a quick circle. There was shouting and clapping and moments later Miranda was surprised to find that she and Viti were in one of the small rooms beside the servery. The room smelt musty and there were piles of spare carpet thrown on the floor. This was carpet that had been taken up to reveal the dance-floor.

Viti kissed her and Miranda responded, her breathing short and husky.

Then came the unexpected. Viti's hands were on her. He pushed her down on to the carpet and his hands pulled at the buttons of her uniform while his lips sought her mouth. Miranda did not know how to respond. She tried to kiss and she tried to talk and she tried to fend him off. She felt his hands on her breasts and then on her thighs and she cried out in pain as he pulled at her clothes. She tried to push and she tried to kick and that made everything worse.

She seemed to retreat to a distant world as Viti opened her thighs and entered her. His weight came down on her and his hands were everywhere.

Moments later she felt him shudder, his head buried in her shoulder and her hair in his mouth, and he thrust and came and she felt his hot sperm. But it was not Miranda that felt this. It was someone else: someone remote.

For moments Viti lay still, simply gasping, and then she tapped him on the shoulder and asked him to shift and release her, which he did.

He lay beside her on the rough uncomfortable carpet and put his arm round her. She moved away from him and in the same movement tried to pull her Polytech uniform down. She tried to sit up and when he tried to kiss her she burst into tears. For some reason the forced kiss seemed the greatest indignity of all. Quick tears led to more tears and suddenly she was racked with sobs. She curled up into a ball and cried. Outside the small room the noise of the party continued.

Viti, who had more or less recovered, looked on and did not know what to do. When he tried to touch her she squirmed away. When he tried to kiss her she buried her face. He had no way of approaching her. This was beyond him. Normally the girls he had taken had sighed and asked for more. He had paid gold coin and there was no harm done. What now was different?

He pulled her dress down gently. 'Did I hurt you?' he asked. But there was no reply.

He stood up and tied his tunic. 'Can I get you another drink?' No reply.

'Well, what the hell can I do?' he asked, suddenly angry. 'You wanted it. You know you did.'

Miranda rallied. 'Just leave me,' she said. 'Just leave me and go back to your party.'

And Viti did just that, but the memory of the crying woman disturbed him.

Ten minutes later he went back to the room but Miranda had gone. The room was stale and tawdry.

That night he got drunk and fell, cutting his face. Later he was carried home oblivious.

Left alone, Miranda tidied herself as well as she could. Her handbag was still in the banqueting-room but she could not go and get it. She gathered up her shoes and found that the heel on one of them was broken and flapped as though on a hinge. She made her way out of the small storage-room by a back door and found herself in the main corridor that led to the kitchen. Mercifully there was no one about. She slipped into the kitchen. An old man, one of the kitchen porters who doubled as a dish-washer, was scrubbing at a large enamel pan. He paid her no attention and she was able to run across the kitchen and through to the women's toilet.

She slammed the door behind her and felt safe.

One of the girls from the city was there, changing from her day clothes into a short and tight dress. She sized up Miranda. 'One of them jumped you?' she said almost matter-of-factly, and Miranda nodded. 'Hope he paid you well for it. Who was it?' Miranda didn't answer. 'Well suit yourself, but you should always get their name. That way they always pay.' Miranda nodded and pressed her forehead against the cool glass of the mirror. The other young woman, who was only a few years older than Miranda, sized her up and wisely and kindly did not press her for more details. She guessed everything. 'Call me Marj,' she said. 'If you want to talk.'

Marj left her hairbrush and a spare lipstick for Miranda to use. She even had a needle and thread and Miranda was able to catch the hem of her uniform and sew on a couple of buttons. When Marj had gone she showered and only started to feel clean when the soap was in her hair and the lather was spattering the floor. She scrubbed herself and noticed where bruises were already beginning to show on her arms and thighs. Then she dried herself and dressed slowly.

Finally she felt able to face the journey home.

At home her mother was waiting up for her, as was Angus. They wanted to know how her first banquet had been received. But Miranda did not want to talk. She claimed tiredness and hurried to bed.

Angus, who had bought a celebratory bottle of wine and who had planned a quiet but passionate tryst under the trees, was disappointed. He sensed that something was wrong and clumsily assumed that he was somehow to blame. Eve *knew* that something was wrong and later that night she sat by her daughter's bed stroking her dark hair while her daughter cried and told her what had happened.

Angus heard too for he had tiptoed down the corridor to Miranda's room, as he had done on many nights, and was about to turn the handle when he heard the women's voices. He could not hear everything that was said, but he heard the name of Viti and he heard the crying. He clearly heard Miranda say, 'But you must never tell Angus.' And he put two and two together and made four.

That night he drank the wine himself and lay on his back naked, staring at the ceiling, and planned a murder.

Angus dreamed up a thousand ways of killing Viti, ranging from the excruciating and refined to the blunt and bloody. It became an obsession. And it didn't stop there. He tortured himself and Miranda by confronting her with his knowledge and then making her describe to him what had happened. He listened with a face of stone. Miranda for her part felt guilty and took the blame on herself. 'I was provocative,' she said. 'I was silly. I stayed too late. He was a bit drunk. I was a bit drunk. It was the music. Oh, I don't know.'

And again she cried and when Angus touched her hoping to offer comfort, she flinched.

If anything sealed Viti's death-warrant it was that moment. Angus felt his life turn sour. The hitherto happy man was filled with anger and hatred – and disgust.

Let it be said: Angus could not admit it to himself but the fact that Miranda had been taken by another man, even though it was against her will, tainted her in his eyes. If he had been challenged on this he would have denied it, but it was true. And this made him surly towards her. Where she needed healing laughter and a patient and casual affection (casual because it could afford to be so, being deep as a header-post and sturdy as a barn), Angus was brittle. He made her be close to him, but he did not make her laugh. He made her feel judged.

And this was his plan.

Viti, having graduated from the Military Academy, could expect to be sent to any one of a thousand outposts of the Empire. He could find himself in northern China, or in Waitangi in Aotearoa, or in the Peruvian Andes. There were always places heating up where the local populations had not been completely pacified or where independence movements were rearing their heads. Indeed all was not well with the vast sprawling Empire which covered the globe like a threadbare fabric.

Angus guessed that during the period before his assignment came through, Viti would want to keep his hand in at the Battle Dome by taking his father's Dragon out for a run. Angus would know of any request since he was in charge of the day-to-day maintenance of the mechanical creatures and it would be an easy thing for him to arrange an accident.

And so it was, in the month of July.

One day while Angus was adjusting the piston linkage on an old steam-driven monster which the Eburacum Military Museum was hoping to use as part of an exhibition of antique armament, a call came through that Viti Ulysses wanted use of the Dragon on the coming Sunday at 10.30 in the morning.

Angus went cold when he heard this. Reacting by instinct, he checked the maintenance schedule and confirmed that the machine was ready for use. He also, trying to sound casual, said that he would be available on that day as he wanted to complete some tests he had been running on the Crab. Everything was confirmed in a matter-of-fact way and Angus went back to his work, but his heart was pounding and his throat was tight.

His plan was formed and he knew just how the 'accident' would occur.

Sunday came and Angus got up at six as was usual on a working day. When he entered the small kitchen to make a quick cup of tea and prepare his lunch he was surprised to find Miranda already up and waiting for him. She looked very pretty and fresh in her early-summer clothes and with her hair drawn back and pinned up the way he liked it.

Miranda was making every effort to mend the breach she knew had occurred with Angus. She had talked to herself at night and had willed herself to run through her indignity in her mind until it lost its poison. She wanted to show Angus that she was still the woman she had always been, and perhaps she tried too hard. Looking at that another way, perhaps Miranda did not realize that she was not the woman she had been and could never be so again.

'Didn't expect you to be up,' said Angus.

Miranda came round the table and kissed him. 'I wanted to surprise you. I want to make your lunch and the tea. I want to come with you today. Like we used to.'

'Well . . . er . . .' Angus's voice trailed away. This new twist to the day's plans he had not expected. 'It's going to be pretty boring. Just looking at fuel lines and circuits.'

'I hoped you'd take me for a run in that thing . . . what was it called?'

'The Porcupine.'

'Yes.'

'It's broken down. Hydraulics.'

'Oh. Well. It doesn't matter. I'll bring my Polytech books and when you've finished for the day we can go for a walk under the trees.' She tried to look mischievous in the old way but it felt uncomfortable and so she simply smiled instead. Silence. She didn't know how to understand the shifty way Angus stood, not looking at her. 'Don't you want me to come?'

'No. It's not that,' he said hurriedly, 'it's only . . .' Silence and then daylight struck him. 'I didn't tell you but that young Ulysses bastard is coming to the shops to take the Dragon out.'

Miranda coloured slightly when she heard this but her voice remained firm. 'He doesn't have to see me. In any case, I've got all that behind me. I'd be glad if he saw me with you.' She turned away and busied herself with the sandwiches and with making the tea.

Angus breathed deeply. 'OK,' he said, and let the matter rest.

In truth his mind was teeming. He wondered if he should abandon his plan. He wondered if he should go ahead. He wondered if he should tell Miranda what he was about. In the event he did nothing and they rode together in silence on the early-morning train out to the Battle Dome.

At the Battle Dome Miranda excused herself and ran to the women's toilet, giving her imminent period as the reason. But that was a lie. She wanted to hide her tears. On the train journey out she had begun to feel that she and Angus were now on different paths. She began to accept that which she had refused to accept before. But still, the time of separation was not yet, and all might yet be well and she still loved Angus despite his strangeness and perhaps he still loved her and so . . . Miranda looked at herself in the mirror, remembering an earlier occasion when she had looked at her crying face. And then she forced herself to smile.

Minutes later she was outside again and took Angus's arm. 'All's well,' she said, and he did not know what to make of that.

Angus invented work for himself. There were no pressing repairs. The only reason he had assigned himself the Sunday shift was so that he could tamper with the Dragon and make it lethal. At half-past nine he had smoko and then said, 'Well, I'd better get the Dragon warmed up for that bastard.'

'Do you want me to come with you. I will if you want. I'm not afraid.'

Angus shook his head.

'Well I want you to promise me one thing. I don't want you being silly and insulting him or anything. He's not part of our world. He can destroy us. Now, promise me.'

'I promise,' said Angus. 'I'll just get the Dragon ready and then I'll come back here. With luck I'll never even see the bastard.'

Angus hurried down the long hangar where the rows of battle-creatures hung in their harnesses. He came to the Dragon and lowered it to the ground. Then he used the auxiliary batteries to power up its hydraulic systems to make sure there were no leaks. The Dragon stood imperiously with head raised and mouth partly open. Quickly he got the flywheel started and connected the high-pressure air line.

Angus climbed up the Dragon's back and opened the trapdoor leading to the driver's cockpit. Inside the machine he slithered down round the control seats and into the area which contained the pistons and rods which controlled the legs, claws and tail.

It took him only twenty seconds to unscrew one small nut at the end of a piston-arm in the lower tail section. He then repositioned a safety sensor and finally sawed into the rod with a common hack-saw. He cut to two-thirds through the rod and then replaced the nut, screwing it down until it was just above the cut. Angus knew that Viti liked to flex the tail, almost making it crack like a whip. Well now, if he did that manoeuvre, the piston-rod would shear, sending the sharp rod, fast as a bolt from a crossbow, directly into the back of the driver. According to Angus's calculations it should shatter the spine about half-way down the back. If luck was with him, thought Angus, the bolt would not so much kill Viti outright as leave him paralysed from the waist down for life.

And afterwards, the inspectors would inspect the maintenance record and would note the number of occasions that the mechanics, especially Angus, had warned that the Dragon should not be driven close to its tolerance. Of course, by then Angus would have doctored the offending rod so that there was no hint of his handiwork.

Angus climbed up to the driver's seat and checked the fly-wheel's r.p.m. It was almost up to speed. It took him only a few more moments to disconnect the air pipe and seal the armoured casing. Then, using only the half-track, he drove the Dragon down the centre of the workshop to the nearest exit bay. He left the beast in the ready mode, holding its tail in the open flex position. This was the normal operating position. He made sure that the security guard saw the Dragon positioned at the exit door. The machine was fully charged and oiled with the giant flywheel spinning smoothly and humming pleasantly to itself. The Dragon was ready for action.

'Viti Ulysses is taking it out for a run,' said Angus, using the security intercom. 'He should be here any time. It's warmed up and ready to go.'

'OK,' said the security guard. 'Is he fighting anyone or just joy-riding?'

'Just joy-riding.'

'Well, I hope for your sakes he doesn't crash it. You boys must be tired of patching it up.'

'We is,' said Angus, and left it at that. He returned to Miranda and ten minutes later he was informed that Viti had collected the machine and was on his way out to the battlefield.

Viti was angry. He didn't know why he was angry except that that morning he had woken with a thick and throbbing head after too much wine the night before. This was becoming a pattern. Also, he was disappointed. He had been waiting for days to discover where he was to be assigned now that he had completed his time at the Military Academy. But no word had yet come to him. Already some of his colleagues were packing their bags and making plans to travel east to Asia or south to Africa or to any one of the thousands of military camps scattered over the face of the globe.

So Viti was not really paying attention when he swung up into the Dragon, slamming the spring-lock doors behind him. He did not notice the hack-saw which Angus, in his nervousness, had left behind after cutting into the bolt. But even if he had noticed it, it is unlikely that he would have conceived of sabotage to the Dragon.

Viti's nose wrinkled as he strapped himself in and fitted the direction harness over his head. It smelled of stale sweat and he made a mental note to tell that big, surly red-headed mechanic to have it sanitized.

Then he adjusted his seat, lowering it until his feet rested lightly on the pedals. He tapped out his call-code to the security guard who acknowledged his signal and then activated the metal door which cranked up slowly revealing the grey light of the Battle Dome. Viti slipped his hands into the control gloves and when the door was sufficiently open he fed power to the half-track system and the Dragon lurched forwards, rocked slightly on its hydraulic shock-absorbers, and then began to crawl out of the hangar.

The tail was hardly clear of the hangar before Viti fed power to the giant drive legs and the beast surged forwards. This was what Viti wanted. He loved the sheer power that the Dragon gave him.

Viti ran the beast out to the centre of the Battle Dome and

there brought it to a swift halt. He made it rear and dip, and tear the air with its claws as though tangling with a real opponent. He made it run and then swerve at speed, combining the half-track system with the powerful rear legs. This was a difficult manoeuvre requiring adroit manipulation of the pedals combined with subtle hand and finger movements. He was oblivious to the thunder of relays as the control rods slammed open or closed at his bidding. Then he set the creature to run with its giant dragon-head held only a few feet above the ground. In this mode the Dragon could achieve a formidable speed and could ram its way through armour-plating.

Just for fun Viti pressed the control switch which would have made the beast jet fire through one of its forward horns. He imagined the plumes of red fire exploding before him and the golden- and red-scaled Dragon galloping through the flames, its jaws wide and its talons advanced. He hoped that one day his father would take the Dragon up to their estate at Farland Head and there let him blaze and burn to his heart's content.

Without slackening his speed, Viti edged the Dragon into a wide arc. Beneath him the ground was a blur. He could smell the hot oil. He could hear the clatter of the well-greased machinery and the deep humming of the flywheel as it was tapped for energy. Viti set course for the practice hills where, on the night of the graduation battle, geysers had played and hot pools bubbled. It was here that he had been defeated by Diana and her Amazons. The memory was still green and painful.

Viti could see that hydraulic engineers had been at work dismantling part of the hill, but the main area was not roped off and he opted to take a chance that it was still safe. He decided to perform a risky manoeuvre: running the Dragon up the hill and then using the tail like an outrigger while he forced the Dragon into a 180-degree turn at the top.

Viti hit the slope at speed and then raised the tail and swung it to one side with a flick of his little finger. At the same time he used the pedals to slow one side. He felt the entire Dragon shudder as its structure took the immense strain of conflicting forces.

Then suddenly there was an explosion behind him. Viti felt

something slam into his back and an immense expanding pain. He bit his tongue. His arms went numb and he felt the Dragon lurch and twist out of control throwing him about in the webbing straps. The Dragon seemed to roll and pitch . . . There was a screaming of strained metal. The screens before him danced in crazy patterns. Somehow he banged his head . . .

Viti's last dying thought as darkness descended was how angry his father would be, for he had surely wrecked the Dragon this time. He felt glad.

Back in the machine-repair section of the Battle Dome, Angus and Miranda were having a cup of tea. Angus was finding it difficult to concentrate on what Miranda was telling him about the new Polytech courses. He was so keyed up waiting for the wail of the accident siren that when the siren call did come he sprang to his feet, knocking over his cup. 'He must have crashed it,' he said, trying to sound matter-of-fact before Miranda's startled eyes.

'Crashed?' said Miranda.

'Viti Ulysses. The Dragon. He's driving it. That's what the siren's all about. There's no one else out there. He must have crashed it. I'll go and see. I'll take the tractor in case the bastard's really smashed it up. Won't be long.'

'Can I come too?'

'*No.*' Angus's voice was almost a shout. He turned away quickly. Then he pressed the intercom relay and announced that he was on his way. Moments later the siren cut out.

Angus raced through the repair sheds and climbed up on to one of the powerful rescue tractors. He disconnected the recharge terminals and threw the switches which fed power to all the tractor's systems. The tractor's lights came on. Oil was pumped under pressure to the hydraulic pistons which supported the tractor's bulk and it slowly rose and began to edge forwards. The door to the workshop rolled up and as soon as it was high enough the tractor trundled out and up, on to the main field of the Battle Dome.

The tractor had large soft wheels in front and a half-track system in the rear. Most of the vehicle's weight came from the giant batteries which were slung in pairs in its mid section and provided its main power. But it also had a diesel engine and oil tanks which could be used as a back-up. All systems could be used together and so powerful was this tractor that it could drag the Dragon back to the hangar if needs be. Angus sat in the cab and gunned the machine to its top speed of 15 m.p.h. It lumbered over the turf, unstoppable.

Angus found the Dragon, canted over on its side, at the bottom of the hill. It was clear that the Dragon had rolled down the hill tearing giant chunks from the turf and exposing the bright yellow high-pressure pipes which had carried the steam and water on the night of the graduation battle.

'Why the hell did the silly bugger come up here?' Angus thought to himself as he trundled towards the Dragon. As he drew closer he noticed that the tail was twisted and he smiled to himself. Undoubtedly Viti had pushed the machine beyond tolerance.

Angus pulled up beside the glossy scales of the Dragon and unhurriedly jumped down from the tractor and then climbed the back of the Dragon. He kicked aside the dog-clips that held the hatch-cover and threw it back. Inside he could see the slumped form of Viti held in the protective harness. He looked dead, and as Angus slung his leg through the hatch to climb down he began to rehearse the words he would use to communicate the news back to the central command area. But then, when he was half into the machine, the slumped figure moved, struggling, trying to sit up, pushing away from the control desk with bloody hands. Viti turned and looked up. There was a cut above his eye and blood was still oozing from his nose but he was able to move and did not seem greatly hurt, let alone paralysed.

Angus glanced round the cabin and noticed that the pressure rod had ripped through the top side of the driver's chair but had then been deflected and was embedded in the wall-padding. It had come within inches of tearing Viti's spine and had he been as tall as Angus it would undoubtedly have killed him. Angus realized the error in his calculations. The truth which struck him most forcibly was that the sheared bolt had missed

Viti entirely. He was stunned and a bit bloody but otherwise whole. 'Get me out of this bloody thing,' he shouted. 'Bloody stupid machine. Craps out just when you want it to perform. Come on, help me.'

Angus instinctively sprang to help, for all his training said that when a Roman ordered, a Citizen jumped. But then he stopped himself. This was the man who had raped his woman. This was the man he had come to kill. Shaking his head in near-disbelief, Angus looked round the cabin for a weapon. Finally, seeing nothing obvious, he wrenched free the heavy link-rod and prepared to brain Viti.

He should have struck quickly but he stayed a moment to savour his act. He let anger master him. 'You bastard. I want you to die slowly. Do you know who I am? Eh? I'm Angus, and I'm going to kill you.'

'Why?' shouted Viti and even as he shouted he was working at the harness which held him. Viti knew from his training that if you can get an attacker talking he will lose the initiative. 'Why do you want to kill me? I like you. I admire you. I think you are very skilled. You've kept the old beast running when I thought I'd smashed it beyond repair. Is it badly damaged now?'

Angus waved the heavy piston-rod. 'No more talking. Do you remember Miranda?'

'No I don't think I . . .' The webbing straps were loose and Viti knew he could move.

'I'm killing you for her.'

'Why? What have I ever done . . .'

'You made her . . . You made her into a . . . You forced her to . . .' Angus didn't have the words. He heaved up the heavy bar and slammed it down on to the seat. But Viti had dodged. He had guessed Angus's relations with Miranda as soon as he heard the name and he remembered the time he had seen them together in the Porcupine.

Viti slammed back against the wall near the view-screens. In his trained fighter's mind he had begun to assess the situation and was prepared to take the initiative. Being smaller than Angus gave him a slight advantage in the confines of the cabin.

Before Angus could recover, Viti swung the control helmet

into Angus's face. Then he swung the control seat round causing Angus to fall off balance. When Angus drew back he found himself tangled in the webbing straps. 'You bastard,' he shouted. 'I'm going to fucking kill you if it's the last thing I do.'

Viti had not wasted his advantage. By the control panel was a small fire-extinguisher and Viti seized this and began to spray foam on to Angus. Holding the extinguisher in front of him he edged round the control seat until he was almost behind Angus. Then he kicked him. It was a vicious jab to the back of the knee and Angus staggered. He reeled free of the webbing and again raised the piston-rod. But before he could bring it down, Viti charged him, hunching his shoulders and with arms locked in front. Angus was caught off guard and completely lost his balance. He fell back against the control panel. When he tried to regain his balance by grabbing at the driver's seat, it swung round and he fell down through the spiral opening which led to the Dragon's working parts. His shout of rage made the small cabin ring.

Viti scrambled up and out of the Dragon. For a moment he almost blacked out as he stood on the Dragon's back. Adrenalin had enabled him to fight, but he was injured. The crash of the Dragon had bruised his ribs and his face felt as though he'd been hit with the back of a shovel. One leg was starting to ache where the muscles had been crushed and there was blood seeping inside his overalls. He was not thinking clearly or he would have slammed shut the small door leading to the cockpit. But he didn't. He began to limp away.

He heard a scrabbling behind him and Angus's head and shoulders appeared from the machine. His eyes were staring and set and his face had a red and crumpled look. Viti recognized the signs of a man possessed with battle-fever and the need to kill. He limped as quickly as he could down the back of the Dragon hoping to make the open ground. Then he would improvise.

Angus saw a thing like a black ape which limped away from him. It seemed to move in slow motion. His hands and arms ached to grapple. There was a howling in his ears. He was not thinking, he was simply reacting and the instinct to fight was in charge. Angus threw himself bodily down from the Dragon straight on to the back of Viti, knocking him to one side. Angus crashed on to the ground on his side but if he hurt himself he didn't feel anything. He was up in a flash. Viti had rolled away and was behind one of the canted legs of the Dragon. He had drawn his knife.

The two men sparred, each looking for the moment that would give him the chance to make a kill. Viti, the professional fighter, had the advantage in experience but Angus was big and strong and passionate and his instincts were brilliant. Once Viti lunged with his knife and Angus managed to grab his wrist by the cuff of his overall. He squeezed and twisted and butted down into Viti's face with his head. Viti held as long as he could but his grip was no match for that of the mechanic. As he released the knife he twisted and brought his knee up sharply into Angus's groin, just missing his balls. For a moment there was blankness for both men before the pain hit and they staggered apart.

Then suddenly there was a figure between them, dragging at Angus, confronting Viti. It was Miranda and she was screaming and crying. 'You fools. You fools. Didn't you know your radio was on? Everyone heard you. Get up. Get up. The security guards will be here in a moment.' She pulled at Angus and he staggered up and looked round. Beyond the big wheeled tractor he could see four or five dark-uniformed men advancing at a run. Only then did the howling he could hear shape itself into a comprehensible sound: it was a siren echoing in the Battle Dome.

'Get up there. Get into that thing and keep your head low. They may start firing.' Angus pushed Miranda up the twisted back of the Dragon.

'What about y—' she began.

'*Move*,' he yelled, and Miranda had never seen such fury in a man's face. She ran up the Dragon's back and climbed inside, more frightened by Angus than by the advancing guards.

And she had good reason. The guards on duty at the Battle Dome on this quiet Sunday morning were neither the best-trained nor the most competent. Indeed, their usual job consisted merely of controlling the locks on doors, making tea for one another and surveying the dome's corridors and passages on a variety of TV screens. Their job was widely regarded as a sinecure. Though armed and trained, they were not expert in roughhouse fighting and they were not expecting trouble and they were not fit.

Angus pulled a long-handled spanner from its magnetic clips in the side of the tractor and swung it like a club. As the first of the guards came round the tractor he received the heavy spanner in his face and went down without a sound. The second came clambering over the tractor and Angus turned to face him. This man had the foresight to have his gun in his hand. Angus swung his spanner in an arc but missed the guard's legs, and the spanner clattered harmlessly on the treads of the tractor. Had the guard had more skill and a cooler nerve he could have shot Angus where he staggered. But the guard gaped, stupefied. And then, just when he had collected himself and was raising his pistol to shoot, a knife, thrown from close quarters, buried itself in his throat and his knees buckled. He tipped forwards from the tractor and crashed at Angus's feet.

Angus stared in amazement. Viti had thrown the knife. 'Why?' shouted Angus. 'Why? You bastard.'

And Viti shrugged. He did not know. He could not have explained. It was not a rational decision.

Moments before he had seen Miranda and the memories had flooded back. He had picked up his knife from the grass and balanced it in his hand ready to throw at Angus. He could have killed the man easily on several occasions, but something stayed him. He saw the guards as they came toiling up and a great revulsion shook him. The guards seemed to represent everything that he hated in himself and in his Roman life. When he threw the knife, he did so without thinking. It was an act of instinctive rebellion.

Both young men knew that the killing of the guard was significant in a deep and personal way as well as in a public way. The guards were running to protect Viti the Roman. All he needed to do was lie back and eventually Angus would be felled. Then, if still alive, he would be sent to a holding prison such as the Caligula Detention and Punishment Camp. There he would remain until, half-starved and weak, he would face his execution at the hands of howling Romans during the next year's battle feast. Either that or Viti could have killed him at his leisure. Viti knew this, and yet he had saved Angus's life. More, with that one throw of the knife he had allied himself with the forces of disorder.

This was Viti's first act of deep rebellion, and like all such acts it came from a depth of his being more profound than reason.

Another guard arrived and was felled by Viti with a short-armed jab to the throat. Then Angus and Viti fleeced the guards of their weapons. Calmly they shot the remaining two guards as they came puffing up to the tractor.

Angus and Viti faced one another, angry and confused by the turn of events. 'Now what?' said Angus. Viti looked at him and then looked beyond him, his eye caught by movements out on the plain. 'Can you get the Dragon to work?' he asked.

'Given time I can,' said Angus. 'The bloody thing's almost indestructible. What are you thinking?'

'I'm thinking that's the only way any of us will escape alive.' Viti gestured towards the far end of the Battle Dome. Angus turned and stared. Black figures of security guards were fanning out across the grass from the machine-shops and hangars. These guards were different, probably brought in from the nearby rail depot. They ran low with a trained stealth and energy and obviously knew what they were about. Accompanying them were three black- and red-painted, spoke-wheeled vehicles, each of which had a variety of different-sized cannon mounted in front. The vehicles had been supplied to the Battle Dome during the previous century to quell disorder should it ever arise. To date they had never been used or needed. The cannon could fire canisters of tear-gas and incendiary shells. They could create a wall of blinding gas if needs be.

'Don't worry about them,' called Angus. 'I'll stop them. Just keep me covered.' And even as he spoke there came the spatter and whine of bullets as they dug into the turf and ricocheted off the plating of the Dragon. Viti returned the fire while Angus sprinted across to the heavy retrieval tractor which was still ticking over.

Viti set up a pattern of firing which resulted in many of the guards pitching forwards and lying still. Others ran and dived. Answering fire came but it was erratic and uncoordinated since the guards were having to advance over open ground and Viti had the advantage in height. But Viti was not lulled by his success. He knew that already there would be crack units of the civic police flying to the Battle Dome and that they were skilled, professional and ruthless and would attack in force from all corners. He hoped that Angus knew what he was doing.

Angus climbed into the cab of the tractor and revved the engine. He slipped it into gear and manoeuvred it round until it was facing the advancing guards and the machine-shops. Then he applied the brake. He extended the tractor's mobile cranes on either side to their fullest extent, like outriggers. Finally he flung open the cap to the diesel fuel tank and tore a length of mechanic's absorbent shoddy from its stand. This he coiled into a wick which he plunged to the full length of his arm into the fuel tank. Drawing out the sodden wick he squeezed it and twisted it and then set a match to it. His last act was to release the brake and the tractor lurched forwards and began to roll towards the oncoming vehicles. Those vehicles fired their first canisters of tear-gas, unaware of the bomb that was lurching towards them.

Angus ran back to the Dragon and climbed up to the cabin. Viti kept firing and retreated backwards after him. Then his guns fell silent and he jumped down into the cabin and slammed the cover closed over him.

Inside the Dragon, Angus settled himself down into the control seat and fitted the drive helmet and gloves. 'Anchor yourselves,' he called to the others. 'Use the webbing straps. Grab hold of anything you can. This may get rough.'

Then he took control of the Dragon. The information panel told him of those parts which had been damaged and which he had, therefore, to protect. The tail, for instance, could be raised to the run position, but it could not be swished. That did not matter. Most of the other systems were in working order despite the crash and the flywheel had hardly lost any energy. Angus tried out several movements and eventually had the Dragon upright again. 'Fucking amazing,' he muttered. Then he glanced at Viti. 'I'll sort you out later,' he said as he fed power to the half-track and heard it graunch and begin to churn.

Within moments he had the Dragon gathering speed, using its central wheels. It required all his skill to drive it for some parts had been twisted when it rolled down the hill. They moved out on to the central plain.

Pouring in through the main gate of the Battle Dome were detachments of security guards equipped with short-range assault weapons. Suddenly there came a massive detonation away to the right and massive chunks of synthetic soil and rock were hurled into the air. The ground shook and the body of the exploding tractor became so many blazing pieces of shrapnel.

'Break through the wall,' shouted Viti. 'Come on. Get this fucking thing moving. Now's our only chance.'

And Angus obeyed.

He turned the Dragon away from the main entrance and set it running for the grey sloping wall of the Battle Dome. As it approached the wall he set its steel claws.

When it was only metres from the wall, the Dragon rose to its greatest height and its front claws lashed out, raking downwards, and the wall of the Battle Dome tore like damp cardboard. The Dragon thrust its head and neck forwards through the hole, and the rest of the body barged afterwards. It tore right through the wall and emerged on the other side.

It faced a wall of trees.

This was the wild wood.

The adventure was just beginning.

8 Events beyond Britannia

Britannia basked in its security. But far away, events were occurring which were to shape the fate and the entire face of the densely wooded islands.

In the small town of Pons Aeni, close to the city which we know as Munich, on a particular market day in spring, it was observed that some of the sheep that were on sale had weeping cysts about their eyes. The sheep were listless and their wool hung lank. The official who managed the market ordered that the infected sheep be separated from the rest and destroyed, which was done. But then, a few days later, came reports that one entire flock in the mountains had been affected and that the poor creatures had run wild in their anguish, scratching their faces on the fences, before finally expiring. Within hours a similar report had been received from northern Gallia and it was obvious that a major epidemic was breaking out. Perhaps worst of all was the discovery that the disease could also affect humans. It was less virulent in humans, rarely resulting in death, but frequently resulting in blindness.

Within days of the outbreak a pattern was emerging and the cause had been found. All the affected flocks had had their winter feed-stocks supplemented with pellets imported from a factory in northern Hispania. Wherever the pellets had been eaten the disease appeared in the flocks after an incubation period of six weeks. By the time the disease appeared the sheep were as good as dead and the only remedy was to kill any affected sheep and burn the bodies. This began in earnest, and as spring edged into early summer the upland fields of the entire continent were stained with the black smoke of the burning flocks and the air was pungent with burning wool. The factory which had produced the infected pellets was itself burned to the ground and the earth scorched for an acre about it. Such was Roman thoroughness.

Quarantine was imposed rigorously. All shipments of sheep-meat from Europe to Britannia were cancelled. Any garments that could have come in contact with the disease were burned and all shepherds' quarters and shearing-sheds were drenched in wine as libations to the gods. The process of contagion was only dimly understood in this world. Experience had shown over the centuries that isolation and fire helped control an epidemic. The factories which spun yarn to make carpets and knitting-wool began to cut back production and ran at half capacity.

Under the hot summer sun the sheep droppings hardened and decayed while the grass grew long and lush. The barns were bursting with hay and the cattle prospered. Agricultural experts from Roma advised that the pastures be left fallow for as long as possible to make sure that the pestilence had died out. They prayed for a hard dry summer. Meanwhile, mutton and lamb became prized delicacies available only to the very wealthy and the black market flourished.

The gods must have heard the prayers, for the high summer became a succession of sun-drenched days which had the wine-makers dancing for joy and talking about the vintage of the century. The hills, once dotted with the white and shaven bodies of sheep, now crackled in the heat and dried to a dangerous golden brown. Prudent towns and villages in the areas which had been affected cut fire-breaks to surround their walls.

Then in the autumn teams of soldiers ignited the grass and the wind carried the flames in ragged lines of orange and red over the hills leaving ash in their wake. It was an operation carried out with surgical precision. It was the kind of operation which showed Roman efficiency at its best. In the late autumn the rains came and the hills recovered though the rivers ran like liquid chocolate, so great was the erosion. Then came the frosts and the authorities began to breathe more easily. As far as they were concerned, fire, famine and frost should have put paid to whatever pestilence had caused the disease.

In the early spring fresh stocks of sheep were imported from the Pennine uplands of Britannia, from the Western Empire and from islands in the South Pacific. With these the European hills were again stocked. As the first warmth of the new year brought the grass on apace, the sheep and their lambs wandered hoof-high in grass in their new paddocks.

When a sudden cold snap came down from the Arctic and covered Europe with a last blanket of snow, the lambs snuggled for warmth beside their mothers under shelters made from bales of hay.

The farmers watched. Agricultural officials watched. Restaurant-owners watched. They all hoped they could heave a sigh of relief that the epidemic was ended. But shortly after the fires from the festival of the Reformed Lupercalia had died down, the first sheep sickened and died. This year the pattern of the epidemic was different. The worst-affected sheep farms were in Gallia, but everywhere, even up to the Russian steppes, the fierce cysts appeared round the eyes of the hapless sheep. Grudgingly it was realized that the epidemic had become endemic at least as far as the continental mainland was concerned. For the second year running, the disease did not appear in Britannia and this was ultimately Britannia's misfortune.

However, we must now turn to other developments which were taking place in the vast Roman Empire. In the province of Gallia, the old Praefectus Comitum, a one-time great athlete called Publius Eudromus Sulpicius, finally died of an internal haemorrhage after choking on a chicken-bone. After much intrigue his place was taken by Lucius Prometheus Petronius, who delighted in being called Trimalchio after the character in the *Satyricon*.

Lucius was a man renowned alike for his beauty and his debauchery. In his final year as a student at the École Militaire at Avennio, he had won the crown as Victor Ludorum with an act of singular bravery. He had thrown himself beneath the feet of his adversary's horse, causing the beast to rear and then stumble. Then he dispatched the rider, dragging him from his horse and garrotting him with the reins. Thus Lucius Petronius won the prize. In the years following he had served first as a centurion and later as praefectus in one of the jungle provinces of the southern continent of the great Western Empire. The popular jest was that he had subdued the entire province through unlimited fornication and that when the women and boys were gone the stables better beware. It was also said that he could drink a regiment under the table and piss as high as a second-storey window.

It was during this period that Petronius published a short book of philosophy called *The Games of Men*. In this he argued that the peace of Socrates only came to the man who knew himself and that the only way to know yourself was to face danger and licentiousness in equal measure. He believed that the truly brave man is the hedonist and that if in the pursuit of pleasure you hurt another human being that is their fault for not being on their guard or for allowing themselves to be put in a place of danger. 'The brave man talks to his mistress, his sword, if Fate frowns too hard,' he wrote. And again, 'Life is to be lived like wine is to be drunk . . . but avoid the dregs of both.'

After twenty years in the jungle he returned to his native Gallia with an immense fortune in gold and silver, ships and slaves. He brought fourteen wives, sundry catamites, as well as enough children to people a town. He established his home in a villa to the north of Massilia, on the banks of the river Durance, and set about creating a settlement totally devoted to the exploration of sensual pleasures. He took special delight in his name Petronius and decided to recreate the grandeur of old Roma by emulating the life-style of Trimalchio.

He set out his thoughts on social philosophy in a small volume entitled *On Nature*. This was a collection of aphorisms and each statement was linked to some public building which he had financed. When he built a fine new high-towered brothel beside the public baths in Avennio, he also added a statue of his mother above the entrance gate for it was said of her that in her prime she could out-Messalina Messalina herself. 'What were the ancient Romans' greatest achievements?' asked Lucius Petronius. 'Architecture and debauchery,' he replied, answering his own question. 'Therefore let architecture be our monument to this brief life, and let debauchery remind us we are living.'

He built hospitals: 'To refresh the wilting and rejuvenate the jaded.'

He built temples: 'The greatest tribute you can pay your god is to desire to copulate with her. The greatest honour you can pay your lover is to see the god shining in his eyes.'

He built homes for the aged: 'Let us acknowledge that when the flesh is past performance, we still have memory to warm us and hence we need comforts to allow us the peace to savour old wounds.'

He built schools: 'What a curse is an ignorant lover. For when Priapus is down, I want you to engage me with your sharp wit.'

And while all this building was going ahead, he set himself to investigate the length and breadth of gluttony. 'I will satiate my palate, yea even to oblivion, and then chew my way out the other side.'

It was at about this time that old Eudromus swallowed his chicken-bone and the position of Praefectus Comitum of Gallia came up for grabs. A private civil war broke out between the rival Roman families which ruled Gallia.

In Britannia, the Roman aristocracy looked on with ironic detachment at the Gallic mayhem. One pretender to the position of Praefectus was found in his bath with his throat slit from ear to ear. Another was discovered drowned, head-down in the latrine of a whore-house. A third managed to blow himself up. A fourth was garrotted when his scarf caught in a ski-lift while a fifth was mashed to pulp when he fell into the gears of a windmill. Yet others, it seemed, threw themselves casually off high buildings or gulped down poison with relish. Such goings-on were not the Britannic way, but they had a certain operatic bravura and the leaders of the province of Britannia applauded.

Word was out in the streets that Lucius Petronius had had a hand in most of these killings though this was never stated publicly nor could ever be proved. Then one day Lucius issued a statement from his villa on the Durance river that he intended to seek the position of Praefectus Comitum of Gallia and would shortly undertake a progress to promote his campaign. Lucius Petronius planned to spend some six weeks travelling through Gallia presenting his argument to the people.

Those who saw Lucius – or Trimalchio as he now preferred

to be called – when he was carried forth from his villa on a litter of black bamboo-canes adorned with tusks of ivory and skins of lion and tiger, those few can still dine out on the story. Trumpets brayed and cymbals crashed as he was borne from his residence.

Lucius's handsome face, which had in his youth caused men and women to swoon and fall on their knees with desire, was still in evidence. His hair was brushed into tight black curls. His eyes were the lazy sultry eyes of Pan. But below the fine face, sensual, cruel lips and finely chiselled chin was the gross body of an ox. The head seemed to float on a sea of flesh.

Dancing before his litter came boys dressed up as Cupid, with fluffy wings at their backs and coronets of bay-leaves on their heads. These had been dipped in sugar and gold-dust and sparkled in the light. The boys fired arrows of pure gold into the crowds and the people fought and swore and kicked and bit to secure the small trophies.

Following the litter came a series of barges, each set up on wheels and bearing casks of rich red wine.

That was Lucius Prometheus Petronius's argument, his platform: wine and gold.

Wherever Lucius went he was met by cheering crowds who quickly became a drunken mob as the booze-barges emptied. The mob's ardour was not even cooled when 'Trimalchio' was heard to say, 'They'd eat my turds if I dipped them in aspic.'

He staged public shows, too, and proposed a new public festival which he called the Fornication Olympiad. This would take place four times a year and would last on each occasion for seven days.

Wherever Lucius went he preached a gospel of liberty, carnality and delight in the *now*. He promised that when he was appointed Praefectus Comitum he would ensure that no family ever lacked for wine.

Of course, Lucius did not have things all his own way and there were members of other powerful families who opposed him. Once at a banquet he was challenged by a senior Roman senator. 'Who will pay for the excesses you advocate?' he asked.

'We can hardly pay for the standing armies that police our Empire. So who will pay?'

All eyes turned on Lucius Prometheus. That man raised his glass of red wine and held it up against the light so that its colours tinted his face.

'The future,' he said, quite simply. 'The future will pay. Those that come after me will pay. They always do in the long run. Only the man blinded with vanity believes he has the strength to stave off the coming darkness, so let us enjoy the daylight while we may. *Après moi, les ténèbres.*' He drank quickly, like a man drinking poison, and then threw his glass the length of the table where it smashed into a thousand glittering fragments. 'I drink to the Future,' he shouted.

That ended the debate, and those who were present remembered the way that all the guests raised their glasses and shouted, 'The Future.'

Inevitably, 'Trimalchio' was elected Praefectus Comitum. He was not, of course, elected by the Citizens, but by the Council of the Roman aristocracy who in their discreet ways wisely listened to the *vox populi*. They did not want to see their estates burned or find themselves pelted with horse-dung. Be it noted that the Citizens in Europe were altogether a more feisty crowd than their counterparts in Britannia.

And when Lucius Prometheus Petronius was installed in the palace of the Praefectus at Avennio he declared that he was going on a fast to restore his youth. He also made it known that he had his eye on the Imperial crown in Roma.

This ambition too was Britannia's misfortune.

Throughout the rest of the Roman Empire there were troubles.

The truth is that the Empire was too big and had been so for centuries. It was ungovernable. The centre could not hold. The Empire was like a giant flywheel that was beginning to wobble eccentrically as its mighty energy ran out of control.

It was widely predicted that the fall of the Empire would cause comets to fly, and people in all parts of the globe watched the sky anxiously. In general, acts of rebellion were matched with repression from the State for that was all the rulers knew, and repression merely rebounded back on itself in the form of resentment, slowness, attrition and cynicism.

In the South Pacific, in a place called Aotearoa which was also known as the Land of the Long White Cloud, a warrior chief called Te Rauparaha had arisen to oppose the Roman forces. His furious invective combined with astonishing military expertise hurled back the Roman mercenaries who had occupied his land. This action sparked a rebellion that now blazed throughout the country.

Across the sea in the vast flat Southern Continent, several legions had been lost in the arid interior. One had been caught in a flash-flood. Two others had apparently wandered away into the desert. Survivors who came crawling out of the bush weeks later talked of dark men with legs like sticks who danced like lizards and birds. When they danced the hills roared and strange winds came spiralling from nowhere at midday and destroyed the camps. They talked of the ground sweating blood and rocks that spoke and rivers in the air that moved like silver snakes. Popular opinion held that these men were crazed by the sun and the dry air. But some wondered.

In Tibet an entire legion defected and became pacifist.

In Africa bandits gained control over sections of the trans-Africa highway and demanded tribute from any travellers who wanted to pass. After many battles the bandits were crushed. But the price which the Empire had to pay to keep the road secure was constant vigilance. Troops were diverted from tasks in the East to man the ten-thousand-mile length of the highway.

At the southern tip of the great Western Continent, the soldiers of an entire legion declared themselves independent of Roma. To show their independence they extinguished the lighthouses which guided the ships to safety through the treacherous waters. Roma reacted with force. Shock troops were sent to destroy the uprising. They succeeded, and the weary and starved mutineers were brought home to Roma to be dragged through the streets before being chopped into joints for the animals in the zoo.

*

However, little of this mattered to the inhabitants of the Britannic Isles where Roman order seemed secure, at least in the towns and cities. The province of Britannia could ignore the rest of the world, for in these lands there was peace and prosperity. The sheep crisis in Gallia meant windfall profits for the Britannic landowners. While the continental farmers pondered their dying sheep, the Britannic farmers rubbed their hands behind their backs and fattened their lambs for profit and slaughter.

Here the wind blowing over the deep forest smelled sweet and pure and the bees bumbled in the gardens among the hollyhocks and camomile.

Everyone knew that here, in Britannia, the beer was the best in the world.

Here common sense and decency prevailed.

Here, during this long hot summer, the sky was blue and the diving swallows caught their fill of insects. If there was a distant rumble of thunder, no one paid it much regard.

Here bat met ball with a solid and comfortable thud on the greens of the many state farms.

The Dragon barged through the wall of the Battle Dome.

The fabric of the dome stretched and ripped, tangling round the claws and neck of the Dragon, trailing after it in long strands which broke with a sound like a whip cracking. Stressed beyond their tolerance, the straps and threads of the dome deformed into tight ringlets which coiled back, giving the hole the ghastly appearance of a blank face fringed with a curly wig or a frozen, open wound. Meanwhile, deep behind in the heart of the Battle Dome there grew a red glare where the synthetic grass was blazing.

So great was the momentum of the Dragon that it almost toppled down into the dyke which surrounded the base of the Battle Dome. Angus made quick adjustments, lowering the tail and drawing the neck and the head back. In this posture, almost that of the Dragon rampant, it teetered on the bank and finally held firm.

Before them was the wild wood. It rose, dark and ominous, some fifty yards in front of them. In the springtime, the trees closest to the dome had been cut down. Woodsmen had dragged the trunks and branches away lest they provide fuel for a fire. Now all that was left was a narrow band of stumps, some jagged and sharp where the trees had fallen before the cutting was complete.

'Those bastards could snag us,' breathed Angus nodding at the stumps. 'Rip the whole underbelly out of us.'

'Can't you walk over them?' asked Miranda.

'I'll try,' he replied. 'I'll use the base-plating to crush a way through.'

'Well you'd better be quick,' shouted Viti. 'They'll be coming round the outside perimeter by now.'

Angus revved the Dragon and made the tail push, edging the beast forwards until it toppled over the rim and slid down into the clearing. Then he made it rise up on to its hind legs but with its neck thrust out. It began to step daintily like a heron but it also had the menacing power of a crocodile. In this way it crossed the narrow band of stumps and finally came to face the packed trees of the forest proper.

'Now where?' asked Angus.

As though in answer to his question a figure in a cloak of white fur suddenly rose from among the stumps at the forest's edge and beckoned them. Angus hit the brakes to avoid crushing him. The man pointed towards a large oak tree and shook both his fists in front of his face, a gesture which suggested both urgency and courage. He was grinning, too. This was, of course, Lyf.

Both Angus and Miranda recognized him, though they did not know his name. They had seen him at the bonfire when the young athletes were jumping through the flames. It was the same man who had calmed a dangerous situation.

Miranda looked at Angus and Angus shrugged. As far as he was concerned his life was out of control anyway, so why not follow the guide of a wandering wild man of the wood? What had he to lose? Miranda felt the same.

Only Viti did not recognize the man in the white fur cloak, though had he but known it, that man was present at dawn on the day that he and Diana made love under a yew tree.

Angus gunned the machine. Although he could not see a way out, he urged the Dragon towards the oak tree. When they came close they saw that one heavy branch had grown into an arch creating a tunnel beneath it. Angus drove towards this. He lowered the Dragon, thrusting its head out even lower and making it crawl.

Once under the branch they found themselves facing a small clearing. The man appeared before them, running with his cloak hitched up and held with one hand. As he ran he waved with the other.

'Who the hell is that?' asked Viti, but neither Miranda or Angus answered.

Angus guided the Dragon carefully under the trees. Sometimes the branches rasped over the back, sometimes they broke. The first clearing led into a second which was larger and which in its turn led into an avenue of sorts where the trees gave way to bracken and scrub growing beside a trickling stream. Here the Dragon could move more quickly and Angus urged the beast along. Lyf ran before them. Once he tripped and fell on his face in the mud and Angus had to stop the Dragon in mid-stride to avoid crushing him. But then Lyf was up again and running before them, waving his fists and punching the air with zeal.

Lyf ran with an easy loping stride. He jumped over fallen logs and plunged under the trailing strands of willow as though he had been running this way all his life. He led them towards stands of trees which looked impassable but which suddenly showed that they had a narrow way through them, just enough for the Dragon.

They zigzagged back and forth, rarely seeing the sky, and suddenly they came to a drop. Here a stream which had been meandering through a glade now became a waterfall which tumbled down over rocks. Lyf urged them downwards and Angus used all his skill to make the Dragon step downwards from one rock platform to another. Water tumbled between the Dragon's legs.

Gradually the dim forest light became even dimmer as they descended into the pit, which showed itself to be the collapsed roof of a deep cave. None of them had ever seen anything like it. At the bottom they could see a domed opening under a massive lintel of stone. The stream tumbled in front of this into a pool which then flowed into the cave. The entrance way seemed very small.

'Hell's bells,' said Viti. 'He must be joking if he thinks we can get into that.'

Angus grunted, his attention entirely on manoeuvring the heavy Dragon.

'I don't think we've much option,' offered Miranda.

The further they descended the easier the manoeuvring became. The slab rocks gave way to shingle and they stepped aside from the tumbling stream. Ferns and long pale grasses grew in the twilight. Finally the Dragon set its feet and slid the final few yards down to the the base of the pit beside the pool.

The cave-mouth was now before them and Angus guided the Dragon under its heavy lintel and into the darkness. They scraped through.

But as their eyes adjusted they discovered that the cave had lights within. Set into the walls were lamps which cast a green glow down on to the cave floor. They also saw that people were scurrying about. They seemed neither surprised nor afraid at the sudden appearance of the Dragon.

No sooner was the beast within than the people began blocking the cave-mouth with rocks and bushes. Some of the bushes had a carefully manicured appearance and looked as though they could have been pilfered from the Battle Dome.

'Anyone would think they were ready and waiting for us,' said Miranda.

'It looks that way,' agreed Angus. 'At least they don't look hostile. Come on. Let's go out and meet them.'

He began to close the Dragon down. The hydraulic pistons hissed as the pressure relaxed and the entire beast shuddered. The giant head lowered until it rested on the floor. The tail creaked as it straightened and finally came to rest partly twisted into a corkscrew shape. As it settled, a dribble of oil ran from some of its lumbar plates and stained the sand on the cave floor. The control dials died except for those that reported system failures and these blinked on and off. They would not stop until the main power packs were switched off at the outside control panel near the base of the tail.

Angus opened the small door above him and threw it back with a clang. He was surprised to find that his hands were shaking. He had been gripping the controls with great force and now worked his hands open and shut to relieve the tension. With elaborate courtesy he helped Miranda to climb up out of the beast. He began to scramble up after her and then paused and looked at Viti. He jabbed a finger at him. 'You'll keep,' he said. 'I'll sort you out later. But don't get under my bloody feet. That clear?' Viti stood up and Angus pushed him back roughly. 'You've had your warning.'

Viti said nothing. The jolting journey down into the pit had hurt him greatly but he didn't want Angus to know that. He had banged his head again and had opened the partly dried cuts on his arms and back. Viti was now suffering. The adrenalin that had kept him going was now draining away and his head hurt and his clothes were sticky and stiff where blood had seeped and partially dried. Had Angus still wanted to kill him now would have been the time for Viti's fighting spirit was dulled. But Angus ignored his opportunity. Perhaps for him, too, action had lost its relish or perhaps he just lacked training.

When Angus and Miranda emerged from the Dragon they were astonished to find that the people they had seen milling about had gone. The cave was almost deserted save for the figure of Lyf. At the cave door was a child who stood, one finger in his mouth and his other hand twisted in his garments, looking at them with frank curiosity. A woman appeared from behind the barrier of rocks and scrub, and scooped up the child hurriedly. It spoke to her, pointing at the Dragon and asking a question. The woman smiled quickly and answered and then hurried outside carrying the child. Lyf was now alone.

He was kneeling on the cave floor, blowing on to a small fire he had started. The yellow flame flared up, making his shadow leap, and the wood crackled and smoke rose. Beside him on the ground was a bundle bound up in a red and white checked cloth.

From their vantage-point on top of the Dragon Angus and Miranda had an opportunity to survey the entire cave. The green lights illuminated only a horseshoe of flattened earth near the door. Beyond the lights, in the depth of the cave, were shadows which merged to simple blackness. The cave was high. Stunted stalactites pointed down from the roof, but they were dry. The cave felt dead. It had finished its growing many centuries ago. The floor was sandy and the stream, the same one which had tumbled down to the entrance way, now meandered between banks that gave the appearance of having been carefully carved. Finally, at the light's edge, the stream flowed into a pool without ripples, where after it flowed away swiftly into the darkness.

'Come yous on down,' called Lyf, beckoning and speaking in the quaint and ungrammatical Latin that Angus and Miranda had heard before on the night of the fire-jumping. They began to descend. 'No danger here. The Roman squaddies is off in another part of the wood chasing an old iron chariot we set on with mad horses. It'll lead 'em a merry dance. They won't stay out after night-down. Romans is afraid of the dark. We own the dark. And we'll set a bonfire in the darkness and sing a song or two about trophy heads and they'll believe a story that we've eaten yous. Yum-yum.' Lyf smacked his lips and laughed. At that moment Viti's head appeared from the hole at the top of the Dragon and he hoisted himself up painfully. Lyf raised his voice a fraction. 'It's a long time since I've eaten a Roman.' He grinned a deliberate stage grin, drawing back his lips, and Angus and Miranda saw with some surprise that his canine teeth at the sides were filed to points.

Viti made no reply but began to climb down from the back of the prone Dragon. Lyf looked disappointed and returned his attention to the fire and to an iron billy which he had filled with water. He settled the billy over the flames and then carefully opened the cloth bundle. Inside were several flat wheaten cakes, a dozen or so small legs of meat black from smoking, some cheese, a few green and wrinkled apples and a couple of jars of wine. These victuals he spread out carefully on the cloth and then added four small earthenware cups.

Viti approached, limping slightly, and Lyf surveyed him from crown to toe. 'Well, you're a bit of a dog's dinner. Been savaged by the invaders, eh? Let's see how bad you are.' Viti began to reply but before he could speak Lyf moved to him and placed the palm of his left hand down on Viti's head. 'Shut up and close your eyes,' he ordered. Viti obeyed. For a few moments there was absolute silence while Lyf moved his hand on the young man's head. Then he checked his pulse, first pressing all the fingers of his right hand against the side of Viti's throat and then moving them down to his shoulder, to the inside of his armpit, to the lower ribs of his waist and finally to his wrist. There his fingers played up and down the lower arm almost like a cellist. Seemingly satisfied he stood back. 'Lucky for you you have a head of bone and a body of iron. Your cuts will heal in their own time. For your mind . . . ? No man can say. Nor can

I.' He looked round the three of them. 'Eat now, all of yous. Wash later. Then new clothes for a new world.' He turned back to the fire where the flames were licking round the billy and the water was starting to steam.

'Who are you?' asked Miranda, speaking suddenly, like someone starting from a dream. And then less certainly she added, 'We've seen you before, haven't we?' She turned to Angus for confirmation and he nodded.

'Call me Lyf,' said the man standing again and facing them. 'That's all the name I have for now in this place. And you may well have seen me before. I'm often round here, or hereabouts. I keep my eye on the Battle Dome. And I know you two. You're Angus the machine-man, and you're Miranda the virgin and this piece of raw meat is Viti who doesn't yet know how to sing. Am I right?'

Miranda shrugged and blushed. She did not know how to take the strange man's remarks about herself. She knew she could have been upset, but at the same time she did not feel he meant any rudeness, though why he should call her a virgin she could not guess. She could not tell whether Lyf was threatening or trying to give secret messages or whether his strange manner was just the result of his speaking a language that was not native to him. But in her innocent, shrewd and intuitive way, she felt trust in him, recognizing a man who neither speaks nor acts without purpose.

Not so Angus. He felt his male vanity pricked by Lyf's humour and his obliqueness. He did not like people making fun of him. A thought flitted through his mind that he could perhaps overpower Lyf while the latter was stooped over the fire, though he did not know what he would do then. 'Make him talk straight, perhaps. Answer a few questions.' But in the event Angus did nothing aggressive. Instead he squatted down and pushed some scattered twigs and sticks towards the fire. 'Why did you save us?' he asked finally.

'Well, did I save you?' Lyf echoed the question, looking at each of them sharply with his head on its side like a bird waiting for crumbs. 'Cernunnos knows. Perhaps I didn't save you, think of that. Perhaps you're out of the pot and into the flames. Time will tell. I don't control things. You see, there are many things that must come to pass. Unavoidable. But how they come to pass . . .' His voice trailed away and he looked at them again with his head on its side. They were clearly mystified by his words and he shrugged. 'Bah, early days yet. Yous just arrived.' Lyf continued to look at them and then suddenly his eyes seemed to smile, though in other ways his face remained impassive after the manner of men with dry humour. 'Sorry if I confuse yous. You see in my world, in the world you are now part of, two and two rarely make four after the good old Roman fashion. We talk in riddles here. We like ambiguity. We think anyone who builds a straight road is a fool. That stands to reason, to us. For the journey is always more important than arriving. Anyway, what is arriving anyway, but another departure? You see?'

'No,' said Angus and this time there was a hint of aggression in his voice.

'Ah well,' said Lyf, turning back to his fire. 'You might one day. Anyway. Now food. For yous.' He gestured with his thumb towards the victuals he had spread out.

All three of them were hungry and began to share the food which Lyf handed round, tearing the bread into hunks, pulling the meat off the bones with their teeth and sitting on the ground by the fire. 'Are you eating with us?' asked Miranda and Lyf shook his head. He opened one of the jars of wine and drank deeply after first tipping a bit of the wine out on to the ground. Then he busied himself with the billy. He took a small sachet of herbs from a bag at his side and shook them into the bubbling water, which subsided briefly and then boiled as vigorously as before while a pungent odour, which owed something to mint and something to ginger, spread in the air of the cave close to them.

Lyf removed the billy from the fire and set it aside. 'When this has cooled you will drink. Taste not too bad . . . a bit flat, a bit like stale beer. Give you the shits, no doubt, and that is good. Shits is good. Shit place outside.' He mimed digging vigorously. 'Cover shit with earth. You'll see. Don't fall in. OK?'

He beamed at them. It was evident he was enjoying this conversation. 'Wash your bum in the stream outside. Not this stream, OK?' He spat into the fire and busied himself with the billy. He nodded to Viti. 'You drink first,' he said. 'You need energy and sleep. Now I'll get you clothes.'

Lyf moved towards the dark back of the cave to the place where the small stream began to race away. He came back moments later carrying three bundles. 'Disguises,' he said, throwing the bundles down. 'Make yous look like woodlanders. Much better for the wild wood. Keep you dry among the leaves when you set out from here. Hey, a bit of advice, OK? You try to be kind to one another. OK? And now I'll leave yous. Farewell.'

He turned abruptly and headed for the door of the cave. Miranda stood up quickly and ran to him. 'Lyf. Don't leave us now. We don't know where we are or what to do. You can't leave us now.'

'I can,' said Lyf, and he threw his white fur cloak round his shoulders. 'Watch me,' he said and stepped quickly out through the small cave-mouth. Miranda chased after him but she could not catch him. The man, totally at home in his world, ran lightly up the scree where the Dragon had skidded and reached the solid rock. There he turned and, much to her astonishment, blew her a kiss. 'Don't worry,' he called. 'You've more friends than you know in this world. Sort out those two silly buggers first and take things as they come. Trust your nature.' With that he sprang up the stones by the waterfall and was quickly gone. All that marked his passing was a scatter of small stones which tumbled down to land at Miranda's feet.

The daylight seemed to be waning and everything seemed darker. Looking up to the daylight Miranda could see where large drops of water were falling from the trees high above. Clearly it had started raining. 'Damp as a tomb.' The thought came to Miranda involuntarily and made her shiver. But despite that and despite her situation, Miranda felt strangely alive. And she squeezed every drop of comfort she could from the final words of Lyf.

She returned back through the cave-mouth and into the deep

green of the underground chamber and found Viti and Angus rowing.

Angus was on his knees by the fire. '. . . And I say we should have grabbed him while we had the chance. He obviously knows more than he's letting on. Bloody mumbo-jumbo. We don't have any friends in this world. This could be a trap and . . .'

Viti sighed. 'You don't grab types like him. Take my word. I know more about fighting than you do. The wiry ones are the hardest to fight. No sooner do you throw them down than back they come, low and fast. He's probably a kick-fighter too. He'd smash your goolies before you could draw breath.'

'Then what do you suggest, smart arse? That we just sit here?'

'Yes.'

'And let them pick us off? Bloody brilliant.'

Miranda joined them. 'You two,' she said. 'I've had enough of both of you. So stop it. We're still alive. We're fed. We're safe for the time being. So shut up. Night's coming outside and its going to be a long cold night, I can tell you.' She looked at Angus directly. 'Angus, you go outside and get more wood. Try to find dry wood. We've got to keep the fire in and I don't want wolves or bears or anything getting in here tonight.' Angus looked at her in astonishment. He had never heard Miranda speak in this way. 'Well move,' she said to his open mouth.

With bad grace Angus got to his feet, his strong shoulders hunched to give an impression of power. He moved towards the cave door. But before reaching it he turned and pointed to Viti. 'If he gives you any trouble while I'm gone, just let me know.' And then he left.

This comment struck Miranda as funny and she just managed to restrain her mirth until Angus had left. Anyone less likely to cause her trouble than Viti was hard for her to imagine. That young man was now hunched over on his side and his back and neck had obviously stiffened. 'Have you drunk any of that brew the woodlander made us?' she asked and Viti shook his head.

'Well get some down you. He said it would help and I get the impression he knows about such things.'

Viti grunted. 'I can't make sense of what he says,' he muttered. Miranda dipped one of the earthenware cups into the billy and scooped out some of the liquid. 'That's just his manner. Some people are gruff when they are kind. My father was like that . . .' Her voice stopped. This was the first time she had really thought about her mother and father since the escape from the Battle Dome. Suddenly the enormity of what had happened was borne in upon her. She imagined her mother's anguished face at this moment. She'd be asking why, why, why, and her father would have no answer. He'd be as upset as she was in his own quiet way. Would Miranda ever see her mother and father again? Would they get into trouble because of her? What had happened? Why was she here?

'Are you all right?' It was Viti asking. 'I know the light's not good in here but you've gone pale as a ghost. And the cup's spilling on the floor.'

Miranda came back to herself. 'I suddenly thought about home,' she said. 'I suddenly felt afraid.'

Viti took a moment or two to digest this. 'Look,' he said finally. 'You're no part of all this really . . . well you are but . . .' The young man became confused and found that he could not look Miranda in the face as he spoke. 'But anyway . . . you're not responsible. Look, what I'm trying to say is that I'd like to help you get back. They can't hold anything against you. The mechanic and I will be put to death if they catch us, but you . . . You can tell them we forced you to come.'

'We'll see,' said Miranda, dipping the cup in the liquid again. 'Here, drink this down and then go and have a wash in that pool like Lyf said. You're starting to smell.' And this was true. He stank of dry blood and sweat, soured with adrenalin.

'Try some yourself,' he said. 'Got a peppery taste. Quite nice.'

'When you've gone.'

'All right, I get the message.' Viti got to his feet slowly. 'By Mithras, my legs are stiff.' He stretched and then stumped over to the pool. 'Hey, there are towels and piles of furs here. Must be for bedding. They've set this place up for us properly.' In the shadows he slipped out of his overalls and dipped his toes in the water. 'It's bloody freezing,' he shouted. 'Oh well. Here goes'. There was a splash followed by a whoop and then more splashing as Viti thrashed about in the water to get his blood pounding. 'It's deep enough to swim,' he called out in gasps.

Miranda, for a few moments alone, peered into the fire. She tried to understand herself. There was sadness in her and excitement too, an awareness of freedom combined with responsibility. Contradictions everywhere. Where will it end? she wondered. At the same time she hoped she would see Lyf again and soon . . . Not that she was attracted to him (she blushed at the very thought, which came to her unbidden and from some unexplored depth in her being) – she guessed that Lyf was more her father's age than her own – but he was a breath of a new world. He excited her and she did not know why. Something to do with his strangeness and his confidence. Miranda sighed. Then she filled a beaker of the liquid for herself and sipped it. Her Polytech training came to her and she tried to identify the flavours. She could detect mint and black tea and something else, something like lemon and something like mushroom. That did not make sense, they were contraries. It was not unpleasant and it certainly was not peppery as Viti had maintained. She drank it down and felt the liquid flow in her. She scooped another mugful and, placing it beside her, edged the embers of the fire together until they flared up. Then she thrust the last of the sticks into the blaze. The fire was beginning to die down and she hoped Angus would be back soon with more wood. The fire made her feel safe.

'L-l-let m-me g-g-get by that f-f-fire.' It was Viti and he was shivering so much that he could hardly speak. He had wrapped a large brightly patterned blanket round his shoulders and held it together at the waist. He came padding over, leaving wet footprints. He seemed to be moving much more easily. 'Oh and there's st-st-stacks of w-w-wood over there in the corner.' He nodded back over his shoulder. 'Enough to k-k-keep this fire going for a w-w-week.'

Miranda held the beaker of herb tea she had scooped for herself up to Viti and he snaked a hand out of his blanket and took it. 'Drink this while I get a real blaze going,' she said and then she jumped to her feet and ran to the back of the cave where Viti had gestured and began gathering an armful of small dry logs and pine-cones. When she returned Viti was struggling into a roughly made shirt with baggy arms and elastic at the wrist. It had a hood with draw-strings at the neck. He had already donned a pair of trousers and these were several sizes too large at the waist, though in length they only came to just below his knees. These too had a draw-string of woven flax at the front.

'Feeling better?' she asked.

'Better.' He pulled the shirt down. 'How do I look?'

'Daft.'

'That's all right then.'

She put the wood in the fire and it began to blaze up, illuminating the cave walls, and at that moment Angus returned, walking backwards, dragging what seemed to be half a pine tree with him. He pulled the branches through the narrow cave-opening with a desperate anger. He was soaked to the skin and water poured off him. 'Bloody rain,' he shouted. 'Bloody river. I fell in. And I've cut my sodding hands trying to break branches.' He turned. When he saw the fire burning brightly he dropped the branches he was carrying. 'And there was me worrying in case the bloody fire had gone out.'

'We found more wood at the back,' said Miranda simply. 'I never thought to look before. Those people who were here when we arrived must have gathered it.'

'Aye. And of course that quare fellow Lyf never thought to tell us,' said Angus.

'Probably thought we'd have enough wit to find it for ourselves,' offered Viti.

Angus looked at him. 'And who asked you?' he said. Then he looked at Viti more closely. 'So what you been doing? Gone native, have you? Think you've got a future here, do you? You look like a prat.' He spat on the cave floor.

'Angus,' warned Miranda.

'Listen Miranda,' said Angus, directing his attention to her and deliberately standing tall with his hands on his hips so that he dwarfed her. 'You don't have to fear him any more, or call him sir or any other fancy name. He's finished. But don't you ever forget what he did to you. Don't ever lose your anger. I've been thinking about things while I was out there lugging wood about. There's probably a price on his head right now. Probably every soldier this side of Deva's out looking for him. He's a danger to us. And there's no love for him and his kind out here in the wild wood. Tomorrow I'll stave his head in and we'll get away. What do you say? You can help. I'll hold him while you belt him if you like.'

Miranda couldn't believe this. This talk was coming from the man she thought she knew. She looked at him and it was Angus in body – big and strong and raw and quick – but was it Angus in mind? She realized she did not know. She was hearing him as though for the first time. There was an ugliness about him she had not known before. And she was afraid. Afraid of what she was hearing which was so alien to the world in which she had grown up, and afraid also that Angus might be right . . . for if so, she was now in a world where the values that had hitherto guided her life no longer applied. 'We'll talk tomorrow,' she said finally. 'Come. Eat and drink and warm yourself and get rid of those wet clothes . . . and your anger,' she added as an afterthought.

Angus grunted but did as he was bid. Soon steam was rising from him as he sat close to the fire with both hands wrapped round a beaker. Silently Miranda brought him dry clothes from the back of the cave.

The thin grey light that had filtered in through the cave door faded away as darkness fell outside. Within the cave the green lights burned steadily. All three sat in silence, hunkered round the fire with the remains of their meal on the floor. Each was lost in a private world. The excitement of the day had been replaced by tiredness, and the first, almost incoherent, murmurings of sadness and loneliness. They felt the sadness of change and abandonment. For each of them the experience was different. Miranda felt the loss of her parents most of all. Angus realized that he had lost an occupation that he loved and an easy place among men. Viti had lost his power and prestige and comfort – and his father.

Each stared into the flickering embers, and in the mind's eye each saw something different for the future. Viti saw himself alone, hunted by Roman death squads until he was finally cornered and cut down by some young commander with a name to make. He saw his blood run from a cut in the throat and spatter on green grass by a river. He felt relief that the brief days of his unhappy life would end.

Angus saw himself alone in the vast forest at nightfall, lost and not knowing which way to turn. As the shadows deepened and the giant trees creaked in the freshening wind he cried for the mother he had never known, not knowing it was a mother he cried for.

Miranda had lived her fear many times and had never given it a name, let alone spoken of it. She feared the dark and the strange panther shapes with yellow eyes that roamed in the darkness where no men walked, baring their fangs. They had growled at her in her dreams, and now she knew in her bones and water that they waited outside, patient as death, certain of their prey. Her.

In the silence Miranda shook herself to break the spell and then she yawned. In this she was followed by Viti and Angus who could not restrain themselves. But none of them spoke.

Viti stood up and moved to the back of the cave and began casting logs and pine-cones over to beside the fire. Miranda brought furs for bedding, tossing them on the cave floor round the fire. Angus busied himself at the Dragon, making sure that all the systems were properly closed down. For each of them the activity helped.

'Lights are fading,' called Angus suddenly. And it was true. The green lights were one by one becoming dim. It was a steady fade, not a fitful dipping and flaring as when a battery is running down. 'Wonder how they power these things?' he asked, speaking to no one in particular. 'They must take quite a charge.' And even as he spoke, the last green lamp blinked out and the only light in the cave was that from the flickering flames. With the darkness every sound seemed to become louder. They could hear the moan of the wind as it blew over the pit outside the cave, sounding like a monstrous pipe, and they could hear the steady gurgle of the river as it raced away into the depths of the cave.

Angus made his way carefully back to the fire and found that Viti was already under his furs and propped up against a rock within easy reach of some dry faggots. 'I'll take first watch,' Viti offered. 'I'm feeling wide awake now.' Angus grunted in reply.

On the other side of the fire Miranda had made a bed. She was now buried under the covers, carefully stripping off the pretty clothes she had donned to please Angus at the beginning of that day. She had found a long woollen shawl among the garments supplied by the forest people. Her dark hair was loose and when her head popped out from the covers, the hair fanned lightly down on to her shoulders and gleamed the colour of dark copper in the firelight. Her skin was almost luminous. 'I'm going to have a wash,' she said.

'Can you see all right?' asked Angus. 'Shall I bring a couple of brands from the fire to light your way?'

'I'll manage,' said Miranda, standing up.

She walked into the shadows, the shawl wrapped round her.

When she had gone, Viti spoke up again. 'So what do you say? Shall I take the first watch? One of us had better stay awake, just in case.'

'I don't trust you,' said Angus slowly.

'Then you're a bigger fool than I thought,' said Viti. 'Listen, we don't know what's out there, but what we do know is that two of us can fight better than one. And if something comes looking for us we'll want the best defence we can give. Have some sense, man. I'm wounded, so do you think I'm going to nobble you in the night? Like hell. I might need your strength tomorrow, and you might need mine.'

Angus grunted as he loosened the tie-strings on his tunic. 'I'll take the first watch,' he said and then added, 'I need a crap.'

Viti rolled over. He lay still and listened as Angus pulled a brand from the fire and then stumbled away to the cave door. He heard a sharp intake of breath at the river end of the cave as Miranda entered the cold water but that was all. He marvelled at her strength and guessed rightly that the cold of the water was helping her in some way with her sadness. And with that vague thought of flowing water and a swimming naked body he drifted into sleep.

Angus was in bed by the fire when Miranda returned. She was shivering and she wriggled quickly under the furs and rolled up into a ball. Angus touched her and her skin was tight and cold as ivory. He tried to caress her and place his lips near her neck, but she pushed his hand away. 'Leave me alone,' she said. 'I have nothing to give.'

She lay shivering beside him, gradually becoming still as her natural warmth returned, and Angus felt a strange loneliness possess him, so accustomed had he become to Miranda needing him and being grateful for the crumbs of his affection. He thought over the day and wondered about the strange man called Lyf. 'Hey,' he whispered, 'that one who calls himself Lyf, what did he mean when he called you Miranda the virgin?'

'I don't know,' she murmured, already drifting off to sleep. 'Perhaps he understood me ... perhaps he knew that I feel a virgin where it counts ... always have ... always will ... even when I've had children (yawn) ... even when (yawn) ... I'm dead ...'

Angus was puzzled and would have asked more. But Miranda's sighing and her soft regular deep breaths told him that she was asleep. Across from them Viti snored. It was a sound such as a cat makes, and was loud in the cave.

Angus drooped despite his desire to keep watch. He could not keep his eyes open, try as he might. He stared at the fire and the dancing flames lulled him. The next snore which broke the silence was his own, but he never heard it.

The fire burned brightly and then burned low. The flames died to a pattern of embers which glowed where the light breeze from the cave door played over them.

Outside, in the wild world, the rain stopped and a wind sprang up, tearing the rain-clouds to tatters. Stars appeared in the rents and a gibbous moon shone out low on the horizon, its grey light, cold and steely, playing over hills and trees.

From above the canopy, the tops of the trees looked like sluggish grey waves as they eased back and forth in the wind. The rain-water which had gathered in the cups of the leaves slopped down to the ground.

Between the trees in the moonlit glades, dark shapes moved with muzzles thrust forward, like javelins. The creatures moved silently and occasionally one would pause and raise its head and howl and then listen while an answering howl sounded from hills miles away. The sabre-toothed wolves were hunting. The pack came to the pit where the cave had collapsed and gathered round its rim. The leader, a creature that stood five feet tall at the shoulder and was covered with stiff white and black fur, sniffed the air, catching the faintest whiff of wood-smoke.

It was about to lead the pack down into the pit when there came a drumming from the trees some distance away. It was a harsh rattling sound and though it was muffled by the trees, it was definitely getting closer. The wolves started and rounded and stared, baring their fangs.

There was movement at the end of the clearing, a bush twitched as it was pushed aside, and into the pale moonlit clearing strode a giant. It was a man. He had broad shoulders and solid thick-set legs and stood an inch under nine feet tall. He wore a cloak of bearskin over his shoulders and the head and snout of the bear formed a cap which made him seem even more huge, adding at least another twelve inches to his height. The paws of the bear hung down over the front of his shoulders and were joined by a gold brooch just above his waist. In his hands the giant held a long staff, the end of which he slapped rapidly against a small wooden drum, setting up echoes in the clearing.

As he approached, the leading wolf snarled, one foot raised, ears flattened and head thrust forward. The giant strode towards it unconcerned, beating out a lively tattoo. It backed off with a growl and the other wolves all withdrew with lips drawn back. At the edge of the slope leading down to the cave the giant banged the drum for one last time and then tossed it back over his shoulder where it hung on a plaited thong. The wolves now stood in a semicircle facing him. The giant drew from beneath his cloak a satchel and from this he removed a lump of meat wrapped in cloth. He unwound the cloth and then threw the joint high into the air and away from the pit.

'Now eat,' he shouted. And as though they were obeying him, the wolves rounded and menaced the meat and tore into it. '. . . And stop bothering me.'

The giant looked up into the sky and his face was caught in the moonlight. He had an ugly deformed face with prominent bulging cheeks and thick lips. But his eyes were bright as chips of glass. His hair was fair and he wore it long, tied back in a pony-tail. He was in his early twenties but his long hair and rough clothes made him seem older.

Satisfied that the wolves were eating he turned and, without a backward glance, headed down into the pit, stepping from rock to rock and using his staff for balance. For all his bulk he moved with grace and ease. He jumped down the last part and came to the cave entrance where he paused, his hands resting on the damp stones. He cocked his head on one side and, hearing nothing except snoring from inside the cave, he ducked down and stepped inside.

The fire was merely a glow and the air was sweet and heavy with the smell of wood-smoke. Silently the giant stepped over to the three sleeping forms which were still as rocks despite the snoring. In the soft glow from the fire he could see their faces. Angus was relaxed and vacant and seemed gentler, too. Miranda was curled on her front like a child and her face was half hidden under the covers. Viti was dreaming and his quick mobile face was scrunched up and his lips were moving.

The giant edged wood into the fire and saw it smoke and then catch. Slowly and carefully he fed the fire and then drew back when Viti stirred. But Viti merely rolled over. The giant crossed the cave, seeming to find his way about with ease. He moved over to the Dragon which looked like a beast asleep. He rubbed his hand appreciatively over the smooth metal plates and tapped them lightly with his knuckles. When he turned away from the Dragon, the drum at his back struck the side of the beast with a clang.

'Who's there?' called a voice. It was Miranda.

The giant glided over to the cave entrance and slipped through without a sound. He climbed quickly up and when half-way to the top stopped and crouched down, becoming invisible among the rocks.

Looking down he could see the cave-mouth partly illuminated by the fire within. After a few moments the wary shape of Angus came padding to the cave door and peered out. He stood for a few moments looking up towards the moonlight, and then, evidently seeing nothing to alarm him, went back inside muttering. There was a soft murmur of voices and then silence again. The giant grinned to himself in the darkness and settled down, wrapping the heavy bearskin round him. He clutched his drum in his arms and prepared to watch out the rest of the night. From far away he heard the howl of a wolf.

11 *Ulysses Weeps*

It was a predictable reaction.

Informed that his son had been involved in some misdemeanour at the Battle Dome, Marcus Ulysses immediately put those forces on whose loyalty he could depend on full alert. He suspected some trickery from the Caesars. The northern legions were solidly for the Ulysses and besides, ever since Viti's trouble with the young relative of the Caesars called Brutus, his father had paid gold to ensure loyalty and to employ spies. Marcus Ulysses was ready to march on Eburacum at a moment's notice.

But then reports arrived linking Viti with some chit of a serving-girl and with one of the young mechanics at the Battle Dome. They seemed to have gone skylarking in the battle-Dragon. There was no evidence of any Caesar involvement. Old Marcus Ulysses was baffled.

He bided his time and later that evening received an Imperial messenger with an invitation to take breakfast the next day with the Praefectus Comitum. This invitation was a kind of code which signified that official business would be conducted in an unofficial manner. Marcus accepted the invitation but made it known in his reply that if he or Viti were harmed or threatened, then he had left instructions for those legions which he controlled to attack Eburacum. It was not an idle threat. Marcus's forces were well armed and mobile and the most effective strike-force in the whole of Britannia. They would be storming the city from their assault crafts and occupying the Imperial Palace by midday unless Marcus Ulysses called a halt in person.

So, the next morning at dawn, Marcus Ulysses arrived in an armoured car at the steps of the Imperial Palace. Tripontifex Britannicus was waiting for him. The man was plainly nervous and kept smiling and dabbing at his lips. 'Glad you could come, Marcus. Lovely morning. Yes, this way. Come right up.'

'Is there anyone else joining us?'

'Yes. Yes. Marmellius Cae—'

'Caesar.'

'Yes. He asked specially if he could join us. He was worried in case you thought that he or any of the Caesars had had a hand in . . . He wanted to assure you himself.'

'I see.'

They entered the State dining-room where a hundred-foot-long table of polished oak stood beneath glittering chandeliers. Incongruously, only one end of the table was laid and this was for just three people. Three boiled eggs stood under their own individual cosies. There was bacon in a silver dish and toast in a rack and warmed red wine.

Marmellius Caesar, the grandson of Julius Caesar XIX, was already seated and waiting. He was a tall, blond young man with an intelligent, well-shaped face and blue eyes. For lack of an alternative he had taken over management of the fortunes of the Caesar family since the death of his grandfather. He stood up when he saw Marcus Ulysses advancing. The two men faced one another, as watchful as beasts at a water-hole. Then Marmellius thrust out his hand showing the palm up. Marcus accepted the greeting and the two men shook hands and then sat down opposite one another.

'I asked Tripontifex to let me be present,' said Marmellius. 'I did not want a civil war breaking out unnecessarily. Your preparations are well known to me. Before you say a word, let me assure you that the Caesars had no part in whatever has happened to your son. Or if I do find that one of my family has been playing games, I will hand him or her over to you for justice. You have my word on that on the soul of my grandfather.'

Marcus looked at the young man, carefully. He could not see any trickery, no obvious sign of lying. And yet . . . He shrugged his massive shoulders which were well braced and padded. 'Shall we eat?' he said, and gestured to the set places. 'The eggs will be cold.'

They ate in silence for a few moments. Then Marcus spoke. 'So. If not the Caesars, then what *has* happened? I have heard garbled reports. What is the news, Tripontifex?'

For answer Tripontifex uncovered a red folder that had been placed by his plate. 'This was prepared for me at four o'clock this morning,' he said. 'It has eyewitness reports. It makes strange reading.'

Marcus took the report and began casually to flip through the pages. It was not a long report and he settled to read it. Tripontifex and Marmellius exchanged glances and both busied themselves with the breakfast.

Most of the report was concerned with the damage done to the Battle Dome. The section that dealt with Viti's disappearance was comparatively short. A survivor, one who had been wounded in the first exchange, described how he had seen Viti draw a knife and throw it, killing one of the guards. Another eyewitness reported seeing Viti firing across the plain. Statistics indicated that Viti had probably killed nine guards. A final report described how he had been seen climbing into the Dragon with Angus. Thereafter the Dragon had charged away, tearing a hole through the wall of the Battle Dome. Finally the Dragon had been lost in the deep forest. The report concluded with the following sentence. 'On the available evidence, it would seem that Victor Ulysses, in company with the Junior Citizens Miranda Duff and Angus Macnamara, deliberately set out to steal the battle-Dragon. It would also seem that they were assisted by persons unknown in escaping from the environs of the Battle Dome. The only conclusion that can be drawn is that this was a deliberate act of sabotage and treachery against the province of Britannia and the Roman State.'

Marcus Ulysses finished reading and set the document down carefully.

'Is this true?' he asked. 'I mean is this a true account? Who prepared it?'

'The Senator Ulpianus in person,' replied Tripontifex, 'who has, as you know, no reason to find against you or your family.'

Marcus grunted. Tripontifex had spoken the truth. The Senator Ulpianus was distantly related to the Ulysses family. And besides, he was known as a man of absolute honour, fearless in his defence of truth, one of the old school. 'Very well then. I hope the search-parties you have sent out looking for them find them. I will add some of my own retinue if I may.' He paused and looked at Tripontifex and Marmellius. Then he said slowly, 'As far as I am concerned my son is dead. If he is found I do not want to look on him. If he is caught alive he is to be treated more harshly than we do our worst criminals. Henceforth he is no longer a Ulysses. He is disinherited. I have said this.' Marcus Ulysses stood up. 'I will arrange for these words to be sent to you in full legal form. And now if you will excuse me I have . . .' His voice trailed away and for a moment the iron jaw worked up and down as though he were chewing on an irksome bit of bacon, but no sounds came out. 'Anyway. I have much to attend to. Much to set in order. Thank you.'

Without waiting for reply, Marcus Ulysses walked away, striding with the measured step he had learned so many years earlier when he was a young officer at the Military Academy here in Eburacum. He paused briefly and blinked in the bright sunlight and then hurried down the steps to his waiting armoured car.

That very day Marcus Ulysses left Eburacum to travel to his estate at Farland Head in the far north.

By evening, as the ruddy sun was setting, he was able to stand looking across the sea to the Isle of Arran. A high sea was running and the waves crashed in, sending spray right up to where the lonely man stood. He was soaked but did not walk away. His only movement was to wipe the cold brine from his face.

12　*The First Day*

It was the dawn chorus that woke Miranda. Even inside the cave it could be heard, a brisk, impatient sound; a calling of hunger and a roaring of wings. Miranda woke first and stretched, only to discover that she was stiff and more than a bit sore where she had lain on the hard cave floor. She stood up giddily and shivered and stepped carefully out of the furs trying not to step on Angus who was sprawled on his back. Miranda realized that her first task was to get the fire going again. She gathered some more wood from the back of the cave, noticing that the green lights had again come on and were burning with a steady but low intensity. She had never been brought up to be curious and so accepted this as part of the new world of which she was a member.

With twigs fed to the white ash, Miranda blew on the embers and was relieved when blue smoke curled up and was quickly followed a few moments later by a small bright yellow flame. For the first time it really struck Miranda just how continuous the vigil must be to keep even something as simple as fire going. She was amazed that the fire had lasted all night and thanked her lucky stars. She added more small twigs and sticks and watched them catch and blaze. And while doing this she suddenly remembered the huge shape she had seen moving in the fitful light of the flames. At the same time she felt a sudden cramping of her body and knew that, fear or not, she needed to go outside and find the place to relieve herself.

Outside the cave she looked up and saw the clear blue sky above the trees. The leaves were pale green and yellow where the sun's rays touched them. The air was crisp and sweet after the rain and even the damp pit in which the cave was located seemed more cheerful. Birds were hopping and darting and arguing everywhere.

The long-drop that Lyf had referred to was a deep trench cut in the ground with a pair of boards for standing on. Miranda now understood the man's warning about not falling in. She crouched, holding her clothes up, and felt vulnerable, imagining eyes in the bushes and up the rocky slope. But all that moved were birds and a curious bumble-bee and a line of ants carrying bits of wood and leaf. She felt herself tickled by blades of grass and told herself, despite her fears, that these were not spiders.

However, something in her spirit responded to the bright living world around her and when she had finished, she felt clean and empty. She saw where a side-stream plunged away, one which did not enter the cave, and guessed that this was the place for washing herself. Someone, perhaps that strange man Lyf, had thoughtfully placed flat standing stones.

Lying on the loose soil near the long-drop was a flattened and hollowed piece of wood which was clearly intended to be a scoop. She picked it up and then dropped it with a scream for a big black spider scampered out from under the paddle and ran up the soil. A marauding bird, obviously unafraid of Miranda, pounced and snaffled up the spider and then flew away. It took a few moments for Miranda to regain her courage and pick up the piece of wood. But when she did, she scattered a lot of soil into the toilet. At the Eburacum Poly she had never been taught how much soil to put down a long-drop. Next she experimented with using the small stream to wash herself. This was the strangest experience she had ever had, and it made her laugh aloud, especially when a black bird with a bright yellow bill perched on a nearby bush and whistled its song to her. But then she hushed herself. She didn't want Angus or Viti to hear her and come to see what was happening.

She need not have worried. When she returned to the cave both men were still hard asleep. She nudged Viti with her foot.

Viti came awake smoothly. Years of training at the Military Academy meant that he slipped from sleep to waking with scarcely a movement. But still his mind lingered in sleep. He emerged from a dream in which someone had shaved off all his hair to the dim light of the cave. 'My turn to watch,' he whispered, almost automatically, and then came fully awake. Miranda was just placing a full billy of water on the fire. 'What's that noise?' he asked. 'It's like a machine.'

'The birds,' said Miranda.

Angus groaned and rolled over. 'What birds?' he muttered.

'Outside. The dawn chorus. Don't you recognize it?'

Both men sat up and blinked as their eyes adjusted.

'Noisy buggers,' said Angus. 'By Jupiter, I'm hungry.' He looked about carefully. 'No sign of your mystery man,' he said to Miranda. 'I told you you were dreaming.'

'I wasn't dreaming,' said Miranda.

Viti looked mystified. 'What mystery man?'

'Miranda saw a giant in the cave. In the middle of the night.'

Viti looked nonplussed. 'What was he doing?'

'Nothing,' said Miranda. 'I don't know. I just saw something.'

'Well I didn't hear anything,' said Viti.

'You were asleep with your mouth open,' said Angus. 'Lot of good you'd have been if there'd really been someone there.'

Viti shrugged. 'Well, I may not have been much good . . . but I had strange dreams last night. Stranger dreams than I've ever had. All about fire. Everything burning, but I wasn't hurt somehow. Then I dreamed someone had shaved my head.' He stopped in embarrassment. 'Anyway. I'm hungry too.'

They all were.

'Is there anything left from last night?' asked Angus.

Miranda shrugged. 'Just some of those herbs, I think.'

'Great,' said Angus, being ironic. 'Can't wait. They gave me the trots last night.'

There was enough of the herb mixture to make a brew, and so they sat by the dying embers of the fire clutching mugs of the hot herb tea and staring at one another while their tummies rumbled.

'Well we're on our own,' said Angus. 'No point in avoiding it. If we want to eat it'll be up to us.' He tossed the dregs of his tea into the cooling ashes of the fire.

He started to get up but suddenly Viti moved with speed and, catching Angus off guard, pushed him sprawling back. Before Angus could do anything, he found himself flipped over on to his face and with his arm in a lock which threatened to dislocate his elbow. 'We've talking to do first,' said Viti. 'Yesterday you wanted to smash my head in . . . I want to settle matters between us now.' Angus squirmed but Viti held him with practised ease. 'Don't worry. I'm not going to kill you. But we're going to talk.'

He released Angus suddenly, rolling him with his knee while he stepped back. Angus sat up, rubbing his elbow and scowling at Viti. 'I wish I'd done for you in the night . . . and don't think I didn't think of it. But Miranda wanted everything quiet.'

'Why?'

'Why what?'

'Why do you want to kill me? Why did you set a trap for me back there in the Battle Dome? I think I know the reason but I want you to tell me.'

Angus cast about. Now that the moment had come he didn't want to use the words that rose in his mind, they had such bitterness for him. 'You made her . . .' he said finally, staring at Viti. 'Do you remember? In that back room . . . the night you had a party you had her . . . you fucked her . . . she told me. I made her tell me.'

Viti, crouching in the ready stance of a wrestler, prepared in case Angus tried to attack him, nodded. 'I know,' he said. 'I remember.' There was a long pause between them. 'Now listen, Angus, to what I'm going to say to you, and show that you've got more than shit for brains between your ears. You were right what you said yesterday – I'm finished in my world – but I'm not dead in this one, and I don't intend to be. I'm a fighter whatever comes. So listen. I'm sorry for what I did to Miranda. But it's done and can't be undone. Anyway, I'm going to leave you two to sort things out together. OK? But don't come after me, Angus. Let this be the end of your feud. OK? I'll take my chance in this world and so must you.' Viti stood up slowly. 'I wish you well.'

He was backing away slowly when Miranda swilled a full billy of cold water over him. Then, before Angus could move, she stepped between them. 'Now listen, the pair of you,' she said and pushed Viti so that he lost his balance and landed flat on his bottom. 'I'm not here in this dark cave because I want to be. I'm here because of both of you.' She turned to Viti. 'You and your silly pride and your silly family and your silly fighting and your cruelty.' Before Viti could speak she turned to Angus. 'And you. You're as bad. You and your silly fighting-machines and your cruelty.' She looked at them both. 'You have cost me a family I loved. You have cost me my innocence. You have cost me things that can never be repaid. Well, I've had enough of you. Both of you. But neither of you is going to go crawling away to be noble and independent. Both of you are responsible and both of you must now protect me. And there'll be no favours and there'll be no more fighting. Is that clear?'

Where had these words come from? Miranda did not know. She just let herself flow and her anger found the words, aided by her necessity.

The two men, one wet, one dry, stared at her open-mouthed.

An hour later they stood at the top of the pit. They had taken anything that might be of use to them from the Dragon and now had a first-aid kit, a pair of binoculars, some hand-tools which could also serve as weapons should the need arise, and a small axe. Each was garbed in the simple, serviceable clothes of the people of the wild wood. For outer garments they wore the furs they had slept in. Angus was tallest and his fur was black, being a stitching – together of two smaller furs. Viti wore the skin of a dappled grey and black creature which might have been a giant goat. Miranda's fur was piebald, brown and white, with a calfskin collar. They felt surprisingly at home and comfortable in their clothing.

Steam was already rising from the grass where the sun shone down through the trees. 'It's going to be a scorcher,' said Angus as he filled their water-bottles from the stream.

Viti, who had had some training in woodland survival, studied the ground. He saw the spoor of the wolves that had gathered there during the night and he saw a single footprint of the giant where the man had paused near the river to throw the meat. He mentioned neither of these but concentrated on the bruised and flattened grass which showed where the people had passed who had been in the cave when they arrived. He could make out where an old path wandered. It led beside the stream-bank for a short distance and then turned right and headed up a shallow hill and into a grove of larch trees.

Viti led the way. He walked with care for he was still somewhat stiff and, though his wounds were healing quickly, they still hurt. The path led through the larch trees and then down into a dell. The grass in the dell grew as high as their arms and the narrow path was like a tunnel. At the bottom of the dell they came to a swampy patch where dark water oozed. Bubbles rose from the deeps, filling the air with a rich smell of eggs and cattle. The small swamp was crossed by a path of shaped stones. This gave them all hope, for the stones indicated a road well trod. They crossed with care for none of them wanted to risk being daubed with the stinking mud. Insects buzzed above the marsh-water and crawled into and over the plants. On a broad-bladed leaf a giant red and blue enamelled dragon-fly opened and closed its wings in the sunshine. Miranda wondered at its beauty for, even on her trips up the River Ouse with Angus, she had never seen one so close.

Beyond the dell the path wove backwards and forwards, steadily making its way upward. Gradually the grass gave way to trees and they entered a dense part of the forest where the tangled shrubs and bushes and dry branches from fallen trees plucked at them and caught in their cloaks. The sky was almost hidden. Beneath their feet the forest floor was damp and soft and their footsteps made no sound, but their breathing was loud and seemed to echo. 'Sh,' said Viti, stopping suddenly. 'Listen.'

They paused with held breath and listened to the silence. About them the trees creaked and popped in the gathering heat but that was the only sound. 'What did you hear?' whispered Angus.

'I don't know. A sort of—'

Viti did not need to finish his sentence for they all heard the steady beating of a drum which seemed to come from somewhere behind them.

'Do you think we're being followed?' asked Angus.

'Is it guards from the Battle Dome?' asked Miranda.

'If it was danger, I don't think they'd advertise themselves like that,' said Viti. 'I don't know. Does it sound threatening?'

This question was addressed to Miranda.

'Not threatening,' she said finally as the distant drum boomed. 'But it is confident. It's saying, "I'm here. Watch out."'

'I say we push on,' said Angus and Viti nodded.

'Yes. We don't know the rules of this place. We don't know what the hell's going on. Come on. Let's hope we find a village or a house soon.' He turned and led the way deeper into the forest.

Occasionally as they tramped they heard the drum, sometimes sounding nearer, sometimes further away, never really close.

Late in the morning they emerged from the forest into the bright sunshine. They were sweaty, tired and scratched. Forest cobwebs had caught in their hair. Angus was sneezing almost uncontrollably as the forest pollens irritated the membranes in his nose. Viti was limping, having tripped on a root and twisted his ankle. Miranda had more than once taken over the role of leader. When the path they were following had crossed other paths, she was the one to decide which way they should go. Viti seemed to defer to her and she did not understand this, nor did she trust it.

Beyond the forest Miranda saw a small brook with grassy banks and she led them to it. 'Here we rest a while,' she said. 'You Viti, soak your feet. Swim if you've a mind to. Angus, bathe your face. Wash your eyes and nose.' Both men did as they were bid. Both were used to taking orders and both in a way wanted to please Miranda. Viti stripped off his boots and then lay on his back with his legs over the bank and his feet in the cold tumbling water. He stared at the sun under the cover of his closed eyes and saw redness. Angus moved further upstream and plunged his head under the water and blew bubbles lustily through mouth and nose. He repeated this several times as though it were a ritual he enjoyed, as though he were flushing out his entire head. At last he drank and gargled and spat out and finally lay back in the soft grass, panting.

'Can you eat grass?' asked Angus suddenly.

'Cows do,' offered Viti.

'Well we might have to if we don't find a house or a village soon,' said Miranda. 'Come on. On your feet. We've got to come to somewhere soon.'

'We might have been going in a circle,' said Angus.

'No,' said Viti, pulling on his boots. 'I've had my eye on the sun. We've been walking east – well, more or less.'

'Then what time is it?' asked Angus somewhat aggressively.

'About midday.'

'Hm. Well listen. I reckon that we should keep walking for another couple of hours or so and then we ought to think about catching some food and building a shelter for the night. We don't want to be stumbling about in the dark.'

'Right,' said Miranda. 'Then the sooner we start—'

'Look,' said Viti, his voice just above a whisper. He was pointing at the stream. They all stared.

Lazily a large brown trout was working its way upstream. It held still against the current, its tail moving slowly.

'Catch it,' said Angus. But his voice was too loud and with a swirl of its tail the fish was gone like an arrow into the shadows on the far bank.

'Now if we'd caught that,' said Miranda pointedly, 'we wouldn't be facing hunger. We've a lot to learn. Come on.'

They followed the stream for some three hundred yards and came to a place where the stream widened and ran over banks of shingle. Here they crossed the river and struck a course which led them up a hillside. There was a path of sorts which burrowed through the bracken. In some places the bracken was so high that it formed an arch over their heads.

After what seemed like an hour of toil they came into open grassy ground at the top of the hill. From here they could look out over the rolling tops of trees. 'Look over there,' called Miranda. She was pointing to where smoke was rising from the forest. 'That's bound to be a settlement.'

'And you look over here,' said Angus. He was pointing behind them. 'Recognize that?'

Far in the distance, rising from the dense mat of trees, was the smooth, alien shape of the Battle Dome. They could not pick out the details but the dome was clearly damaged. Part of the curved roof was blackened. Looking through the binoculars they could see where the surface was blistered and torn. Something sparkled in the sunshine. It was a flyer gliding down the magnetic pathway from Eburacum.

'The blaze must have been spectacular,' said Viti, almost wistfully.

'They'll soon rebuild it,' said Augus, and his voice was somewhat hushed as he felt a pang of sadness. How much he would have loved to be part of the rebuilding.

'Come away you two,' said Miranda. 'We'll wonder about that when we've found food and a place to sleep.'

They plunged down the slope away from the Battle Dome and in the direction of the blue smoke that Miranda had seen rising. Soon they found themselves lost in a maze of thickets. The path seemed to have petered out or they had missed a turning in their scrambling. Every direction was identical. 'Now where?' muttered Viti.

For each of them there was a sudden feeling of panic. Without the faint path to guide them the forest seemed to press closer. It was claustrophobic. They could wander in circles. With the wild grasses almost up to their necks and the roots tripping them and the thorns scratching at their hands and faces, no one would ever find them.

In desperation Viti pushed through some blackthorn and suddenly slipped. He bumped down a bank, crashed through some bramble and found himself sitting on a narrow lane which was like a tunnel under the trees. In front of him, brazen and aromatic, was a pile of fresh horse-dung. It was already the focus of attention for a myriad bottle-green flies. The walkway was obviously in frequent use. Up and behind him Viti could hear Miranda and Angus calling for him. Their voices came to him muffled by the dense thickets though they were no more than a few yards from him.

'Down here,' he called. 'Take your time. I've found a path. A real one. I'll keep calling. Work your way along. You find an easier way down.'

Minutes later Angus and Miranda broke through the bushes at a place where the blackthorn was less dense. They stood, panting and scratched, on the soft loam and gravel of the lane and stared up and down as though they couldn't believe their eyes.

'This way,' said Viti. 'The smoke we saw was over this way.' And he set off at a brisk walk.

About half an hour later the trio heard children singing ahead of them, and when they rounded a bend they found themselves facing a high gateway which closed the entire lane. The singing came from beyond.

The gate was made of stout timber planks which had been woven together and lashed with hempen rope to thick uprights. At each end of the gate, thick tree-trunks were sunk into the ground and these supported the gate's weight. Each of the trunks was carved as a totem pole with grotesque images of faces. To each of these trunks were joined walls of woven saplings which stretched away under the trees of the forest. These became part of a high and dense hedge. The construction would not withstand an army or a fire, but it would, as Viti observed, keep animals at bay. The gate was topped with staves of wood which had been sharpened to points and hardened in fire. Set high between the staves and each in its own niche were human skulls which stared down at the trio balefully. The skulls were decked with chains of flowers.

'Romans,' said Angus to Viti, nodding to the skulls. 'Bound to be. Come on, lift the latch and we'll go in.'

But it was Miranda who raised the rough wooden hasp. Then Angus put his shoulder to the gate and it swung inwards easily and they walked through and into a village. The gate swung closed behind them under its own weight. They found themselves standing beside a playground which obviously belonged to a small schoolhouse. This building nestled under the branches of a giant beech tree with pale green leaves which grew just beyond the village walls. In front of them, and following the gentle curve of the lane, were neat houses made of timber, some with thatched roofs and some with shingles of dark shiny wood.

The children in the playground stopped singing when they saw the three and gathered at the fence facing on to the lane and stared at them. Viti, who since his discovery of the well-kept lane had taken on something of the role of leader, asked the children if there was an inn in the village where they could get food and lodging. Hearing him speak, the children burst into gales of laughter and several of them spoke to him in a soft, fluid language complete with animated gestures. This was the language of the woodlanders and Viti, Angus and Miranda looked at one another baffled. The children pointed at the schoolhouse and moments later a young man wearing glasses, and whose wispy hair told of premature baldness, sallied forth, calling to the children. He stopped in his tracks when he saw Viti, Miranda and Angus. But he seemed to size the situation up very quickly and when he spoke to them it was in halting Latin but with a pleasing lilt.

'You are sent by Lyf?' he said, turning the statement into a question. 'You will see Madame Bella.' He pointed down the road. 'Food.' He mimed eating. 'Drink.' An exaggerated gurgling accompanied this. 'Sleep.' A snore. 'Madame Bella will help.'

'Which house is hers?' asked Angus.

'You can't mistake Bella,' said the schoolteacher, clearly not understanding the question. 'She is . . .' he made a gesture which might have been suggestive of large breasts and an ample figure. He smiled. 'Sorry, I have not the words. She is a head-man round here. You will find her. No mistake.' He began shepherding the children back into the schoolroom. 'Go now. She is waiting,' he called, and then disappeared after the last of the children into the schoolhouse and closed the door.

'He's a bloody nut-case,' said Angus.

'Well at least we seem to be expected,' countered Miranda.

'Then how did they knew we were going to end up here?' he asked. '*We* didn't. We could have wandered in any direction.'

Miranda shrugged. 'Perhaps they can read the future,' she said simply.

Angus sniffed. 'Well good luck to them. But it doesn't take too many smarts to figure out we'd be hungry and tired. So I say let's go and find this Belly or whatever she's called. I could eat a horse, and probably will.'

They walked on down the road away from the school. Gradually the plan of the village became apparent. Essentially it was a crossroads set in a large clearing in the forest. Giant beech trees surrounded them, towering beyond the wooden walls, marking the perimeter of the clearing. Wooden houses faced on to the road, each with a small enclosed area in front where vegetables and flowers were growing. Small fences kept chickens and occasionally pigs and goats from wandering into the gardens or out on to the road. Most of the houses were built in two storeys with the lower rooms open. It was here that the bigger animals slept.

Above, and reached by narrow steps or a ladder, were the rooms where the humans dwelt. As they passed the first of the houses a woman appeared at one of the windows and looked down at them. The heads of numerous small children joined her, staring down into the street with the sober unselfconscious gaze of the deeply curious. The woman called something but not one of the three could understand her. Then she put her fingers to her mouth and blew a piercing whistle. Immediately people came tumbling out of houses further down the street. There was a wizened old man with only one leg who hobbled on a crutch into the middle of the street. He danced in a circle before them and had, as Miranda observed to herself, the cheekiest face she had ever seen. His eyes were bright and his face was the colour of tanned leather. There were tall, big-breasted women with masses of copper hair held back with tortoiseshell combs. They laughed boldly and scratched in their armpits while children hung round their legs and stared. Young men with their hair tied in pigtails and their faces smudged with soot, young women with flour on their hands and arms, old women with bandy legs and nutcracker jaws, older men with wavy white hair and fierce angry faces: all gathered and stared and watched and called as the trio passed down the lane towards the small square which marked the town centre. The smell of the village, a mixture of smoke, cooking and animals, struck them as they advanced down the roadway.

At the centre of the square there was a single boulder made of a reddish stone in which small pieces of quartz glittered. It

193

was a bulky but smooth rock with deep score-marks on its surface and came up to Angus's shoulder height. None of them had seen its like before, which was not surprising for this rock had begun its slow journey to Britannia from the far northern fiords thousands of years earlier. It had fallen from an exposed rock-face on to the back of one of the creeping glaciers and had been carried all the way to this part of the land.

Close to the stone, a spring of bright clean water bubbled up to the surface of the earth. Low gutters guided the water in a spiral round the boulder and away through the village.

The trio stood near the boulder while the village square filled with people. Crowds arrived from all quarters of the village to stare at them. Finally Viti took the initiative. 'We are looking for the house of Madame Bella,' he said. His speech was greeted with laughter and the old man who had danced before them reached forwards with his crutch and poked Viti in the midriff. He spoke to them quickly and excitedly but the only word they could understand was Bella. The old man grew impatient and said something to the crowd which made all the young people laugh and the women cover the children's ears with their hands. Finally he pointed with his crutch to a house which stood alone at one of the corners of the square. It was a larger house than any of the others and as they turned and looked the large upstairs door opened and a shortish woman with fiery red hair emerged. She wore a green dress which was hitched up with a golden sash. On her feet were blue sandals. Her face was merry and bold. She beckoned to them and spread her arms wide in a gesture the meaning of which was obvious and friendly but which also seemed to have something ritualistic about it. Then she called a few words and the crowd parted and many hands urged them forwards. They came to the low gate outside the house.

'It's a bloody knocking-shop,' murmured Angus.

'Sh,' said Miranda, 'she'll hear you.'

'Bah. So what. She won't speak our language.'

The woman laughed down at them and in faultless and accentless Latin said, 'Welcome to the house of Bella. And I'm sorry, no it's not a knocking-shop, well not officially, but an inn. I hope you'll stay here all the same.'

'You speak Latin,' said Viti somewhat incredulously.

'Of course. An innkeeper must have many tongues. But come on in. There's water for washing and food on the table and soft beds for sleeping.'

'What about the cost?' asked Angus abruptly.

'Already paid for. Lyf paid. Didn't he tell you?' They shook their heads. 'Well isn't that the man all over? Never tells the left hand what the right hand is doing. No matter. Come on in, you look like something a dog's chewed up.'

The three moved towards the gate which led into the small garden in front of Bella's inn. Suddenly there came a commotion in the crowd behind them. A bovine-looking young man with tight curly reddish-brown hair had pushed himself to the front of the crowd and now knocked aside the restraining crutch which the old man held in front of him. He pointed at Angus and said something obviously insulting.

'So what's his problem?' said Angus squaring his shoulders.

Madame Bella called something down to the young man but he just spat on the ground and again addressed his question to Angus.

'He wants to know what you think of this village,' called Bella. 'He doesn't like the way you've been looking at things.'

'Well tell him to get stuffed,' said Angus, a sudden anger flaring in him.

And indeed, anger was now a part of Angus. Since his departure from the Battle Dome, the constraints which had held him in check and made him kind were removed. A wild spirit, quick to anger and quick to fight, had emerged, liberated by the wild wood. 'Tell him to mind his own fucking business.'

Bella shrugged and with a glance of sympathy towards Miranda made ready to translate. Members of the crowd, sensing rather than understanding what was to happen, drew back. But before she could so much as clear her throat, Viti stepped forwards and raised his hands. 'Tell him we're tired, we're hungry and we're friends of Lyf. Tell him we're grateful for friendship, slow to anger, pitiless in rage, lovers of wine and connoisseurs of a fine soft bed. Tell him if he wants to "talk" to us later he is welcome. Perhaps he'll share a drink with us, but he might have to listen to our snores.'

Bella laughed and translated, speaking the words with Viti's emphasis. The crowd laughed and looked at the young man with the curly hair and angry mien, for the next move was now with him. He looked angry for a moment, then confused and finally he laughed. He called out some words which Bella translated as 'He says that he and his mates'll get you pissed-under-table another night.' She paused and then waved her arms like a woman shooing chickens away from a bucket of corn. The crowd began to disperse, talking loudly among themselves and with many a backward glance as they returned to their varied occupations in the village. 'And now you come on in,' she said. 'Come up these steps. Don't worry any about the pigs and goats. They won't hurt you.'

Bella's inn was surprisingly large. It extended from the small garden near the road right back almost to the perimeter fence. Inside the wooden front door Miranda, Viti and Angus found themselves in a large open room with tables and chairs. 'This is where all the guests eat,' said Bella. 'You serve yourself from whatever's on offer.' She pointed to the far end of the room where hung a large, heavy metal flat-plate. It was suspended from the roof on four chains. Black cooking-pots stood on the plate puffing out steam. A boy of about ten years, perched up on a stool, was stirring one of the pots. Angus paused. The mechanic in him rebelled against what he was seeing. 'Where's the heat?' he asked. 'Where's the fire? How do you keep those pots hot?'

Bella frowned. 'The usual way,' she said. 'Electricity. We tap the forest. Like with the lighting. What do you think we are, savages? You've a lot to learn, my lad.'

Tentatively Angus touched the range with the tip of his finger and pulled his hand back sharply. The boy looked on in astonishment. Then, carefully, he spat on to the range and the spittle frothed. He spoke one word, 'Hot', and then shook his finger at Angus as though admonishing a child. So serious was the young boy that they all laughed, even Angus.

'Satisfied?' asked Bella. 'Now come on, you can eat later. I'll show you your rooms.'

At the end of the room, beyond the cooking-range, were three doors. 'That door,' said Bella pointing to the door on the left, 'leads down to the byre. Sorry about the smell but you'll get used to it. Good for a hangover so I'm told. Makes you feel warm and safe on winter nights, too. Now this door,' she pointed to the door on the right, 'leads down to the bakehouse and laundry and communal baths. You'll all be going down there shortly, I shouldn't wonder. And this way,' she opened the middle door, 'leads up to the bedrooms. Now I take it you two men don't mind sharing a room. You can sleep top to tail if you want. It's either that or one of you can go in a hammock down below.' She turned to Miranda. 'You've got a room of your own,' she said and looked at her kindly. 'That is if that is what will please you the most. Lyf gave no directions. I'm reading your mind.' This was said so directly that Miranda did not know whether it was literally true. 'I prefer a room of my own,' said Miranda quickly.

'Right, follow me.' Bella led them through the middle door and up a short ladder. They came to a maze of corridors. Green lights glowed in the dark corners. The building had clearly been improvised as it was being built and new rooms had been added on as necessary. 'This is the room I've put you two in,' she said to Angus and Viti, throwing open one of the doors. 'It's my son Gwydion's room, but he's not here at present and he won't mind.'

The room was simple and unadorned. The walls were white-washed and a single window looked down into a corner of the byre where a rooster, perched on a fence, cocked its head and looked up at them. The bedroom had one large double bed covered with a brightly coloured woven spread. 'It's all aired so you should be all right. You can decide how you want to sleep.'

Angus threw his sack down at one side of the bed. 'This'll do for me,' he said. 'I reckon I could sleep on a rope if I had to.' Viti shrugged and moved round to the other side. 'Fortune acquaints one with strange bedfellows,' he said. 'Or something like that.' He spoke to Bella. 'You are very kind and we are grateful. Don't worry. We'll make out.' Angus looked up at the ceiling, but said nothing.

'Well, when you've had a chance to settle in and have a wash, come down for a drink and some food. There's not too many guests expected tonight.'

She closed the door. 'We'll let them get used to one another,' she whispered to Miranda with a wink. 'Now this way.' She led Miranda up more steps and along a long corridor and finally round a corner to the right. She threw open a small door. 'Here we are, this is your room.'

Miranda stepped inside and immediately felt a tightness in her throat. She wanted to cry. The room was bright and cheerful. There were flowers in a vase and their perfume mingled with the comfortable smell of linen that has been warmed in the sun. To one side was an alcove in which was a simple tub with a tap and the wide rose of a shower. Opposite was a single bed tucked into a corner under the angle of the roof, and a bunch of dried herbs was pinned to the wall near the pillow. On the floor was a rough mat and the late afternoon sun poured in through the half-opened window. Miranda heard the sound of birds squabbling over crumbs and the deep lowing of cows, gathering in the long grass, knowing that milking-time will soon arrive. Somewhere a dog barked and a cat squawked, but these sounds seemed far away. She cried at the sudden security after the doubt of the journey and the strangeness of men. She cried and solid arms went round her and held her close. 'I'm all right,' murmured Miranda.

'Of course you are all right. But I thought you'd like a place of your own, a place where you can unwind.'

'You are a mind-reader. This is so like my own room at home.' She sat down on the bed and felt the quilt with her hands, exploring the different fabrics. 'Everything is so strange and yet . . .' Her voice trailed away and she looked round the room, taking in its simplicity and comfort. 'I feel at home.' She blushed at how childish and inadequate her words seemed. 'That's silly isn't it? Perhaps I'm just tired.'

Bella stood solid as a gatepost and with her hands twisted in her golden sash. 'Once I was caught in a thunderstorm up on the Moors. Dark as evening it was, though it was only eleven in the morning. The lightning was dancing on the hills and the rain came down like arrows of glass. I'd never seen anything like it and I was all alone. Well I found a hole in a bank under a clump of bracken and I poked my bum in and settled down. I felt at home there. I watched the storm come and I watched it pass a day later. Home is where you feel safe, that's all. Nothing mysterious about it.'

Miranda looked directly at Bella. 'Do you know what has happened to us?'

'I know some of it. Enough. I know when people need to let go.'

'Did you know we would be arriving here?'

'I knew it would be here or elsewhere or nowhere. I'm honoured that my inn was chosen.'

'You sound like Lyf.'

'Is that bad?'

'I don't know. I don't know anything. I'm afraid and I'm not afraid.'

Bella crossed and sat down on the bed beside Miranda. 'You know, in this village I'm called one of the wise women. I can cure warts and such. I can set bones and rub away pain. I can join with birds and spiders and my house is a house of peace because I have walked into the grave so far and have seen through the door of death.' Miranda, wide-eyed, began to speak but Bella hushed her and held her hands. 'Listen, child. Release the past. Forget the future. Cry when you need to but BE. Be blessed. Blessed be.' Then Bella wet the middle finger on her left hand with her spit and touched Miranda's eyes and the mid-point of her forehead. 'There. A bit of witchcraft to put you at ease. There are many trials ahead but you will never be given more to suffer than you can bear and if it is your parents you are thinking about, I can get a message to them to put them at ease.'

Miranda smiled at that and nodded. 'I would like that,' she said and looked round the room with a sigh. 'I feel better now. Thank you for talking to me. This is a room I can rest in.' Her gaze travelled round the bare white walls. 'Why are there no pictures?' Then she noticed something above the lintel of the door. It was a hole, like a small cupboard, but far too high and small to be of any obvious use. 'What's that?' she asked, pointing.

Bella stood up and crossed the room and, standing on tiptoe, was just able to reach into the niche above the door. 'This is where the guardian of the room lives,' she said and lifted down a human skull. The lower jaw had been wired in place and all the teeth were intact. 'This is why you feel at home. This is the skull of my great-grandmother. Her name was Polly and she was a powerful witch for the times. With her on guard there's nothing can come in here that could cause you harm. Here, hold her for a minute.' Bella handed the skull over and Miranda took it gently and gingerly. 'Go on, hold it properly. It won't bite you and it won't break. But don't you drop it all the same.'

Miranda held the skull and looked into its vacant orbits and the cavity which once held the soft tissues of the nose. She rubbed her thumb over the solid bone where the chin had been. She tried to imagine the face as it was in life, laughing at a joke perhaps or serious at a wake; and she failed. 'What did she look like?' she asked.

'A bit like me but taller and bigger all round. Same hair, though. She was a right tyrant, with a temper on her that could blister the paintwork. I can just remember her. She died when I was seven.'

'Do you have all the heads of your family?'

'Not all of them. But quite a few. Some are in the foundations. Some are in the walls. Some are dedicated as guardians, that is if they wish it. Polly did.' Bella took the skull back and rubbed her hand over the crown fondly. 'So there you are. That's why you feel safe here.' She crossed the room and reached up and popped the skull back in its niche. 'Now you rest. I'm sure you've got a lot more questions, but they can all keep. All will be well. You'll see.'

With that Bella closed the door, and Miranda for the first time for what seemed an age found herself alone. After a few moments she crossed to her window and pushed it wide open.

The sill was a solid beam of timber and she could perch easily and look out.

Her room was at the very back of the house and set off to one side from the main body of the building. Looking back and down she could see under the house to the byre where the cattle and pigs lived. Most of the rear of the inn was built up on stilts and Miranda could see the pillars and beams which supported the building. They were of stout oak and were polished to a glossy nut-brown where the pelts of the animals rubbed against them. Looking the other way Miranda could see over the perimeter fence and out into the wild wood. Movement caught her eye. Stepping under the trees came a creature the like of which she had never seen. It had the head of a cock but the body of a lizard. It dragged its length along and came right up to the perimeter fence and there began pecking at the loose foliage that grew between the interwined stakes. Miranda hardly dared breathe. In the gentle light under the forest canopy the feathers that made up the creature's neck and crown shimmered turquoise and bottle-green. Once it raised its head and opened its beak and uttered a clear high note. Then the creature moved on, oblivious of Miranda, and with a final swish of its scaly tail disappeared under the trees.

Miranda came to herself with a start. She realized she must have been dreaming. She looked in vain for any sign of where the creature had passed, but the shadows were growing dark under the trees as the evening advanced. Men and women were moving in the byre under the house. The pigs and piglets had been driven back to their quarters and the four cows were gathered in a shed where they were being milked. Miranda could hear the spurt of the milk as it frothed into the bucket. She looked at her own hands which were dirty and her fingernails black. 'A wash,' she thought decidedly and stripped off her clothes.

As she sat in the tub with the warm water round her there came a knock at her door and a girl of seven or so popped her head round the door and then came in. She carried clothes which she deposited on the bed with great care as though they might break. She was a serious child and she spoke to Miranda with a torrent of liquid sounds to which Miranda nodded although she did not understand a word. Apparently satisfied, the child withdrew.

Some time later, feeling refreshed and wearing a bright blue blouse and skirt and a red shawl, Miranda left her room and made her way down to the dining-room. She was starving.

When the door clicked shut the two men found themselves staring at one another.

'Now don't you go getting any funny ideas,' said Angus. 'I'm putting a pillow in the middle of the bed and if you so much as touch it, I'll bloody belt you.'

'What are you afraid of?'

'Nothing.'

They glared at one another.

'And I don't want any snoring either.'

'I don't bloody snore.'

'Yes you do.'

'Bloody don't. You snore.'

They glared even more angrily.

'Oh, what the hell,' said Viti finally. 'This is ridiculous. I'm going for a wash down below.' He stamped out of the room.

Minutes later he was standing under a stream of warm water which cascaded from a wooden pipe. He was in a communal bath-house which seemed to have been modelled after the Roman pattern. Other men were there whom Viti guessed were newly arrived guests of the inn. After a short time Angus joined him.

'Do you smell that food?' he asked. 'God, I've never been so hungry all my life.'

When they returned to their room they found that fresh clothes had been provided. They pulled these on, and feeling slightly self-conscious for the clothes were not the best of fit, they made their way down to the dining-room.

There they ate and drank their fill of stew and wine. And when they were wiping their plates with the last of a loaf of coarse wholemeal bread, Miranda entered.

She was so beautiful she almost seemed to glow. They made

room for her, clumsy in their desire to be gallant.

But it was not a happy meal. Tiredness was heavy upon all of them and when Miranda had eaten they nodded and yawned and by mutual unspoken consent made their way to bed.

That night Miranda lay still in the darkness and listened to the silence. Her window was open. Occasionally she could hear one of the cows stamping and blowing. Somewhere far away a man was singing and the sound of his voice came to her fitfully on the breeze. She heard the trees creak and rustle and they seemed to speak softly to her, telling her to sleep. In her dreams she was a child again, and a woman with a firm jaw and hair the colour of flame was telling her a story about a magic waterfall.

In the men's room two figures lay back to back in the gloom. They snored almost in unison but with difference of pitch, creating harmony. Neither moved.

So ended the first day.

13   Incidents at the Inn during the First Few Months

Within days, life at Bella's inn settled into a routine for Angus, Viti and Miranda. They were each given jobs about the inn and that gave them a sense of purpose and a feeling of belonging. They also started to attend, for two days a week, the small school they had encountered on their arrival at the village. They began to learn the language of the village. This language was quite different from the Latin they had learned as part of the Roman world. Not only were the sounds different, but they had to learn new letters. They were also greatly taught by the children who were tireless in teaching them slang, rude words, the names of trees and the words of songs.

They progressed. None of them was particularly gifted with language but gradually they began to get a grip on their surroundings and to rely less and less on Bella for translation. They also began to fit into the life of the small community and discover themselves in other ways.

Miranda in the kitchen

Miranda turned her catering skills to good use, and soon sweet and savoury sauces and garnishings began to add variety to the roast meat and broiled fish, stew and soups that were the staple fare of the inn. She also grew accustomed to the frank sexuality of the woodlanders. The women who worked in the kitchen talked about love and sex all the time. They exchanged frank details of how well their men were performing in bed or who had cast eyes at whom or how long couples had spent out under the trees. There was easy rivalry too among the women and they joshed Miranda about Angus and Viti, teasing her for details about what they were like as lovers. When Miranda said she was having nothing to do with either of them, the women in the kitchen cast their eyes to heaven as if to say, 'What a waste!' Some gave her advice about the men of the village, who to watch out for, who to keep clear of and who was fancying her. Sometimes it became a trial for her, but by and large Miranda kept her sense of fun. But when she could, she spent time alone in her room or out walking under the trees or talking to Bella, who kept an eye on her.

Bella arranged for a message to be sent to Miranda's mother and father telling them that she was well and that she hoped that some day she would have a chance to see them again. And in this there was deceit, for though Bella said the message was delivered and a verbal message carried back of love and tenderness, and that all was well at Miranda's home, the message never reached the mother and father for they were no longer in Eburacum.

Within hours of the escape from the Battle Dome, Miranda's mother and father had been rounded up and charged as accessories to the crime. They were evicted from their house. Their goods were sold at auction and at about the time when Miranda. Viti and Angus were entering the village, Eve and Wallace were on their way to the Caligula Detection Centre, chained to the walls of a prison wagon. The law of the Romans was swift, inflexible and ruthless. We shall meet Eve and Wallace one more time before the end of the tale.

Bella reasoned as follows: 'How will it serve Miranda now to know what has happened to her parents? There is nothing she can do except grieve. Later, when she is stronger, she can face the truth. Perhaps wiser heads than mine can tell her.'

Glad to know that all was well with her parents in Eburacum, Miranda relaxed and chattered to Bella as though she were a cross between an elder sister and a grandmother. Bella found this charming and flattering, and did her best to help the turbulent young woman. When Miranda told her about her dream of the cockatrice, she was thoughtful, for she well knew that such creatures existed though they were rarely seen and then only by people with special sight, inner sight, spiritual sight:

people with eyes that could not be fooled. She watched Miranda with care, and at night and in the morning she prayed to the great mother that lives in all things to protect her and guide her and keep her whole.

Viti in the byre

Viti worked in the byre under the house, mucking out the pigs and cattle, gathering eggs from the hen-house and keeping the stables sweet. The byre was a warm place of rich smells and ooze. At first the smell made him gag but gradually it became part of his life. To protect the byre from evil, branches from a rowan tree were tacked to the beam above the entrance.

In the morning Viti drove the four cows that were owned by the inn out through a gate in the perimeter fence and into an enclosure under the trees. Here the grass was long and succulent and the cows could roam at will and scratch their hides on the forest trees. In the evenings he brought them back for milking. Viti's last chore for the day was to sweep out the byre, spread fresh straw and then cart the muck out to an allotment where a wizened old man dug it into the ground.

Viti's special responsibility was to feed the pigs and keep them clean. Slowly he discovered, much to his astonishment, that he had a natural way with animals and especially pigs. A story best illustrates this. One night the sow rolled in her sleep and crushed one of her litter of piglets. In the morning when Viti brought her food, the giant beast was beside herself with grief and kept nosing the small dead form. The danger was that she would become so preoccupied with the one dead piglet that she would neglect the others, and this indeed started to happen. The surviving members of the litter ran round her screaming and squealing for the nipple, for food; but she ignored them or kicked out. Viti knew that the dead piglet had to be removed from the sty and, since there were no other men about to help, it fell to Viti's lot to swing his legs over the stout fence which restrained the pigs in their sty and advance on the crazed mother. She eyed him through staring eyes. Her head lowered and began to sway from side to side ominously. And Viti sang to her. He didn't know what made him do it. His song was a natural crooning, a mixture of soft sounds and repetition, a bit like a lullaby. The sow paused in her swaying, and then she backed off with a series of short sharp grunts and ran fast and low round the enclosure. Viti thought she might charge but instead the creature returned to the dead piglet and pushed it with her snout as though urging it to wake up. Viti advanced until he was no more than an arm's reach away from the sow. She looked at him with glittering eyes. At this moment the man was at his most vulnerable. Had the pig chosen to charge, she could have bowled him over like a skittle and then gored him. But she stayed still, grunting to herself. Slowly Viti bent down and, without taking his eyes off the sow, grasped the small carcass. He lifted it to his chest and cradled it. Then he began to walk backwards, crooning softly all the while, until finally he felt the rough fence in his back. Holding the dead piglet firmly in one arm, he reached up with the other arm and gripped one of the support bars. Using the muscles that had been hardened in him at the Military Academy, he hoisted himself up and was able to jump back and out of the sty. He was none too soon, either. For as he jumped down on the far side, the giant sow squealed and ran and a hundredweight of muscle and grief charged through the place where he had stood.

There was no one to witness what had happened and Viti sat for several minutes with his back to the sty fence and thought about how foolish he had been to take such a risk. But then he heard squealing from the sty and when he looked, he saw all the little piglets feeding at the teats and the sow standing still, just chewing. He thought no more about it except to find a small corner of the cow-pasture where he could bury the small body.

Occasionally, as he moved in the byre, Viti saw Miranda at her window and sometimes he watched her when she went for a walk. Their past lives seemed so remote. Almost they seemed to belong to other people. Viti would have liked to say something to Miranda but he did not know how to begin or even what he wanted to say and so he left it. As far as he was concerned, the past was a sleeping dog.

Then one day a man called at the inn and left a folded paper for Viti. It was a broadsheet with a full-face picture of Viti and a large-print caption: WANTED. Below this was an announcement that old Marcus Ulysses had publicly disowned and disinherited his son and that henceforth the boy was an outlaw with a price on his head. 'So you'd better grow eyes in the back of your head from now on,' said the man with a smile and went his way.

Angus in the tall trees

Angus became a woodsman and general handyman. His natural aptitude for machinery came in useful not only at the inn but in the village. He repaired and improved a windmill that drove a water-pump close to the village square. He improvised a rheostat in the kitchen of the inn and this made the cooking more predictable, especially the baking of bread. Indeed so successful was the rheostat that demand for the small gadget grew in the village and Angus ended up spending some of his time working with a local craftsman called Damon and turning the rheostats out by the dozen. This led to a friendship and Angus found himself enjoying the company of Damon, who maintained the electrical system of the village.

Try as he might, Angus could not figure out or guess why the current flowed the way it did or account for the strange fluctuations that occurred in the lighting and heating at Bella's inn. Roman education had never equipped him to think in a theoretical way. If a thing worked he could apply that knowledge in a variety of logical ways but beyond such certainty lay theoretical fog. This was frustrating. One of the effects on Angus of his departure from the secure world of the Battle Dome was that he began to ask questions. His brain started to come alive. After all, it is only a short leap from asking why the power in a line fluctuates to asking why food distribution is erratic. Or given that there is a simple law which describes magnetism or the effects of gravity, why is there no simple law to explain human beings? Or is there? Is it perhaps that our social customs conceal the law? In the first few weeks after his arrival in the village, such questions did not form themselves distinctly in Angus's mind, but they were shaping. He began to think for himself.

One day, frustrated that a power line which he had connected to a lamp in the byre kept failing, he called on Damon and asked the man to show him how the power system worked. 'I'll show you,' said Damon, 'but it won't make you happy.' Angus blew a raspberry at that. 'Bugger happiness. I want to know why the fucking lamp keeps going on and off.'

In Damon's workshop Angus was able to study the living cables which Damon grew by the mile. The cable was grown from a plant like supple-jack and was started in tubs which were fed with a brown slurry which contained a high quantity of iron and some traces of copper chloride as well as other minerals. Also living in the water were small organisms not unlike yeast which had an important effect on the growth of the supple-jack. 'Get the proportions wrong,' said Damon, spitting into the brew, 'and it starts to stink and nothing can grow.' Angus nodded and thought back to the Channel Bridge he had known so many years ago when he was a boy. He remembered the careful way the kelp was forced to grow.

Angus cut one of the mature cables in section and found that the wood was very fibrous. Moreover at its core were lines of blue-black fibre. By experiments he was able to determine that only these fibres carried the current and the external fibres were insulation. He also discovered that a severed cable died, and as it died it lost its ability to convey electricity in a coherent way. So life was important to the transmission of power. That astounded him. It did not explain the fluctuations but it gave him an inkling, for was not life itself one of the most erratic and unpredictable things of all time?

On one occasion Angus accompanied Damon when he was cabling up a new house. Two years earlier when the house was planned and the garden prepared, Damon had started some cables growing. Each week since then he had visited the cable-tubs placed near the foundations of the house and had checked that the plant-food was correct and that the cable was growing steadily. As the months passed he guided the supple-jack out through the perimeter fence and towards a tall beech tree several hundred yards into the forest. As the supple-jack cable grew Damon trimmed off any side-buds or root fibres and wrapped the wounds in a cloth soaked in the growing-medium.

At the selected beech tree the supple-jack was guided up the trunk in spirals. Damon had bedded pegs into the tree so that he could climb. When Angus visited the tree, the supple-jack was just reaching the top of the tree and was ready to be connected.

The two men climbed together. At certain places Damon stopped and performed a ritual that Angus did not understand. He pressed his forehead against the tree and then the palms of his hands. He muttered words to himself. Angus watched him and finally asked, 'Who are you talking to?'

'The tree.'

'Huh. Ask a silly question and . . . Why? Why do you talk to the tree?'

Damon rested back against the trunk and thought for a while. Obviously he had never asked himself the question before. 'It feels like the right thing to do,' he said finally.

'But why?'

'Why! Why! I don't know why. I just do it. Because I was taught to. Because it feels right.'

'All right, all right. Keep your hair on. It's just that I've never seen anyone talk to a tree before.'

'Well you have now.'

Pause. Angus scratched his jaw. He wanted to laugh but knew that would not be very politic. Besides, he was not sure of Damon's temper and they were forty feet up in the air. Finally, as they began climbing again, working their way round the thick branches, he said, 'Can I ask you something else?'

'What?'

'Does the tree ever answer you back?'

'Are you trying to be funny?'

'No. I'm serious. You've stopped and talked to the tree several times, and then we've moved on and I want to know what – er – feedback you're getting from the tree.'

They reached a narrow platform that Damon had built some

months earlier. From here on he had attached rope-ladders into the tree and the climbing would be easier but more dangerous. Moreover, at this height they could feel the movement of the tree as it flexed in the wind. They were in the power of the tree, totally dependent on and subject to its strength. Damon squatted down on the platform with his back to the next climbing-branch. 'Trees don't talk, but you can feel whether what you are doing is right. I sometimes think that simply asking the question, "Can I go on, with your leave?" gets you in the right frame of mind and that is what is important. The frame of your mind. You've got to feel both respectful and open. Don't you ever do things just because they feel right?'

Angus shrugged. 'I've not had much experience of such things. When I build a machine it either works or it doesn't. And if it doesn't I sort it out.'

'Aye well, next time try talking to it and see what happens.'

'I'd feel daft.'

'That doesn't matter. Don't think of a tree being a human being or anything like that. That *would* be daft. Just think of it being part of everything, like the wind and the rocks and the wolves and you yourself, and that you are in its space. So you say, "Do you mind me climbing?" And then if everything feels OK get on with your work.'

'Have you ever stopped climbing? I mean have you ever felt it was wrong, that the tree didn't want you? That it wasn't right?'

'Yes I have. Often. You don't have to think twice if you get a message. You feel it in your stomach and in your throat. You know . . . you just know and you can't go on. Funny really, I suppose. Anyway, one time, let's see, about three years back, I was doing this job for a woodsman. I was way out in the back-end of nowhere. I suddenly got this bad feeling just when I was about to make some final connections and so down I went. Aye and I was high, too. Anyway, about the time I got to the bottom, a right storm blew up. There were branches coming down and hailstones as big as your fist and lightning dancing about. Even t'squirrels had a hard time. So I hunkered down in a hollow and when the worst of the storm was over I managed to get to the woodsman's hut. Then next day when I went up t'tree again, I found that one of my platform branches had broken right off and the platform had fallen. So there you go. If I'd tried to weather it out up there at t'top either I'd have fallen or I'd have been marooned and no one knew where I was. That's a true story. There's plenty of others, too.' Damon stood up. 'Well, let's get this last bit over. You follow me, and go steady. No smart-arse acrobatics.' He gripped the ropes and tested them and then began to climb steadily, feeling out the wooden rungs with his toes and instep and bending his body to keep his centre of gravity low. The rope-ladder swung out from the tree and Angus noticed that Damon never took his eyes off the branches above and that his lips were moving. Steadily he climbed while the ropes sang and stretched under his weight. Finally he was able to grip one of the high branches with his arm and then step over into a place where several branches started. 'Now you,' he called.

Before he started to climb, Angus looked down through the branches to the ground below. Then, feeling foolish, he said, 'Tree, I hope you don't mind me climbing up here.' There was, of course, no reply and if Angus had expected some sudden moment of enlightenment he was, of course, disappointed. Except that a moment after he had spoken the wind blew and the branches shifted and the entire tree eased so that Angus seized the trunk with both arms and hugged it for fear he might fall. Was that an answer? Angus did not know. He did not know what he thought beyond that he was in uncharted sea as far as he was concerned and there was no going back.

'Are you coming or aren't you?' It was Damon from above.

'I'm coming,' said Angus, with some of his roughness and bravado returning. He took the rope-ladder in his strong mechanic's hands and began to climb, hand over hand, never taking his eyes off the branches above. He felt calm as the ladder swung out. His life was on trust.

The place where several branches started was a natural platform. This was as high as they could climb. From here on the branches were too small to bear the weight of a man swinging on a ladder, but they still might have to shinny up higher, for the electrical coupling had to be made at a point as high in the tree as possible.

Looking out from this eyrie, Angus could see into the canopy of the forest. He had never experienced anything like this in his life. He felt safe because the tree was so strong, but frightened because one slip would send him plunging down some hundred feet to the forest floor.

'Here's where the cable is now,' said Damon indicating a place where the supple-jack had formed itself into a rough coil. 'Now watch what I do.'

Damon took a sharp short-bladed knife from his belt and cut several notches into the vine, measuring the span between the tip of his little finger and the end of his thumb between the cuts. Then he took from his satchel several cuttings of a black-leaved ivy. He inserted the tips of the ivy-cuttings into the notches and secured them with tape. 'Now we come to the difficult bit.' Damon took the growing-end of the supple-jack in his mouth and gripped it with his teeth. Then he began to shinny out along one of the branches. Angus saw the branch bend and was about to call out but restrained himself. Damon was not the type to show off and Angus did not want to distract him.

When Damon had gone as far as he dared, he gripped the branch with his legs and, lying on top of the branch, began to spread the cuttings of black ivy into as many of the small side-branches as he could. Where the cuttings encountered firm wood he bound them. His last job was to stop the tip of the climbing supple-jack with a bite. He spat the small cutting out from the tree. Then he worked his way back down the branch securing the creeper and the black ivy whenever he could. Finally he again stood beside Angus. 'Now, if we're lucky and I've done it right, the ivy will begin to bed into the beech tree for it's a parasite. It'll spread through this part of the beech tree and it'll respond to whatever current is flowing at this altitude. I'll come back in two weeks' time to see if it's taken. Now let's get down and connect the base.'

'Is that all there is to it?' asked Angus.

'Well, what more do you want? Sparks and blue flashes? We've tapped into the tree's electrical circuit and, at a height such as this, there's a big difference in potential between here and the ground. You take my word for it. From now on, whenever light hits the leaves of this tree or when it opens its pores to take in or give out gases, or whenever the wind blows, a current will flow and eventually there'll be enough to light and heat the house back there.'

They climbed down the tree and Angus was surprised at how soon they were once again on the ground. When he looked up, the platform where he had stood was lost among the leaves and branches.

'Now, what we do down here is pretty much the same as what we did up top. Do you want to have a go?' Damon handed Angus the short knife and a bunch of cuttings of the black ivy. 'Now be very careful. Don't be ham-fisted. If you cut the cable too deep you'll kill it. And that'll be three months' work wasted.'

Angus had watched carefully. He opened up the supple-jack and inserted a cutting of the ivy and bound it. Damon nodded with approval. Then Angus took the ivy and trailed it round the bole of the tree. And as the ivy touched the trunk there was a crackle and Angus shouted and jumped back. He landed on his bottom and sat there rubbing his hand. It was not the first time he had received an electric shock but he had never been so surprised before.

'Now you can see why we connect up the top part first. There's already a hell of a charge building up. Come on, I'll show you how to do it so you don't get a bang.'

Damon made the connections and, being careful to hold only the supple-jack and not the ivy, trailed the fronds of ivy over the roots of the tree. There was plenty of crackling. Then he gathered some leaves and used these to handle the ivy. He cut nicks into the tree's bark and rammed the ivy home. 'So there we are. That's how it's done.'

'But why does it work?' asked Angus.

'Nay, search me,' said Damon. 'I understand about differences in potential. But why differences in potential produce the effects they do, I have no idea.' Then he added slyly, 'Perhaps you should ask the tree.'

'Aye. And 'appen I'll get more sense from it, too,' responded Angus.

With that they trudged off back through the forest.

Three weeks later they returned to the tree and saw that the ivy had grown and had already inserted its own short white roots into the bark of the beech tree. It appeared to be thriving. 'Will I get a shock if I touch it now?' asked Angus.

'No, probably not. It's earthed itself now.'

Angus touched one of the black leaves and then favoured it between finger and thumb. He did not flinch. 'I can feel a tingling,' he said, 'but nothing more.'

'That's probably your electrical field,' said Damon. 'The black ivy is very sensitive. But everything's alive.'

Angus nodded. 'Right. Well now I'm going to try and find out why the electrical system at Bella's inn isn't working as well as it should.'

And he succeeded. One morning he traced the supple-jack cables which supplied Bella's inn with electricity and found himself standing at the base of a giant ash tree. It was almost completely overgrown. The ivy at the base of the tree had climbed so high that it was starting to interfere with the ivy from the top of the tree which had grown down. They neutralized one another when they brushed against one another in the breeze and that was the cause of the problem. Angus cut back the ivy. He climbed the tree, following a path that was many centuries old. He hammered in new wooden climbing-pegs and built several small platforms. He hung ladders and swaying bridges. He was able to study the ways in which the tree had adapted itself to the climbing-paths.

After some days he knew his way round the ash tree as intimately as he had once known the work-room in the Battle Dome. To his astonishment he found himself talking to the tree without actually thinking about it, chattering as he might to a mate. Before attempting something dangerous he would press himself against the tree's rough bark, gripping it with his arms as hard as he could, and he would mutter, urging the tree to help him and telling it to stay firm.

Finally, after repairing a short wooden ladder, he came to the place where the top connections were made. Here, some of the ancient supple-jack was as thick as his arm and the black ivy was as dense as a thicket. Some branches had rotted and Angus cut them free and watched them fall down through the giant ash. They crashed with a dry rattling sound on the ground below. Then Angus made repairs and new connections. He was careful not to give himself a shock for this electrical system was powerful and well established and the jolt could have killed him.

Finally, grimy from the accumulated muck and bird-droppings at the top of the tree and sticky with the sap from the cut ivy, Angus was satisfied. The pruning was clean and symmetrical. The black ivy-leaves were spread evenly. The effect looked vigorous.

When Angus returned to the inn all the lights were glowing brilliantly and the ovens were hot. Everyone noticed the difference. Everyone complimented him, and when Bella saw Angus she gave him a kiss.

That evening Miranda told him how glad she was that he had been able to improve the systems at the inn. Her face was flushed from leaning over the hotplates and her hair was drawn back tightly with just a few wisps escaping from the bands. Her eyes sparkled merrily as in the old days, and with a mounting hope Angus asked her to go out with him that night into the woods. Miranda frowned as though she had not heard him correctly and then declined his offer and retreated to the kitchens. Angus sat alone in the inn that night, torn apart, by admiration and rejection. Angus was hungering for the woman he had known in the early days in Eburacum, but that woman was dead and nothing could bring her back to life. Angus could not accept this and so consigned himself to days of jealousy and nights of frustration.

Relationships

Angus watched Miranda, and if she looked at another man passing in the street outside or smiled while serving one, Angus scowled. His one consolation was that she seemed to treat Viti with the same disdain as she did him. But when the anger became too great for him to bear, he took his axe and went out into the forest and vented his rage against a tree, exulting as the chips flew. Once, by chance, he was close to a stream and downwind of some deer that came to drink. He threw his axe at the deer and solely by luck felled one of them when it turned directly into the path of the tumbling axe. He was able to kill the stunned deer with a blow to the throat and felt an amazing complex of emotions as the creature died before him. He carried it back to the inn and did not mind the fact that its blood soaked his shirt. 'Food,' he said at the kitchens. 'Fresh. Just killed. For today.' But Miranda was not there to witness his triumph.

Having believed that Miranda was somehow 'his', Angus was still suffering all the pain of discovering that he was not wanted. Sometimes at night he realized that he did not love her but that what he truly wanted was for her to love him. He wanted the envy that comes to a man who is loved by a beautiful woman. Sometimes, in the mornings when the inn was just stirring into life, he felt a vast emptiness inside him. This was terrible, and he stumbled out of the inn as fast as he could and took his axe or else, when opportunity presented itself, he sought out the company of one or two women who lived in the village and would go out under the trees with him. To Angus, it was still a matter of astonishment that the women of the village had at least as much freedom as the men and that they seemed to be in charge of so many areas of life. He gained a reputation as a frantic and aggressive lover.

Tension between Angus, Viti and Miranda was manifest at all levels of their relationship. And in this Miranda was no saint, for at times she provoked the desire of the two men for no reason other than to assert her sexual power. At times she remembered how fierce and joyful had been the nights in Angus's arms and she longed for those simple, uncomplicated times while knowing they could not be again. When she looked at Viti something in her stirred, for she could scarcely recognize in the dung-shifter who came in each night tired from his duties in the byre the cruel and arrogant Roman who had raped her. Even so, when she thought back over those times, she immediately wanted to be alone for something had been damaged in her, some freshness, some immediacy, and only solitude could heal her. Or so she believed.

Still being a healthy woman with healthy instincts and a temperament disposed to passion, she often sighed for one of the young men of the village, a man whom she'd watched perhaps as he casually lifted a sack of beech-nuts up on to a dray or lay back in the sun at midday with a blade of grass in his teeth, or whom she'd accidentally caught relieving himself behind a tree in the forest. Perhaps she longed for an abstract man, a laughing concoction of salt and sinew, who could be there and ready when needed and gone when unrequired. And to be sure, there were many men in the village who would have liked to see if their feet could fit such slippers.

Sex and spilt milk

And what of Viti, whom people called 'the silent' for the very simple reason that he spoke seldom? Viti, though no one would have known, found himself nursing a passion for Miranda which at times was as sharp as needles. He did not know what to do with his feelings and did not understand them. Sometimes at night, as he lay beside the sleeping Angus, he drifted into sleep believing that she was beside him, breathing in the darkness. One morning he woke to find himself tangled up with the still sleeping Angus and extricated his arms and legs gently so as not to wake his bedfellow, who was surely living as erotic a dream as he himself had just enjoyed. In embarrassment Viti slid over to his half of the bed and snored deeply when Angus shifted.

However, Viti was afraid to make his feelings for Miranda known lest, as he deeply feared, she were to reject him. So he was content to sit down and day-dream in the byre among the animals, or stretched out in the barn on the bales of hay among the wild mint. Had he but known it, Viti was finally growing up, enjoying the moody and private adolescence which is every child's birthright. His fantasies about Miranda all centred on his saving her from some calamity such as a swiftly flowing river or wild beasts or fire. And when the danger was over, she came to him and thanked him and thanking led to a kiss and a kiss to passion and passion to— Here the day-dream broke down, snarling and snagging on the truth that the one time he had made love to her he had been drunk and violent and his only clear memory of the entire incident was of her anguished and passive face, turned away from him as he tried to kiss her.

This memory was lodged deep inside him and he did not know how to shift it. Now if ever, Viti needed a father or a mother to turn to, but there was no one.

Then one day, at noon, Miranda came down to the byre with a jug for milk. She climbed down the ladder, not knowing that Viti was working over at the chicken-coop, mending the door. He looked across when he saw movement and was rocked by the memory of seeing Miranda descend from the mechanical beast so many months ago. The memory was like a physical assault and he sank down out of sight.

'Viti,' called Miranda. 'Bella wants some fresh cream. Where are you?'

Viti peered round the side of the coop. 'Oh. Hi,' he said as casually as he could manage.

'What's wrong with you? You look as though you'd seen a ghost.'

'Eh? Oh, er. You startled me. I didn't know anyone was here.'

'I want some cream for Bella.'

Silently Viti went to the cool-vats under the building. He filled the jug and was handing it back when, at that very moment, both he and Miranda became aware of the other's physical presence and that they were alone. Miranda backed away, her hand going to her throat. Viti released the jug too soon and it fell to the ground and broke.

'I'm sorry,' said Viti.

'I'm sure Bella's got another jug,' said Miranda quickly.

'I don't mean that. I'm just sorry, that's all. Sorry for . . . all of it.'

'I know. Don't . . . I don't want to talk about it.' Then she turned and ran back to the ladder leading up to the house and was gone. Viti began to clear up the spilt milk. For some reason his heart felt lighter and he was amazed to discover that he was breathless.

Minutes later Bella's younger son appeared with another and larger jug. 'Mum says to be careful this time. Jugs don't grow on trees and she's docking the cost of the other one from your wages.'

'She doesn't pay me any wages.'

'Well anyway, she's hopping mad so I wouldn't go up for a while.' He grinned.

Viti drew off the cream and handed the brimming jug to the boy. 'There. Tell her I'm a butter-fingers.'

A Fight

One evening a group of young men came to Bella's inn to drink. The drinking grew boisterous and the men began to arm-wrestle and challenge one another to feats of strength. Viti was seated in a corner watching proceedings quietly while nursing a beer. Occasionally one of the young men, a raw-boned specimen with spiky hair, a lantern jaw and broken front teeth, would nod in Viti's direction and then say something in broad dialect and they would all laugh. Viti could not quite hear what was being said but the meaning was clear enough.

Finally, feeling uncomfortable, Viti stood up to leave, and the raw-boned one called, 'Hey Roman, how do you like working down there with the animals?'

'It has its moments,' said Viti and moved on.

A different voice called, 'Hey Roman, hear you like a slice of pig's bum. That right?'

Viti paused and smiled. 'No, I leave that to turds like you,' he said and again moved on.

That response caused a laugh. Then another voice chimed in: 'Hey Roman, how's this for a bit of Latin?' The voice adopted an exaggerated falsetto. 'I fuck your sister. He fuck your sister. We fuck your sister. Everyone fuck your sister.'

There was an expectant silence after this and Viti, who was

half-way to the door, paused and turned. He looked at the drunken leering faces and though he tried to control his temper and find a quick reply, he felt something start to smoulder inside him and the smouldering burst into flame. His reaction had nothing to do with his sister but everything to do with human stupidity and how you cope with it.

'Now which of you dickheads said that?' asked Viti, advancing slowly.

'Me,' said the raw-boned one, standing up. 'What's it to you?'

Viti faced him, keeping just beyond arm's reach. 'Well, you've got just five seconds to apologize before I smash your face in.'

That brought laughter and the tall man spat on his hands and balled his fists and said, 'Well you'd better grow a bit first, Titti.'

The others drew back and pushed back the tables, clearing a space. They began to chant.

Five . . .

Viti felt his body flood with adrenalin. His muscles knit as they had so often in the fights at the Battle Dome.

Four . . .

Training dinned into him over years took over. He noted the balance of his opponent . . . that he was left-handed . . . that he wanted to punch . . . that he would try and stun Viti with a single wild blow . . .

Three . . .

Viti knew that his opponent knew nothing of his training and this was his best advantage and hence should not be revealed.

Two . . .

He saw five points of weakness. Two of which would be instantly fatal if he chose . . .

One . . .

He saw the blow coming . . .

. . . and stepped back and parried it as though by accident. The momentum of the punch carried the big man round off balance, and when Viti pushed him he fell sprawling over a table behind which were some of his companions. The table tipped. Two water-jugs toppled. Their contents swilled into the laps of the men who howled and dived to one side.

With a roar the big man turned round and unleashed a punch

that would have broken an oak door or lifted Viti's head off his shoulders, if it had connected. But Viti had dived to one side and retreated to the end of the room. From here he had a view of the whole room. He was at the place where the kitchen pans and brushes were stored. There was also a large vat of vinegar.

The big man came at Viti with arms outstretched. Viti picked up a mop that was still stale with beer. He brandished it in the man's face, jabbing it at him and taunting him. The man tried to knock it aside only to find it jabbing him in the stomach and balls and then back into his face. Finally he managed to wrench it from Viti's grasp and throw it away.

More wary now, he stooped into a wrestler's crouch and Viti imitated him but with variations. He made a noise like an ape, distorting his face and scratching under his armpits. The man hurled himself forwards, expecting Viti to retreat but suddenly Viti advanced, dropping low so that he was inside the man's guard. Before the man could grapple and squeeze, Viti straightened up with all the strength of his legs and his head smashed into the man's jaw. Then, partly concealed by the big man's size, Viti unleashed two punches, one high, one low, which bruised the heart and then the bowels of the man and left him windless and senseless. It all happened so quickly that the drunken companions who had been shouting for blood were astonished to see Viti hoist the unconscious assailant up on to his shoulders and tip him face down into the half-empty barrel of vinegar.

The noise of the brawl had not gone unnoticed. The door leading to the living-quarters burst open and an old man poked his head in. He found himself pushed right into the room by the press of guests and staff who wanted to see the action. They were not disappointed.

The drunken friends of the man who was now gargling in the vinegar-vat had begun to sort themselves out and were advancing on Viti. Viti had picked up a heavy ladle which he passed from hand to hand. At his feet was a three-legged stool which he hooked in his instep and then kicked up to the ceiling. This was unexpected. The stool hit the ceiling and bounced down, proving just enough distraction for Viti to jab the blunt end of the ladle into the teeth of the foremost of the attackers while reaching up and grabbing one of the others by the hair.

Viti's plan was simple. He wanted to enmesh them all in a general mêlée during which he could pick them off one by one. Already the man who had tasted the ladle was showing less interest in the fight and the one whose hair he had pulled was thrashing out wildly. They made a heap of fighting, pummelling men and at that moment the door to the inn opened and in walked Angus. His face was murderous. Having had a frustrating time in the village, he was just spoiling for a fight. It took him a moment to size up what was happening and then with a whoop he dived in and started to punch and kick indiscriminately. He had not seen that Viti was involved.

Now Angus had a reputation as a fighter and his presence tipped the balance. Those who had been keen to belt the smaller and less aggressive-looking Viti considered discretion the better part of valour when it came to dealing with bull-headed Angus. They began to pull back.

Viti meanwhile had managed to squirm out from the heap of bodies and take refuge under one of the dining-tables. From there he was able to climb up on to a bench and watch proceedings, limiting his engagement to reaching out with his ladle to bop any heads that came within reach.

He was thus engaged when Bella arrived in her night-gown, her hair streaming, and armed with a pickaxe handle. She waded into the mob, jabbing and shouting and sending them scattering so that finally all that was left was Angus, bloody-knuckled and panting, standing in the middle of the inn-room pawing at the air with one of his eyes bruised and closed.

In the sudden silence Bella dressed him down right royally. She called him a cretin, a pea-brain, a dildo, a piss-pot, a vulture, a turd, a scarecrow, a bed-louse. He looked at her vacantly while she likened his ancestors to things that crawl out of rotten meat and his relatives to the garbage that is fed to pigs. 'Cute,' she ended, 'cute. You think you're so cute. Well let me tell you, you're about as cute as a shit-house rat and you'll pay for all this . . . you and this bad bugger.' She indicated the big, raw-boned man who had started the fight and who now stood groggy and streaming with vinegar, his mouth opening and closing vainly.

Viti started to speak but Bella rounded on him. 'And as for you. I thought you had more sense. Why didn't you stop them?' She addressed the general crowd. 'Honestly, *men*! You can't trust them for a minute out of your sight. And what are you all gawping at? Come on. Get cleaning this place up. We begin breakfasts in a few hours.'

And clean they did. Under Bella's watchful eye the vinegar-vat was thrown out of the inn door to crash in the street. The floors were mopped, the tables set up and the broken pots and jugs lined up for tally. Finally Bella was satisfied and she sent all the men outside to sort themselves out, relenting so far as to give them a last jug of beer.

No one can remember quite what was said as the men passed the jug round. But from that day on no one tried to pick on Viti and the number of anti-Roman jokes uttered in his presence declined.

Kidnapping

After the fight, life in the inn settled down quickly and both Angus and Viti were astonished that Bella seemed to forget all about the scrap. They noticed also that fights in the village were frequent among the men and women but that they hardly ever led to lasting resentment unless death occurred, in which case the village elders, of whom Bella was one, got together and settled the matter. The people they were living with seemed to laugh and then fight and then laugh again with hardly any awareness of how incongruous this behaviour was to those brought up in the civilized Roman world. But while the villagers might fight among themselves, they united if there was any threat to the village.

One night, the entire village was woken up by a great hulla-baloo. The village gates had been set on fire and a group of men from a neighbouring village had attacked one of the houses, kidnapping two sisters. Within minutes men and women were swarming out of their houses and into the moonlight. Some carried cudgels made from branches of blackthorn, some had bows and quivers of black arrows, others were strapping on antique swords. Pitchforks were pulled from the eaves of the low houses. Viti and Angus joined them and were welcomed. Blazing torches were handed round.

The village dogs which were used to hunt wild pigs in the forest were loosed and barked and snapped round the house where the kidnapping had taken place. Soon they had a good scent and were straining at their chains. They led the way and a war-party consisting of many of the men and women of the village departed after them at a run. They were led by the father of the two girls, a big, black-bearded man called Solem.

It was strange and thrilling and new for both Viti and Angus to run through the night as part of this grim posse. The road, similar to the one they had followed to reach the village, twisted and turned under the trees and hedges. When they came to crossroads the dogs howled and sniffed and departed like arrows. Once they found part of a woman's night-shirt and set up a clamour which echoed loud under the trees.

Then, ahead in the darkness, they saw the flicker of fires and the entire war-party began to howl and holler and run to attack. Both Viti and Angus were caught up in the frenzy. Any thoughts they might have had that the battle was not in earnest were dispelled in the first charge. They saw limbs cut with swords, and bodies savaged by dog-bites. The gates of the village were forced and the first house they came to was set on fire with the occupants within. Arrows whistled and thudded, lethal in the darkness, and Viti saw one of the young men, one of those who had been prominent in the scrap against him, go down with an arrow through his throat.

Soon they were fighting in the streets. The village they were attacking had a stream running through it and it was at one of the bridges over the stream that the battle was at its most intense. Here, after several attacks and counter-attacks, there was finally a stand-off. There seemed to be an argument taking place among the villagers on the far side of the stream and finally the crowd parted and an old man came forward. He was carrying a young woman in his arms. The gash in her throat was visible for all to see and a howl went up from all the villagers. Behind him came the other young woman and two young men with downcast heads.

Solem, the father of the two girls, stepped up on to the bridge to receive the body. He took it into his arms and sank down on the bridge above the swift-flowing stream.

'It was one of your arrows,' said the old man, carefully. 'None of our doing.' Then he turned and motioned the other daughter to join her father on the bridge. Viti noticed that she walked like a zombie, with staring eyes, uncomprehending.

Finally the old man pushed the two young men forwards. 'My grandsons,' he said, and stood waiting.

Solem howled and rocked. Everyone watched and waited patiently.

After a time his grief gave way to sobs and finally he could speak. 'Why?' he asked.

'Love,' said the old man, when it was obvious that neither of the two young men would speak. 'The boys loved the girls but the girls wouldn't have them.'

'Not true,' piped up one of the young men. 'They wanted us. They came to us when we called in the forest.' He paused and the brief flurry of spirit died in him. 'But this shouldn't have happened.' He nodded towards the dead girl and then began to cry. The old man put his hand on his shoulder.

There was a pushing in the crowd on both sides of the bridge and young men came forwards carrying stretchers on which were lain the bodies of those who had died in the skirmish. In all there were seven.

'We will talk more about this in the days to come,' said Solem and motioned for the litter on which his daughter lay to be lifted.

'The boys will go with you,' said the old man, and turned his back and made his way from the bridge and back into his village. The crowd parted for him and then began to disperse, taking their own dead with them.

'Rum way to end a scrap,' whispered Angus to Viti.

'It's not ended yet,' murmured Viti, 'you mark my words.'

Nor was it, though there was no more killing.

The war-party which an hour earlier had been in full cry became a funeral procession. First came the women, keening and crying out. Some of them had gone into the forest and pulled down branches of elder and willow. These they swished back and forth before them and beat on the ground and struck across their backs. Behind them came Solem, his head bowed and his chin on his chest. After him walked his daughter with one of the women, who held her close and never stopped whispering to her though what she said no one could hear. Beside them walked the two young men who had been mainly responsible for the kidnapping, and they carried the dead girl. Last came the young men of the village, many of whom were wounded and limping. They carried the other two dead companions on stretchers. At the very end of the procession walked Viti and Angus. Angus had been hit in the chest by a staff and it hurt when he breathed. Viti had a fine cut which ran from elbow to shoulder where an arrow had grazed him. Round all the people ran the subdued dogs, their heads down and their tails between their legs.

Back at the village old women were already waiting to take up the wailing and a bonfire was being prepared in the village square. Burning torches stood outside the houses, casting a fitful light. Everyone, young and old, was up and the children stood in the doorways wide-eyed and serious. The smoke drifted through the village streets.

Bella's inn became an impromptu morgue. The dining-tables were joined up and fresh linen was brought from the store-room. Carefully the three bodies were laid out. Viti and Angus were surprised to see Miranda setting to and working beside Bella. They cut away the clothes stiff with blood and began to bathe the hardening flesh.

'You two off and find something to do,' said Bella pointing to them. 'And you, Angus, get that chest strapped up. There'll be Lyf the healer down at the square. Go and find him.'

Angus muttered something about bossy women but did as he was bid, and favouring his arm across his chest stumped out of the inn and down the steps.

'I'd rather stay and watch,' said Viti. 'Don't worry, I won't get under your feet and I can carry the hot water and whatever else you want. I'm only scratched.'

Bella looked at Miranda and Miranda shrugged as if to say, 'I don't care.'

'All right, you can stay. But keep well clear. You can start by making us a cup of tea.' Viti nodded.

Outside the inn Angus breathed deeply enjoying the strange taste of the night air. Then he wandered in the direction of the square where torches were burning and some men were unloading piles of brushwood from a dray. They were obviously planning on having a very hot fire. 'Hey, Angus. Give us a hand with these logs.' It was Damon calling from the top of the dray. Angus tried to lift his arm but the pain made him wince.

'Sorry,' he called. 'I think I've cracked a rib.'

'Right,' said Damon. 'Get away over to the fountain. Lyf's arrived and set up shop. He'll see you right.' Then he went back to tossing down brushwood and logs.

Angus thought, 'So that old bugger Lyf's turned up. Reckon he can smell trouble.'

Lyf was by the fountain fixing a dressing to a man's eye. He was wearing his full fur coat and wore a cap to which the antlers of a young deer were attached. He nodded when he saw Angus. 'See you're still alive then,' he said and tapped the man he had been treating on the shoulder to show that he had finished. The man stood up and thanked him and walked away.

'Just,' said Angus. 'Got a poke in the ribs. Hurts when I lift my arm.'

'Let's have a look at you.'

Quickly and expertly Lyf touched Angus's chest and back and located the damaged area. 'You won't be sleeping on your side for a while,' he said. 'There's two cracked ribs. Breathe deeply.' Angus did and coughed with the pain. 'Bad bruising too, but I don't think the lungs are damaged. Here, sit down and I'll strap you up. Drink some of this. It'll ease the pain.' Lyf handed a flask to Angus's good side.

Angus hoped the drink was alcohol but he tasted something that was like the water you find at the bottom of a stagnant ditch. Still, it eased the pain almost immediately.

'Settling in OK?' asked Lyf.

'After a fashion.'

'How are the other two?'

'We're not close. Ask them.'

'I will.' Lyf pulled the bandage tight round Angus's ribs and began to wrap it over his shoulder. 'What do you think of our world?'

'Rough,' said Angus. 'But interesting. Lots of surprises.' Then he changed tack. 'What's going to happen to the two young men we brought back, the ones who kidnapped the girl?'

Lyf shrugged. 'Don't know. That's over to Solem. He can demand a life for a life, or a life can be given. This is a complex case. We'll have to see.' With that he tied the bandage tight and asked Angus to move his arm.

Angus could, but only just.

'That'll take a few weeks to mend but after that you should be as right as a rooster.' There was already a queue forming of other people that wanted Lyf's attention. 'We'll talk later if you are interested. I'll be around for a few weeks. For the moment I'm busy. Next.'

Angus grunted in thanks and moved away to watch the fire being stoked.

Back at the inn the two women worked side by side with Bella explaining to Miranda how to straighten the corpses and wash them and dry them and close the gashes with wadding and press down on the bodies to force out the air and then block up the orifices. Miranda worked with a quiet intensity and only paused briefly when one of the bodies broke wind. 'Pay no mind to that,' said Bella. 'All dead bodies belch and fart a bit. That's why we have to press the air out of them first and then close them up. Even so the gases build up. I'm always for a quick cremation. Cleaner. Back to the earth and back to the sun.'

No sooner were the bodies washed than there came a knock at the door of the inn. Viti opened the door and found some children waiting. They were carrying clothes from the families of the dead. They brought them in and set them down on a spare table and would have lingered to stare and ask questions but Bella shooed them out. 'Tell your mums and dads to come in an hour. Everything'll be ready then.'

Viti poured himself a glass of beer and watched as the bodies were dressed. 'Why am I watching this?' he wondered. 'Why am I so interested? I've seen death before. What in me is being fed by watching these last rites?' He made himself more comfortable, stretching his legs out on the bench where he sat. He found himself admiring the quick strength of Bella as she turned and rolled one of the young men and worked his shirt down over his uncooperative body. He saw the way that Miranda observed Bella and then imitated her moves. 'The lives of women,' thought Viti. 'How clear and structured. Maidens then mothers then mortuary workers. They learn from one another. Always with a function. They bring us into the world in the beginning and they see us out at the end.'

These were strange thoughts. He shook his head as though to clear it from a ringing. Viti felt strange, unreal to himself. 'Must be tired,' he muttered and set his glass down on the table and closed his eyes, hoping to doze. But his eyes would not stay closed. He watched Miranda and Bella and was surprised to see that they had been joined by another woman who now stood by, watching them. He hadn't heard her come in. Surely he hadn't fallen asleep in that small space of time? But then the woman turned and looked at him and Viti was astonished to see that she was the same woman who now lay dead and washed and clothed on the table. She looked very much alive. Viti tried to speak, but though his mouth opened, he could make no sound. He felt trapped in a dream. Neither Bella nor Miranda seemed aware of the woman as they tugged and pulled at the body of one of the men. Viti watched as the woman walked round the room and looked down at the faces of the dead men and then her own face. She shook her head and pointed and seemed to be talking to someone else that Viti could not see. Then she turned and seemed to walk towards Viti but as she did so she seemed to grow smaller and started to fade. Within seconds she was gone and Viti found himself released from whatever had held him. All he retained was the final image of the woman's face. He let out a loud gasp of air and both Miranda and Bella looked up.

'Have you been asleep?' asked Bella.

'No. Did you see her?' He pointed at the table. 'That one. She was here. She was walking about. As real as my hand. I saw her.'

Bella looked about the room. 'I can't see anyone,' she said.

'No. She's gone now, but she was here. She looked down at herself. I swear she did.'

'Did she look happy or sad?' This from Miranda.

'Neither. Surprised more than anything. She seemed to be talking.'

Bella snorted. 'Well that's all right then. She's on her way.'

'What do you mean?' asked Viti, but Bella would not explain.

'Another time,' she said when he protested. 'Too much to do now. It'll be dawn soon and we can't be late.'

Minutes later there came a loud knocking at the door. Viti attended after a quick glance from Bella and the parents of the young people that had died filed into the room. They brought bread and wine. They were followed by mourners who were keening, and friends and relatives. Everyone packed into the inn-room until the floor was creaking.

Viti found himself squashed over against one wall and he climbed up on to a stool so that he could see. The wine was passed round, and cakes which were still hot from the oven. Occasionally someone would stand up and speak for a few moments standing near one of the bodies. They told stories, recounting events from the young people's lives. Some were comic and Viti was interested to see the way that laughter and tears could mingle.

He could not help but compare the pomp and ceremony which surrounded death in the world where he was born with the simple rites he was now watching. Uncomplicated, human, focused . . . He looked at the faces about him: women with wrinkled faces like old apples, wide-eyed children standing between the legs of their mothers, men whose gaze was all inward, they—

Viti was suddenly aware that everyone in the room had turned to him and was looking in expectation. Bella was speaking and he caught the last of her words.

'. . . that you saw her in here walking and looking. Tell them.'

Viti understood and in halting language began to describe the woman and how she had looked and moved and her graceful care. Where he was stuck for a word, Bella or one of the mourners helped him. The parents of the young woman nodded and when Viti finished they thanked him formally and several people grunted in appreciation. A glass of wine was passed back to him. Much to his surprise Viti had found the talking easy. He lacked vocabulary but he did not lack shape or ideas and had spoken with a flow. He noticed Miranda looking at him with an expression of surprise on her face and he looked away.

Then, suddenly it seemed, the windows of the inn were grey and then pearly blue as dawn built in the east. The father of the young woman spoke for the last time and an old woman took up the keening. Bearers lifted the three bodies and gently carried them out of the inn and into the fresh morning air.

In procession the bodies were carried down to the square where the fire had become a heap of glowing charcoal across which scampered flames of blue and green. The heat was so great that no one could approach closer than three or four yards. Sticks thrown on to the pyre burst into flame before they touched the embers.

Above the village the sky was now bright, almost luminous.

Lyf took charge of the ceremony. Wrapped in his furs and defying the heat he chanted in front of the fire. He cast garlands made from ivy and honeysuckle on to the glowing coals and scattered sweet-smelling oil on to the embers at the fire's edge. The oil blazed.

Then, when he had finished, men of the village tied each of the bodies on to long frames of wood. The frames were such that they could be raised up on their ends and toppled over so that the body and the frame fell into the heart of the fire. First the men were burned. As the bodies blazed, cries went up and the people cast objects of value into the fire.

Then the body of the woman was raised high above the crowd and a great wailing went up. The frame toppled and fell, crashing into the fire, and sparks flew and flames leaped. Suddenly there was commotion at the edge of the blaze and one of the young men who had been brought from the neighbouring village, the one who had cried for love, ran and dived directly into the fire. He clawed at the frame as his hair blazed and his flesh steamed and then all movement ceased. He burned like a statue coated with pitch and finally collapsed into ash beside the ashes of the woman he had loved.

The first rays of the sun probed into the clearing and people began to drift away from the funeral pyre and make their way home. The fire would be left to burn until it was completely out and the ashes cold. That might take days. Then the ashes would be gathered and taken out into the forest and scattered.

Viti went to bed but found that he could not sleep. Angus was already there on his back and snoring fitfully. He was sweating and Viti guessed he was in pain.

Viti wandered round the inn for a while, feeling dislocated, and finally sought out his favourite nook in the byre. It was a corner between the chicken-house and the pigsty and he had made it comfortable with a couple of bales of loose hay and some sacks. Here he could sit and think without fear of being disturbed. Except that this day, Bella came down to the byre in the early afternoon and found him sleeping with a straw between his teeth and a half-drunk jug of ale at his side.

She woke him gently and sat down by him. Viti had the sudden and terrible fear that Bella had come to tell him that he had to leave the inn. But she smiled at him and he relaxed.

'You're a strange one,' she said. 'You see more than you say, and you think more than you tell. I thought I'd come down and explain what you saw last night. I thought you might be wondering.'

'I am,' said Viti and yawned despite himself.

'Have you ever seen spirit life before?' Viti shook his head. 'Well, that's what you saw. You saw the spirit of the woman. When someone dies their spirit stays close for a while, sometimes for days, before moving on.'

'Have you seen them, then?'

'Yes. I've laid out many a stiff. Sometimes you can even see

233

the spirit rise from a body at the moment of death. It is very beautiful. Like watching a birth.'

'Bloody hell.' Viti thought for a moment. 'Did you see her last night?'

'No.'

'What about the two men?'

'I saw none of them.'

'Did Miranda?'

'She sensed them. Several times. She wanted to see them but she is not ready yet.'

'What will happen to her?'

'Who? Miranda?'

'No. The woman I saw. The ghost. The – er – spirit.'

'Well now.' Bella settled herself more comfortably into the hay. She was enjoying herself. 'Our beliefs are a bit different from you Romans. To us there is no such great gulf separates the living from the dead. That lass'll spend some time in the spirit world. As long as she needs. And then she'll probably be born again. Perhaps it'll be round here, methinks. It might even be in her family. I know Solem and Polly want more children. She might come back as a new daughter, or a son.'

Viti didn't know whether to laugh or take this seriously. But a glance at Bella's fine face told him that laughter would be unwise. As far as Viti was concerned, when you were dead you were dead and that was the end of the matter. The idea of coming back to life again in another body and perhaps as a different sex was inconceivable to him.

Bella picked up the jug of beer and took a swig from it. She wiped her lips. 'Well there we are. I don't expect or ask you to believe anything I've said. You make up your own mind. But just accept for the time being that we who live here believe and have done so for many generations. OK? And think over what you saw last night. You were very privileged. You have a destiny.' She stood up and picked the straw from her skirt and hair. 'Don't want to give people the wrong idea, do we?' she said and cackled. Then she turned to leave.

'Can I ask you one last thing?' said Viti, getting to his feet. 'Why did you ask me what expression she had on her face?'

234

'One of the hardest things a spirit has to accept is that their physical body is dead . . . especially if it has been a violent death. The spirit is shocked. Sometimes it tries to deny everything and becomes set in anger and resentment. But she was talking, right?' Viti nodded. 'You see, she was talking to someone who loves her. And she was looking at her dead self. That is very important. She had accepted that she had passed on and now she was free.'

'And what'll happen to her next?'

''Appen you yourself'll find out one day.'

Viti realized that Bella was teasing. 'Aye, 'appen I might,' he said, imitating Bella's broad accent. 'Thanks for telling me. I guess what you say makes sense. That is if any of it makes sense.'

Cormac

After the cremation Lyf stayed round the inn for a few weeks. It was noticeable to all that Bella suddenly took more care with her appearance and her step had more of a spring to it. Many winks were exchanged behind her back. The inn had not been built for privacy and those who wished to listen could hear Lyf and Bella at their noisy love-making. Miranda heard and smiled to herself and felt sexy. Viti and Angus pretended not to notice.

Then one morning Lyf was up very early, and when Viti tottered down to the byre to begin the day's chores he found that Lyf had already chopped the heads off two chickens and had them strung up to bleed in the lemon trees and had selected a young pig. He'd run it down to the far end of the byre and had it resting between bales while he fed it.

'Hush. Don't startle it any more than I have,' said Lyf. He continued talking to the pig and scratching its back and tugging its rough bristle while he slid a slim-bladed knife into his hand and down and under the pig's neck. With one movement he stroked the pig at the shoulders and brought the blade up, slicing through its throat. It didn't even grunt. Only its eyes blinked as it died.

The blood he caught in a bucket, and then hoisted the carcass up on to a frame and began to butcher it.

In answer to Viti's unasked question he said, 'Tonight we have a singer coming for the night. He's travelling down to the south coast. His name's Cormac. Have you heard of him?' Viti shook his head. 'Ignorant sods, you Romans. They didn't teach you anything important. Well, if we're lucky and put on a good spread we might get a song or two out of him. Get a good place though, early, if you want to hear. It'll be standing-room only.'

And so it was. In the early afternoon the inn began to fill up with casual visitors. They sat about drinking as though on holiday. Then shortly before sunset there was a commotion in the street outside accompanied by much cheering. Angus, who had been asked to do extra kitchen duties, looked out through one of the windows and saw an old man in a battered hat climbing stiffly down from a donkey. Round him were many of the village people and they called to him and touched him. On his back was a large black canvas bag and this seemed to be all the luggage he had. He gestured vaguely to the people and then, assisted by Lyf, came towards the inn. 'Is that what all the fuss is about?' thought Angus, and he went back to turning the roast parsnips.

Indeed a feast was presented in Cormac's honour, and the interesting thing as far as Angus and Viti were concerned was that Cormac ate alone and in silence. All the other guests fed early on and then the dining-room was cleared and swept. Only one table was left and this was dragged to one end of the room and covered by a fine cloth, which anyone with an eye for such things could see had been stolen from some fancy Roman villa. Then the table was laid with golden plates and dishes brought from a special lock-up at the back of the inn. Angus scratched his head as he helped carry the heavy dishes.

'All this just for that old bugger. Doesn't make sense.'

'He's a singer,' replied Viti, as he helped heft a heavy wine-vat up on to a trestle.

'So? What's so special about a singer? You pay them to give a bit of entertainment. Anyone'd think he was one of the top brass.'

Viti shrugged. 'They think he's important, anyway.'

Lyf had overheard their conversation. 'He is more than royalty. He's the closest thing you'll ever meet to a god. You two watch him close and behave yourselves or I'll boot you out.'

Angus began to reply but thought better of it and got on with his work. To show willing he rigged a special light above the splendid dining-table.

After he had rested, Cormac was escorted to the table in the middle of the inn. Everyone else crowded round in silence to watch him eat and Cormac studiously ignored them. First came wheatcakes and wine served by Bella. These were followed by slices of chicken in sauce with fresh brown bread. These were served by two of Bella's children. Cormac ate with his fingers and used bread to scoop up the gravy. After each course he washed his hands and dried them daintily on a napkin. Both Angus and Viti noticed that his hands were small and delicate, like the hands of a girl, but brown as though stained with tannin.

When the roast pig was brought in by Lyf, complete with all the trimmings and slightly burned parsnips, Cormac tucked in with relish and tore at the meat with his teeth. He was as oblivious of the people about him as if he had been dining on thin gruel alone on a winter's morning in the depths of the forest. He took all the meat he wanted, and the sauces, and then pushed the rest away with a casual gesture round the room. Immediately Lyf carved the rest of the pig and Miranda appeared from the kitchen with a pile of warm pottery plates of the kind normally used at the inn. The meat was served and passed round the room and everyone had a share, even if it was no more than a piece of crackling. Still no one spoke. There was fresh bread too, small loaves as big as your fist, and freshly churned butter. When Cormac had tasted one of them the rest were handed round. Last came a pie made with apples and cloves and dried apricots topped with brandy and butter. This was Miranda's special contribution, learned at the Eburacum Poly, and she served it. Cormac took a large slice and then pushed the rest away.

'He can certainly pack away the food,' whispered Angus to

237

Viti. 'You'd think he hadn't eaten for a week. Perhaps he hasn't at that. Looks like a scarecrow that's been sleeping in a ditch.'

'Shh,' said Viti. 'Watch what happens.'

Cormac ate the last of his pie and wiped his lips and then belched profoundly. Immediately Lyf proffered a large tankard full of beer. This vessel normally hung above the serving-counter. It was called the bard's jar and could hold just seven gills of beer. Cormac emptied it at one go and held it out for more.

'They'll be lucky to get more than a snore out of him if he swallows much more like that,' whispered Angus.

'Shut up,' hissed Viti.

After drinking deeply once more, Cormac finally placed his tankard on the table and looked round the room. It was at this moment that Miranda re-entered.

'Welcome, Moonbeam,' said Cormac. These were the first words he had uttered since entering the dining-room. His voice, unlike his appearance, was young and vibrant and melodious. It was a voice that would always stand out in a crowd, a voice that commanded attention. Miranda blushed, finding herself the focus of all eyes. 'Come and sit by me.' Miranda hesitated, not quite understanding, for Cormac's voice, though clear, had an accent that was strange. 'Don't worry, I don't bite. Well not in a way that you need worry about. Or is there some swain with more bollocks than brain you'd rather sit by?' Cormac glanced round the room and his gaze rested for a few moments on Viti and Angus before moving on. Both of them felt as though they had been looked through and felt uncomfortable.

Bella gave Miranda a nudge and whispered to her and pointed to the vacant seat by Cormac. Miranda nodded and crossed to the chair, noticing for the first time that Cormac was wall-eyed. One eye looked straight at her, the other looked away towards the chimney. As she approached he removed his crumpled hat with a flourish and revealed a mass of grey curly hair which stood up all round his head. He looked comic and Miranda laughed despite herself and then blushed again. 'Laugh away, Moonbeam. Don't mind an old man's feelings. I'll soon be worm-meat anyway and then you can have an orgy of giggles.'

He spread his arms to the crowd. 'Then you can all get your own back on me for the things I've said about you over the years.' Miranda sat down and Cormac addressed her. 'You know, old age is not quite the blessing it's cracked up to be. The older I get the more I forget. When I go for a pee I often piddle down my leg and get my boots wet. I bet you don't have that problem, do you?' Miranda shook her head in astonishment. 'When I find myself in bed with a young woman, which happens often, let me tell you, I usually find myself discussing technique rather than practising it.' Several people in the audience laughed at this. 'You see, they have the same problem. Age makes philosophers of us all, but philosophy, no matter how sweet, is no compensation for the wild spirits of youth. And tell me, how does it happen that you are working in this trollops' den?' Before Miranda could reply, Cormac hurried on. 'How do you find Dame Bella? Is she treating you well?'

'Very well.'

'Good. You know, a hundred years ago when I was young and so handsome that the willows wept for me and the ivy climbed the wall with desire, Bella and I were in love.' There was again laughter at this from the audience and Bella shook her head and looked up at the ceiling in mock disbelief. 'She taught me everything I know. True. You may find it hard to believe but Bella was once young and beautiful, especially by candle-light and after a few flagons of ale. At least I thought she was beautiful and still do, especially when I don't have my reading-glasses. But those were the days, weren't they Bella?'

'Yes. Especially if you liked garlic and honey,' replied Bella cryptically.

Cormac continued as though he had not heard. 'We used to make love. The forests were full of ringing bells and paths of sunlight when we made love. The wolf lay down with the lamb and the worms gave up their nibbling and came out and stretched in the sunlight. She used to cry out my name, Beith Cormac, and all the birds of the forest would take to the air with a great rush of wings. And any passing Romans used to beshit themselves with fear. She used to string my harp morning noon and night. Then Lyf arrived from out of the sunset to spoil

everything. He was a randy little sod even then. Smelt like goat
. . . looked like a goat, too, and he'd try to swive anything that
moved. I tell you, in those days even the chickens walked with
their wings over their bums when Lyf was about. Isn't that right,
Lyf?'

'They still do,' called Lyf.

'You, my dear Moonbeam, must be careful and watch out
for him. Anyway, when Lyf arrived on the scene it was bye-bye
Cormac. Bella only had eyes for him.' Everyone groaned in mock
sympathy.

'Not true,' called Bella.

'And that is the story of my life. Now what is your story?'

Miranda was astonished to see that Cormac's one good eye
was fixed steadily upon her. The question was not rhetorical.
There was something compelling about that one eye. 'I call you
Moonbeam because you shine in the darkness, but you must
begin by telling us what your mother and father called you.'

'I was called Miranda Duff.'

'A good name with good rhyme. Rough, stuff, tough, muff.
Tell us more.'

Then, with careful prompting from Cormac, Miranda began
to talk. She described growing up with Wallace and Eve in
Eburacum and then attending Eburacum Polytechnic. Bit by bit,
Cormac drew her story from her. But when she came to the bad
bits of her life she halted. At the same time, she felt a curious
relief at telling her story, even in this public manner. She did
not give details but she gave a sense, an outline. She mentioned
Angus.

Cormac looked round the assembly. 'Ah, he's the big
gormless-looking one at the back, isn't he? The one who's just
reaching for another beer.' Angus froze in his tracks.

And she mentioned Viti. 'There he is,' said Cormac, pointing.
'Looks like a ferret, doesn't he? A right Roman ferret. A chip
off the old Ulysses block. Do you think there's hope for him?'

Miranda shrugged. And lastly she talked about the escape
from the Battle Dome and the arrival at Bella's inn and how
happy she was working in the kitchen.

'So that is your song up to now, is it? Well hush now and

pour me another beer please, that is if Angus has left any in the pot, and listen to what an old singer makes of your song.'

Cormac reached behind him and lifted up the black canvas bag. He undid the buckles and removed a stained but well-polished stringed instrument which in shape was not unlike the old Greek cithara. He pushed his chair back from the table and wet his thumb and quickly tuned the instrument. Resting it on his knee he began to pluck the strings gently, exploring rhythms. Miranda watched as Cormac's eyes closed, and the old man began to sway as he strummed and then the strumming took on urgency. Suddenly Cormac was pulling sounds out of the instrument which were sweet and sad and driving, and his arms cradled and raised his cithara as though it were part of his body. At that moment he began to sing. He sang the song of a moonbeam that fell upon water, upon the surface of a pool deep in the forest. Animals of the forest, the bear, the wolf, the deer and the wildcat, came to drink at the water for all nature knew that this water had the power to heal and bring eternal life. Fishes and eels came up from the deep of the pool and tried to eat its silvery beauty. They tried to drag the moonbeam down under the surface, down to the mud where the weeds grow. As they fought at the surface the pool was disturbed and the moonbeam was broken into a thousand fragments. But finally they tired and the pool became still and the bright silver light filled the water with wonder, and the bright silver light caught the ripples that wandered, and the bright silver light held the night in its spell.

The last chord died away and Cormac set his cithara down on the floor and reached for his beer. For a while no one spoke. In their imaginations they had all been there, at midnight in the magic grove in the heart of the forest.

Miranda opened her eyes last of all. 'Thank you,' she said simply. 'Did you make that up just now?' Cormac nodded. 'It is so strange. I was there. I saw myself. I saw my life . . . my life that has been up to . . . Can you tell the future too?'

Cormac shrugged and grinned. 'Thank Brigid and Branwen, no. I never know what's going to happen from one minute to the next. But I'm of a morbid temperament, anyone will tell you that, and so I am never disappointed when it pisses down with rain on a summer's day. I leave optimism and brightness to the young. For me, the next beer is a blessing, a warm bed is heaven; but if it's water in the morning and bracken at night, that too is OK, savvy? The only thing to care about is not to care about anything. Especially not the future. No, sorry, music and a good song are worth caring about and so is your good nature. Anyway, forgive me for rambling. I'm glad you liked the song.' He felt in one of the pockets of his coat and pulled out a small knot of wood through which a cord was passed. 'Here, this is for someone who worries about the future to remind them of tonight. It's a balm-knot made from the root of a nuin tree. Wear it if you've a mind. I found it in the north in a cave when the Romans were after me many years ago.' Miranda accepted it. 'Now I want to sing a few more songs.' He smacked his lips. 'I'm feeling in the mood for some music.' Miranda knew that this was her cue to depart. She slipped away from the table and joined Bella and showed her the wooden pendant. Cormac continued speaking. He seemed to be in beaming good spirits. 'Are any of you thirsty?' he called. Many of the assembly nodded. 'Well Angus and Lyf will serve you, won't you lads?' And while they were so engaged Cormac reached inside his black canvas pack and removed some sticks and skin and wooden hoops. From these he quickly fashioned a small flat drum which when he struck it had a bright hard sound. He strapped the drum to his left leg and then reached for the cithara again. He struck two chords and quickly everyone fell silent. He began to tap out a martial rhythm on the drum.

Cormac's next song was an old favourite. It told of a battle many centuries earlier when a Roman legion was routed by a band of the Parisi who were out on a drunken picnic. The song had a chorus which required first stamping with one foot, then with the other, then slapping of the elbows and finally a clap of the hands between neighbours. Everyone joined in the chorus. Viti was pushed forward by rough hands during this song and had to endure standing and listening. He held his ground steadfastly. The song ended with a cheer signifying the complete rout of the entire legion.

'Do you Romans have songs about us?' asked Cormac. 'If so, be my guest.' He handed the cithara over to Viti who took it and was amazed at its weight.

'I don't know how to play.'

Cormac reached across and with his strong brown fingers plucked four of the strings making a chord. Viti tried and found the strings stiff and hard. The sound was weak. A few people laughed and Cormac shut them up with a glance. 'Now hold it up,' he said. 'It won't break. It's over a thousand years old and good for another thousand. It's made of duir, coll and oir. Hold it firm. Hold it like you hold a woman you love. And be bold with the strings. Like you're bold with a woman you love. Pluck them.' Viti tried the chord again and made a better sound.

'But I don't know any songs,' he said.

'Sing this,' said Cormac. '"I come from over the bounding seas, My name's not Cuchulain but Ulysses, I'll sing my own song under your trees, And if you tread on my shadow you'd better say please, Sings Viti."'

Viti did as he was bid, accompanying each beat of the verse with a chord.

'Sung like a true Celt,' said Cormac. 'That's put them in their place. Given time, patience, a long life, strong wrists, a sense of rhythm and new vocal chords we might make something of you.'

Viti handed the cithara back and saw the way the instrument almost seemed to snuggle into Cormac's shoulder. 'Now listen to this one,' said the singer. He played a melody with one hand while plucking out chords with the other, and then began to sing in a high controlled falsetto which occasionally descended into a growl as the emotion of the song grew.

It was a sad song of love about a boy who ached for a girl who was a fairy and who lived in the depth of the forest and who could only be with him at twilight and in the grey time before dawn. One morning he held on to her for one last embrace and the sun touched her and she began to age rapidly. Each breath was a summer and soon all he held was grave-dust.

This was followed by a rollick, during which Cormac got to his feet and danced some complicated heel-and-toe-steps while still playing. He got Angus to join him and Angus, who had always enjoyed dancing and whose inhibitions were lifted a bit by the alcohol, danced with his hands on his hips, letting his legs and feet do the work, stamping and kicking out the rhythm, and whooping.

'Look at that,' said Bella. 'Who would have thought it? He's a natural footer. Ee, I love to see the men dancing. It gets me right here.' She slapped her midriff.

Other men of the village jumped up and joined in. Soon a contest began to see who could leap the highest and dance the fastest and perform the most outrageous steps. But there was no winner. One man, Brennar by name, the same raw-boned man who had taunted Viti some weeks earlier, lost his balance and grabbed Angus who in his turn grabbed another man and they all ended in a heap.

This led to a break in proceedings. Cormac went to relieve himself and while he was gone the table was removed and chairs and benches brought in. More men and women arrived too, and children managed to fill all the small spaces between legs and under arms and on laps.

'It's great isn't it, eh, Moonbeam?' said Angus to Miranda, hefting a bench up over the heads of a couple of old women who were knitting and talking. 'We never had owt like this back in Eburacum. Reckon Viti ought to get himself one of them 'arps. Might make us a bit of money on the side.'

Two pregnant women found places at the back near the door and Miranda overheard them saying how much they hoped they could give birth that night after the singing – or during it, so one said.

Cormac returned, cracking his knuckles and complaining of thirst. He'd changed his shirt and now wore a gown of white trimmed with green. Beneath this he was bare-chested and showed an old man's paunch and an old man's breasts. For all that, he looked vital and strong. Miranda could not help but wonder what he had been like as a young man. She asked Bella, 'Was that true what he said about you two being in love, when you were younger?'

Bella burst out laughing. 'How old do you think I am?

Cormac's old enough to be my grandfather, great-grandfather possibly. He looked like he does now when I was a girl. No, you see it's one of the functions of a singer to tease and take people down a peg or two. He was just having fun and he must have heard word about me and Lyf. There's not much misses him even if he does live most of his time in the forest. When he comes into a town he can say anything he wants. True or false. You never argue with a singer 'cos they are always right even when they're wrong. If you see what I mean. That's what it means to be a singer.'

Before Miranda could reply, Cormac struck three chords to gain attention. 'Welcome to all the children and newcomers.' Then he spoke several words in a language which Miranda had never heard before but which caused a sudden burst of applause. 'What did he say?' whispered Miranda.

'This is a rare song. Did you hear that language?' Miranda nodded. 'That's the language of the people who lived in this place before my people came. The language of the people who set up the great monoliths. Listen, he'll translate. There's nobbut a few know that language now.'

Cormac struck three more chords. 'Here's a song from the time of the great black-backed glaciers and the animals that lived in their shadow. It is a song of the hunt.' He began to play a steady pulsing rhythm and alternated strums on the cithara with fast, flickering drumbeats. The song was not a song as we know it but more an invocation to the spirits of different animals. First there was a small furry creature which Cormac called a purru and which lived in burrows on the stony margin left by the retreating glacier. Cormac became the hunter and he seemed to be calling the purru and to have left a baited cord at the mouth of the burrow. Then, even as he called the purru, Cormac seemed to transform into the small creature with darting eyes and nimble gestures. He looked about, timid and ready to flee, and finally took the bait. Then Cormac mimed being the creature as it was caught. Then he became the hunter again, biting the neck of the purru and spattering some blood on the ground. No sooner was this accomplished than a large horned beast hollered on the moraine and approached the pool of glacier-water. The hunter crouched. The beast moved slowly, snuffling the wind and uttering an unearthly noise from deep in its throat. It lowered to drink and at that moment Cormac became the hunter again with slingshot in hand. He whirled the sling and loosed the shot. But the great beast tossed its head and trotted away, shaking its great spread of horns. Why had it moved? What had alarmed it? The hunter looked round, and there facing him just a few yards distant was a shaggy-pelted wildcat with giant fangs. This was a shis-traa (or some such name) and it bared its fangs and howled. It advanced with lowered head and lips drawn back, and pounced.

And there the song ended, with the hunter smiling and stroking the wildcat's fur which adorned him.

To those who had never seen this kind of singing and performing before, Cormac's ability to transmit the essence of the creature he was describing was unearthly. Miranda in particular found the experience frightening and turned to Bella.

'There you have a breath of the real old world. A time of magic, just before the time of the giants,' said Bella with a strange kind of pride. She obviously felt exhilarated by the contact with the early world as did most of the people in the room.

'How does he know such songs?'

'Handed down, mouth to mouth. Cormac is the latest in a line of singers that goes back to the time when this country was joined to Gallia. He can speak the old tongues. Some say he can speak the languages of the elves and the dryads too.'

More songs followed as the night wore on, until finally dawn showed in the sky. Then Cormac led those that were still awake, which was most of the people, outside and into the village square. There he paused at the fountain and sang a blessing on the water and on the town and on all who dwelt in it. He stood where the fire had blazed only a few weeks earlier, consuming the bodies of those who had died in the fight against the neighbouring village. He sang in his clear, loud voice a song to the spirits of the departed, bidding them peace from this earth of woe, joy in the everlasting and ease of passage if it were their fate to return to this earth. For this Cormac received the tears of gratitude of the mothers and fathers of the young.

And at the end of that he lowered his cithara for the last time and yawned hugely. The singing was at an end. One by one the people departed for their homes. Before leaving they bade Cormac farewell and good fortune in his travels. They pressed presents of money and valuables upon him and Cormac accepted all with an easy grace. Miranda noticed that for a while he had seemed like a giant standing there in the middle of the village, but now he was once again a frail old man.

'Can I carry your cithara?' asked Viti and it was duly handed over with an admonition not to drop it.

'Here, rest on my arm,' said Miranda and Angus almost in unison.

'I haven't had a singsong like that for years,' said Cormac. 'Must be something in the air of this place. By, but I'm dry. I could drink a river.'

'You've got your robe a bit mucky,' said Angus.

'It'll wash.'

'I'll run ahead and get you a drink ready,' said Miranda and hurried away.

'She's a pretty lass, that one,' said Cormac when she had gone. 'Light on her feet and a bit of a rogue I'll bet . . . but I don't have to tell you lads that, do I?'

A short time later Viti and Angus climbed into bed. Without their being aware, the open enmity between them had dropped away. They were talking about the singing. Angus said, 'But that song where he became those animals. That put the wind up me. I tell you, Viti, there are strange things going on here. Strange happenings. More than you or I know.' Viti grunted agreement and drifted into sleep with the image of a shaggy wildcat hissing in his mind.

It seemed that their heads had only just touched the pillow when both men found themselves jarred awake and with their hearts beating. They could hear a heavy dragging and scraping sound outside in the corridor and a sound of harsh breathing which could have been a panther or a man after a fight. Then the catch on the door was lifted.

In the gloom of the corridor stood a giant figure with a great hunched back. Neither Viti nor Angus moved as the figure approached the bed. There was a thump as something heavy and metallic hit the ground. Then the figure grunted and climbed up on to the bed and collapsed down between them, half crushing them. The bed creaked in protest as two strong arms pushed Angus and Viti away to the very edges of the bed. The figure breathed deeply and a noise that could have been a growl, but was in fact a humble snore, made the curtains tremble. Neither Viti nor Angus dared move.

The return of Gwydion

After ten minutes of trying to lie still listening to the noise, Viti decided to worm his way out of bed. He was just moving his leg when the hand that had pushed him to the edge of the bed gave a sudden hard shove and he fell completely out of the bed. The same happened to Angus. They were rolling on the floor when the curtains they had closed against the dawn were thrust back and early sunlight flooded the room.

Both men felt themselves suddenly seized and turned round.

Facing them was a golden man. He was stark, mother naked except for the torque of gold about his neck which was twisted like rope and ended with the gleaming heads of two horses. He was lightly tanned. His face had the fierce intensity of a creature that had come in from the wild though the high cheek-bones and clear brow would not have shamed a classical hero, a Jason, say, or an Achilles. The hair and beard fell in curls of pale amber. His angry eyes were smoky grey-green and his eyebrows were dark as a raven's wing. Tattooed on his forehead was the image of a small snake. The lips were full and sensual. However, any impression of effeteness they might have given was dispelled by the muscles which stood out on the man's neck and arms and chest. Pale scars on his body told of a fighting-man who was casual about his beauty.

'Now listen,' he said. 'I know what you two are up to and I've no objections, but *not in my bed*. Savvy?' He shook them as he spoke. 'So scarper. There's a spare room'll be empty down the end of the corridor.' With that he gave them another shove and bundled them out of the room and slammed the door.

Angus and Viti found themselves standing in the corridor.

'You take the room,' said Viti. 'I'm too tired to care. I've a place down below.' And with that he stumped off.

In the byre Viti found his comfortable nook. He was settling in when he heard movement. Turning, he was able to see down to the stables where one of the animals was being led out. Viti kept very still as Cormac led his donkey past him. The old man's hood was up, but still it seemed to Viti that the face he could see in the gloom was bright-eyed and whiskery like the face of a giant vole. This shocked him, so vivid and strange was the perception that he scarcely dared breathe. But then Cormac emerged out from under the byre into the light of the garden. He was again just an old man in a threadbare coat and with a black canvas bag at his back. He trudged down to the gate which led directly out to the cow-pasture in the forest. At the gate Cormac paused and suddenly turned. 'Goodbye Roman,' he called softly but distinctly. 'We'll shape a song again some day.' Then he swung up on to his donkey and the gate closed and clicked behind him and he was gone.

'That's one tough old bugger,' thought Viti as he settled and snuggled. 'But I hope I'm not going crazy. He's had no more sleep than ... What a wor— ... Singing mice and dancing rats ...'

Upstairs in the inn, breakfast was being prepared though there were few takers. Piled up neatly on one of the tables was a pile of gold coins and rings and brooches. These were the gifts given to Cormac. On them was a note which read: 'A singer travels light, or not at all. Blessed be.'

'What I don't understand is this,' said Angus to Viti. It was evening and the inn was crowded but subdued. Most people who had dropped in for a meal looked as though they had just got up and as if they intended to go back to bed as soon as possible. 'What I don't understand is why everyone feels hung over. I mean we didn't drink all that much. Not really. But I feel as if I'd been orgying for a week.'

Brennar, who was at a neighbouring table, leaned across. 'It's always like this,' he said. 'The singing always knocks the shit out of you.' Then he went back to his stew.

Miranda came in, and finding no other spare places joined Viti and Angus.

'You not eating?' asked Angus.

'Not hungry,' said Miranda.

'Even Moonbeams ought to eat something.'

There was a commotion at the kitchen end of the room which, had this been a normal day, would have gone unnoticed, but in the subdued atmosphere seemed loud. It was Bella talking excitedly. '. . . And when did *you* get back, you mucky little stay-away? Honestly, you disappear one morning, don't show up for weeks . . . Never a word. No thought for your poor old mother. You're just like your father. You could have warned me. You're not injured again, are you? I could have got your room ready and everything. Oo, but it's good to see you, love.' This was followed by a loud kiss and then Bella came into the room. 'Look everyone,' she called, beaming. 'Gwydion's back.'

Gwydion followed her and had to stoop slightly to get into the room. If Angus was tall, Gwydion was a good two hands taller. He was carefully groomed and the curls of his hair and beard seemed sculptured. He wore a simple, green short-sleeved shirt fastened with a gold belt. Attached to the belt was a dagger with a tapering blade like a kris. On his feet were Roman sandals. Gwydion waved round the room and was greeted by many calls.

'What's it like in the far north?'

'Heard you stole one of those flying things and went overseas to Egypt. That right?'

'Did you have any good fights?'

'Did you kill many Romans?'

'What presents did you bring back?'

Gwydion raised his hands again. 'All in good time. For the moment I'm too knackered to talk. I only made it to shore last night. Had to swim half-way across the North Sea. Bloody boat went down.' Shouts of good-natured derision greeted this but then Gwydion was left alone.

Bella brought Gwydion over to the table to join Angus, Viti and Miranda.

'This is my eldest son, Gwydion,' she said.

'We've already met,' said Angus and Viti.

'Oh.' Bella seemed surprised. 'Well, I'll leave you to get acquainted a bit better. But I'm afraid you men'll have to bunk in together for the next few weeks. We're going to be full. There's a lot of coming and going.' While she spoke she tousled Gwydion's hair with her fingers in absent-minded affection. 'So you've just come back in time, my lad.' Gwydion groaned in mock anguish and Bella bustled away.

Angus looked at Gwydion and found himself in contradiction. Gwydion, having showered, had rubbed aromatic oils into his skin and smelt . . . well, he didn't smell like a man should smell in Angus's code. Also, there was no mistaking that he was wearing make-up. His lips were redder and his eyebrows were edged with dark blue. 'What you looking at?' asked Gwydion and Angus was disturbed to notice that the man's eyes darkened even as he spoke and his voice had an edge of challenge. Angus had lived long enough in this world to recognize the danger signs.

'Nothing. Just didn't get a proper dekko at you, last night, what with the dark and all.'

'Well you can see me now.'

'Yes.' Angus looked away and changed the subject. 'Anyone want any more stew?' No one did so he went to serve himself.

Viti nodded to Gwydion and Gwydion fixed him with his eyes. 'So you're the Roman kid all the fuss is about. I heard about it in Gallia. It makes a good story.' Viti nodded and shrugged. He was trying to place Gwydion. Somewhere he had seen him, or his like, before. And then he remembered. In Africa, when he was on his grand tour, there had been slaves kept for their wrestling ability. Some had this same golden look. They had to fight trained animals and sometimes one another. But they were branded on their arm. Viti glanced at Gwydion's arm but there was no brand-mark, just a swirling tattoo of interlocking patterns. Still, the resemblance was there. Viti guessed that Gwydion had many stories to tell and wondered how old he was. Mid-twenties, he guessed: but older, far older in the ways of the world. He seemed so at his ease, so assured: a man in control of his life. Despite himself, Viti felt a pang of envy. How he would have liked an elder brother like this. Some-one to horse about with. Someone to help him.

Miranda was appalled at herself. She sat silent and dumb and with eyes downcast, feeling silly. Like Angus, she was caught in contradiction. She saw Gwydion's casual good looks, his vanity in his curls, his male pride in his muscles, his seducer's glad eye, and felt that she ought to be able to dismiss such as mere show (after all, how many offers had she refused?) . . . but when Gwydion walked across to their table, something in her, very deep in the darker parts of her, moved like a waking animal. It took her breath away. Her grey rational mind screamed danger, but her intuitive self, older and greener than the intellect, woke up and opened. Gwydion terrified her and she hoped he would not make her look into his eyes, for she feared what that might do to her.

And Gwydion, what did he make of things? Gwydion had the spirit of a horse and was passionate in all things whether it were battle or love. He had long ago given up trying to control his life and so was free to follow its sensuous curves through light and dark, through danger and tranquillity. When he looked at Angus he saw a man whom he would inevitably one day have to fight. That was the way of things. Toward Viti he felt compassion, for to him Viti was like a walking wounded. And for Miranda he felt simple, uncomplicated desire. Gwydion's sexual appetite was not contaminated with guilt and he had in his life loved many women and many men.

When Angus returned with his plate of stew he found Gwydion deep in conversation with the others, describing one of his adventures which he had had tattooed on his forearm. It was an adventure at sea, and when he drummed his fingers on the table, the muscles in his arm rippled, making the sea move. Both were laughing, for the story Gwydion told was against himself and about a black-bearded dwarf who had pushed him overboard when their frail boat was threatened by sharks and how Gwydion had been swallowed whole and had only escaped by dancing a jig in the shark's belly.

Viti laughed, delighting in the nonsense, and Miranda found that she could look at Gwydion, for when he smiled and was telling stories he was no threat at all, but was simply merry.

'But it's not true, is it?' said Angus, when Gwydion finished. 'I mean those things never happened, did they?' There was an awkward silence.

'Well maybe they did and maybe they didn't,' said Gwydion finally. 'Anyway, who cares? Too much of your kind of truth makes a story leaden. Who wants facts? Life's too full of them.'

'Tell us another one,' said Miranda, with a deliberate warning look at Angus.

'Right,' said Gwydion, 'cop this then. Literal truth, not a word of a lie, bone-hard fact. OK?' Miranda and Viti nodded.

'It was a dark and stormy night . . .'

And so the night went on. People left the inn to wander home. From the kitchen came the rattle of pots being scrubbed. Gradually Angus and Viti found themselves edged out of the conversation as Gwydion addressed himself more exclusively to Miranda, and she had eyes only for him. They mumbled their good-nights and received nods.

On their way through the kitchen, Angus stopped and examined the rheostat which controlled much of the power in the kitchen. 'I invented that,' he said to no one in particular and for no apparent reason.

When they got to their room the two men found that an extra bed had been jammed in. It was sheeted and Gwydion's clothes lay neatly washed and pressed on it, thereby staking a claim.

Later they lay far apart staring up into the darkness. Viti felt torn apart by his feelings though there was nothing he could say to relieve his agony. Sitting opposite Miranda he had been in a position to notice the dreamy, far-away look on her face as she listened to Gwydion, and her quick laughter. She was like a different woman. At the same time he couldn't be angry with Gwydion, finding him attractive and appealing and fun. So he lay still in silence.

Finally Angus said, 'If he's . . .' and then his voice trailed away.

'If he's what?'

'If he's in bed with her . . .' Another pause.

'You'll do what?' An even longer pause. Then Angus changed tack as another preoccupation carried him away.

'Still, he's obviously bent.'

'What!'

'A poofter. A pansy. A brown-hatter. You know, one of them, a queer. The way he dresses up in that thing like a skirt and smells like a whore. And did you see he had lipstick on? I've a good mind to . . .'

Pause.

'What?' There was no reply. 'Listen,' said Viti finally, lifting up on to his elbow. 'You can't have it both ways—'

'Bet he does.'

'Shut up. If he *is* a poofter, which I doubt, then he's only having fun with Miranda. If he *isn't*. . . then I don't think there's much we can do.'

'We could jump on him together. Belt the shit out of him.'

'Then what?'

'That's a start.'

'Oh aye. Well, I'll hold your coat if it's all the same to you.'

'Are you yitten, or summat?'

'No, but I've got more sense between my ears. I mean, if you want to go walking up to that one and say, "Listen you raving pansy, keep your thieving hands off Miranda or I'll belt the cream out of you," well, you're welcome to. I'll stick about and help you pick up your teeth. I mean, he'll fucking murder you. Those scars on his body aren't love-bites.'

'Well. We've got to do something.'

'Why?'

''Cos we just have to. That's why. It's driving me crazy, thinking about him putting his hands and fingers—'

'SHUT UP.'

There came a banging at the wall and a sleepy voice from

254

next door warned them to keep the noise down.

They lay silent for a moment and then Angus whispered, 'I'm going for a pee.'

He tiptoed out into the corridor. When he came back he whispered, 'They're still up. Bella's there too. Still jawing.'

'Go to sleep,' said Viti. 'There's nothing you can do for tonight. Accept it.'

'Bah.' Angus turned over.

Minutes later they heard tramping in the corridor and their door opened. 'Good night,' called Gwydion.

'Good night,' came the voice of Miranda, and they heard the quick patter of her feet as she ran on down the corridor to the passage that led to her room.

Bella spoke in a loud whisper. 'Now you be up betimes, young Gwydion. There's fences to mend and a new drain-channel needed. You can teach that young Viti how to handle a saw.'

'Yes, Mam.'

'But welcome home, son.'

There came the sound of a loud motherly kiss and then the door closed. The light came on dimly. 'Hey, you two gay sparks alive?' He kicked their bed. 'Come on, you're not in Roma now, you know. You're in the real world. You can sleep tomorrow. Look what I've got.'

Angus and Viti blinked in the light, both pretending to be more asleep than they were. Gwydion was rummaging in his bag of belongings. He took out a pair of gold candelabra, a statuette of a peacock with bent feathers wrought in silver, an assortment of gold spoons and knives, some jewellery, a pair of knuckledusters with wicked spikes on them, and three goblets of brightly polished silver. Finally he stood up holding a black bottle. 'Now get a taste of this. A Roman red from thirty-eight. I hope it's not too shook up. This was intended for the table of the Praefectus of Gallia, but I liberated it instead.' He removed the cork with a pop. 'Now, here's to the dead,' he said and poured the wine into the goblets.

Angus drank quickly, quaffing it down.

Viti sipped and slurped appreciatively.

Gwydion held it in his mouth till drips ran into his beard,

then he swallowed and breathed out lustily. He threw open the small window of their room and peered out into the black night.

'Now is that a wine or isn't it?' he enquired.

For all of them the second glass went down quickly.

To Viti the experience of drinking stolen wine in the dead of night was strange and exciting. The wine seemed to soak through him, staining him red. It made him merry. He speculated on how his life had changed from the days at the Eburacum Military Academy. He kissed his balled fist as though offering a challenge to Fate and laughed at nothing in particular.

Angus felt the wine hit his stomach and then bounce back up to his nostrils and thence to his brain. Angus became sad and wanted to sing, but Gwydion pushed him down and threatened to sit on his face if he so much as offered a peep.

Gwydion felt . . . well, Gwydion made his feelings known as he measured out the last of the rich warm wine.

'By, that Miranda's a cracker, isn't she?' he said. 'I'd like to get her between sheets. Bet she'd go all night given the chance.' He knocked back his wine after swirling it in the goblet and looked across at Viti and Angus who were staring at him, their expressions inscrutable in the dim light. 'Still, I'm surprised you two haven't had a go at her. She's only down the corridor.' Then he added thoughtfully, 'Of course, it could be that you're not interested.' He grinned wickedly.

'Now you listen, Gwydlium,' said Angus, wine-brave. 'I want to tell you once and for all that we're not—'

And at that moment Gwydion threw a pillow at him, knocking him off balance. 'Tell it to the Greeks,' he said, and reached up and switched out the light.

So ended the first day of Gwydion's return.

But let us not forget Miranda. She lay in bed and wondered if she could still smell the strange musky perfume that Gwydion had worn, for at one point, at the height of one of his stories, he had flung his arm round her shoulders and squeezed her. She wondered what she would do if she heard him in the night coming into her room. Would she cry out to waken Bella? Would the ancestor above the lintel protect her? Miranda wondered if she should lock the door and even got out of bed. But then she thought that was silly. Gwydion was Bella's son, he wouldn't come prowling down to that end of the inn . . . not unless he was really desperate and lonely, and she couldn't imagine him being either desperate or lonely.

And then suddenly, in one of those twists of understanding to which all of us human beings are prone, she realized that it was *she* who was desperate and lonely. She rolled over and rocked. She so wanted that man's arms round her, and she let herself imagine. She thought of Gwydion's broad chest and the snake he had tattooed on his forehead and how nice it would be to kiss that snake. She blushed at her own thoughts and finally drifted to sleep feeling delicious and warm and happy and sad and somehow at peace with her own deep self.

Gwydion and Miranda

Next morning when Angus and Viti woke up they found that Gwydion was already gone and that the gold and silver ornaments had disappeared, too. About mid-morning Gwydion returned to the inn, having delivered his booty to one of the village metalworkers. But both Viti and Angus noticed that Miranda was wearing a silver pendant with a fine purple stone.

Later that day, when Gwydion went out to help launch a new river-boat that had been built on the bank near the village, he just happened to pass through the kitchens and it just happened that Miranda was there and was not too busy to accompany him. Angus decided to climb a tree and Viti chose to swill out the pigsty.

At the river-bank, Miranda joined some of the other women of the village as they watched the menfolk heave the boat to the slip and then knock away the chocks and ride it down into the stream. When the boat hit the water they dived overboard and swam to the shore whooping and fighting.

'Where's Angus and Viti?' asked some of the women. 'Don't know,' said Miranda, and added to herself, 'and don't care, either.'

In the evening there was a picnic by the riverside with music and dancing. Fires were lit as a chill dampness spread up from the river. Inevitably tales were told and Miranda sat close to Gwydion while he talked about his most recent adventures. He was a born story-teller, and if she closed her eyes she could see the events he was describing, whether it was waves swamping a small ship or a fight in the dark of a mine or an orgy in a taverna in Athenae. She noticed that in most of his stories Gwydion made fun of himself. But he gave news too. The listeners learned what was happening in distant Gallia, about the sickness that was afflicting the sheep and about the grape-crop that was rumoured to be the best for wine for years. Gwydion also reported exotic yarns told by mariners from the South Seas.

Suddenly it was late and the fire was burning low. She shivered and Gwydion offered his cape. She looked away when he relieved himself into the embers of the fire but was strangely flattered that he did not treat her with false courtesy. Couples drifted off. Down by the river Brennar and one of his mates, both having drunk too deeply, lay with their arms round one another.

Gwydion offered Miranda his hand and she stood up feeling slightly stiff.

'You tell wonderful stories,' she said. 'The things you've done. The places you've been.'

He smiled in the dark, 'Aye well, it's a strange old world out there. Buggered if I know what's going on half the time. Come on, I'll see you home.'

They walked and as they walked they bumped and Gwydion slipped his arm round her shoulders and she slipped her arm round his waist. They walked by the river and approached the inn by way of the water-meadow where the cows chomped and tore the grass. They let themselves in by the small gate.

Viti was there, asleep in his snug corner, and they tiptoed past and up the stairs and into the sleeping inn. Bread for the morning had been baked and the heady smell of yeast filled the air.

They kissed in the kitchen.

'Shall I stay with you tonight?' asked Gwydion and Miranda

held him close and nodded though she could not speak.

They tiptoed past Gwydion's room, unaware of Angus who lay in there, bright-eyed and angry, listening to every creak of the old inn and enduring a thousand nightmares.

In Miranda's room they stripped off quickly and were under the covers in minutes.

And Miranda started to cry. She could not help herself. She cried and did not know why and said she was sorry and then cried again. Gwydion, perplexed, held her close to him and felt the wetness of her tears on his chest.

He stroked her hair and kissed her forehead and told her not to worry, though he did not know why he said this. He did not try to touch her intimately, sensing somehow that this would be wrong. He let the woman kiss him and cry. Finally Miranda murmured, 'I don't think I want to make love. I'm sorry. Do you mind?'

'Dunno,' said Gwydion. 'So long as you're all right.'

'I'm all right. I'm just me.'

Gwydion nodded, sage in the darkness. 'Ah, it is your moon-time coming on. I understand that.'

'No.'

He thought for a moment, surprised. Then, 'Are you feared of a baby?'

She laughed and shook her head. 'I hadn't even thought of that! But no, I am not "feared" of a baby.'

'Then don't I smell nice, taste nice?'

'You're lovely. It's just . . .' Miranda's voice trailed away, unable to explain. 'Please, just hold me close.'

Gwydion did that and lay thinking in the darkness. Suddenly he smiled. 'Ah,' he said. 'Now I understand. The goddess is not with you tonight. Is that it?'

And Miranda nodded. Gwydion held her close, and she held him, and within minutes they were both asleep.

At about half-past five when the birds were stirring Miranda woke up and was aware of the man asleep beside her. Gently she kissed his forehead and could feel the hairs of his chest on her breasts. He did not wake though his arms tightened momentarily round her. She looked at him and saw how the golden torque had pressed its rope shape into his neck. She kissed his neck, pressing her nose into the curls of his beard.

Her arms were round him and she felt herself come alive and moisten as her hands explored downwards.

Then he shifted and when she looked at him she found his green eyes wide open and looking at her seriously.

'She is back?' he asked.

'She is,' said Miranda.

And that was that.

And did the sun shine brighter the next day?

For Miranda I believe it did, and for the next day and the next and the next. She warmed inside. She was like a woman come home to herself. She recovered her virginity through an outpouring of lusty love that made even an old campaigner like Gwydion put his finger to his lips.

For Gwydion perhaps the sun shone brighter too, though that strange and most passionate of men was himself largely unmoved by passion. He was content to be used, and when Miranda called out in her passion, 'I love you. Love me,' he did his best for her, but he did not speak. For Gwydion had a perception of his life. He believed that he was a servant but not a master though he did not know *what* he served. He speculated that perhaps it was Life itself. At all events, he knew deep inside him that Miranda would move on from him and speedily, too. He knew this with the certainty of a man who can feel the sheer age of the spirit that resides in him and who has trod this path so many times before. Sometimes Gwydion wondered if he would ever find a mate with whom he could be simple and true and final. He hoped, but he doubted, too.

For Viti and Angus the sun did not shine. When Gwydion crept back to his bed at night after loving Miranda, they heard him mutter prayers to whatever gods he admired and then sigh, 'What a woman. Bloody hell. She's fantastic. Fucking magnificent. Phewwww.' Then he'd stretch and fart and punch his pillow and finally fall into the deep sleep of the innocent and just.

*

So life at the inn settled into a new pattern.

Lyf moved on, claiming he had business to attend to in the far north.

Gwydion, Angus and Viti worked together during the day building an extension to Bella's inn. Gwydion taught them how to measure and saw and how to tell a good piece of timber and how to secure shingles. They also dug drains and cleaned fences.

Bella was thoughtful for a while after Lyf's departure but within a couple of days her spirits returned. And besides, the inn was almost full with guests every night, and that meant more washing, more provisions, more bookkeeping and more hours in the kitchen. 'At least it keeps you young,' she said to Miranda as she stirred one of the cooking-pots. 'Work, I mean. At least that's what they say.'

Roscius the renegade Roman

Among those who stayed briefly at the inn and made life busy and interesting was a man called Roscius. He arrived one night, unannounced, and with a retinue of bodyguards, attendants and students. They occupied all the spare rooms and some of the students had to sleep on the tables in the dining-room. Roscius arrived unannounced for a very good reason. He was a wanted man among the Romans and hence kept his movements secret.

Roscius was a high-born Roman and an intellectual. He had renounced his position shortly after coming into his inheritance and had escaped into the wild woods to join the woodlanders. Before taking this drastic step he was careful to stash away gold and silver and put his lands in trust. Roscius did not intend to live mean. He wanted to live the fine life enjoyed by his ancestors in the days when Roman civilization was still thriving and expanding, and Latin was a language of poetry, scholarship and wit. Eventually, after roving round the famous historic sights of Britannia, he had established a splendid settlement close by the mysterious small town called Stand Alone Stan high on the Wolds and there he had built his library and set up his printing-press. For Roscius was a historian, a social philosopher and above all a teacher. His books were subversive. Possession of one within the Roman domain was a capital offence. Even so, the books circulated.

What had made Roscius reject Roma and her ways? Well, to understand that you would have to read his first slim volume called *Chains*, which begins with the immortal words, 'Man is everywhere born free, but is everywhere in chains.' As a student of history he had quickly seen that Roman military might had crushed beautiful civilizations wherever it had trod. Where others of his kith saw only the glory of conquest, Roscius saw only the waste of suppression. This led him to write his *Hymn to Liberty* and his sad ballad *On the Execution of a Free-thinker*.

While writing these idealistic and Utopian works, Roscius could not ignore the fact that the will to dominate and the urge to power somehow seemed endemic in mankind. He blamed social conditioning and he blamed the patriarchal order which, lacking any natural authority, backed its assumption of power by force.

His researches led him to elaborate a theory of individual freedom which rejected all civic codes and religious systems. As he stated in his pamphlet *De Profundis*, 'The deep moral nature of humankind can only come into its own when it is able to make decisions free from law, lore and cant.'

Roscius also developed a theory of history according to which the struggle for individual freedom would ultimately lead to the overthrow of all monolithic states. After a period of chaos a new social structure would arise, resulting in the establishment of a vast network of small interactive homesteads. Women would be in charge of these and they, in consultation with the men, would be the main decision-makers. Men, so Roscius believed, would largely be left free to roam where they wanted and to make what living they could. With the women in charge of social affairs and with no dominant power-structure to distort their natures, men would be free to become what in their hearts they truly are: doers, makers and supporters. As mates they would be selected for their intelligence, their strength and, most important of all, for their compassion.

On this particular night he arrived at the inn carried on a

stretcher hefted by two mighty women. He was suffering from an ulcer on his leg and could hardly bear to put his foot on the ground. He was weary from travel and sick with pain.

The women carried him right into the middle of the dining-room and then helped him up and into a large comfortable chair brought in by one of his bodyguards. Roscius was not a big man but he exuded an immense psychic energy. This was manifest in his eyes which were large and blue and which could be merry as a summer sky one minute and cold as chips of ice the next. These almost luminous eyes were set in a face that was friendly and clownlike. He had a big red nose and was completely bald on the big, domed front and crown of his head. His hair behind was the colour of dirty carrots and stood up like a kind of frieze, giving the impression that he was in a permanent state of fright. He had narrow shoulders and a pot belly, thin legs and large feet. In age he was in his mid- to late fifties.

'Let there be no mistake, I am aware that I am not beautiful,' he had said more than once. 'Beauty I leave to those that need it. There is no great virtue in bedding a man or woman if you have the looks of a Venus or the equipment of a stallion. Now when *I* take a lover, I have to strive, and the battle is fierce and the climax in every sense tumultuous. After such efforts, the delight in my astonished lover's eyes is more than reward for my ungainliness.'

Needless to say, many women and men found Roscius irresistible and he never lacked for bedmates, though his interests tended to the solitary and the academic.

He settled at a table at the inn and when offered wine refused. 'Is that medicine man called Lyf in the neighbourhood? I'm sure he knows how to relieve this pain.'

'Lyf went to the North a few days ago,' said Bella.

'Bugger. I could do with some of his magic to get me back to Stand Alone Stan.'

'Perhaps I can help.'

'If you can I shall be your servant for life. Meanwhile, food and drink for my gang and paper and pen for me. We will continue our symposium while we eat.'

At this there were some protests. It was not that people did not want to study and talk but that they were concerned for Roscius who was animated with a feverish energy. Eventually he quietened them with the words, 'If Socrates our father could keep on teaching while he drank hemlock, then I'm sure I can teach despite an ulcer. Consider it this way: when I teach I think, when I think I am happy and when I am happy I forget about pain. Thinking is the greatest sensual pleasure I know. Ergo to teach is to make me forget pain. Quod erat demon-bloody-strandum. Now where were we? We were considering the implications of some of the works of Lao-tze with regard to the present dilemma of the Roman State. And we were agreed that though he wrote some twenty-four centuries ago, and though he is not often thought of as a political philosopher and though the society he confronted is not the society we know, nevertheless he has much to say of value to us. Especially regarding the moral Way and the shabby bag of precepts which the Romans call order. Let us consider the following . . .'

And so, while food was brought and wine served, Roscius recited and translated from the works of Lao-tze.

While his foot was bathed and dressed he talked about paradox. 'The mind that cannot cope with paradox is poorly equipped to face the reality of the human condition. Paradox tears classifications apart at the seams and truth spills out. Listen to Lao-tze . . .'

Those guests at the inn who were not part of Roscius's retinue sat and listened, weighing up the strengths of his arguments and just imbibing ideas and words they had never heard before. Among those was Angus. At first he thought Roscius was absurd, he looked such a weakling and his high nasal voice sounded affected. But gradually Angus listened, and as he listened he became intrigued and he faced questions that he could not answer but that seemed important.

'Finally,' Roscius said, 'Lao-tze does not deny that there is an absolute truth, but he does insist that the only way to truth is through personal understanding. "Avoid all delusion," he says. "Find your own way." "Keep a clean house." "Find the spirit in all things." We could all do worse.' And with these words he closed his book. 'Any questions?'

264

Many guests at the inn began calling out questions and Roscius answered them, entering into dialogues that were sometimes comic. Finally Angus plucked up courage. 'I've never heard of Lao-tze and I don't know much about history, but I can't accept what you say about Roman order being false. I was brought up in the Roman world and as I understand things the Romans brought peace wherever they trod. They found chaos and created order. That's what I was taught.'

Roscius looked at him with his bright blue eyes. 'Now there's an accent I didn't expect,' he said. 'I haven't heard anyone speak like you for years. Where do you come from?' And he added in Latin, 'Are you an escaped prisoner from the Caligula Detention Centre?'

'Never you mind who I am or where I'm from. Answer my question.'

Roscius shrugged. 'I can answer your question,' he said. 'But I wonder if you can hear my answer.'

'Try me.'

'All right. What is better, to travel or to arrive?'

Angus thought for a moment and then said, 'I don't understand.'

'Well, let me tell you something. In everything that matters there is no such thing as arrival. There is only the journey. But the Romans don't know this. They are obsessed with progress, with getting there, with achieving higher and higher states of success. But they never get anywhere. Only when you stop worrying about arriving do you start to travel. Does that make sense?'

Angus shook his head. 'Sounds like more of that Lao what's-his-face.'

'All right. Try this. Why build straight roads?'

'To get where you want to go. Quickest way possible.'

'Exactly. Now. Show me a straight line in nature. There aren't any. Straight lines are an abstraction. So is Roman order. Straight lines are an imposition and so is Roman order. The price of Roman order is death of the spirit in man. When men begin to live by abstractions they soon begin to wither.'

'Words,' said Angus as though with derision, and stood up.

'Aye,' replied Roscius, 'Words. Just about the only things we

265

have to show the depth of our consciousness. Words let us think.'

'Well I don't need your words. I can think for myself.'

'Maybe you can. Maybe you can't. But a wise man is not afraid to admit his own ignorance. The day you truly start thinking for yourself is the day your journey will have begun and there'll be no mistaking it. Travel well, stranger.'

With that Angus left the dining-room. He felt angry and confused. That man Roscius was too clever for his own good. Angus wanted to thump him. But at the same time he knew that Roscius had not tried to put him down or be rude. So why was he angry? He realized suddenly that he was angry because he felt inadequate. He'd wanted to engage in the word-play and the ideas. He wanted passionately to think. Questions tumbled upon him. Why had he got into an argument? Why hadn't he just sat quiet and listened? Why had he tried to defend Roman order, for hell's sake? That was plain stupid. He was merely mouthing things he'd learned when he was at kindergarten. Why was he so ignorant? That question stopped him in his tracks. Why *was* he so ignorant? He could hardly remember his own mother and father but they must have taught him something. He'd learned to read but reading was just part of the training to be a mechanic. There were hardly any books other than technical manuals and the *Daily Citizen's Paper*. And here was this Roscius with bags full of books. Books for reading, books for writing. Old books with black ink. New books. Some books written in languages that Angus could not understand. Even the students who travelled with Roscius had books.

Angus began to get undressed. A strange thought struck him. 'I wonder if I could read a book if I didn't know what it was about. I mean . . . I wonder if I could understand a book if it was about something other than mechanics?'

He climbed into bed and lay back with his hands under his head. 'I bet I could. I bet I bloody could. Then I'd have that Roscius on.'

Angus mused. 'That's a funny name, Roscius. Wonder why he's called Roscius? Wonder why I'm called Angus? Why did I work at the Battle Dome?' He sighed and yawned. 'Hell, once you start asking questions there's no end, is there?' And at that moment, as though in confirmation of his thought, there came a gale of laughter from the dining-room where the talk was still going on. 'Could be fun, too.'

Next morning Angus made himself useful about the inn. He helped to repair the woodland cart that Roscius used when travelling through the forest. He helped the attendants repack it and wondered at the library which Roscius seemed to carry with him.

One box was broken and some books tumbled out and on to the ground. One fell open and Angus picked it up, and of course, following the instinct of all literate people, he could not help but read a few lines. It was the end of a chapter and these words met his eye.

> The worth of a State, in the long run, is the worth of the individuals composing it. A State which dwarfs its men in order that they may be more docile instruments in its hands, even for beneficial purposes, will find that with small men no great thing can really be accomplished and that the perfection of machinery to which it has sacrificed everything will in the end avail it nothing.

What did it mean? He stood for a moment thinking about dwarfs and machinery, and jumped when someone tapped him on the shoulder. He turned and found himself looking down at the the slight figure of Roscius who had hobbled up and was leaning on a crutch.

'What are you reading?' asked the scholar.

'Dunno,' said Angus. 'It fell out of the box.'

Roscius took the book and turned it over. 'Ah, Jane Sara Mill's *Essay on Liberty*. A bit indigestible. But she was way ahead of her time. Black slave brought from Africa about five hundred years ago. Keep the book if you want to.'

'Can I?'

'*Fiat lux,*' said Roscius with a wink. He took a pen from his pocket and carefully crossed out his own name on the flyleaf. 'Who shall I say now owns it?'

'Call me Angus.'

'Right. "This book is now the property of Angus, given by me, Roscius."' He handed the book over. 'And if ever you are at Stand Alone Stan, call at my villa. You have a sharp brain if last night's exchange is anything to go by, but it needs some real food, not the pap they serve you in the Roman kindergarten. Farewell.'

A few minutes later the boxes were packed, the attendants were mounted, and Roscius was perched in his carriage.

The party moved off. Angus followed them to the gate leading out of the town and waved as they disappeared into the dappled sunlight under the forest. Within minutes they were lost to sight. It was as if they had never been. But the small book was solid in Angus's hand.

That night he started to read, and he found it hard.

The Attack

The attack came at four o'clock in the afternoon. At the time when men and women are just starting to relax after the day and before they they have begun to think seriously about the evening.

Angus was deep in the forest. He and Damon had been working together repairing the power system which supplied the small school and which had been damaged by a storm. He was just packing his tools and thinking of a cool glass or three of beer when he heard the wailing. It was harsh and discordant. The sound a saw makes when it bites on a thick nail or a pig that knows it is about to be slaughtered.

Damon, who was climbing down the tree in front of Angus, froze with one arm round a branch. 'Storm-troopers,' he said. 'They're in the village. You keep clear.' Then he was gone, scampering down the tree with all the agility of a monkey.

Angus did not know what to make of it.

Then the raucous siren cut out and the silence seemed to echo. But before the peace of the forest afternoon could reassert itself, a harsh metallic voice broke though, shouting orders. Angus could not make out the words, but then he heard the rapid firing of the small forearm guns favoured by the front-line soldiers of the Roman army. He climbed down quickly and, keeping to the deepest thickets, cautiously approached the small village.

Gwydion and Viti were replacing sewer-pipes. It was a job that Gwydion had put off and put off until Bella threatened to cut off his booze ration, and that got him moving.

Tree-roots had damaged the pipes which led from the first settling-tank, in the latrine, down to the second treatment tank, with the result that a foul-smelling slurry was seeping into the garden. To replace the pipes the men had had to remove the wooden covers from the simmering, microbe-lively, anaerobic brew where the shit was slowly being converted into useful fertilizer. To get to the pipes they had put planks over the settling-tank.

The stench that accompanied this work could have blinded the gorgon. They worked quickly and tight-lipped, their noses protected by rags dipped in rose-water.

The last pipe was just in and cemented and buried when the sudden raucous sound blasted their ears. It was like being hit by a tumbling axe. The noise made the teeth at the back of the head ache. Viti dropped his shovel and clasped his ears and almost fell into the slurry. At the same moment, grey, flat-bottomed assault vehicles came crashing through the branches of the forest canopy.

Gwydion sized up the situation in an instant.

'Get in there,' he shouted at Viti, pointing to the boards over the settling-tank.

Viti looked at him in surprise and opened his mouth to speak.

Gwydion didn't waste words. He balled his fist and his punch crashed into Viti's jaw before that man could so much as turn. Gwydion grabbed the slumping body and lowered it on to the planks. Then he threw the wooden covers over and locked them.

He stooped down under the eaves of the latrine and crept through the doorway which led to the sitting area. There was no one there, naturally, and the smell made him gag since the natural cleansing airflow had been interrupted by their work and the gases had accumulated. He pulled his shorts down and sat and pressed the palms of his hands against his ears.

At that moment the shadow of one of the giant assault craft passed over the latrine and stopped. The noise of the siren was like hammer-blows. And then it cut out. Gwydion released his ringing ears and heard the clump of soldiers landing on the roof of the latrine. Moments later the door of the latrine was kicked in and the figure of a Roman assault trooper in full battle-gear was revealed. He fired at random round the walls and Gwydion dived for the ground. A bullet grazed his shoulder, leaving a mark like a whiplash.

Another soldier appeared at the door. They grabbed Gwydion by the hair and dragged him out of the latrine and pitched him against the steps which led up to the inn. Gwydion felt the butt of an electric whip placed behind his ear.

'Where's the Roman kid?' a voice asked. Gwydion mumbled, playing stupid. 'C'mon fuck-wit, or do you want me to turn your brains to slime?' Again Gwydion mumbled. One of the soldiers kicked him. 'Where's Viti Ulysses? We know he's here. We'll kill every one of you if we have to.' Gwydion tried to squirm round.

'Give the cunt a taste of the whip. That'll sharpen his wits.' Pain exploded in Gwydion's head, making him draw his knees up into the foetal position, and he twitched uncontrollably and made guttural sounds through his mouth. Then he shuddered and lay still. 'I didn't say kill the fucker.' He kicked Gwydion. 'Shit a brick. Bang goes an informer. He looked a likely lad, too.'

'There'll be others.'

Miranda was working in the kitchen with Bella and some other women preparing the evening meal when the sirens blared. Miranda saw Bella turn white, to a blotchy paleness. 'What's that . . . ?'

She looked out through the window and was just in time to see the flat-bottomed assault craft smashing their way through the tops of the trees surrounding the tiny village. There were so many and each had a loudspeaker mounted which sprayed the ground with the harsh wailing. When the craft hovered, doors opened in the sides and ropes snaked down. Even before the ropes had straightened, assault troops came swinging out of the craft, sliding down to the ground, some firing from the small guns they had strapped to their arms.

One of the assault ships paused directly over the garden of the inn at about the place where Viti and Gwydion were working. Miranda saw the ropes come down and the black-uniformed soldiers after them. She screamed and turned and at that same moment Bella thrust nettles in her face.

'Rub yourself,' she called, 'rub yourself with the nettles. Sting your face and arms. Lift up your skirt, sting your legs, sting the inside of your thighs.'

'Why—'

'Just do it. They rape. They kill. They'll be here.'

Miranda did as she was bid. The white blotches of nettle-stings appeared over her body.

'Now rub this on you.' Bella and one of the other women had quickly mixed up a potion using vinegar and some herbs. 'It'll hurt but do it.' While she spoke Bella was also frantically stinging herself and splashing the water up her arms and into her face.

The blotches became livid and puffy and Miranda found she could hardly close her fingers. Her face felt tight and swollen. She could feel the skin as it swelled. She looked in the mirror quickly and did not recognize her own face.

From the streets came the rattle of gunfire. Below them, where the steps from the byre led up to the inn, they could hear shouting and the breaking of wood and many feet tramping. Then the door to the kitchen was kicked off its hinges and three soldiers burst in. They advanced, but when they saw the women they stopped and one of them swore. 'Poxed-up fuckin' whores. All right, where's the Roman kid? Tell us or we'll burn your shop down and you with it.'

The women said nothing but huddled together.

On the stove was a pot of stew and one of the soldiers, the one who seemed to be the leader, kicked it over so that the steaming brew spread out over the floor.

'We'll find him and when we do, we'll fucking crucify you lot upside-down and with your arses in the air.' He turned to one of the others. 'You stay here and don't let them out of your sight. And don't try any silly business, either.' Then he left with the other soldier.

In the corridor there was the tramping of more feet and some laughter followed by shooting. The noise told that rooms were being wrecked.

Outside, smoke drifted past the window and the sound of screaming could be heard.

Angus made progress slowly. Once he hid himself in the middle of a clump of hawthorn trees and waited, scarcely breathing, while a detachment of the black-uniformed soldiers, beating the undergrowth, passed by him.

Then, close to the village, he climbed up one of the giant beech trees and was able to see down into the village. The school was on fire. The schoolteacher lay dead in the playground and close to him were two small bodies. Other houses were burning and Angus watched as some of the men of the village, chained together at the neck, were marched down the street towards the central square.

Wherever Angus looked there seemed to be black-uniformed soldiers milling about. The village was being taken apart. Bedding was thrown from upper windows to land with a thump in the street. Furniture was tossed out of doors and broke as it landed. A thorough search was being conducted and it did not take Angus too long to work out the object of the search.

Angus could see that about thirty assault craft had taken part in the attack. All these had now landed and had all their doors open. One which seemed to be a mobile prison was also serving as an interrogation centre and screams told that torture was taking place inside its dark grey walls.

It was all so quick. Angus could not believe what his eyes were telling him. As a mechanic working at the Battle Dome he had encountered the ritual violence of combat, but this ruthless cruelty, this delight in injury and humiliation, he had not seen before. The troops that were carrying out the destruction of the village were about as far removed from the attendants at the Battle Dome as it was possible to imagine. He watched with a mixture of anger and awe, for there was something in Angus that would have liked to kick and beat other human beings, and burn houses. But the gang rape of a young girl whom Angus knew, for she occasionally served at table at Bella's inn, made him feel sick. He wanted to see blood, Roman blood. They tied her down to a table in the street and raped her successively while the screaming mother was forced to watch. Then one of them shot the girl in the neck and left her. Then he shot the mother. But she would not die, despite wounds, and held to the dead body of her daughter crying and cursing before finally she toppled over and lay still.

Angus began to climb down. He had seen enough.

In his pocket was the book which Roscius had given him, and it seemed to bump his side as he climbed as though reminding him to think.

Viti woke and was aware of the taste of blood in his mouth. The dried blood had stuck his hair and cheek to the plank. He could hear shouting and his military training again came to his aid. The stink in the latrine was bad but bearable, for the natural airflow had begun again and fresh air was wafted on to his face. He was in near-total darkness and the only light in his chamber was that which came down through the seat-holes in the latrine. It was from here that the sweet fresh air arrived also.

Viti lay and listened but could not make out the words that were being shouted. Finally two soldiers came into the latrine and one of them peed down through one of the seat-holes and the stream of urine spattered only a couple of feet from Viti's face. They were talking about the raid, using the gutter Latin of the regular soldier.

'Too late. We should have hit this place a week ago when we first got the word that he was hiding out here. He'll have gone by now.'

'So much for the fucking bonus. That'll have gone too.'

'I was hoping to buy my way out of the army. Get a plot of land somewhere south, maybe down in Hispania.'

'Better be a fucking good piss-up tonight. Have you seen some of the women round here, for fuck's sake? All got some kind of pox. Stick your end in there and the fucker'll drop off.'

'I'm tired of the fighting. Tired of the killing. It's lost its . . .' His voice trailed away.

'Lost its what?'

'Fuck knows. But I'll tell you this much. If I got my hands on that Ulysses kid, I'd cut his fucking head off and I wouldn't tell anyone, and I'd stow it in my pack until I could show it to his dad. Then you'd see me smile. Eh?'

'Away. Stop dreaming. C'mon, let's see if that big blond-haired cunt's come round yet. He should be good for a bit of sport.'

Viti could not tell what happened next. Obviously the two soldiers turned away from the latrine but then he heard grunting and a sudden gasp of air and a brief gurgling sound.

The next thing he saw was Gwydion's face, thrust down through one of the latrine-holes and peering about for him.

'Viti. You there?' hissed Gwydion.

'Yeah.'

'Well stay there. I'll get you out later. Here. Take this.' Gwydion's long arm came reaching down. It was holding one of the forearm machine-guns. 'Only use it if you have to. Right, here's some company for you. Shit for the shit.' Gwydion lifted one of the lavatory seats and moments later a black-uniformed body slid head-down into the stinking ooze. It was followed by another. Both were dead and their limp bodies flopped. 'Use one of the planks and try and push them under or to the back of the tank. Don't let them be seen. Good luck.'

'Where are you going?'

'For help. See you.' Gwydion lowered the seat and was gone.

The leader of the assault troops made Bella's inn his HQ for the night. He was a blond young man in his early twenties. He had all the people caught in the inn, visitors and workers alike, parade before him naked.

He sat back, his feet up on the table and a glass of red wine in his hand, and addressed them.

274

'We have evidence that the wanted man called Viti Ulysses was here. If you tell us where he is now, I will let you go. If not, let me tell you that I will have one of you killed in this room in thirty minutes. Two of you killed thirty minutes after that. Four killed thirty minutes after that. And so on. You get the progression.' He glanced at his watch. 'We'll call it six o'clock now. That means that unless one of you sees sense, we'll have killed, let me see . . .' He pretended to do some calculations on his fingers. 'We'll have killed eight thousand one hundred and ninety-one of you by half-past twelve. That's more than your entire village, isn't it? Including the children. So perhaps we'll have the whole thing finished by ten-thirty, say eleven o'clock at the latest. Anyway, it is up to you.

'Now, lady of the house, I'll try some of your food. I'll have soup first followed by roast pork and some good wine, please. And you, little pig-face' he pointed to Miranda, 'you are one of the beloved daughters of the house, I believe. Well, I select you to taste the food before me.' He looked round. 'All right, chop-chop, come on, I'm hungry. Get cracking.'

At 6.30 exactly, the blond captain looked up from his food and glanced round the naked people who still stood in the dining-room. Finally he pointed to an old man. This was one who had arrived at the inn the previous night and who was travelling north.

The old man looked round and then cleared his throat and spat with astonishing accuracy on to the young captain's plate. Then he ran straight at one of the guards, screaming and with his arms outstretched. He was shot down but his momentum slammed him into the guard and his blood stained the neat black uniform.

'You are extraordinary people,' said the captain, pushing his plate off the end of the table. 'You never seem to know when you are beaten. Well, I shall teach you. The next two will be hung up by their feet with wire. Unless one of you wants to talk. You have, let's see . . . twenty-six minutes. At least, *two* of you have.' He looked at Miranda. 'Come on, little pig. Bring me clean plates.' He turned to the guards. 'You,' he said to the one that had shot the old man. 'Take this dead meat out and throw it to the pigs.' He turned to the other guards. 'You others find some wire, the finer the better, and tie it up to the rafters. I'm told that women can withstand pain longer than men. Let's see if that is true.'

The minutes simultaneously dragged and raced away. Miranda, sitting near the blond captain, was in agony. She imagined that everyone was staring at her and accusing. She did not know what to do. Should she confess everything? She caught Bella's eye and Bella stared at her as though reading her mind and shook her head minutely.

Then at seven exactly the captain pointed at one of the women who helped clean the rooms and to a young man who had called in to the inn to collect some food to take home.

'Start with the woman,' he said. 'Sit her down. Place the wire round her ankles. That's right. Pull it tight. Good, now start to hoist. Let's see what kind of chattering she makes.'

They hoisted and the woman bit her tongue as the wire began to take her weight and cut into her flesh.

'No. No. Let her down again.' The captain waved his hand languidly. He addressed the assembly. 'Now you can stop all this happening by just answering a simple question, "Where is the young Ulysses?"' Silence greeted this. 'Why protect him? You owe him nothing. He has brought suffering on you. And he will bring more suffering, for make no mistake, the hunt is on and we don't care how many of you we kill. So come on. Talk to me. Save this lovely girl.'

Outside the window of the inn, as though to mock the horror inside the walls, a bird sang in the early evening. It was a chirrupy, cheeky song. The young captain's face lit up and he crossed to the window and looked out, but he could not see the bird.

One of the men in the inn cleared his throat. 'I'll talk to you,' he said. He was a man skilled in working silver and who had a shop in the village but who lived alone and so dined at Bella's inn on an evening.

The captain looked at him with interest. 'Go on.'

'That bird told me. It said, "Here's a man who doesn't know who he is or what he is or why he is." That's what the bird said.'

'Meaning?'

'You are trapped. You come here to our village and start killing people, but that Viti whatever-his-name-is doesn't mean anything to you. Not really. You don't really want him. You're just obeying orders. You're trapped. Just like you are trapped in this room.'

Again the bird whistled lustily outside the window.

One of the guards lifted his gun and pointed it at the silversmith's face, awaiting the order to blow him away.

'Well, well, a philosopher. How quaint. Nothing traps me. I do what I want in my own way. I kill because I like it. I'm like that bird. I'm free.'

The bird sang again and the man pointed at the window. 'I saw it that time. It's a golden bird.'

Quickly the captain crossed to the window and opened it. He leaned out, and then staggered back with a scream. Sticking out from his head were two darts. They had plunged into his eyes and jammed in the bone.

The guards were so astonished that they lost the initiative. They were overpowered and kicked to the ground. The helmets were pulled off, revealing faces of young men barely out of their teens. In the middle of the room the blond captain staggered back and forth. He could not bring himself to touch the darts which were lodged in him and so just wandered in a circle with his hands and mouth open.

From outside there was suddenly a tumult of shouting. It was a terrifying screaming, like devils loose from hell. The door to the inn burst open and in stepped Gwydion. He was daubed with blood and held a machete. In his eye there was a light which to those who are aware of such things betokens a man with the blood-lust upon him, a man who is fearless of death. Gwydion walked up to the captain and whistled in his face. It was the bird-song. Then with one swing of his arm he severed the head from the body and it fell with a thump on the floor.

Outside in the village the black-uniformed troopers were on the retreat. They had stayed too long. They had given the people who lived in the forest time to group and now every shadow held an assassin. Suddenly, or so it seemed, the people of the village had pulled themselves together and attacked.

As the late-evening sunshine entered the grove which held the village, the people began to burn their own houses. Smoke stained the pale blue evening sky. Men and women, sometimes armed with nothing more than farm implements, ran at the soldiers and overwhelmed them by sheer weight of numbers. And always there was the shrieking.

The troopers stared in disbelief as children ran from houses and tossed incendiary bombs into their carriers. With their assault vehicles burning, some troopers tried to escape by running out of the village and there Angus was waiting.

He had caught one of the troopers and strangled him and taken his weapon. Now he stood at the side of the lane and as the troopers ran out they were torn to bits by Angus's gunfire. The gun burnt his hands but he didn't notice. And when it stuttered to a halt he collected another. He began to advance into the village.

Despite the sudden reversal, several of the grey carriers were able to lift above the forest and retreat.

And suddenly there was quiet save for the whoosh of flames. The entire village was burning.

Angus came running through the flames and reached the inn and ran upstairs.

'They're burning the whole bloody place. Why? The soldiers have gone!' He saw Miranda and squinted at her. 'Is that you? What the hell happened?'

'I'm all right. This,' she gestured to her face and arms which were now covered with small pustules and scabs, 'was to protect me.'

Bella bustled in. 'Come on, help. We're clearing the inn.'

'What the hell is happening?'

'They'll be back. We're abandoning the village. Taking what we need and burning the rest. You help Gwydion. He's down below.'

Though he still did not understand, Angus went below to where Gwydion had opened a hole in the ground and was removing objects of gold and silver. These he was packing into wicker boxes.

'You can fill that,' Gwydion gestured to a cart that was standing by the chicken-coop, 'with the harnesses and milk-churns and whatever can be saved.'

'Where's Viti?'

'Having a wash in the river.'

'Why?'

'He fell in the shit over there. Bit dizzy with the pong. He was climbing out and he tripped.' Angus looked over at the latrine and could see where the covers over the settling-tank were thrown back and one of them lay broken.

'Is that where he was hiding? Bloody hell! Were they after him?'

'They were. Now enough of your questions, get lifting.'

Minutes later Viti came running into the byre still dripping from the river but with his clothes on. Without a word he began organizing the livestock.

Incredibly, within an hour, all the detachable items in the inn had been removed and stacked on three stout horse-drawn carts. The chickens were in cages tied to the back of the carts and the cows were tied in line. Most of the pigs had been slaughtered and their singed carcasses hung on the outside of the wagons. Some of the women carried small piglets in their arms.

Gwydion tied some straw into a knot and dipped it in oil. Then, accompanied by Viti, he walked through the rooms igniting oil-soaked rags against the walls and leaning out from windows and setting fire to the straw thatch of the roof. Soon dark smoke was billowing through the open windows and round the eaves. Occasionally a flickering redness could be seen deep within the smoke. As the fire in the inn caught hold it began to find its voice. It started as a whisper and grew to a roaring. Timbers cracked and sparks exploded. Then flames of yellow, white, green and blue rose and Bella's inn became an inferno.

Bella watched dry-eyed.

As the walls of what had once been the kitchen collapsed with an explosion of sparks which mounted up to the high oak trees, she said, 'Farewell old house. Welcome the new.' And that was all.

Minutes later the carts began to move down the lane and joined other carts heading out of the village. On every side houses were burning. Angus walked beside one of the carts. He watched everything and knew that the people were burning their village as a kind of sacrifice. They would leave nothing that the Romans could count a triumph. They would carry their stories and their skills to new villages. Some might start a new village somewhere far away, in a new clearing.

Miranda rode on one of the carts, sitting beside Bella. She carried the skull of Bella's great-grandmother in a box. It was a gift to her and now more than ever before she needed it. Miranda felt a mixture of anger and guilt and looked neither left nor right. Her skin was clearing rapidly and her former beauty already peeped out. But she was heedless of that. Also, Gwydion had not spoken to her since the attack and she could not understand why he suddenly seemed remote.

The small convoy left the village, passing by the still-smouldering school. The bodies of the schoolteacher and the two children had been removed.

Soon they were in the pitch-dark under the trees. The men led the horses and the only sound was the soft plodding of the hooves. At crossroads the men would light torches and hold a brief conference. Then some carts would separate off, heading for whatever destination they had chosen. Eventually, only the three carts which held the contents of Bella's inn remained together. Led by Gwydion they had followed a very winding road and Viti and Angus had completely lost any sense of direction.

Hours later the moon came up, filling the forest with its pale eerie light, and Gwydion led the horses off the road and made camp in a dell filled with holly trees. In the moonlight the leaves were shiny and black. After the horses were watered and fed, the women slept atop the belongings in the carts and the men made beds for themselves between the wheels. Still people only spoke in whispers and sleep came quickly.

At some point in the night two figures approached the camp: Lyf and the giant who had drummed to the wolves so many months earlier. They spoke softly and then the giant glided away into the night while Lyf made his way carefully through the carts and whispered to the horses which stamped and blew steam. A figure rose up from the ground, Gwydion, but he settled again when he saw it was Lyf and the camp became silent.

'I'll watch,' whispered Lyf. 'You sleep. We'll have need of your strength in the morning.' And so it was.

Dawn was misty and with a fine rain filtering down which gathered and dripped from the leaves. A quick breakfast was made of wheatcakes, heated on a griddle over embers. Then Bella called everyone together. She and Lyf and Gwydion had spent the first part of the morning huddled together discussing plans and no one was allowed close. Now she would say what would happen.

She looked at Viti first. 'We were surprised by the attack. We did not realize how much they valued you. Well Lyf tells me that one of the Roman dead, one about your size, has been stripped and burned in a manner that suggests a sacrifice. We hope they will think it is you.'

'We have left other signs,' chimed in Lyf. 'But you are no longer to be called Viti for Viti is now dead.'

'What name would you choose?' asked Bella.

Viti shrugged. All names seemed vacant and all equally meaningless. He glanced round. The holly trees looked oppressive but beyond them he could see an elegant tree which seemed to have many trunks starting from the ground. One tree; many lives. 'What's that tree called?'

'That's the hazel tree. We call it coll.'

'Mmm, Coll, Coll.' Viti tested the word in his mouth. It had a simple sound. Down to earth. No nonsense. 'If I must change my name, call me Coll.'

Lyf nodded. A pan of clean spring-water was brought and some leaves from the hazel tree were placed in the water. Viti was made to kneel in front of the pan so that he could look down and see the reflection of his face. 'Now ask the tree to let you use its name.' Viti did this. 'Say the name as you look at your reflection.' Viti murmured the name Coll. 'Louder.'

'COLL.'

'Now drink some of the water.' Viti did, leaning forwards until his nose, mouth and face were under the surface. Lastly Lyf gathered some of the water in his hands and scattered it on Viti's hair and shoulders. 'Viti is dead. Coll is born again. Stand up and find your way, new man.' Coll stood up feeling slightly foolish but no one was laughing. 'Gather some leaves from the tree over there, the one that gave you its name. Carry them with you.'

'Now for the rest,' said Bella. 'Time is short. We have decided it is too dangerous for you to travel with us. Time is moving fast again. Your journeys must continue. The Roman attack came to remind us of that. Life was becoming too easy and secure. We think you should move to Stand Alone Stan for that is a place of great learning and from there you can depart again.'

Miranda looked alarmed. 'But I thought I—'

'You are strong and yourself again. Our love is with you but you have a life in front of you now. Likewise Angus. Likewise Coll. At Stand Alone Stan you will find new directions.'

'What will happen to you?' asked Angus.

'Don't worry about us.' Bella laughed briefly. 'We have a place to go to not too far south of here. It is called Brind. We'll be all right. We'll start another inn. We'll hope to see you again.'

'Who will travel with us?' asked Miranda shyly, and it was obvious she was wondering about Gwydion.

'No one. It is not far from here to Stand Alone Stan. You will be safe. Lyf has sent word ahead. And now it is time to move.' She stood up briskly. 'Time for all to move.'

Angus was struggling to understand something and suddenly he comprehended. They were being pushed out, like birds from the nest. They were on their own again. He looked at Viti, now called Coll, and at Miranda who had her head down and who was cradling a box. They were not exactly strangers to one another, but each had grown in new and different ways and now they had to work together again. Then he thought of Stand Alone Stan. Was not that where Roscius lived and taught? Angus felt a surge of hope. Perhaps Roscius could help him understand what had happened in the last twelve hours. Moreover, Angus had finished reading the short tract *On Liberty* and had more questions than he could list. 'How long will it take us to walk to Stand Alone Stan?' he asked Lyf.

'Two days and a night. Barring accidents.'

'Is it an easy road?'

'There will always be places to show you the way.'

'Right, well I'm ready,' he said and swung his kit up on to his back. 'You ready Viti . . . sorry, Hazel . . . sorry, Coll?'

'I suppose so. It is all very quick. I want to say some goodbyes.'

Miranda had walked to one side and was in close conversation with Gwydion.

'Will I see you again?' she asked.

'Of course.'

'Will we still be lovers?'

'I hope so.'

'Do you love me?'

Gwydion could not answer. 'Love' did not seem to be the correct word for what he felt. 'I think you are magnificent,' he said cautiously. 'But you don't need me. Or you won't. But I'll be there if you do. If you see what I mean.'

Miranda didn't. 'Are you sending me away?' she asked.

'Yes and no. But don't look at me like that. It is always this way. It is not me that is cruel, it is this . . .' He gestured about him, trying to find the right words. 'Life.' His big arms fell to his side. 'Sorry. That doesn't sound very adequate either. There is no good way of saying these things.'

'No. Did you use me?'

'I gave you my best.'

'Very well.' She reached up and kissed him. 'We're equal then.'

Coll was speaking to Bella, Lyf and some of the other people who had worked at the inn. 'I want to say thank you and farewell. *Ave atque vale*, more or less. But I want you to do something very special for me. Try to tell the people who were relatives of those that died when my people attacked the village that I am sorry for what they have done. I would have given myself up rather than have happen what happened.'

'We know. And you mustn't feel guilty. We had our eyes open when we took you in and besides, you can't take responsibility for the system you inherited.'

'No. But I don't have to accept it either. I want to fight it. But I don't know how. Yet. I will. Anyway, all I want is for you to tell everyone wherever you go that Viti Ulysses is dead and his descendant will hope to redeem his name.'

'Spoken like a true Roman,' said Lyf, and despite his earnestness, Coll had to smile.

Lyf called the three of them together. 'Your way lies true east. Follow the road and remember some of these names: Berry, Bird, Grindal, Lutton, Weaver, Butter, Fox. These are towns where people will help you if you get lost. At Fox you go south by east to Thwing and thence by secret track to Stand Alone Stan. Good luck.'

'What is Stand Alone Stan? How will we know it?' asked Angus.

'It is a tall stone, a standing stone, planted by our ancestors, long before your people came to these islands. It is a place of learning and safety. Now on your way.'

Miranda stood alone, her few belongings in a bag, the box securely tied, hung at her shoulder.

Coll picked some leaves from the hazel tree and stuffed these in his pocket. Miranda smiled at him.

Angus lifted his roll to his back and waved.

Together they left the grove and then Miranda turned and ran back. She spoke to Bella and they kissed and Bella whispered something and sent her on her way. When Miranda rejoined the two men, her step was lighter.

The three walked into the mist and the light, drifting rain.

To be continued in Book 2 of
A Land Fit for Heroes:
STAND ALONE STAN